Edward William Dirom Cuming

With the Jungle Folk

A Sketch of Burmese Village Life

Edward William Dirom Cuming

With the Jungle Folk
A Sketch of Burmese Village Life

ISBN/EAN: 9783744768290

Printed in Europe, USA, Canada, Australia, Japan

Cover: Foto ©Andreas Hilbeck / pixelio.de

More available books at **www.hansebooks.com**

MAH PAN AT THE LOOM

With the Jungle Folk

A Sketch of

Brumese Village Life

By

E. D. Cuming

Author of " In the Shadow of the Pagoda "

Illustrated by a Burmese Artist

London
Osgood, McIlvaine & Co.
45 Albemarle Street, W.
1897

PREFACE

A FORMER book on Burma was so kindly received that my indulgent critics must be held responsible for the appearance of this commonplace story of Burmese village life.

Imagination has little part in it, save in the dacoit chapters. If I have made mistakes in these passages, correction by any one having dacoit experience will be gratefully received. I have no desire to "inform," but wish still less to misinform.

For many useful hints and suggestions I have to thank Moung Gyee, son of Moung Kheen, and Pho Thin.

I beg indulgence for my artist, who, as a "son of the town," is at a disadvantage in portraying jungle scenes.

By the advice of my publishers, the majority of the pictures have been reproduced exactly as drawn, in order to preserve their character.

Lest they should mislead the reader, it seems
advisable to point out that this method of re-
production also serves to illustrate a conspicuous
trait in the character of the race to which my
artist belongs. His houses in many cases are
disproportionately small : this is not because jungle
village houses are very minute, but because it is
less trouble to draw a little house than a big one.
I had requested the artist, moreover, to represent
one or two night scenes to correspond with the
text, but he objected that as you could not see
things in the dark you could not paint them.
The light of day is therefore shed upon a few
incidents which occurred at night.

E. D. C.

LIST OF ILLUSTRATIONS

WITH THE JUNGLE FOLK

CHAPTER I

Moung Pho Lone squatted on the platform of the little watch-hut puffing his cheroot, while he gazed blankly over his knees at the night. Before, and on either hand, the whispering grain waved in moonlit billows through deepening dusk to the jungle outlined black and ragged against the purple sky, a grey sea murmuring in the night wind. Now an owl chased its shadow over the paddy as it ranged for rats ; now a beetle boomed past ; and now the pariah curled up on the ground below the hut growled in his sleep as if the sambhur belling on the wooded hills behind disturbed him. A bunch of thin coir ropes tied round a bamboo at Pho Lone's feet starred away like limp telegraph lines on the poles which carried them over the paddy ; and the moon picked out the dangling bamboo clappers which by day scared birds from the ripe ears.

Pho Lone, swathed in his pasoh, his arms on his

knees and his chin on his arms, stared out at the skyline.

"You do not sleep," said a drowsy voice inside the hut.   "Why do you not sleep?"

Pho Lone took his cheroot from his mouth, and without turning his head, answered that he did not wish to sleep yet.

"It is courting time," said another voice, also drowsy, "therefore Pho Lone must remain awake."

Pho Lone shifted his feet uneasily, and said, laughing, that Moung Yeik was one of the wise men who could tell what another's thoughts were. But the creaking of the bamboos showed that he was roused from those thoughts whatever they might be.

You could not move in the hut without making it creak and tremble all over.   It was only required for two or three weeks while the grain was ripening, and a bundle of bamboos and some brushwood serve to build a hut that will give shelter from sun and dew; it was not much larger than a big dog-kennel and was perched on a platform as high as your hand could reach.

"I think Moung Maw is now in Mah Hehn's house sitting at Mah Pan's side," said Moung Yeik presently.

"I think so too," said Pho Lone; but the bamboos creaked again and louder.

"Never mind, my friend," yawned Moung Yeik, "when the field work is finished, I will go with you every evening to Mah Hehn's and sit with deaf ears."

Pho Lone replied that it was very good, and that he should remind Moung Yeik of his promise; then to escape more teasing he got up and crept in to his mat.

The night was chilly, and he was glad to draw his old red blanket over his head; but for long after the others were snoring he lay awake thinking jealously of Mah Hmway Pan and Moung Maw. He could imagine them sitting side by side in her mother's house, while young Tha Tway, Moung Maw's brother, squatted on the verandah looking another way. Last year Pho Lone had enjoyed the weeks spent guarding the paddy before harvest as much as any one. It is pleasant to lie all day in the shade smoking and chewing betel, with nothing to do except give the clapper ropes a pull now and again; and as birds come to feed only in the early morning and evening, the watcher may sleep all through the heat of the day. But last year Pho Lone was not in love with Mah Pan, and that made all the difference. The hut was a great way from Myothit village, and the baying of the pariahs sounded quite faint in the distance. By daylight one might walk nearly in a straight line to the village along the low bunds which divide the fields, or go round through the shady jungle, which was the pleasanter way though three times as far. Neither path was good after dark; the bunds were full of holes in which you might break your legs, and it is not well to walk in the jungle at night because of demons and evil spirits. In any case it was too far to go merely to see a girl, and Pho Lone only felt that it was bad luck Moung Maw's being able to visit Mah Pan at young man's time, while he himself could only see her by day when women are not sweet. However, in a week or so the paddy farthest from the village would be cut and he should be able to live at home again, when he would make up for lost time. But the paddy must be protected: how late it was now, the moon shining in through the chinks like that. Moung Maw must certainly have left Mah Hehn's now; it was a pity Moung Maw was a carpenter; if he had been a cultivator he would have to come and guard his crops. Pho Lone was asleep.

The deer stole like ghosts from the blackness of the jungle and stood in the shadows snuffing and pricking their ears; only the complaining screech of the owls above the scream of the crickets disturbed the night, and they stalked slowly down the grass slope and across yesterday's stubble to eat their fill of the standing grain. Then the wild swine, like the shadow of a cloud, came out for their share. There was plenty for all, but two young hogs fell to quarrelling and woke the pariah, who ran out and barked both deer and pigs back to the forest before Moung Yeik shouted to silence

him. Then the owls and crickets had the moonlight to themselves again.

The other two were still asleep under their
blankets when Pho Lone awoke in the morning
and sat up on his mat to look out. It was very
cold. A white shroud of mist lay on the flats,
hiding all but the crowns of the distant trees;
the paddy drooped under the weight of dew, and
water dripped heavily from the roof. The red
sun, just peeping over the jungle, gave no warmth,
and Pho Lone, shivering, was half inclined to roll
himself up again and wait till one of his friends
should wake and light the fire. But they seemed
so sound asleep and he was so cold that he folded
his blanket over his head and shoulders and crept
out over the wet bamboos, down the ladder, to the
blot of ashes whereon lay the charred ends of three
logs which were being burned whole to save the
work of cutting up. The logs were still smouldering under the feathery ash, so Pho Lone tucked
his pasoh about his hips and went to work. They
were thick as his thigh, and in length twice the
stretch of his arms; but standing astride he knit
his fingers underneath and swung the glowing
ends together; then, having laid a few sticks
against the embers, crouched to blow up a blaze.
He had to stop for breath many times before he
got anything but a lazy curl of smoke, for the
sticks were green, and damp with dew besides:
but in about the time needed to boil a pot of rice

flame burst up, pale in the brightening sunshine, and Pho Lone sat back on his heels to warm himself.

The fire had begun to burn briskly when the creaking of bamboos made him turn to see Shway Toon coming down the ladder.

"You always wake when there is fire," said Pho Lone a little crossly.

"Yes," answered Shway Toon with a chuckle. "Ho, neighbour! there is fire."

Moung Yeik came out at once, wrapping his blanket about him. He squatted beside Pho Lone and, looking in his face said gravely it was much trouble to light the fire on such a morning. Pho Lone did not answer. Moung Yeik was chewing betel, so it was plain he had been awake for some time.

The sun rose higher and rolled away the mist to see a shining golden sea where the moon saw a cold grey one: the dew-fall from the roof grew slow and stopped, and the diamonds vanished from the grass. A family of crows came and perched on the hut to see if there was anything to steal, and finding the rice-pot not even on the fire, flew away scolding, towards the village. Then a chattering flight of parrokeets swept like a bow down from the jungle and dropped into the grain.

"Birds," said Shway Toon. Moung Yeik, who was nearest, shook off his blanket, and reaching

OUT ON THE KWINS

for the ropes overhead, pulled till the clappers rattled and rag streamers danced. A flutter, a swelling roar of wings and the parrokeets poised to fly off shrieking. There was no breakfast for them on the kwins nowadays; cobwebs of scares stretched from a dozen little huts peeping above the paddy like rocks in the sea.

It is only for a little while after sunrise in the cold season that the fire is pleasant, and the young men, who had already begun to edge away from it, now threw off their blankets and twisted up their hair. It was time to think about morning rice, so Pho Lone filled the chatty and set it on the fire; they were not going to work until the people came out from Myothit.

Rice had been eaten and cheroots smoked before the screeching of cart-wheels told that the villagers had set out. Pho Lone, looking round from time to time, followed the carts by the dust-cloud.

"There are many people coming I think; hear the wheels."

"Yes," replied Moung Yeik, smiling at him, "every one in Myothit comes to-day, except the carpenter."

Pho Lone laughed. Moung Maw was very busy just now repairing his neighbours' paddy boats which had been drawn up on the creek bank ever since the end of last hot weather. There was always something to be done to each before it was ready to launch again ; new oar-posts to put in, split planks to replace, or perhaps a crack to caulk and clamp in the great hollowed log which forms the lower hull. Several of the village boats were already in the water waiting for the cargoes of grain they would carry to Bassein for sale at the English mills, but Pho Lone knew that Moung Maw had still many days work to do on Moung Byoo's big boat, which carried fourteen hundred baskets of paddy. Pho Lone took particular interest in that boat for Moung Byoo was Mah Pan's father.

The screaming and groaning of the wheels on their ungreased wooden axles began to grow louder again after being nearly lost by distance, and the carts could be seen coming round in the jungle shade. The heavy water-buffaloes moved slowly, but presently you could hear the *tong tong* of the bells at their necks and then the voices of the young men and women. At last they clattered down the bank into the stubble while the girls, packed tightly in the carts, clung to each other, screaming and laughing by turns. The drivers unyoked the cattle and sent them away in charge of the little boys to graze, while the girls shook out their tameins and waded through the long straw to the hut where Pho Lone and his friends squatted awaiting them.

"I think everybody in the village has come to-day," Pho Lone called to Mah Pan who, with one or two other girls, was sitting down in the scanty shade to light her cheroot. He had not moved when she approached and she did not seem to see him, though she knew quite well he was there. She glanced up now and smiled, so he took courage and went to sit near her. She looked very pretty this morning : her working dress, an old cotton tamein of faded pink check, left her plump arms and shoulders bare to the breast, while its single fold hinted the soft curves of her figure. Three white blossoms set off the blackness of her smoothly coiled hair, and in her ears she wore yellow glass nadoungs thick as Pho Lone's finger. Very few girls of her age could wear such thick ones, for stretching the holes the borer makes with his needle is painful. Mah Mee, who sat beside her, wore nadoungs no thicker than a paddy straw ; but then Mah Mee did not think so much about her appearance; her skin was much darker than Mah Pan's, and her mother used to say she had a nose as big and as thin as an Englishwoman's ; so it would have been odd if she had thought herself pretty. Nevertheless, everybody in Myothit liked Mah Mee.

"Why do you stay out here on the kwins?" Mah Pan asked Pho Lone who sat staring at her.

Pho Lone replied that she knew he came on account of his old father ; if he did not do the

scaring his father must and he always got pains
in his bones if he slept out in the fields.

"I do not like to stay," he added looking at
her.

Mah Pan did not believe that; she thought he
liked the easy life. Anyhow it showed that he
did not care to come and see her.

Pho Lone protested, but she would not listen,
turning her back on him to talk to Mah Mee.
Of course he was not going to court a snub before
everbody, so he went to sit with some of the
neighbours who sat smoking and talking till the
kullah coolies should come before they began
work.

The Myothit cultivators could not get in their
great crop of paddy without help; so at each
harvest they sent to Bassein to hire the big, black
Strangers from the West, who were always eager
to earn money. There is no work for coolies in
the rice mills until the grain is brought to market,
and they were glad to come to the jungle and
help reaping. They could not speak Burmese,
but that did not matter as they knew what they
had to do and nobody wanted to talk to them.
They were not at all like Burmese people. You
could see that now as they filed along the bunds
on their way out. They walked one behind
another, a long line of men, solemn as buffaloes
and as silent. All were dressed alike: a dirty,
blue rag about the loins, and another round the

head, and a string with a key tied round the waist, was the dress of each.

"What does a kullah keep in his box?" asked Moung Yeik, as the coolies streamed off the bund and squatted in a group a little apart.

"Clothes and pice," suggested a neighbour.

"I think he wears all his clothes," said Moung Yeik, coming nearer the truth than he supposed.

"I know what he keeps there," struck in another man. "I can tell."

"Tell!" said everybody turning to him.

"He keeps things belonging to Men."

"Moung Pay thinks of the big bundle of cheroots a kullah stole from his boat at the mill last season," laughed Moung Yeik. "He could not tell which one took them."

"How can one tell?" asked Moung Pay. "The animals are all alike."

"They are," agreed several men. "Their black faces are all quite the same."

"Now then," said Moung Byoo, going to the coolies and pointing to the paddy, "work! work!"

The strangers blinked at him stupidly for a minute; then one grunted and took up his sickle, like a great bird's claw stuck through the end of a handle. The villagers watched them working for some time before any one thought of moving; when you can hire kullahs who seem really to like work it is stupid to exert yourself more than

you must. But presently Ko Moung Galay, the
headman of Myothit, jerked himself upon his
feet, saying, "Go!" And the rest got up slowly,
tucked up their pasohs, and drifted out to reap.
Pho Lone was the last to go; he lingered on,
hoping Mah Pan would speak to him. But she
would not look his way, and at last he rose in a
huff and went to take his place in line with the
rest, who were cutting paddy in intervals of talk
and laughter.

Reaping is very hard work, because after the
paddy has been laid by dragging a bamboo over
it you must stoop to cut off the ears, and stooping
with the sun on one's bare back is tiring; so
naturally you stop pretty often to stretch yourself and see how your neighbours are getting on,
or to take a few pulls at a cheroot. The coolies
did much more than the village men. When Moung
Byoo threw down his sickle and strolled back to
the hut to rest, their line was far in front. But
then they had been promised an extra rupee each
if the work were finished quickly, and, as Moung
Yeik said, a kullah will do anything to have a
few more pice to count before he goes to sleep at
night.

Pho Lone sat down near Mah Pan, but he did
not speak to her and tried not to look that way.
Two or three times she spoke of Moung Maw so
that he might hear, but he took no notice even
when she told Mah Mee that Moung Maw was

going to row in her father's boat when they took the paddy to Bassein.

"Moung Maw!" exclaimed Mah Mee, "why does he row in your father's boat?"

Mah Pan laughed. "I think he likes to do so this year," she said.

"I think you will go in the boat," said Mah Mee.

Mah Pan was not sure, but thought perhaps she should go one trip. Moung Byoo would certainly go three or four times, and her mother intended to accompany him to see that he did not gamble away all the money.

Pho Lone could hardly keep still while he listened to this. Mah Pan meant him to hear what she was saying; he could tell that by her voice.

"Your mother grows very careful," said Mah Mee after a pause. "Why is she so careful?"

"She wishes to earn Merit," answered Mah Pan. "She says she must gain *koothoo*, and wishes to build a little kyoung."

Mah Mee took her cheroot from her lips and stared. Mah Hehn had often said that she should like to perform this Work of Merit; but so had many other women and men in Myothit. It was news that she really meant to do it, though one does not save money without a purpose. The village hpoongyee was always telling his supporters that the person who built him a new monastery would

thereby gain very great Merit and much honour.
But the work would cost three or four hundred
rupees, and nobody had thought seriously of it.
Certainly the kyoung in which the holy man now
lived was very old and ruinous. It leaned over
to one side, there were great gaps in the plank
walls, and the boards in several places were so
hollowed by white ants that you could push your
finger right through. Ko Moung Galay, Moung
Byoo and other men had gained a good deal of
merit by making repairs when they had wood and
leisure to devote to the task ; but they were
content to stop at that, though each one agreed
with the hpoongyee that a new monastery would
gain far more for the builder than for the priest
who consented to dwell in it. It would have been
strange had they denied it, when everybody knew
that to build the kyoung would be an action so
meritorious that the builder might make his
mind tolerably easy about future existences ;
while the hpoongyee could gain nothing by
moving from his old ruined dwelling into a new
one. The only wonder was that some one had not
seized such an opportunity long ago.

At any other time Pho Lone would have been
quite as much interested as Mah Mee in Mah
Hehn's project ; but just now he could think of
nothing save what he had heard about Moung
Maw ; and when the shadows, creeping under the
hut, told that it was time to resume work, he went

out into the field without having spoken a word
to Mah Pan. He was not going to talk to a girl
who slighted him as she did, and he would not go
and see her any more after this. He grasped his
sickle and sawed off great handfuls of ears as
though cutting himself free, but he heard her gay
voice above the hum of talk about him and felt
like a fish in a net.

By-and-by the women came to gather up the
cut paddy and pile it with the grain inwards to
await the sleds and carts which would carry it to
the threshing-floor. Pho Lone's heart gave a leap,
for he heard Mah Pan's voice behind him. There
were fifty swathes to choose from and she had
chosen his or one very near it. He did not look
round ; every sheaf she collected brought her
nearer, but he went on cutting without turning
his head ; she should not think he knew she was
there.

"You work very hard."

Pho Lone nearly dropped his sickle half way
through a bunch of straw, for Mah Pan was sitting
close behind him. She smiled as he stood up
straight and turned.

"Everybody had breakfast in your father's
house this morning," she remarked.

As Moung Let was chief partner in the twenty
acres of land he farmed with Shway Toon and
Moung Yeik, and it was their paddy which had
been reaped to-day, it was hardly necessary for

Mah Pan to come for the express purpose of telling him that. If Moung Let had *not* invited his
neighbours to eat the morning rice at his house
when he asked their help, it would have been very
strange—quite unheard of in Myothit or anywhere else. Moung Let would never neglect the
civility expected by ancient custom. Pho Lone
said yes, he supposed so, and stood turning his
sickle in his hands.

"In whose boat do you row this season?" Mah
Pan asked suddenly, after a silence.

Pho Lone did not know; he had not thought
about it yet; there was plenty of time.

"My father is already engaging rowers," said
Mah Pan drawing a straw through her fingers.

Pho Lone thought it was wise of her father;
he wanted many rowers for that big boat.

Mah Pan thought so too. He had engaged
nearly all his crew now she believed: Moung
Gyaw, Poh Sein, Loo Oung, Zah Nee, and—and
several others. Her father always liked to
engage his rowers early and so get the best
oarsmen of the strong young fellows in Myothit.

Pho Lone observed that he had a very good
crew last season; and, as Mah Pan did not seem
to have any more to say, balanced his sickle as if
to begin work again.

"If my father asks you to row, will you come?"
she asked smiling.

Pho Lone tried to hesitate but could not. He

smiled back and said he would take an oar if Moung Byoo wanted him.

"It is very good," said Mah Pan, "he will ask you; I will tell him. I am going in the boat."

She smiled again and got up to rejoin the other women; for the sun was low now and the little boys were already dragging the buffaloes by their nose lines to the carts.

CHAPTER II

"Stop then!" cried Pho Lone pulling at the driving lines. "Stop!"

The screeching of the wheels died in a groan as the buffaloes answered the tugs at their noses and stood still, sawing their necks against the yoke. Pho Lone uncurled himself to push one beast's quarters out with his foot that he might get down, for Shway Toon, who sprawled on top of the load, was calling that paddy had fallen off. He went back, raked up the scattered ears with his fingers and packed them into the cart, grumbling.

"Can't you hold it on better?" he asked his friend who peered down at him. "Four times now paddy has fallen and we have come a very little way."

Shway Toon squirted a mouthful of red betel juice and replied that he could keep the load firm if the cart were properly driven; he thought his young friend could not drive buffaloes very well.

Pho Lone grunted contemptuously and told him he had better come down and drive himself. But Shway Toon only rolled his chew and smiled; it was pleasanter to lie up there on the paddy than squat on the cart-pole jamming one's back against the load to avoid being shaken off.

Pho Lone climbed back to his perch on the pole between the buffaloes' buttocks and poked up the cattle, bawling his opinion of Shway Toon above the squeal of the axles. It was impossible for any one to drive smoothly over the kwins. The long stubble hid places where the ground was so soft that the wheel sank half-way to the hub, shooting off great swathes of paddy in spite of Shway Toon's outspread arms and legs. A rope would have saved much trouble but they had forgotten to bring one. Besides the soft spots, there was a bund to get over at every stone's-throw; straw and earth had been heaped against each to make a path, but nevertheless the clumsy cart bumped and jolted till it seemed that the axle must surely snap.

"I wish we had a sled," sighed Pho Lone as he pulled up again to collect more fallen paddy, "a sled is much better."

"Yes," agreed Shway Toon, with the air of one regretting good advice thrown away, "it is a pity you did not make one."

Pho Lone took no notice of this speech. While he had been helping Moung Byoo to build his sled, Shway Toon had lain in his house just opposite, looking on. When urged to get to work, he always answered that it was foolish to bother about the harvest while the paddy was green; so, as Pho Lone was never able to begin a job by himself, the time came to go and live out in the watch-hut before a single bamboo had been cut. A sled is far more suitable than a cart for carrying in the grain; it is easier to load, carries more, and above all, it slides safely over the mud-holes and bunds. A dozen of them, like rude ship gangways, might be seen on the kwins to-day, for all the crop was cut and everybody was bringing his grain to stack by the threshing-floor behind the village.

The buffaloes waded slowly through the stubble, heeding their driver's stick as little as the glistening flies which swarmed about their eyes and nostrils. The air was hot and still but the fields were full of life. Fat bronze lizards basked on the bunds, too lazy to move even when the shadow of the passing cart fell on them; now and again a snake peeped above the grass and sank again with a whispered hiss; in the wet corners of the fields, little red land-crabs trundled out of the way to draw into their holes. Overhead a kite floated, whistling sadly, as if calling his mate to join him and go to the coast where kites spend the dry season.

It was hard work dragging the heavily laden cart over the fields, and the buffaloes stopped of their own accord when they came to the threshing-floor on the edge of the waste land.

Preparations for threshing were going on all round. The boys and women were unloading the sleds, and piling the paddy from each holding in a low stack by itself. A party of young men were sweeping the floor clean with branches and bunches of straw, for it would be wanted to-morrow if not this afternoon. That floor had existed as long as any one in Myothit could remember. Oo Yan, the oldest man in the village, used to tell how his father said it was a fine floor when he was a young man; and that was in the time when there were no white men and no mills in Bassein, and the Myothit paddy land was only enough to grow house-rice. It was a good floor, whatever its age, made of earth and dung mixed and trodden down; each rainy season left it a round patch of evil-smelling mud, honeycombed by the hoofs of wandering cattle; but when the monsoon was over in October, the holes were filled up and the surface smoothed so that the floor sloped from centre to rim like a paper umbrella, and a few weeks' sunshine baked it hard as a road. A stout post, grooved deep by the buffalo ropes, stood in the middle; that had been renewed in Pho Lone's time, for the rains and white ants work havoc with wood. A little way off, men were clearing the stubble and weeds from a round space which was to serve as a second floor; for the harvest was heavy, a full sixteen anna crop, Ko Moung Galay said, and two floors would be required if the grain

was to be ready when the market opened at the
end of January. A bare spot, from which the
paddy can be swept up when the buffaloes have
trodden it out, is really all that is wanted for
threshing. Some distance from the floors Moung
Maw and other men were putting the last touches
to the winnowing stage. It was finished save for
the ladders, and looked like two steps of a giant's
staircase, the first a man's height, the second as
high again. The older men were sitting in the
shade of a stack, chewing betel and smoking; a
live ash would have put an end to the calculations they were making on the out-turn of the
threshing, but the chance of fire did not occur
to anybody. Life would not be worth living if
one were always thinking of misfortunes that
may happen.

Pho Lone looked about for Mah Pan, but he
could not see her. He did not feel at all happy.
Her father had asked him to take an oar in his
boat and two days after, Mah Pan had said she
was going with Mah Mee in Ko Moung Galay's
boat. Ever since he heard this Pho Lone had
been trying to exchange with one of Ko Moung
Galay's rowers, though his friends advised him to
keep his oar in Moung Byoo's.

"She says this to tease," Shway Toon sagely
observed when Pho Lone spoke to him about it.
"If you exchange with Bah Thet she will say, 'I
go with my father.'"

But Pho Lone was not satisfied. It was quite possible that she did intend to go in Ko Moung Galay's boat, for his daughter Mah Mee was her particular friend; and he had determined to ask Mah Pan the next time he saw her what she really meant to do. He was sitting in the shade of the cart-tail smoking gloomily, when Mah Mee came by and called saucily that he "must go to her house." He laughed in reply, but when Mah Mee was out of sight he got up and, shaking out his pasoh, sauntered towards the village.

Myothit was not a pretty place: two rows of low brown houses, shaded here and there by clumps of giant bamboo, facing each other across an uneven strip of naked brown road, which shrank into a jungle track at either end of the village. On the left ran the creek, almost at the street-level now the tide was high; the long prow of a boat, riding light at its moorings, peeped between the houses. In the rainy season Myothit was under water for days together, and the people went to see their neighbours in canoes. Behind the village, waste land inclined gently up to the kwins, so that the paddy was not flooded though the street were waist deep in water. Much work was going on in the village to-day. Men and women sat about the roadway, with mallet and block beating out bamboos to plait into matting for paddy bins. Sheets of new mat glared white in the sun, and finished bins, like immense drums, stood about ready to be set on the stands among the houses.

Pho Lone went down the street to Mah Hehn's. As he came near he heard the loose clatter of the loom and knew where to look for Mah Pan. Her father's was one of the largest houses in Myothit, but was built on the same plan as all the rest, open in front, with two half storeys, the lower before and the higher behind, with a short flight of stairs to connect them. There was nobody on the lower floor, but through the lattice-work between it and the upper story Pho Lone saw Mah Pan at the loom which stood on the ground under her sleeping room. He went round and squatted on the ground near; somebody was moving about in the room over Mah Pan's head so he could not go under the house close beside her; it is not good to have anybody's feet over your head, particularly a woman's; and as Moung Byoo was out on the kwins, the person within could only be Mah Hehn. Apart from this, it was well, in the interests of propriety, that Mah Hehn should be within hearing, for no well conducted young woman would allow a man to sit near her were nobody else by.

Mah Pan paused in her work to turn and smile to Pho Lone and then bent over the frame again. Mah Hehn was very proud of her daughter's weaving. Old Mah Too's was the only work in the village which could ever have been compared

to it, and now Mah Too's hands were shaky, her
weaving was not what it used to be.   When Mah
Pan finished a tamein or pasoh the gossips would
come and sit round, drawing the cloth through
their fingers and admiring its even texture.
Mothers told their daughters to learn to weave
like Mah Pan, and fathers and husbands and
brothers told their women folk to roll cheroots like
Mah Pan's; and by consequence the girls did not
love her very much.   It is not altogether well to
have the cleverest fingers besides the fairest skin
in the village.   Pho Lone was quite content to sit
in the shade of the bamboos, smoking, and feasting
his eyes upon her, as she leaned against the bar-
seat and passed the shuttle, singing softly to
herself.   But presently she stopped and turned
to him.

"I think they will begin threshing to-day," he
said, feeling obliged to say something.

"Does the elder brother think so?" asked Mah
Pan.

Pho Lone understood by this rather formal
mode of address that she meant to keep him at
his distance, just as if he had come at young
man's time.   The smash, smash of mallets all along
the street seemed to beat all ideas out of his
head.   He wanted to know what she meant to do
about going to Bassein, but did not wish her to
think he had come merely to ask.   He picked up
a stick and pushed it slowly down a rat-hole, then

drew it out, scratched his neck with it, threw it aside, clasped his arms about his knees, and blinked at her wistfully.

"The elder sister does not work in the fields this morning," he said at last.

Mah Pan's head was beating a little to-day, so she stayed at home.

Pho Lone said he was sorry to hear that; and having said so, relapsed into silence, wishing she would begin weaving again. While she remained leaning against the loom-seat looking at him he felt he must talk; but he could not do all the talking himself, and she seemed to have less to say than he had. From sheer embarrassment he plunged into the question he had come to ask.

"Will the elder sister go in Ko Moung Galay's boat?"

Mah Pan thought not; she had made up her mind not to go to Bassein at all this season.

Pho Lone's patience gave way at this. "I shall be off!" he said, and lurching on his feet, walked away. He went slowly, half hoping she would call him back; but before he got round to the front of the house the clack of the loom began, and with it Mah Pan's song. Hearing that, he quickened his steps, and passing between the opposite houses went straight out to the threshing-floor.

Mah Mee saw him coming, and waited.

" Is she kind to-day ? " she asked roguishly, as he came up.

" She is not," replied Pho Lone, who was in no mood to be teased. He would have passed on, but Mah Mee, telling him to stay and tell her all about it, sat down on the bund.

Her tone was kind, so Pho Lone stopped, and sat near her.

" She is very proud," said Mah Mee soothingly. Though she did laugh at Pho Lone a great deal, she really liked him, and she saw he had been vexed.

" She is much too proud," he agreed warmly ; and went on, raising his voice as he thought of his wrongs :—" She is very proud, and also very changeable ; she has a new mind each day."

" She plays at changing her mind," said Mah Mee.

She spoke so kindly that Pho Lone opened his heart, and told her how Mah Pan altered her plans so often that he did not know what to do.

It was consoling to learn that Mah Mee had heard nothing of Mah Pan's wish to go in Ko Moung Galay's boat, and still more satisfactory to be assured that there would be no room for her if she did wish to go. But when Mah Mee, having set his mind at rest on this point, proceeded to rate him for believing everything he was told, Pho Lone could only chew a straw and look unhappy.

"She is sweet to Moung Maw," he said dismally.

"Moung Maw is wiser than you," retorted Mah Mee. "Yesterday we sat together, Mah Pan and I. Moung Maw came. 'Go away,' says Mah Pan, and Moung Maw went. 'Come back,' says Mah Pan; but Moung Maw looks over his shoulder and laughs. Next time Mah Pan will not say 'Go away' to him."

"I think Moung Maw has worked magic," said Pho Lone, looking round to see nobody was near enough to overhear.

Mah Mee did not know whether he had worked magic or not; if he had, he would not have told. She did know, however, that he had given Mah Pan a silver ring—a beautiful ring worth quite four rupees.

"I gave her a string of beads for the neck," said Pho Lone, sadly remembering that he never saw those beads on her neck, while she always wore that ring. "The price was two and a half rupees."

"She loves beautiful ornaments," remarked Mah Mee.

"I expect she does not like what I give her," sighed Pho Lone. "I also gave her a pink silk kerchief which she never wears."

"I expect she thinks you are a *loo mike*," retorted his companion, sharply. "You have no spirit: you behave like a little puppy, which

rolls on its back to a big dog. Who will love a
young man like that?"

Pho Lone was too much depressed to answer;
he let Mah Mee get up and go away without saying a word, and presently went to work by himself, unloading the paddy which they had
brought in an hour ago. He did not feel inclined
to join the people who were shouting uproari-
ously over the first threshing, though he often
stopped to look on and wish he were as light-
hearted as his neighbours.

In virtue of his position as head-man of the
village, Ko Moung Galay had his stack threshed
first; consequently he looked on and directed
matters while his daughter took her share of the
work with the rest. It was very hot, but
nobody minded that; the young men and women
ran to and fro carrying great bundles of paddy
to the floor, round which ranks of buffaloes, eight
abreast, plodded heavily, up to their dewlaps in
rustling ears. There is always great fun over
the first threshing. Mah Gway, trying to throw
a sheaf, fell into the deep loose bed, and was
buried by her neighbours before she could
scramble out with her hair down and full of
straws. Little Poh Chin, dancing wildly round
the floor, got in the way, and Moung Yeik, crying
"Here is fine paddy!" tossed him into the litter,
where he lay kicking till the buffaloes came
round, and he had to struggle out as fast as he

could. Tha Tway and the other small boys were
enjoying themselves hugely. They rode the
buffaloes, and bullied them as monkeys might
elephants. If a beast dared lower his head to
sniff the grain through his basket muzzle, little
naked heels drummed on his ribs, the stick
rained blows on his shoulders, and he was scolded
till his great flat horns lay back to his withers
again. The people bustled backwards and for-
wards between stack and floor like ants, till the
cattle pushed a wave of paddy before them, and
Ko Moung Galay cried, "There is enough!"
Then everybody went and sat in the shade to
recover breath and coil up hair, leaving two or
three old women to hobble round the floor with
forked sticks, pushing the paddy within tread.

Round and round toiled the buffaloes, switch-
ing their tails, and blowing through their
muzzles, while the straw whispered against their
legs, and the yoke-ropes creaked on the centre
post. Having ceased work, nobody was anxious
to begin again; so when the first puffs of the
evening breeze stirred the hot air, the mass on
the threshing floor was trodden to litter, and you
heard the loose grain crunch beneath the buffaloes' hoofs.

The women went home to prepare evening
rice, and the buffaloes were loosed and unmuzzled
that the boys might take them to wallow in the
creek before being picketed for the night. Then

the men girt up their pasohs again to clear away
the chaff, and sweep up the paddy which lay a
finger's depth upon the floor.   There was a large
heap when it was collected, and Moung Maw
remarked to Pho Lone, who had come now to do
his share, that they should begin winnowing to-
morrow.

"If Ko Moung Galay wishes it," said Pho
Lone.

"If he wishes, of course," assented Moung
Maw. "Come to my house to play to-night,"
he continued. "Shway Toon and other fellows
will come."

"I go to Mah Hehn's," replied Pho Lone. He
had had no thought of going to see Mah Pan
again that day, but now he resolved to in sheer
defiance.

"Come afterwards, then."

From the way Moung Maw spoke one would
have thought that Mah Pan was no more to him
than any other girl in the village.   Pho Lone was
very jealous of him, and the thought that Moung
Maw was not jealous of himself made him angry ;
but he was afraid to quarrel, for the carpenter,
besides being masterful, was bigger and stronger
than he was.   He mumbled that he would come
and play later, and turned homeward feeling very
bitter against Moung Maw.   Certainly he must
have procured a good love-charm to be so sure of
Mah Pan's favour.   He was pitted with small

pox and had been known to get drunk; that was
not the sort of man to attract a pretty girl or
make a good husband. Plainly he must have
worked magic. Well, if one suitor could do that
another might, and while the Wise Man still lived
near Ngatheing, half a day's paddle down the
creek, there was no need to be anxious.

Myothit looked very peaceful now after the
busy day. The street was littered with shreds
of bamboo, telling of the work laid aside; thin
trails of smoke curled up from before every
house, and every pot was on the fire. The women
moved about getting dinner ready, while the men
squatted in groups smoking and talking. Passing
Mah Hehn's, Pho Lone glanced in. Mah Pan was
not to be seen, but her mother was there and called
to him to hasten, for Mah Tsay was waiting.

Mah Tsay, Pho Lone's mother, had had an
accident twenty years ago, when he was a baby,
and her back was crooked. In consequence, she
could not do much of the house-work; she could
sweep the floor and sew, but could not clean rice
in the mortar nor lift the pot on to the fire.
When Moung Let and Pho Lone were absent the
neighbours took care of her, but this evening
nobody had thought of helping because both were
at the threshing close by. She was sitting on
the verandah, a wide shelf waist-high above the
street, and began to scold as soon as Pho Lone
came within hearing.

"Lazy one!" she cried. "The sky is shutting, and there is neither fire burning nor rice in the pot. You stay gossiping and forget your old mother."

"No," said Pho Lone very gently, "I thought my father had returned."

"My man forgets me too," whimpered Mah Tsay; "he is not come. Now hasten, lazy fellow! I am hungry."

Pho Lone set to work to cut up sticks and build the fire on the ground a few paces from the corner of the verandah where his mother sat. It is not good to cook quite near the house because the smell of fish and vegetables cooking is unwholesome. One must cook on the verandah in the rains, but then the fire-place, a shallow box of earth, is put where the wind can blow the smoke clear of the house.

"It is a very good harvest," he remarked, setting up the three stones for the pot. "Now all is brought in you can see how large our stack is."

But Mah Tsay did not care to hear about the harvest this evening; she only asked, as she often did when cross, why she had no daughter but only a lazy son. Pho Lone took no notice, but fanned the fire till the flames licked all round the pot.

"There, good mother," he said cheerfully, "soon you shall eat."

c

"The neighbours are eating," grumbled Mah
Tsay. "Only I, the broken woman, am hungry."

It was dark now. All along the street the
firelight dancing on the smoke showed men sitting
at rice. The village was very quiet; the lapping
of wavelets on the mud slopes mingled sleepily
with the slow murmur of voices. Now a crooning
song rose to hush the wail of a child, or a dog
whined for the remains of the rice to be thrown
to him. Mah Tsay sat grumbling to herself till
Moung Let appeared, when she roused herself to
scold him. The rice was ready at last and father
and son hastened to eat, for Mah Tsay was repeating every minute that she was sick by reason
of her empty belly.

Leaving his father to smoke on the verandah
Pho Lone lighted the lamp, a shred of wick in a
saucer of treacly oil, and went to change his dress;
for he could not pay his visit in a faded old cotton
pasoh and nothing else. The upper floor was
partitioned by rough mat walls into two rooms,
one of which Pho Lone had to himself. It was
dark even at mid-day, for the one small window
on the floor level looked into a leafy clump of
bamboo; but that did not matter because he could
find everything with his eyes shut. There was
not much to find certainly. The furniture con-
sisted of a small teak box without a lock, the lid
of a biscuit tin which served as a mirror, and a
low board bedstead with mat, blanket and wooden

pillow, under a tent of thin cotton mosquito net which hung by knotted scraps of coir from the rafters. The head of the bedstead prevented the door opening properly, but Pho Lone never thought of moving it. How could he change its position without disrespect to his parents who slept in the adjoining room? A dutiful son must lie with his feet turned away from his father and mother, and Pho Lone's bed was placed so that his head was nearest them when they slept.

Pho Lone spent some time in his room this evening, and the biscuit-box lid was in much request. When he came down his mother had eaten her rice and sat smoking in the dark, with her bent back against the wall, and her arms hanging over her knees. As he stepped carefully down the rough stairs holding the light before him, Mah Tsay took the big green cheroot from her mouth and looked him over with admiring eyes.

"I go to see Mah Pan," he said; and setting the smoky light on the stairs he drew himself up to show off his clothes.

"She is a lucky young woman," said Mah Tsay, whose ill-temper had yielded to dinner. "She is lucky that my handsome son should go to see her."

Pho Lone did look smart. He wore a rustling silk pasoh of red and yellow tartan, which reached his ankles, and a snowy linen jacket fitting very

close, with tight sleeves made long to wrinkle
from wrist to elbow. His hair was neatly coiled
on top of his head, and a yellow silk kerchief was
loosely twisted about it with two corners sticking
up. As he stood for his mother to admire him,
he threw the long loose fold of his pasoh over his
left shoulder, making the bunch of keys tied to it
jingle again. Every self-respecting man carries
keys thus when he wears his best clothes. People
look after him and say, "What quantities of
valuable property that young fellow must have
locked up in his boxes at home!"

Now if Pho Lone had been wise he would have
asked Shway Toon or somebody else to come with
him to Mah Hehn's. It is the custom to take a
friend with you when paying a visit of this kind;
not so much for propriety's sake, as the young
lady's mother is sure to be at home though out of
sight, but because the presence of another man
makes it appear as if you had just dropped in
casually. The friend always sits outside the
house with his back turned, so he is not the least
in the way; and as Shway Toon was a most
obliging fellow, and, moreover, had sometimes got
Pho Lone to accompany him where he went to
see Mah Mee of an evening, there was really no
excuse for Pho Lone's going by himself. Surely
it is better to be chaffed a little by your friend
than to give the girl you love reason to think
lightly of you?

Moung Byoo's house was a much finer one than Moung Let's; it was larger and better built : the partition which hid the sleeping rooms on the upper floor stood back from the edge, leaving a wide space on which you could sit and look down on the lower floor out of sight of people passing along the street, unless they came close up to look in. As Pho Lone stepped on to the verandah he saw by the light behind the partition that Mah Hehn was at home, and the murmur of voices told him that Mah Pan and her younger sister Mah Noo were sitting on the upper floor just outside their mother's room.

"Come in," said Mah Pan in a tone of pleased surprise when he asked leave to enter ; and Pho Lone crossed the bare floor and waited while Mah Noo got up and vanished into the room behind.

"I will light the lamp," said Mah Pan, rising. Pho Lone would have been quite satisfied to sit in the dark ; but she had more respect for social usage, and in a few minutes an old lamp with a rusty reflector and cracked chimney was hanging on the wall. If she had not been so surprised at his visit, Pho Lone would have thought she expected him ; for mats were spread, trays of cheroots and betel-nut stood at hand, while Mah Pan wore her best tamein and neckkerchief, and had fresh flowers in her hair.

"It is a very good harvest," he said, squatting

as near her as politeness permits—about an arm's length—" quite the best for several years."

" My father tells me so," replied Mah Pan very graciously. " The men who passed down the river from Ladaw village this morning said the people there had also a fine harvest, but there was trouble owing to cattle-disease."

" Yes, we heard that they had lost very many buffaloes in the rainy season."

There was a long pause after this. It is all very well to begin a conversation thus, but a man can't talk to a girl for a whole evening about the crops and foot-and-mouth disease : at the same time when she has snubbed you wantonly a few hours before it is rather difficult to get any further than neighbour-talk. Pho Lone was not clever enough to lead the conversation as he wished, and the two might have sat in silence till it was time for him to leave if Mah Pan had not begun to speak of the pretty things she meant to make her father buy for her when they went to Bassein a month or six weeks later. She let it be understood that, whatever she might have said before, she really intended to go, and thus the ice was broken. From the jewellery Moung Byoo was to buy, to the attractions of Mah Pan who was to wear it, was a very short step. Pho Lone found it so at all events, and the two got on so pleasantly that if their lowered voices had prompted Mah Hehn to peep through a crack in the partition she would have seen that the young man had moved a good deal nearer her daughter.

Which of the two was to blame for the act which so suddenly ended the visit nobody can tell. Pho Lone told his mother he thought Mah Pan would not have minded after what had passed between them ; and Mah Pan assured her mother that she had neither said nor done anything which could explain Pho Lone's insulting conduct. Both gave the same account of the matter : briefly, Mah Pan was reaching for another cheroot from the tray which lay between them, and Pho Lone took hold of her hand ; not only held it, but pressed it in both his own. If he had touched her by accident, she said—even if he did so very carelessly, she would have forgiven him. But when he took her hand like that, of set purpose, she could think of only one way to treat him : she drew herself into the furthest corner and bade him leave the house at once.

CHAPTER III

PHO LONE, ordered out of the house, stood on the road pleading in a cautious whisper for forgiveness, while Mah Pan let down the great framed mats to convince him that apologies were useless. He felt forlorn indeed when the last fell squeaking on its cane hinges, and he could no longer see into the house. Light streaming across the road, and eager voices from a house a little way down the street, reminded him suddenly of Moung Maw's invitation, but he had less wish than ever now to join the party. His one thought was to get home unseen as quickly as he could, that he might think how to repair his blunder. The affair was not likely to end with the loss of Mah Pan's favour : to-morrow, without doubt, Moung Byoo would come and tell him that he must not visit his daughter any more; that was the least he could expect. And if Moung Byoo were very angry he would make formal complaint to Ko Moung Galay, who would certainly inflict a fine; for the headman was strict, and put down doings he considered discreditable to the village with a firm hand. Worst of all was the gossip which would make him a byword among the neighbours, for of course every one would hear how he had insulted Mah Pan while visiting her at young man's time. He knew he had been very foolish, but as he hurried home on the dark side of the road, so that he need not pass Moung Maw's house, he somewhow felt that he was not altogether to blame.

Their own house, like nearly all the rest, was shut, but the lamp shone through the loosely-made mats, and he crept in to find his mother still sitting against the wall where he had left her.

"Well, then, my son?" she began pleasantly, "was she sweet to-night?"

Pho Lone swallowed something in his throat, and dropping on his heels at her side, told her all about it. Any other young man who lived with his mother would have done the same in his place. Of whom should you ask advice, if not your mother?

Mah Tsay said she quite understood how it had happened, and abused Mah Pan for a bold-faced coquette. She tried to comfort her son by recalling similar cases which had occurred within her experience. There was Moung Tha Nyo's for instance: sitting by Mah Way one evening at a poay in the street, he playfully caught her

by the wrist, and being summoned before the
Myooke at Ladaw, he had to pay twenty-five
rupees.

"I think Moung Byoo would not take me to
court," said Pho Lone, not much comforted by
the story.

"He would not," assented his mother, "unless
Mah Hehn makes him."

Pho Lone sighed that he did not know what
to do; and his mother, admitting that she did
not either, reminded him that the fault had been
committed, and there was no use moaning over it.
Whatever was going to happen would happen,
and that was all that could be said. She was
tired, and it was quite time to go and sleep.
Pho Lone snuffed out the lamp with a bit of
stick, and went up to his room. The shame that
would be his troubled him more than the breach
with Mah Pan, and naturally enough. It would
be foolish indeed to make oneself miserable about
a girl when one had the rupees to buy a love
potion. Before he went to sleep he had resolved
to go the next day to Ngatheing village, and
consult the famous wizard, Oo Boo Nah.

If Pho Lone could have heard what passed
between Mah Pan and her mother after he had
gone, he would have been relieved. Mah Hehn
was a shrewd woman, and told her daughter that
as she had not screamed at the moment it would
not be wise to scream now. In other words, they

had better hush up the affair. Pho Lone was not likely to tell any one but his parents how grossly he had insulted her. He had lost his head, and behaved very badly indeed; but as he had asked forgiveness, she thought Mah Pan had best over-look the affront, and, while remaining friends with him, make him keep his distance for the future.

"Every girl in Myothit is jealous of you," she concluded, "and you may be sure they would not put all the blame on Moung Pho Lone."

Mah Pan saw the wisdom of this counsel, and agreed to follow it; not altogether blind to the fact that the secret would give her a certain advantage over the young man.

Pho Lone was awakened before daybreak by the sweet lingering note of a gong which rang out mournfully at intervals and nearer at each stroke. It was Oo Yan on his way to the pagoda; he had no idea of disturbing his neigh-bours, but the good spirits of the air may over-look a meritorious action performed in dim moon-light, so upon that account it is well to beat a gong. Oo Yan's house was at one end of the village, and the pagoda stood on the margin of the jungle at the other, so all but the heaviest sleepers knew what he did, whether the *nats* remarked it or not. "Tang!" The echoes of the *kyee-zee* quivered along the street, and the pariahs howled acknowledgement. Pho Lone got

up, went downstairs, and pushed his way out
upon the verandah, just as the old man came by.
On his shoulder Oo Yan balanced a bamboo, from
whose fore-end hung the little brass gong, like a
halbert head, still spinning and humming from
the last stroke; from the other end hung a
lacquer tray with plantains and rice for offerings.
Oo Yan's gait was that of one who carries a
burden and sees the end of a long journey.

"Cold," said Pho Lone.

"Cold," agreed the old man poising his mallet
for another blow; but he pressed on towards the
pagoda looming ghostly in the sinking moon
without pausing or turning his head. His face
was very grave; probably he was reckoning up
the amount of Merit he had still to acquire to set
off against the sins of his seventy years. The
hpoongyee was wont to speak with special
emphasis of the state of his kyoung when Oo
Yan was among his visitors; but Oo Yan suffered
from deafness at times: his wife Mah Khin took
care of his money. He disappeared in the white
mist and Pho Lone drew his blanket about him
and yawned. He meant to take Shway Toon's
light canoe and start early for Ngatheing, because
when one goes to consult a sayah it is wise to do
it secretly; otherwise somebody may employ
greater magic to defeat your ends. When the
harvest work is going on everybody must do his
share, and Pho Lone knew that if he were seen

paddling off he would be questioned. It was too soon to go yet, however; even had there been light in the sky, the tide was still running up and would do so for some time. So he went back to his mat resolved to stay awake until dawn came and the tide turned.

When he woke again the sun was high, the mist had cleared away, and the people were gathered at Moung Byoo's house eating the morning rice. Pho Lone started when he saw the crowd there, for he did not at once remember that Moung Byoo's paddy was to be threshed to-day, and that Moung Byoo would of course invite the neighbours who helped in the work to breakfast. There was no chance now of slipping away quietly, and the journey to Ngatheing must be put off. It was very unfortunate, because the house-rice, as it happened, was nearly finished and he must spend the evening cleaning a fresh supply; that meant getting up late next morning, for two long hours of work at the paddy mortar makes the legs stiff and the whole body so tired that early rising is out of the question.

He could not muster up courage to go to Moung Byoo's, so boiled and ate his own rice at home, uneasily eyeing the throng of neighbours whom he felt sure must by now know what he had done last night. Presently Shway Toon came sauntering down the street to ask what he was doing. Pho Lone explained that he had slept late and

therefore did not go out to breakfast: had Shway
Toon been to Moung Byoo's? Shway Toon had,
and had heard their host ask Moung Let where
his good son was. Pho Lone could hardly believe
his ears. Clearly Mah Pan had said nothing of
his rudeness, feeling no doubt that she had been
very much in fault. So relieved was he that for
the space of a breath he thought of asking his
friend to clean a little rice for him; he refrained,
however; Shway Toon would be sure to consent,
but equally sure to ask why he wanted it done.

It was their turn to work at the winnowing
stage to-day, and when they arrived they found
Moung Yeik and others waiting for them. Shway
Toon and Moung Yeik stood on the lower platform, receiving the baskets of grain from the
heads of the women who brought it from the
threshing-floor, and swinging them up to Pho
Lone who squatted on the upper stage. All he
had to do was to pour the grain down and toss
the empty baskets after it. The day was a good
one for blowing paddy as there was a little wind;
and soon a long grey cloud of dust was floating
far across the kwins, while the grain, freed from
straw and light rubbish, crept up the stage posts
in a golden heap. From his high place Pho Lone
could see everything that was going on. He saw
Moung Maw squatting idly near the old floor
where Mah Pan was working, and presently he
saw that she left off carrying paddy and sat with

him. He watched them enviously; they seemed quite taken up with each other, never speaking to the people who passed and re-passed close by. He felt sure Mah Pan was telling Moung Maw of the insult offered her last night, and the thought made his knees shake, for the carpenter's temper was hot when roused. His attention was so much occupied that he did not look what he was doing and threw the empty baskets down anyhow. At last one fell on Mah Sein's head.

"Hé, you!" she cried, throwing it off, "take care what you do."

Pho Lone said he was sorry, but his companions laughed so much that Mah Sein got angry and began to call him names. He did not mind being told he was a fool and a stupid, nor did he answer back when she called him a dog's son; but when she screamed again and again that he was a blind leper he grew angry in his turn, and told Mah Sein he should report this to Ko Moung Galay as soon as the sun was overhead.

Mah Sein looked very much afraid when, the people having ceased work for the mid-day rest, the village elders sent to her to come before them. She had been in trouble ere now for using bad language, and it was disagreeable to be brought before the elders with all the neighbours sitting round; for everybody came to look on. It was quite a formal affair. Ko Moung Galay and three other old men squatted in a row on the verandah

of the headman's house and the people assembled
in a half-circle in the roadway, Mah Sein being in
the space between. When Ko Moung Galay
asked why she had used these shameful words to
a clean and healthy young man, she made excuses,
saying that Pho Lone threw the basket upon her
purposely. No, she had no quarrel with him.
She was much hurt: the skin on her shoulder
was cut as all might see. Mah Tsay, from the
crowd, said it was a very little cut for there was
no blood. Mah Tsay had been abused by Mah
Sein a short time ago, and besides she did not like
her son to be called a leper. Pho Lone denied
having thrown the basket at Mah Sein; it was
quite an accident ; he said he was sorry when she
complained. Shway Toon and Moung Yeik, from
the crowd, confirmed: Mah Sein had a bad tongue
and deserved punishment. Mah Sein, kneeling
in supplication, would not offend again : she was
angry, being hurt. Moung Pho Lone was not
blind, nor was he a leper, his fine skin showed not
one white spot as large as a grain of sand. She
was a poor woman.

Elder Oo Yan, having expectorated betel juice,
wiped his mouth with the back of his hand and
delivered his judgment. It was very bad ; words
of abuse were forbidden by the law ; he thought
Mah Sein should pay ten baskets of paddy to
Pho Lone. Elder Oo Shway, having emptied his
mouth, concurred. Elder Oo Ket Kay thought

Mah Sein had had provocation. Mercy was enjoined by the law, and he was of opinion that admonition would meet the case. The neighbours did not approve of this; they reminded each other, and Oo Ket Kay, that he was Mah Sein's husband's partner; but Oo Ket Kay chewed his betel nut, seeming not to hear. Ko Moung Galay, as head man, gave judgment last; he said he would not allow unlawful words of abuse in his village; Mah Sein was a scold; she had been cautioned before, and must pay ten baskets of paddy to Pho Lone.

Everybody but Moung Hlaing and Oo Ket Kay thought it was very good, and said so. Moung Hlaing was Mah Sein's husband, and as the loss fell upon his partner and himself he could not be expected to approve. The court, foreseeing discussion, had adjourned after giving its decision, and the members were already on their way home for the midday nap, so Moung Hlaing appealed to Pho Lone. Pho Lone, now very sorry for the shame he had brought upon Mah Sein, did not want his friend's paddy; but he must tell his wife not to call a fellow bad names in future. Moung Hlaing considered this arrangement very good; it should be as Pho Lone said, and if ever he or his father or mother wanted the work of his, Moung Hlaing's, hands they need only ask for it. Pho Lone saw his chance and took it. He might then, he said, mention that his mother was even now

D

out of house-rice and required one basket cleaned
that night. Moung Hlaing repeated that the
work of his hands was his friend's.

So Pho Lone slept early after all. Moung
Hlaing slept early too, for that matter; the dull
thumping under his house, where Mah Sein toiled
at the paddy mortar till long after all the world
was quiet, did not keep him awake.

The mist was slowly peeling from the creek
next morning when Pho Lone pushed off and
drove the canoe out into mid-stream to get the
full strength of the ebb. The boat was a very
light one; and as he sat, with one leg doubled
under on the flat stern-piece, his weight threw
half its length out of the water, so that the pointed
prow was nearly at the level of his head. Shway
Toon and Moung Maw had taken great pains over
that canoe: it took them half a month in the
first place to select the tree in the jungle opposite
the village (certainly it sometimes happened on a
hot day that they fell asleep in the shade of a
tree they were considering); and they spent the
whole of one rainy season making it when the log
had dried. The marks of tools and fire still scored
the inside, but the outside had been smoothed and
polished with oil till the canoe slipped through
the water like a racing boat. Pho Lone paddled
hard until he was round the bend and out of sight
of Myothit; then, safe from the curiosity of chance
early risers, he stretched out his legs and worked

"ON URGENT PRIVATE AFFAIRS"

more easily. The last wisp of fog was floating away, and the oily water, a narrowing streak which seemed to end in jungle, glinted in the sun. There was little of life between the dense walls of forest : a kingfisher flashed, purple and red, along the margin and vanished into a hanging bush to watch for prey; a slow flight of paddy birds rose and flapped with trailing legs across to a fresh bared patch of mud, and the doves hidden in the trees cooed sleepily. By-and-by Pho Lone laid down the paddle and opened the leaf of cold rice he had brought. He ate that and, after scooping up a few mouthfuls of water, set to paddle again, singing, for the winding creek was lonely and, now the sun was high, very quiet. Reach after reach was deserted, for at harvest time few people leave their villages even for a day. It was quite an event when he came upon a boat piled high with red earthenware chatties moored to the bank in waiting for next tide ; he stopped paddling and drifted by to exchange greeting with the strangers.

" Ho, neighbours ! Where are you going ? "

" Ladaw village and beyond. You ? "

" Ngatheing village."

The chatty pedlars lay down to sleep again and Pho Lone went on, with only the plunge of his paddle and the tinkling ripple before the belly of the canoe to break the stillness.

At length the forest drew back from the brink,

wavered for a bowshot, and then swept inland,
leaving naked mud slopes with overhanging rags
of turf. Pho Lone steered in to look for a landing
place ; he could see Ngatheing ahead now, but he
did not wish to go to the village itself as Oo Boo
Nah's house stood alone a little way on this side.
Sayahs never dwell among ordinary folk. Charms
and spells cannot be wrought with any success
except in strict privacy. Moreover the nature of
the business brings all kinds of nats and sohns
about, especially at night ; and it would not be
agreeable to have living in the village a person on
intimate terms with spirits bad as well as good.
For all reasons it is best that sayahs should live
apart.

Paddling along under the bank, Pho Lone came
upon a log half buried in the mud, and turning her
prow inwards, drove the canoe high up beside it.
A wide rolling plain of grass dotted with bushes
faced him when he had scaled the bank. Not even
a buffalo was to be seen ; a lonely plover in charge
of the landscape piped mournfully overhead, as if
asking what he wanted there, for a belt of jungle
hid the village and there was not a house in sight.
Squatting, and looking round under his hand, Pho
Lone saw the grove of bamboos and jack-trees
which hid the wizard's dwelling, and going in that
direction soon came upon a thin thread of a path
winding through the herbage. Following this he
came to the grove into which it ran. Here the

way was closed by a bar; a child might push it aside, but he were a bold man who visited a wizard unannounced. The track wound so that the house was hidden, but the creaking of boards told that Oo Boo Nah was at home; so Pho Lone sat down, and, making sure his rupees were safe, screwed up his courage to call out:

"Ho, Great Wizard!"

"Who speaks?" asked a hollow voice.

Pho Lone gave his name, his father's, and their village, and asked if he had leave to enter.

A clever sayah has generally so much business that he has to keep visitors waiting. Oo Boo Nah, as everybody knows, has a very large practice; so Pho Lone was agreeably surprised when, after a short pause, the Wise Man replied that he might come. Stepping carefully over the bar he crept in an attitude of respect up to the verandah. But for the smell, which reminded Pho Lone of the burying-ground between the villages, where the dogs fought after a funeral, Oo Boo Nah's was like any other small jungle house: low pitched roof, thatched with dhunny leaves, and mat walls. The sayah was a little old man with thin grey hair and weak eyes; he wore only a pasoh, and his shrivelled arms, breast, and shoulders were covered with curious tattooings and lumps hiding bits of metal and bone which had been inscribed with charms and pushed into slits made in the skin. He sat in the shade on the low verandah, listening with the

air of a doctor while Pho Lone, with palms pressed
together, crouched in the sun outside and explained
the object of his call.

Oo Boo Nah considered the case with great care.
He could not have been more exact in the information he required if young men suffering from
love-sickness were the rarest and not almost the
commonest of his clients. Pho Lone was quite
ready with the answers to those questions he knew
would be put. Moment of birth ? About one
betel-chew after the third crowing of the cock on
the fourth night of the waning of the moon of
Tawthalin, in the year 1232 ; it was a Thursday.
Then could he tell about the time *she* was born ?
Of course Pho Lone was unable to speak with
precision as to the moment of Mah Pan's birth.
There is no knowing what mischief an evilly disposed person might do if he knew exactly the
moment of another's birth. He said at once he
did not know ; she was born on a Wednesday, and
he believed on the 9th or 10th of the waxing of
Tabodwai, year 1234. Oo Boo Nah pursed up his
lips and referred to his calendar. It was the 10th
day, he said ; the 10th was Bhoodahoonay, Wednesday ; he preferred exactness, but knew these
particulars were difficult to get, and would do his
best with the information supplied. He asked a
few more questions : when Pho Lone had gone to
the monastery as a little boy ; how long he remained there ; the exact day and hour when his

hair was cut off on taking the robe, and one or two other things. Then he went into his house, and letting down one of the mats so that he could not be seen, began a sing-song chant while he seemed to be pounding something in a joint of bamboo. Pho Lone sat outside listening eagerly, though he scarcely dared raise his eyes to look up into the darkness of the little house; the chant and the smell and the loneliness frightened him. The pounding noise stopped after a time, and the sayah ceased his incantation to ask more questions. He wanted to know how much land his visitor's father farmed; how much money he made last season; and how much he gave Pho Lone. It was difficult to see what these things had to do with the preparation of a love charm; but of course the wizard knew best.

"We sold our paddy last year for three hundred and eighty rupees," replied Pho Lone. "My father gave me eight rupees and a new silk pasoh for a present, I having given much work in the fields."

"Ah, eight rupees he gave you?" said Oo Boo Nah, looking round the mat.

"Eight rupees. But by ill fortune I have lost money playing, and have but four and a half rupees left. I beg leave to honour you with this very insignificant sum."

Pho Lone crept nearer the verandah and counted out his money, two whole rupees and a small heap

of silver and coppers, while the sayah, without
even glancing at it, handed him a little packet
wrapped in green plantain leaves and tied with
bark string. Pho Lone received the packet and
held it respectfully with both hands above his
knees as he squatted to hear the wizard's whispered advice.

"As much as your finger and thumb will hold
in the food she eats or in the water she drinks." He
dropped his voice still lower : " Keep near her by
day : think of her by night."

Pho Lone repeated the prescription twice, at the
sayah's order, that he might not forget it, and
still holding the packet carefully, asked if there
was leave to go. For answer the wizard looked
all round mysteriously, and beckoned him nearer
that he might whisper in his ear. Pho Lone felt
more than ever that the place was full of spirits,
and went away satisfied that he had got his
money's worth.

"Put a pinch into her water or her food, without letting her or any one else see. Keep near
her by day and think of her at night."

Pho Lone repeated the wizard's instructions
over again and again as he paddled lazily homeward
on the flood. They were easy enough to carry
out, because the big water chatty in Moung Byoo's,
as in every house, stood in the corner of the
verandah where any one passing could reach it,
The only thing was, all the household drank from

that chatty. Suppose Mah Noo was influenced ; or worse, Mah Hehn ? Pho Lone was so staggered by this reflection that he stopped paddling. Suddenly he bent forward, took a longer grasp, and put his strength into the stroke as if to banish thought by work. Had not Oo Boo Nah warned him that the very best charm would fail if he had not faith in it ?

CHAPTER IV

IT was still early when Pho Lone got back to Myothit. None of the people had come home from the kwins, and the few who remained in the village were busy; so he was able to run the canoe ashore near his father's house and land without being seen. It was not a convenient place to land, because the jungle was heavy there, but he was anxious to get home unnoticed for fear of being questioned; and, further, Oo Boo Nah had advised him to put the charm in a place of safety as quickly as possible. A love potion is not like doctor's medicine which may be carried about everywhere without being any the worse; on the contrary, there are several ways in which it may be utterly spoiled, and that too without your being a bit the wiser. Thus, it is always advisable to be very careful of it. If you are not going to use the charm at once the best plan is to place it on the top of the post where the *aing sohn* dwells, that is, close under the rafters in the comb of the roof: the guardian spirit of the house will see that no harm comes to any-

thing given into his care. Of course it is understood that you are on good terms with him; nats
are easily offended, but so long as you treat them
with ordinary consideration their good offices
may be relied on in cases of this kind. Pho Lone
had no reason to suppose that their *aing sohn* was
otherwise than well disposed towards himself;
but as he intended to seize the very first opportunity of bewitching the drinking water at
Moung Byoo's, he thought it was not worth while
taking the trouble to climb up the post, and
adopted another plan which has the approval of
all sayahs, and also has the merit of greater convenience. He ran up to his room and taking the
packet in both hands balanced it on the left hand
post at the head of his bed. Opinions differ as
to which is the better post of the two, and in
choosing the left Pho Lone followed Oo Boo
Nah's advice. The pillow is a safe resting-place if
you do not possess a bedstead; the great point
being to treat the charm with respect. This is
the reason why you must not put it on the floor
nor at the bottom of your bed where it would be
close to your feet.

Pho Lone was very impatient to use the potion;
but he could not do so yet, for as he came round the
house from the creekside he had seen Mah Hehn
sitting on her verandah talking with one of the
neighbours. Nobody must see him bewitch the
water, for if it should come to Mah Pan's ears, the

charm would naturally fail of its object. When
he came in again after taking the canoe back to
its place among the other boats, he found his
mother had returned.

"You come home early, good son," she said,
laying aside the stout stick on which she leaned
when she walked.

"I come from Ngatheing village," said Pho
Lone.

May Tsay smiled, "A love potion?" she
whispered.

"Do not speak of it, good mother. I fear that
my friends will guess the secret."

"We will say that you went to the sayah to
buy a new medicine for me," said May Tsay, as a
bright thought came to her; "we will tell neighbours who ask questions that you went for that
purpose."

Pho Lone thought that a very good idea. The
neighbours might certainly well believe he had
been to get medicine for his mother's back, as
poor Mah Tsay had spent more rupees than they
could afford on charms and spells to make it
straight again. Some of the wisest wizards and
doctors in the district had prescribed for her, but
all without success.

The shadows were long now, and as Pho Lone
was hungry after his long journey, he bestirred
himself to get the rice ready. His mother came
to squat in her usual place on the corner of the

verandah whence she could watch the cooking, but he did not talk to her this evening; his mind was too full of the charm on the bed-post upstairs, for each time he raised his eyes he saw the great water chatty at Moung Byoo's and Mah Hehn and her visitor sitting close by. It seemed a long while before the gossip got up and came down the street and Mah Hehn went in.

"She goes to get rice to boil," thought Pho Lone, hopefully, for Mah Hehn always did her cooking on the other side of the house out of sight of the corner where the chatty stood, and once she settled down to work it would be easy to stroll by and drop in a pinch of the charm unseen.

He waited till the smoke rose and then, asking his mother to come down and watch the pot, went to his room. Between eagerness to use the potion and curiosity to see what it was like, his fingers trembled, and as he squatted, holding the packet with one hand and pecking at the fastenings with the other, he was near dropping it several times. After unrolling many leaves he reached the charm itself: half a dozen pinches of pale brown powder. It occurred to Pho Lone as he sat staring at it that the charm Shway Toon procured to protect himself against death by dah-wound was very much like this, and he was a little disappointed. Even with Oo Boo Nah's final instructions ringing in his ears he could not

at once make up his mind to touch the powder ;
but at length he screwed up his courage to take
a big pinch, and, balancing the open packet again
on the bed-post, went down to the street. Many
of the neighbours had come in from threshing
and winnowing now, and were loitering about
waiting till dinner should be ready. Of course
when they saw Pho Lone they wanted to know
where he had been, for a man does not leave the
village for a whole day during harvest time without good reason ; and equally of course when they
heard he had been to see Oo Boo Nah upon his
mother's account they closed round to ask about
the visit ; for everybody knows the great wizard,
and little details concerning the private life of
famous men are so very interesting. Pho Lone
began to fear that Mah Hehn would have boiled
her rice before he escaped from his friends, they
had so many questions to ask ; and certainly
one might have chewed a betel nut before he got
away.

He strolled up the street, the precious powder
growing damp in his fingers, keeping careful look
out lest he should pass anything bad. What he
had particularly to fear was passing the lower
garments of a woman ; there is something about
a tamein or sandals when they are not in wear
that is fatal to the virtue of charms. Belonging
to a female they are debased, in a manner of
speaking ; and though you may carry a charm

BEWITCHING THE WATER

through all the women in the village without its
taking hurt, if by accident or carelessness you
bring it near a tamein hanging to dry, or a pair of
woman's sandals which the owner has left outside
her house, its virtue fades at once. The odd thing
is that neck-kerchiefs and jackets are quite harmless; it would not hurt the best charm to be
wrapped up in either. Only the sayahs can
explain why this is.

It was rather a dangerous hour, because, as
usual, many people were bathing after the day's
work; men and women bathe in the pasoh or
tamein they have worn all day, and replace it with
a dry one on the bank afterwards, so it was pure
luck that no girl came up between the houses
from the creek side carrying her wet skirt.
Fortune was kind, however, and he did what he
intended, dropping the pinch safely into the
chatty in the act of stepping up to the verandah,
as if to see whether any one were at home. Then,
in sheer bravado, he went round and told Mah
Hehn that he would take leave to come in that
evening; it is wonderful what confidence magic
gives a fellow.

"Come," said Mah Hehn, cordially. "You
were not at work to-day?"

"I went to Oo Boo Nah to get medicine for my
mother," replied Pho Lone.

"More medicine! Mah Tsay throws money in
the creek when she buys medicine now. She has

spent enough," said Mah Hehn, pausing to gesticulate with a burnt stick, "enough rupees to build a pagoda."

"I think so too," said Pho Lone, for Mah Hehn spoke what had been often in his mind, "but it is her wish."

"Why does she not go to the great English medicine-house at Bassein?" asked Mah Hehn, lifting the pot-lid to see how the rice got on, "they would cure her back there."

"She does not like to; nobody knows what they would do to her. We have heard that they cut off people's legs and arms."

Mah Hehn had heard the same story but did not believe it; was it likely, when nobody would speak to a person with one arm if they could help it? Moung Pho Lone might depend upon it those stories were not true.

She turned to the rice-pot again and Pho Lone got up to go home; he bore himself very differently now.

"Pho Lone walks like a peacock this evening," said Moung Yeik to Shway Toon as he passed their house.

"Sweet words make some proud," rejoined Shway Toon grinning good-naturedly. "I saw him come from Moung Byoo's."

Moung Yeik shook his head and smiled pityingly. "I will bet a silk pasoh on the chance of Moung Maw," he said. "Moung Maw is ugly and gruff, but I will bet a new silk pasoh that Mah Pan prefers him."

"Marries him?" asked Shway Toon.

Moung Yeik nodded.

"The bet is made then, friend. I do not believe she will marry him."

Moung Yeik wished to know why, but Shway Toon only laughed and said Moung Byoo's daughter was not like other girls; more than this Moung Yeik could not draw from him.

Meantime Pho Lone, in the highest spirits, was squatting in his room tying up the charm again; he promised himself that he would bewitch the water afresh to-morrow, and every day he could get the chance until the magic powder was finished, and he laughed with delight as he thought how Mah Pan's favour must from this evening turn from Moung Maw to himself. He had just put the parcel into the pocket of a linen jacket that hung on the wall, as a safer place than on the bed post, when his mother called to him to come and eat his rice. He expected that his father would chaff him about his visit to Ngatheing, but Moung Let, who was already eating, had too much to say about the news the Bassein paddy broker's runner had brought that day.

"Moung Choe said 'there are many ships now waiting and the price will be very high at first,'" he observed, through a large mouthful of rice.

E

"Moung Choe says those words each year at this time," grumbled Mah Tsay from the darkness behind. "It is his business to speak thus that poor jungle-folk may bring their paddy quickly, when the white merchants will buy it for a little price. I do not believe the words of Moung Choe."

"You speak wisely," said Moung Let; "but when there are many ships——"

"I believe there are few ships," struck in Mah Tsay, who, to do her justice, was less easily dazzled by the fine stories of broker's men than her husband. "It is not yet the time when many ships arrive."

Before Moung Let could reply, Shway Toon appeared at the verandah, and stepped in. He came to say that Moung Maw had asked him to tell them there would be play at his house that evening and would they come.

"To lose rupees," murmured Mah Tsay, "to play and lose many rupees."

"Or win, good mother," rejoined Shway Toon, "this son of yours always wins:" which was true; Pho Lone was very lucky.

Hearing that the young man had not yet eaten, Moung Let asked him to join them; they had been eating in the dark, but when Shway Toon sat down before the heap of rice Mah Tsay rose to get the lamp. There was no oil in it, so she told Pho Lone to make the jungle travellers' light, which consists of pieces of wax burned on a stone. It is not at all safe for use in the house, because the blazing wax runs; but it would be very inhospitable to let a friend eat his rice in the dark merely because you are afraid of an accident.

Moung Let said he would go to Moung Maw's, but Pho Lone declined at first: he was going to see Mah Pan.

"You go too often," said Shway Toon with the air of a man who understands women. "Girls do not prize what they have too often."

"That is what I say to him," remarked Mah Tsay.

"They should be kept hungry," said Moung Let, "it is good to keep them hungry."

Pho Lone wavered. Oo Boo Nah had specially told him that he must be with the lady as much as possible in order to let the charm take full effect; but then Oo Boo Nah did not know that she was angry: it might be wise to give her time to forget that little unpleasantness of the other night. On the other hand, he loved play, and having spent all his money on the charm, was glad of the chance to win some.

"You will come," said Shway Toon. "Look here, if you do I will come with you to Moung Byoo's another night."

"Very well," said Pho Lone; and rice being now eaten, they got up to drink before going out.

If Pho Lone had remembered, he would have put back the charm upon the bed-post before he put on his jacket and followed his father and Shway Toon; but he forgot it until he reached Moung Maw's, when he did not feel inclined to go back. It did not matter, he thought; nobody but his mother knew he had the charm, and there could be nothing to hurt it in a house where only men lived.

Play had begun when they entered, but Moung Maw at once stopped rattling the dice and politely begged them to join the circle on the floor.

"Give Ko Moung Let place on the mat," he cried; for Moung Let being elderly was entitled to be called "Ko" by young men though they often forgot it. "Neighbour, there is room for you there by the bottle." Everybody laughed at this, for Shway Toon had been known to drink more English spirits than was good for him. "Moung Pho Lone, there is a place for you where you stand."

Room was soon made for them, and the game began again. The house was very bright, for Moung Maw had borrowed lamps from his neighbours; they were wanted, for the dice were so battered from continual use that the pictures could only be seen in a good light. Beside the usual cheroots and betel, there was a bamboo bucket of toddy and a square black bottle half full of gin, with a cracked English tumbler of thick green glass to drink out of. The men of Myothit said that the carpenter was a capital host; the women thought his play parties very bad, and used to urge Ko Moung Galay to stop them; but the head-man always said he would not interfere because no harm was done: he ought to have known for he often joined them himself.

"I shall throw!" cried Moung Maw kneeling to overlook the circle, and shaking the dice in a brass bowl. "Neighbour, will you call?"

"Elephant!" said Moung Let, putting down his two annas, "the elephant for me."

"Mother!" shouted all, as the big dice skipped over the floor and settled. "What luck: double Elephant!"

Moung Let laughed and swept up the pice which were pushed to him from all round. It was great luck to begin by winning a doublet. Shway Toon called next, but Dog did not turn up; so he paid all round and sought refuge in the green tumbler.

The Sixteen Animal game is a popular one for evening play among friends, as any number can take part, and any one can stop when he pleases without disturbing the rest; furthermore it is very simple, and you can make a great deal of noise over it. Six large dice having on each face the picture of one of sixteen animals and birds are

shaken in a bowl or box by an appointed player,
who asks each man in turn to name a creature
before he throws. If the beast or bird named is
among those which come uppermost, the caller is
paid the amount of his stake by each of his fellow
players, and if it is not he pays them. If two
Dogs or Pigeons turn up to a call of Dog or
Pigeon, the caller wins double his stake from
each of the others. A good deal of money may
change hands in an evening's play, though the
stakes are only one *moo*—two-anna bit—as they
always were at Moung Maw's, and though there
is no betting—which was not always the case at
Moung Maw's.

The toddy bucket and gin bottle passed from
hand to hand, and the game grew noisier and
noisier, till the caller had to shout his loudest to
make Moung Maw hear. Uninvited guests,
whose disordered dress and streaming hair showed
they had been roused from sleep, came in and
joined the game or sat round outside the circle to
look on and bet. When a man won he jumped
up to dance and sing, and as callers had great
luck this evening there were often half a dozen on
their feet at once slapping their thighs and
shouting, while the rest roared to make themselves heard above the din. Pho Lone, though
he did not drink, grew as excited as the rest, and
when he won, which happened often, made rather
more noise than anybody else.

THE SIXTEEN ANIMAL GAME.

"You sit in a lucky place," shouted Moung Maw, not for the first time, when he won his second doublet.

"Yes, certainly," agreed Pho Lone, out of breath. "I have won now eight and a half rupees." He sat down as he spoke, and suddenly remembering the charm, put his hand to his breast to feel if it were safe ; it might have fallen out during his capers for he had quite forgotten it.

"I asked you to sit there because it is a lucky place," shouted Moung Maw. But he laughed so strangely that two or three men looked up in surprise.

"I think our friend must be a little drunk," remarked one young man. " His words are very good, but he looks at Pho Lone as if he would kill him."

"Now then," bawled Zah Nee, who was throwing the dice, " Play, play ! Neighbour Shway Toon, call ! Ho, Shway Toon ! "

For Shway Toon had withdrawn from the circle and was sitting by himself against the wall with his eyes shut.

"Call, Shway Toon ! " cried several.

"Ber-r-randy," said Shway Toon at last, opening his eyes and shutting them again.

The laughter at Shway Toon's choice of animal became a roar, when somebody leaned over and held up the gin bottle mouth downwards ; but some of the older men quickly grew grave and began to get up and adjust their pasohs. Moung Let was the first to move; he did not like his partner to get drunk before half the men of the village. It may be all very well for low-class people in towns to drink too much, but in the jungle the man who does that soon loses his character.

"I think it is time to go and sleep," said he, when the men had ceased bantering Shway Toon; and without more words he shook out his pasoh and went, followed by most of the older men. Pho Lone would have gone too, but his neighbours held him down, crying that he must not leave yet; he must stay while he smoked only one cheroot. He always found it hard to refuse, and at last consented to stay, though, as he said, he was tired after his long paddle and wanted to sleep.

"Just three turns," said Zah Nee, who had been throwing the dice latterly, and had now persuaded Moung Yeik to do it. "Just three turns, to let me win a little. There are only six of us, and the lamps will last."

Though the front of the house was half open, the air within was hot and bad from the smoke of the expiring lamps, which hid the dingy bamboo rafters and drifted down, making the men cough and wipe their eyes.

"Play, then, play! Ho, let us play!" shouted

Moung Maw, kicking his heels on the floor as Moung Yeik rattled the dice.

Pho Lone seconded him with a yell of "Play, play, play!" But somehow there was no life in the game now. The dice tripped noisily over the floor, and the only word spoken was the caller's. From silence grew ill-temper. Zah Nee, who had had bad luck all night, objected to Moung Gyaw's calling Buffalo after first calling Dog, because double Buffalo turned up. Moung Gyaw retorted that the dice were rolling, and that he said Dog by mistake; whereupon Zah Nee, saying Moung Gyaw was a cheat, went away in a huff. The next round did not improve matters. Moung Gyaw declared Moung Yeik was not shaking fairly; and Moung Yeik told Moung Gyaw he was a little drunk, for how could he shake unfairly when he did not know what animal would be called? In short, his guests grew so quarrelsome that Moung Maw said the lamps were going out and they must stop. They were sensible enough to take the hint, and went away to their own houses, each remarking as he went out that all the world was quiet, as though surprised that it was so late.

Pho Lone was the last; he stayed to gather up the pile of copper money he had won and tie it in his head-kerchief.

"You have had great fortune," said Moung Maw, standing over him; "yours was the lucky seat."

Pho Lone said it was, and hastened to finish tying up his money, for there was something in the carpenter's manner that frightened him.

"Stop a bit," said Moung Maw, as he lurched on his feet. "I want to show you something."

He reached up, and taking a lamp from the wall squatted to turn the flame higher, while Pho Lone stood twisting the bundle in his hand, wondering what he meant. Moung Maw having made the lamp blaze, threw its light upon the roof over the spot where Pho Lone had been sitting all the evening.

"Do you see anything there?" he asked, shaking with glee.

Pho Lone's heart beat against his ribs like a smith's hammer, and his hand clutched at the charm, for stuffed between the beam and the rafters he saw a dingy bundle.

Moung Maw, who had watched his movements, put the lamp on the floor and his mirth broke loose in a peal of jeering laughter.

"You brought it, you brought it! That is good. Throw it away, then, neighbour, throw it away! That is the tamein Mah Htone wore when her little one was born last month. That is the very cloth."

Now a tamein that has been worn at childbirth is the worst of all; and Moung Maw had taken the trouble to obtain it secretly from his sister's house.

Pho Lone looked at him for a moment in doubt, for how could Moung Maw know that he had a charm at all? Then, stung by the carpenter's sneering laughter, he raised the weight of coin in his hand and aimed a savage blow at his head. Had it fallen Moung Maw must have been stunned, but he jumped back in time and rushed at Pho Lone, who turned and fled from the house, threatening to kill him. The chase was short; Pho Lone being the fleeter kept ahead, never for a breath's space ceasing his threats to cut his pursuer in pieces, till Moung Maw, catching his foot in a litter of rubbish left by a maker of bamboo matting, fell heavily, bruising his knee on a loose stone. When he got up Pho Lone had disappeared into his father's house, so he limped home, vowing to punish him next day.

His anger did not last long; while turning out the lamps which still burned, his eye fell upon the tamein he had borrowed from Mah Htone, and the thought of Pho Lone sitting below it in the "lucky place" quite overcame him; he squatted on the floor and laughed until he was tired. He was so pleased with the success of his trick, and so much amused at Pho Lone's folly in bringing the charm with him, that when he lay down he had quite forgotten the attempt to strike him.

It was not very wonderful that Moung Maw should have guessed the secret, as Pho Lone admitted to himself that night.

The carpenter's work upon the village boats kept him about the creek side, and he had noticed that Shway Toon's canoe was absent from its place. Hearing later that Pho Lone had not been seen all the morning, he asked Mah Tsay casually as he passed where her son was, and she replied that she supposed he was at the threshing-floor like everybody else, proving that she did not know where he had gone. Therefore, when Pho Lone gave out that he had been sent to Ngatheing by his mother Moung Maw was not deceived like the rest of the neighbours. He had heard from Mah Pan how she had been insulted, and knew as surely as though he had been there the real purpose of Pho Lone's visit to Oo Boo Nah; it was just what any other fellow would have done to regain her favour. When he made his trap and sent to ask Moung Let and Pho Lone to come and play, he did not know the nature of the charm; it might have been a spell engraved on a scrap of bone and let into the skin of the young man's breast, in which case the tamein would "kill" it, since the skin had not had time to heal up. Before Pho Lone had been long in the house the movements of his hand betrayed him, and then Moung Maw had to hide his delight by making two men's share of the noise.

Had he known that the charm had already been used he would have been less happy.

CHAPTER V

"I DROPPED the packet while I ran last night; otherwise I might wash my head and scent the charm and repeat the *mandras* to restore its virtue as you say," said Pho Lone. "But it is lost, and I shall not trouble about it any more now."

"Your words are foolish," said Mah Tsay, not unkindly. "You have charmed her, and should obey the sayah. You must keep near her at the threshing to-day."

"But I am afraid of Moung Maw," objected Pho Lone. "I think Moung Maw will beat me."

Mah Tsay, having heard what happened last night, thought it possible; but most likely he had forgotten, and, at any rate, as she reminded her son, he could run away. He could run faster than Moung Maw.

"It is true," sighed Pho Lone with a touch of pride, "I can run faster, but I am much afraid."

Mother and son were crouching over the fire before their house. The sun winked through the

rolling mist, but the air was chilly. Everybody
in the village was up and sitting over the fires
which smoked all along the street, but there was
no sound beyond the crackling of sticks and an
occasional yawn. The children, scarcely awake
yet, nestled their nakedness under the blankets
of their elders, and the pariahs circled about the
groups seeking warmth.

"I do not think it is any use to try and keep
near her," said Pho Lone, who had been thinking
it over, "because Moung Maw will certainly tell
her that I have worked magic and that he killed
the charm."

"Not so," replied Mah Tsay, "he will not do
that. Will he speak of the means by which he
killed it? Do men love to sit under a woman's
rag? No, good son. Moung Maw's tongue will
be silent." And Mah Tsay nodded wisely across
the fire. "He will not let the men know what
he did."

Pho Lone had not thought of this. Of course
the neighbours would be very angry were they to
hear that a woman's tamein had been above
their heads all the time they were playing.
Moung Maw would keep it secret for his own
sake.

"You speak wisely, mother," he said more
cheerfully. "There is no fear of his speaking of
the charm."

"There is Moung Maw," said Mah Tsay, who

sat with her back against the house. "He goes to sit at Shway Toon's fire. See! he walks with a stiff leg."

Pho Lone looked over his shoulder, remarking that the fellow tumbled down last night when chasing him. Without doubt he was drunk to fall on the smooth road.

"It is good, for he cannot beat you while he is lame," said Mah Tsay. "Do not be afraid of him, my son."

"I am not afraid," replied Pho Lone, and, springing to his feet, he doubled his left arm and slapped it in defiance, crying : "Hé! Moung Maw! Hé, hé! you are the son of a she-dog!"

"He is afraid," said Mah Tsay, when Moung Maw did not look round, "he is afraid."

"Yes, he is," agreed Pho Lone, sitting down again. "I shall certainly throw stones at him to-night when the sky shuts."

Though Pho Lone's challenge had not reached the ears of Moung Maw the neighbours near heard it, and among them Ko Moung Galay, who got up from his fire and came over.

"You shout Hé! and an evil name at Moung Maw," he said sternly.

"Not very loud," pleaded Pho Lone, "not too loud. I think he was too far away to hear." For he thought of Mah Sein, and did not wish to be disgraced as she had been.

"You also incite to breaches of peace," con-

tinued the head-man, who knew English law-
language. "Why do you strike the arm at
Moung Maw?"

For a breath's space Pho Lone thought of
telling the head-man how the carpenter had
treated him last night. But he changed his mind
in time, and said he was very sorry; he was sure
Moung Maw was too far away to hear, or he should
not have done it. He would not do it again.

"The day before yesterday," said Ko Moung
Galay, "you complained of a woman's bad tongue,
and we fined her ten baskets. Look, then! If
anybody complains of yours I shall fine you thirty
baskets."

Pho Lone shiko'd meekly, hoping that the
neighbours who were watching did not hear what
the head-man said; and Ko Moung Galay, settling
his blanket about him again, stalked back to his
own house.

Moung Maw, unconscious of Pho Lone's
challenge, limped along to Shway Toon's fire,
where room was at once made for him.

"You have a sick leg," remarked Shway Toon
huskily.

Shway Toon did not look well this morning;
his eyes were bloodshot and his face was yellow.
Already he had said to his friends that he should
never again drink English spirits. But he had
said the same thing often before, and now they
only laughed at him.

"I fell last night," said Moung Maw, spreading his hands to the blaze.

"Over the bottle?" grinned Shway Toon.

"No, friend; or I had had a sick head."

Shway Toon joined faintly in the laugh against himself, and said he should never again drink anything stronger than the water of the cocoa-nut. Then, adding that his head beat very much, he got up and went to his house to lie down. Three or four other men who had been very silent followed his example, and Moung Yeik remarked that it was curious how a little of this English berrandy, which looked just like water, should be so bad. For his part, he believed it was poison.

"English men drink it themselves," said Moung Maw. "How otherwise could I have bought that bottle for one rupee in the shop at Bassein."

"Did you buy it at the shop?" asked Moung Gyaw, taking his cheroot from his mouth to put the question, and everybody looked interested.

"It was more expensive at the shop," said Moung Maw modestly, "but I know it is not good to buy from the Talouks in the bazaar. I have seen English shipmen drunk on liquor the Talouks sold them."

"Shipmen are always drunk," remarked Moung Yeik, sagely, "very many times I have seen them in Bassein falling about the streets. Once I saw one lying on the road and the Tall merchant came past in his pony-cart and stopped. I said to him, 'Sir, I think this gentleman is dead,' he answered, 'I will see,' and got down to look. He put his face near the shipman's very close, like this, and said to me, 'Bring much water.' I brought two great oil tins of water, very heavy, from the well which was near, and at the Tall merchant's order I poured both on the shipman's head and body."

" Was he dead ? " asked Moung Maw.

"The shipman got up," continued Moung Yeik, bubbling over with laughter, "and ran at the Tall merchant ; they ran a long way, but the shipman did not catch him ; he fell down again, and when the Tall merchant came to him, the shipman cried very much."

" Why did he cry ? "

" I cannot tell," said Moung Yeik ; " when the shipman jumped up, I ran through the ditch by the roadside and looked on from the other side, being afraid."

" What happened then ? "

" The Tall merchant took the shipman's arm with his hand, thus, and led him to the creek side ; there he called a kullah boatman and gave him money to take the shipman to his own fire-ship."

"The English are very curious people," remarked Moung Maw, thoughtfully.

"Very curious, indeed," agreed Moung Yeik,

"I saw a strange thing once, years ago, when I was at Wahgyee, driving a bullock cart for the Government-side."

"What was that?" asked Moung Gyaw, who knew Moung Yeik liked to be pressed to tell a story.

"It was the strange way of the English. The kullah soldiers, after many weeks hunting in the jungle, had caught Boh Hpay, the dacoit, and three of his followers; they were all much wounded, and the soldiers carried them into Wahgyee in carts, for they could not walk. Well, they put those four dacoits in the medicine-house, and an English doctor tended them for many weeks, giving them much English medicine both for the stomach and for their wounds; a kullah who pulled a punkah at the medicine-house told me he saw this daily with his own eyes. And when the four dacoits were quite well, the English tried them in court, and Boh Hpay and one man were shot. I saw it with my own eyes."

"After keeping them in the medicine-house and making them well!" said Moung Maw.

"After taking so much care to make them well: just as if they were English soldiers."

"I saw them shot," continued Moung Yeik, "and that too was a strange sight, but also very funny. The dacoits stood against a wall and ten kullah soldiers with guns stood in a line a little way off. An English sitboh gave orders; a young sitboh

with no hair on his face.   Well, when the dacoits
stood up, I with many others stood near, and I
could see the young sitboh's face very white and
his hands shaking as though he had fever.   He
gave orders, and, when the kullahs pointed their
guns, he turned his back to give the last.   Then
he looked to see that the dacoits had fallen dead,
and walked away as if he were drunk."

"That was very strange," said several men, for
there was quite a crowd round the fire now.

"You said it was funny," said Moung Maw,
"why was the shooting of the dacoits funny?"

"The backs of their heads came out," chuckled
Moung Yeik.   "Ho, ho! The back of each head
jumped off and hung by the hair.   It was the
funniest thing I ever saw," and he fairly rocked
with merriment as he thought of it, while his
hearers agreed that it must have been a very
amusing thing to see.

Mah Doh, Ko Moung Galay's wife, was now
calling that rice was ready, so the people left
their fires to gather at the head-man's house.
Moung Maw noticed that Pho Lone put himself
forward, showing much politeness to Mah Doh,
and remarking upon it to a friend, heard that the
young man had been scolded that morning by Ko
Moung Galay, and why.

"He called you a bad name, and beat his arm
at you," said the friend.   "Many people near
heard him."

"If I had heard it, I should have killed him," said Moung Maw, calmly plunging his fingers into a heap of steaming rice. "I do not love quarrelling, but if he does it again I shall certainly kill him."

Pho Lone, anxious to regain the favour of Ko Moung Galay, was helping Mah Doh and Mah Mee with the rice-pots; but he overheard the words, as Moung Maw intended he should, and decided not to do it again.

"You did not come to see me last night," said Mah Pan to Moung Maw rather loudly. "Why did you not come?"

The carpenter was a proud man and did not like to be spoken to thus before the neighbours, even by the prettiest girl in the village.

"I forgot," he answered with his mouth full.

Mah Pan's ears tingled, for she heard the girls giggling. She turned her back on Moung Maw and talked to Mah Mee about whom Pho Lone was hovering. She had not spoken to Pho Lone since the evening when he insulted her, but now she caught his eye and gave him her sweetest smile; Moung Maw must be punished. The smile did its work and Pho Lone was at her side.

"You are too busy to speak to one this morning," she said.

"No," said Pho Lone, casting a fearful glance in Moung Maw's direction. "No, not too busy

now. But I think there will be much work presently with the paddy."

"I think the elder brother no longer wishes
to talk with me; no longer cares to speak to me,"
said Mah Pan, with a glance.

Moung Maw was not looking; he was laughing
with some other men. Pho Lone dropped on his
heels, and made the most of the time. He was
very happy indeed when the party broke up, and
began to drift out to the threshing-floor. Mah
Pan had been sweeter than she had been for a
long time past, and Moung Maw had not even
looked at them. Without doubt that was a
wonderful charm Oo Boo Nah had given him;
a single pinch had done this. How lucky
it was he had lost no time in putting it in the
water!

Moung Maw, having finished his work on the
boats, came to the threshing, but more to enjoy
the society than to use his hands. He did not
once go near Mah Pan, and did not seem to
hear, even when she asked Pho Lone to let her
drink smoke from his cheroot. As Pho Lone
told his mother afterwards, he had to keep near
her, whether he wished to or not; for what was
a fellow to do when a girl kept asking him to
help her lift sheaves, and told him he must sit
with her when she got tired? Mah Sein said
the way they flirted was shameful, and though
everybody knew Mah Sein was bitter against

Pho Lone, no one contradicted her. Yet Moung Maw, playing with the little boys by the threshing-floor, did not seem to see or hear. Pho Lone's head was quite turned by noon when work stopped. He had told Mah Pan of his luck at play last night, and had received her permission to buy a silver necklace with his winnings. He felt that such a present as that must complete what the love charm had begun so well, and so excited was he that at a nod from Mah Pan he would have beaten his arm at Moung Maw again out there on the kwins.

"I cannot get the necklace till we go to Bassein," said Pho Lone, as they walked back to the village together; "but I shall certainly buy it then."

"That will be quite a month," pouted Mah Pan.

"I shall play often again before then," said Pho Lone quickly, "and shall win many more rupees; perhaps so much that I shall have enough to buy you a dahleezan."

A dahleezan is the ornament of all others to please a girl; it is a mat-work of links and plates and drops of silver to wear round the throat. Mah Pan replied that if it were a dahleezan she could certainly wait a month.

There was a little stir in the street when they arrived. Moung Paw Thin, the policeman, had arrived on patrol duty, and was squatting on Ko

Moung Galay's verandah awaiting the head-man's return. You could see at once that Moung Paw Thin's was an important position; everybody who passed made a little shiko to him, which he did not appear to notice. When he visited the village for the first time, people were pleased to see him, and crowded round to hear the news from Ngatheing and other down-creek villages, whence he had come; they did not do so now, and there was that in Moung Paw Thin's face which said it would not be good to offend him. Even Ko Moung Galay, when he arrived, showed respect to the constable, and hastened to offer him a mat to sit on.

"I have walked very far," said Moung Paw Thin, as he allowed the mat to be put under him.

"Is it your pleasure to eat rice and a little dried fish?" asked Ko Moung Galay anxiously.

It was Moung Paw Thin's pleasure; he also liked ngapee; so Mah Doh had to light a fire and cook food instead of going to sleep as she usually did when she came in from work. Their guest was hungry, and after he had asked twice whether the rice were not ready, Ko Moung Galay himself went to tend the fire. The first stir had subsided, but there was an air of uneasiness all along the street, groups of men and women gathering between the houses to talk instead of going in to sleep at once.

Moung Paw Thin did not mention business until he had eaten and had accepted a cheroot which his host crouched to light for him. Then he inquired what news there was of bad characters.

"By reason of the great vigilance of the police," said Ko Moung Galay, "the district is quiet. We have heard no word of dacoits for many months, since you last came."

Moung Paw Thin gave the ghost of a nod, as much as to say he knew there were no dacoits in the neighbourhood, and the reason assigned by Ko Moung Galay was the right one; but all he said was, "The book!"

The head-man brought the official book which he kept in his box, and after rummaging for a time, found the ink-bottle and a rusty pen. A drop of water made the ink fit to use, but Moung Paw Thin scowled when he took up the pen.

"I cannot write with that," he said angrily; but he crossed his legs, and resting the book upon them, took a dip of ink from the bottle Ko Moung Galay held, and made much display of inability to write. "I shall report that the Government property at this village is not properly cared for," he said, throwing the pen down after a moment.

It was Ko Moung Galay's own pen, as Moung Paw Thin knew very well; but the head-man was wise, and said he feared it was not fit for a police officer to write with. Would Paw Thin do him the great favour to bring a new pen next time he came? Perhaps two rupees——

Moung Paw Thin consented to buy it, if he remembered, and tucked the two rupees into his waist-cloth, adding that he did not know the price, but no doubt that would be enough. Mah Doh, who had been looking on, remarked that two pens cost half an anna, but Ko Moung Galay signed to her to be silent, and Moung Paw Thin did not hear.

"With your honoured leave, I shall write in the book the words you command," said Ko Moung Galay, rubbing the pen on the floor to get the rust off. "I am your clerk, to write at your order.

Moung Paw Thin pushed the book off his lap, and between the puffs of his cheroot, dictated: "I arrived in Myothit village at a little past noon. Asked the head-man if there was news of dacoits. He said there was none. Left at two o'clock."

Ko Moung Galay scratched away at the book, repeating the words as he wrote them. It *was* a bad pen, and spat ink too much, as he confessed to Mah Doh afterwards; but one could write with it.

Moung Paw Thin signed the entry, quite forgetting how bad the pen was, and when the book had been put away, he cleared his throat, and said there was another matter. He was informed there was much gambling in Myothit, and that many people were thereby in debt.

"Several owe money to the kullah chetties," admitted Ko Moung Galay, "but not because they have gambled away their money."

"I have orders to arrest gamblers," said Moung Paw Thin. "It is your duty to give information about persons who break the law. My order is that you tell me the names of men who gamble."

Ko Moung Galay gave a little awkward laugh.

"Shall I read to you the names upon the village tax-roll?" he asked, in respectful play.

Moung Paw Thin looked at him from under angry brows.

"At Thigyoung village last month," he said, "I gave this order; whereupon, like you, the head-man laughed and read to me the names upon his tax-rolls, beginning with his own. The head-man of Thigyoung has lost the favour of the Government."

Ko Moung Galay did not wish to lose the favour of the Government. It would be bad for himself, and also for the village. He knew quite well what the Government wanted, but he would not get any of his people into trouble if he could help it. Still, he was not in a position to object. In every village on the creek it was well known that the Ngatheing people had got into trouble on a charge of harbouring dacoits, whom they had never seen, because Ko Bah Too, the surly head-man, had refused to order men to take the Government in a boat to a distant village. He had a printed notice in his box, which said in beautiful language that head-men were to at once report attempts at extortion to the Assistant Superintendent of Police at Bassein; but Bassein was far away, and one could not leave the harvest to make a report, and an enemy at the same time. Besides it was a great deal too much trouble, all for the sake of a few rupees.

"The men in my village play only very little," he said at length.

"You know it is against the law to play at all," replied Moung Paw Thin. "Give the name of one player."

"Well, then, Pho Lone, son of Moung Let, plays," declared Ko Moung Galay in desperation. After all somebody must suffer; Pho Lone had had all the luck lately, and the winner of rupees was the only gambler the Government wanted to see.

"Anybody else?" demanded the constable.

"No other man has been winning more than a few pice for a long time," sighed Ko Moung Galay. "As I have told you the men here do not play very much; they are poor."

The people were all lounging in their houses by

this time, but they looked out now and again towards the head-man's. The patrol constable was a new institution and nobody thought him a good one ; he came about once in each month to ask for news of dacoits, and never went away without a present. Oo Yan grumbled most at these new fangled ideas. What, he asked, could one policeman do if there were news of dacoits ? Go back at once and report ! Well, if he did the dacoits would be miles away before he got to the police thannah. Yes, yes, he knew that the patrolling frightened dacoits, and that three or four times gangs had been traced and broken up owing to the news taken by patrol constables. But what of that ? It was an accident in each case. Who could say it was not ? Besides you never knew that dacoits would attack the village ; they might not. Myothit had not been attacked for years. But the constable came each month as surely as the full moon and always took money. They must give him money, or worse happened. The people generally agreed with Oo Yan. He was old, so his words were naturally held in respect, particularly by those men upon whom the patrol constable had happened to call at any time.

Hence, when Moung Paw Thin, followed by Ko Moung Galay, went down the street to Moung Let's everybody looked on much relieved. Moung Maw lay in his house shaking with laughter. It was in his mind to go to Moung Let's and tell the constable exactly how much Pho Lone had won; but he did not, partly because he was good natured and lazy, and partly because the neighbours would have thought badly of him. So he lay quiet with his chin on his hands, listening, like every one else, to Mah Tsay's shrill abuse of Moung Paw Thin and to Pho Lone's frightened protests. Moung Let squatted against the wall smoking calmly; he could do no good by joining in, and might get himself into trouble.

The head-man and the constable were a long time in the house, fully two betel chews, and never for a moment did Mah Tsay's tongue cease. When at last they came out Moung Paw Thin carried, rolled up under his arm, a silk pasoh, which every one recognised as Pho Lone's, and fingered the fold of his own red cotton one where a man keeps his money. They went back to Ko Moung Galay's, and after a while, when it was thought the constable would be asleep, the people crept stealthily over to Moung Let's, for they were all dying to know what the visitor's words were and what he had done. Mah Tsay's account was so long and loud that her husband had to make her be silent for fear the Government should come back again; it was also rather confused, and that was why every one assembled at Ko Moung Galay's when the sky shut, soon after Moung

Paw Thin had gone, to hear him speak on the matter.

Ko Moung Galay sat on his verandah, above the people, and spoke wise words. In his opinion Pho Lone had had a very lucky escape; he had been gambling, as everybody knew. Everybody assented doubtfully. He had won money from several neighbours. Several agreed bitterly. And since gambling was against the law, the constable would only have done his duty had he taken Pho Lone to prison. Pho Lone would have been tried in court and perhaps sent to prison where all his hair would be cut off and he would wear chains on his legs. Everybody said "Mother!" in a tone of sceptical awe. Yes, that might have been the fate of Pho Lone. Instead of arresting him, however, the constable had been content to confiscate (a rumbling chuckle passed through the crowd)—to confiscate the rupees he had won; nine rupees and some copper coin. And such was Pho Lone's gratitude (somebody laughed and many found their throats required clearing) that he begged the constable to accept his best pasoh as a present. It was a lucky thing that Moung Paw Thin was not a hard man. Gambling was not good. The village had lost the work of an afternoon owing to the constable's visit; he hoped his friends would eat rice at his house next morning.

"He is the head-man," said Moung Yeik to

Shway Toon as they strolled home afterwards,
" and he must say those words because he receives
Government-side pay.   He knows it is all nonsense
and that the constable is a thief: he will say so
to one but not to many."

CHAPTER VI

I<small>T</small> was a full month since Moung Paw Thin's visit
to Myothit. There was no mist in the morning
now and fires were only needed to boil rice. The
cold season was over and men and women went
about in great leaf and canework hats to guard
against the sun, which glowed a dull red ball in a
pale sky. All the paddy was in ; the granaries
were full and great yellow heaps caught the sun
behind every house. The yield was the largest
Oo Yan could remember, and as reports said the
harvest was good everywhere, the men were
anxious to market their grain early before heavy
supplies should bring down the price. Hence
when Oo Boo Nah was requested, as usual, to
ascertain the propitious day for starting all were
glad when he determined a very early date.
Every boat was laden down to the gunwale and
ready to start for Bassein ; there had been some
talk of dacoits lately, and owners had decided that
it would be safe to make the voyage in company,
so there was none of the hurry to get away first
which Myothit had so often seen.

There was no striving to be first, but ten or twelve boats cannot start on the first trip of the season without some bustle, and the bank was alive this morning. Men were wading, swimming and climbing on board, to vent their high spirits when they got there by capering and shouting. Every boy in the village who was old enough to do what he ought not was where he was least wanted. The men and women who were to remain at home, sat on the top of the bank against the piles of baskets which had been tossed aside after loading, and screamed messages to their friends; those who had no messages to give, shouted because it seemed good to make a noise. Pho Lone was dancing wildly, singing and slapping his thighs as though he had not a care in the world, and Mah Tsay, sitting in a basket with her chin on her knees, screamed cheerfully at him from the bank. She was glad to see him so happy again; for he had been dull and mopish ever since the patrol constable took away his money. Pho Lone cared no more for rupees than another man: money was not a thing to trouble about so long as a fellow was happy. When he lost at play he did not care, because the excitement was the same, losing or winning: if he won, he was ready to toss a friend for every coin and was repaid in due measure by the fun of it. At any other time he would have thought little of his loss; he would have called the constable bad

names for a day or two when the subject was
mentioned, and then in his natural wisdom would
have ceased to regret what he could not help, as
neighbours had done before in like cases.   What
weighed upon him was his inability to buy that
silver necklet which he had promised Mah Pan
and which was to complete what the charm had
begun so well.   It had been very plain that since
his loss he had made no progress in her favour,
though in obedience to Oo Boo Nah he had kept
near her as much as he could ; while on the other
hand, Moung Maw had been taken into favour
again and that in spite of his seeming indiffer-
ence.

However, he was joyous enough now.   He was
on Moung Byoo's boat, and Mah Hehn and Mah
Pan were on it also, while Moung Maw, almost at
the last moment had exchanged into another boat,
to Mah Pan's hardly veiled anger.

"Push ! push ! push !" roared the man who sat
on the high steering chair.   "Ho ! clear those
oars there.   Push away !   She goes ! she goes !"

"Loo la, youk kya, Loo-la-heeey !" sang the
men straining at the poles, "Loo-la, loo-la, heeey,
heey !   She floats !" and all sang together as the
poles sank and the great boat glided clear of the
crush at the bank.

"Oars, oars !" shouted the steersman ; for the
tide was just turning and Moung Byoo did not
wish to drift too far ahead.   The rattan-tied oars

creaked and splashed and the pointed prow swung
up stream, a few paddling gently to hold her so.
Moung Byoo would take the steering paddle himself presently, but just now he was busy with
more important matters, as a careful boat owner
should be when starting on a trip. He was
crouching in the attitude of respect on the prow,
holding in his hands a lacquer tray containing an
offering while he muttered prayers to the nats.

The creeks, like the fields and jungles, and the
air itself, are full of spirits, and very touchy spirits
at that. The water-nats are particularly huffy ;
the least little thing offends them, and when
angered or annoyed they are capable of any mischief. They will put a snag in the shallows
where the boat must pass, cling to the smooth
bottom when the rowers are tired and so double
their labour ; make a split in the hull to let in
water and spoil the paddy, steal oars when you
forget to secure them on mooring, or play any of
a score of tricks, even to pulling a boat bodily
under water with all her crew. On a long trip
when men cannot go ashore they must give offence
to the nats ; and for this reason it is good to pro-
pitiate them at starting. Offerings nearly always
put them in a good temper, though cases have
been known of boats coming to grief in spite of
the most liberal treatment in this respect. Moung
Byoo was far too sensible a man to risk giving
offence by any appearance of meanness. His tray

PROPITIATING THE RIVER SPIRITS

was laden with rice, plantains, betel-nuts, chillies, tender shoots of bamboo and flowers. These he offered freely, murmuring his prayer for the nats' protection and indulgence, and asking forgiveness in advance for any acts on the part of himself or his men that should give them pain. Mischievous and irritable as nats are, it cannot be said that they are greedy; indeed their appetites are very delicate : they swarmed round in invisible crowds to eat of the *ngway*, the essence of the good things on the tray, thereby signifying acceptance of Moung Byoo's bountiful offering. Even stingy Mah Hehn, did not object to her husband's lavishness in this matter ; because when the nats had taken all they wanted the men ate the rest.

Boat after boat slid out from the bank and hung against the ebb in a lengthening chain, while the owners propitiated the nats, and men girt their pasohs tightly about their hips and poured water on the oar fastenings that they might work easily. On most of the larger boats the oars were tied to short uprights, which stood up like the ends of ribs. Moung Byoo's had a knee-high bamboo rail on either side to which the oars were lashed, but then his boat was the pride of the village; the carved steering-chair with its little sun-roof had cost a hundred and seventy rupees, and the great gilt and red eyes on the prow gave it a very fierce look. There was not such another boat on the western creeks

between Ngapoota and Mazalay. When people
of other villages boasted of their boats all a
Myothit man had to say was, "Moung Byoo's
boat is mortgaged for two thousand five hundred
rupees." Then the boasters exclaimed, "Mother!
is that so, neighbour?" and were silenced. The
boat was mortgaged, but Moung Byoo had raised
the money from the English merchant to whom
he had sold his paddy for the last twenty
seasons. It is much wiser to mortgage one's
boat to a white man than to a grasping Madrasi
money-lender who asks three per cent. a month
and will foreclose in a minute if you happen to
lose at play the rupees you had saved to pay his
interest. Moreover, the Englishman will lend
the full value of a boat, while the chetty will not.
Of course you have always to sell your grain to
the merchant who holds the mortgage; but no
hardship arises from this, because all the merchants agree among themselves to pay the same
price, fixing the rate for a week or so at a time
during the season.

All this time Moung Byoo's boat had been
dropping slowly down the creek, and was now
round the bend out of sight of the village. One
by one others crept, stern first, into view, so that
a message could be passed from boat to boat
right home to Myothit a mile away. Moung
Gyaw had given over charge of the steering
paddle, and Moung Byoo, with Mah Pan at his

side, squatted on the perch watching the movements of the fleet. Presently much splashing
and shouting on a boat just drifting round the
bend caught his eye. "All the boats are out,"
he said, laying his cheroot aside. "Give me
room, good daughter." Mah Pan got out of the
way of the tiller, and he pressed it forward with
both hands.

"Now, my sons, put her round, round, round !
Pull Moung Gyaw's side, back Zah Nee's !"

"What great splashing !" said Mah Hmway
Pan, as the boat turned. "The water leaps even
up here."

"All together, now ! Pull away, pull away !"

Moung Gyaw and Zah Nee at the stroke oars
glanced at each other to set the time, and the
fourteen rowers stepped forward like one, throwing themselves back with arms at full stretch.
The boat swept forward to their short, slow stroke
with a creak you could hear above the rowing
chorus, and Moung Byoo picked up his cheroot
again to smoke gravely as becomes a boat-owner.

Mah Pan settled herself comfortably, sought
Pho Lone among the rowers below, gave him a
laughing nod, and turned to look behind.

"All the boats follow now," she remarked. "I
think they are racing."

"Is Moung Let's first ?" asked Moung Byoo
with a chuckle.

"No," replied Mah Pan, facing round at once ;

for Moung Maw was rowing on Moung Let's boat, and she knew what her father meant.

It was pleasant to sit on the steering chair high above the deck and shaded from the sun, getting the best of the breeze from the motion of the boat. Not a leaf stirred in the jungle which hedged the glistening creek from the brink. The men had ceased singing now and talked as they swung the oars. Every one was in a good humour, and presently Zah Nee, who was married and ought to have known better, began to say pretty things to Mah Pan. Others put in their word, saying she was the queen of the boat: this was very agreeable, and Mah Pan soon forgot Moung Maw's desertion. When Zah Nee had no more to say to her she began to make eyes at young Hpo Chit, who pulled the oar behind Pho Lone's. This was great fun, because Hpo Chit, being very bashful, did not know where to look, and Pho Lone, thinking her glances were meant for him, looked so absurdly happy.

As the strength of the ebb increased the boat went faster, though the oars were scarcely more than dipped. Off Ngatheing village they stopped and shouted to the people on shore, for the Ngatheing boats were all ready to start, and, it appeared, had been waiting since yesterday for those from Myothit. The Ngatheing men pushed off as they drifted by, and all went on together, a noisy crowd spreading across the

stream from bank to bank. There was no jungle
to hide the country now, but there was nothing
interesting in endless stubble fields, and Mah Pan
was growing tired of her cramped seat.

"We shall come to Tawchoung on this tide,"
said her father, whom she asked where they
should moor, "and go on again with the next
ebb. That will take us to the river, and we shall
go up to Bassein on two tides."

Tawchoung was still two hours away, so she
let herself down by the deck-house roof below and
went in to sleep.

The fleet glided on. Past the village of the
Karen Mission stockaded down to the water;
past endless ranges of bush jungle so close that
not even deer could harbour; past a weed grown
waste which had been paddy land, and past the
charred posts peering above the herbage, which
was all that remained of Thippingyee village after
the dacoits attacked it three years ago. The men
were growing tired and only paddled with their
oars, letting the current do the work. The creak,
creak of the cane fastenings at every stroke was
enough to send one to sleep; now and again
when a bird screamed you felt how still it was
save for the oar-squeak from the twenty boats
astern. Moung Byoo sat with his hand on the
tiller looking fixedly ahead; the tide was slacken-
ing and when it began to turn they must stop;
men never row against the tide in the creeks of

the Delta ; the progress made would not be worth
the toil.

"Pull away," he said cheerily, for they had but
little distance to go now, and the water being
nearly dead the boat was creeping like a log.

Pho Lone struck up the rowing chorus, and the
rest joined in, but as men who are weary. At
last the boat rounded a curve and a long low
spit where two creeks met ran out from the left
bank. "Tawchoung !" cried Moung Byoo, and
soon the oars were trailing against the boat's side
and the anchor was dropped. The rest of the
fleet anchored as they came near ; and, the sun
having now sunk behind the trees, the men began
to boil their rice.

Moung Byoo's rowers were fortunate ; they
could sit down to rest and smoke, because the
women were there to cook for them. Pho Lone
was the only one who did not rest. This was the
time to which he had looked forward so eagerly,
and no sooner did Mah Hehn put out the pot than
he went to help. He got a dah and cut up the
sticks while Mah Pan measured out the rice, a
double handful for each man ; for rowing seven
hours together gives a great appetite. Pho Lone
helped her to set the pot on the fire-stones, three
pointed lumps of blackened clay buried in a
shallow box of earth ; and then, having set the
fire alight, squatted to help her watch the rice
boil. They did not talk much ; but now and again

Pho Lone glanced at his father's boat which lay on the other side of the creek, and wondered if Moung Maw were sorry now that he had not come in Moung Byoo's.

The sky had shut; all had finished eating and sat in groups smoking and talking. Mah Pan left her father and mother in the little cabin, and found a quiet corner in the stern where she settled herself comfortably to smoke.

"I have made a plan to get a little money," said Pho Lone, appearing, as it seemed, from nowhere, to sit near her.

Had he? What did he want rupees for so much? That necklet? What necklet? O yes; she had forgotten. And Mah Pan puffed her cheroot lazily, looking out over the fleet of boats sleeping on the black water.

"Shall I tell what the plan is?" asked Pho Lone meekly; she did not seem very sweet to-night.

"Tell," she said, as a mother might speak to a child.

"I will help to measure my father's paddy," said Pho Lone eagerly, "and I will cut each basket."

Mah Pan did not understand; so he explained, very proud of having thought of such a good way of making rupees. She knew how paddy was measured? It was taken out of the boat and heaped in the godown; then a square wooden box, called a basket, though it was not a basket at all, was used to measure it, box by box, into another heap while Moung Let and one of the black strangers of the godown kept count.

Mah Pan understood quite well; but she did not see how Pho Lone could make money by helping to measure.

No? Well he would show. He would handle the measuring stick himself; each time the box was filled, the paddy was levelled off with a short round staff as thick as a man's arm at the shoulder. By stretching the fingers as you drew this staff over the box you could scoop out quite a lot each time.

But would the godown stranger take short measure?

Kullahs, Pho Lone explained, were often stupid, and when not stupid, could be made so by a little present; he did not expect any difficulty there. After the paddy had been measured he should tell what he had done, and his father, being much pleased, would give him a present.

Mah Pan thought the plan very good. Moung Let's boat carried four hundred baskets, but if Pho Lone could cut each as it was measured it might turn out a good deal more. She hoped Moung Let would be generous, for she wanted very much a silver necklet to wear. Now she should go in to sleep.

The moon peeped over the black tree-shadows down upon the boats straining to the flood; the

water gurgled and lapped under their prows as
they slowly swung; the crickets shrilled in the
jungle and fluttering bats chased each other to
and fro; now a fish plunged, sending silver rings
to break in moonlit diamonds on a boat's side;
and the fire-flies floated among the bushes over the
banks. A thread of smoke trickled up from a late
fire, but every man slept with his pasoh between
his body and the stars.

The tide had turned and had been running
down for quite an hour when Moung Byoo awoke
and crept out on deck; the moon was shining
brightly, and all the men were still sound asleep.
He stepped among them carefully hoping that
something would soon happen to make a noise and
wake them; but nothing occurred and he sat
down again to wait. Fortunately the men on the
boat anchored just above, being still half asleep,
were very clumsy and in starting managed to
bump up against Moung Byoo's. The squeaking
and groaning as she rubbed by was enough to
wake everybody, and in half a betel chew the
anchor was up and they were on their way to
Moogyouk where the Tawchoung creek enters the
river. There was not much talk as the men
rowed, but a good deal of yawning. They reached
Moogyouk just after the sun rose, and anchored
again to eat rice while they waited for the flood
which would carry them up the river. Moung
Byoo reckoned that they should arrive at the

little village of Kyouksay on this tide, and get up to Bassein on the next with half a tide to spare, unless there was wind, in which case they would hoist the sail and arrive at the end of the journey on the first tide. He had made the trip three or four times each season for so many years that he knew exactly what to expect.

Every one was glad when, after rowing a very little way, Moung Byoo cried from the steering chair to raise the mast. You could see the dark ripple far away, and when the breeze came it filled the sail hanging ready from its slender yard of spliced bamboo and left the oars to spurt tiny fountains as they trailed alongside. It was not worth going to the trouble of lifting the oars and tying the blades to the bamboo rail; the wind might drop and then the work would be wasted. Moung Byoo's boat sailed fast and gradually drew ahead of the rest which, also under sail, were stringing out as far as you could see. Nobody was afraid of dacoits now the broad river was reached; it was different in the creeks where dacoits could hide on the banks and shoot you in the middle of the stream.

Mah Pan climbed up to sit by her father again. She had been to Bassein before, certainly, but that was some years ago and she remembered only enough of the sights to make her eager to see them again. There were the ships; great ships with three masts and more ropes than any man

could count; three passed them to-day pulled by
little fire-ships which fussed along groaning and
throbbing as though angry with the lazy vessels
behind them. And the way the men on board
crowded to the side to stare! You would have
thought a paddy boat was as strange a sight as
their own great vessel. Then a large fire-ship
passed up; it rather frightened Mah Pan, it
came so close, and there was such terrible thunder
in its inside; moreover it kicked up the water
behind in a most violent way. While the fire-
ship was passing a very surprising thing happened: a gentleman with hair all over his face
leaned over and putting bottles to his eyes, cried:
"Ho, Moung Byoo! Where do you go?" in Burmese.

"He knows your name!" exclaimed Mah Pan;
and the rowers echoed, "The gentleman knows his
name!"

Moung Byoo shouted back: "To Bassein," and
laughed; but it was easy to see that he was a
little proud of the white man's calling him by
name. "I know the gentleman," he explained to
Mah Pan, "he is not a real shipman; he lives at
Bassein and earns much money by steering ships
up and down the river. I forget his name, but
he is a very kind gentleman. Once when the
wind was strong against us, he told me to tie my
boat, this very boat, behind the fire-ship which
was about to leave the godown, and towed us
right down to Mougyook. Then he pretended

that we must follow out to the sea, many tides distant, but when we laughed he bade the ship-men loose the rope."

" Do all Englishmen say, ' Ho, neighbour !' like him ?" asked Mah Pan.

" Not all," replied Moung Byoo, hand on tiller, eye on sail. " When a white young stranger cannot speak it is not good ; when they learn to speak well it is best ; they are then very polite and love to joke."

" Yes, usually they are kind," he answered to her next question, " but if they are made angry they become dangerous. Once I saw Thaw' thekin in a rage ; it was when he caught Bah Loogalay cheating. Mother, how fierce he was ! He beat Bah Loogalay till he howled."

Mah Pan took a note of the incident. Pho Lone was nothing to her but she did not wish him to be beaten.

The wind freshened as the sun rose higher, and now the boat rushed through the wavelets, up-right and steady, while the double bamboo mast bent groaning to the rounded sail. The trailing oars were raised and looped to the rail, and the men, delighted that they need row no more, sat about the deck smoking and chewing betel. Pho Lone looked up at the steering chair now and again, sighing. He was the only person who was sorry there was wind ; he would gladly have rowed all day for the sake of another evening like the last. He hated Mah Hehn because she was rejoicing over the rice she had saved.

Round the last gentle curve in the river, and the mills with smoking chimneys, the ships waiting for rice, and the pagoda which overlooks the town, all came in sight together. "In another betel chew we are there," remarked Moung Byoo contentedly, "it is the quickest journey I remember."

They ran past two or three godowns, before he said, pointing with his cheroot, "Thaw' thekin's," and gave the word to let down the mast. The tide was just on the turn now, so the men waited till the boat was abreast of the godown and half a stone's throw from the bank, before they let fall mast and sail together. The sail flapped and bubbled, and it was while they were trying to keep it from blowing over the side, that the accident happened to Hpo Chit.

Nobody saw exactly how it came about, but there was a cry, a bump, and a splash, and Hpo Chit's feet were seen disappearing into the water. He came up once, a bamboo's length astern, but went down again. Then every one, saying "He is hurt; he will drown," squatted to watch.

"I think he struck his head falling," said Moung Byoo, leaning from the steering chair to look round the high stern-piece; "he will certainly drown. His mother will be very sorry."

The black kullahs on the bank shouted and ran

H

to the water's edge when they saw the accident, and their voices brought from the godown a white man in white clothes with a little ship-dog at his heels. He smoked a cheroot, and strolled out with his hands behind him; but when he heard what the coolies were saying he dropped his cheroot and ran out upon the jetty where the ships lay to load, shouting to Moung Byoo's men.

"Back! back your boat quickly; very quickly back her!"

"That is Thaw' thekin," said Moung Byoo, shikoing.

"What does he say?" asked Mah Hehn.

"He says to row back. What is the use? Hpo Chit will certainly drown."

Mr. Thorpe seemed very angry about something. He stamped with his foot and roared, "Back her, you fools! Back three strokes hard, and you save him! Back! will you?"

"Row back a little," said Moung Byoo, slowly; "it is Thaw' thekin's order."

The men got up and freed two oars, but both on the same side; all laughed at this mistake, and Pho Lone, ever anxious to please, went to make ready one on the other thwart.

"One oar, your honour?" he asked, crouching respectfully, "or more?"

Mr. Thorpe did not answer; he spun round on his heel, ran back, and sprang from the jetty on to the stone-strewn bank, and in three steps was in the river, his dog behind him.

" Why does he swim ? " inquired Mah Pan.

" I expect he swims to catch Hpo Chit," answered Moung Byoo, sucking at his cheroot which had nearly gone out.

Seeing what the gentleman did, the rowers let go their oars and squatted again to look on.

" Where is he ? " shouted Mr. Thorpe, swimming hard, hand over hand down stream.

" I cannot see him now, your honour," replied Moung Byoo ; " I think he has sunk."

Mr. Thorpe stopped swimming and trod water for several minutes to look about, letting the tide carry him down ; then he turned, swam slowly ashore, and dripped up the bank.

" He does look very funny," said Zah Nee ; " and hear the water in his boots ! How the little ship-dog shakes himself ! "

The men laughed much at the way Mr. Thorpe's skin showed through his wet clothes ; but they laughed quietly, for they had dropped down to within the gentleman's hearing, and they did not wish to appear rude.

" Hpo Chit's father and mother will be very sorry when they hear he is drowned. It is very unfortunate indeed. Pull away there ! We must go alongside the godown. I am very sorry about Hpo Chit."

CHAPTER VII

MOUNG BYOO's boat was not kept waiting to unload. In fact, the ropes had scarcely been made fast before long planks were quivering between bank and thwart, hatch coverings were off, and coolies were trotting up and down, carrying on their heads the baskets filled for them by the rowers. Beside the steadily growing heap in the godown Moung Byoo sat surrounded by most of his men; he had come from making his shiko to Mr. Thorpe at his office, and all wished to hear about the interview.

"He said to me, 'Why did you not back your boat quickly when the boy fell in the water?' and I replied, 'Your honour, I did not think of doing it.' Then he said, looking sad and cross, 'Did you not love this boy, that you all sat still and watched him drown?' To that I answered, 'I loved the good boy much; we all loved him, and his drowning is a great sorrow to us.'"

"Yes, yes, that was true," murmured the men, " we are all very sorry that Hpo Chit is drowned, very sorry indeed."

Moung Byoo went on, raising his voice in imitation of Mr. Thorpe's. "He said, 'I cannot understand you people!' and laid his face on his hand. I think Thaw' thekin is much grieved. He has sent his little fire-boat to look for the body of Hpo Chit."

"That is very good, very good," said everybody."

"Yes," sighed Moung Byoo; "but I am much afraid they will not find him; for the river is deep, and there are many crocodiles and great fish."

The men smoked in silence for a few breaths, and then, Zah Nee, clearing his throat, and moving aside from the dust of the paddy, began to speak.

"I remember when I went to the pagoda at Rangoon, at the Taboung festival, many years ago, the white police chief was very angry about an accident. He called me and other men fools and animals, using very hard words; he was an old chief; but he could not speak except through the mouth of a clerk."

"Tell about it," said Moung Byoo.

"It happened thus," said Zah Nee, "a very high ladder of bamboos had been laid against the pagoda, and two men climbed up to do work at the top. While they worked, many of us sat watching; presently the bottom of the ladder slipped a little on the pavement and stopped; but the shaking made it slip again; then it slid slowly past our very feet, and slipping more and more quickly, the two men came falling down a great way, their heads struck the pavement and burst, so that they died."

" But why did the police officer say hard words to you?" asked several.

"The policemen who carried the killed men away said, 'You must come and give evidence how their fall happened;' so we went. The police chief said to us, ' You sat still while the ladder slipped past your feet, and not one of you put out a hand to stop it?' And when we said, ' Yes,' he grew very angry. He said loudly, ' You are fools and sons of fools; by putting forward a foot you could have saved the lives of these poor men.' It was true; but we answered that we did not think of doing that. At this the police chief said, 'I wish that I could send to prison all who sat and watched the accident.'"

" That was very unjust," said Moung Byoo warmly. "Go!" he added, rising, "the measuring kullahs and tallyman wait."

The group broke up; some of the men stayed to help with the measuring, others went to sit outside and wait their turn to fill baskets in the boat. Mah Pan wandered away with Pho Lone to see the marvels of the mill. Jungle people who have never been in a rice mill have no idea how wonderful a place it is, with its great wheels and bands making the earth shake.

The measuring was over; Moung Byoo had compared his tally with that of the kullah, and all he had to do now was to get the godown clerk's note, on which he would be paid at the office. Moung Dway did not happen to be near at the moment, so he sat down to wait and listen to Mah Pan, who had much to say about the mill; the English engineer had been very kind and let them go everywhere, up to the top. Pho Lone squatted near, staring at her; she was covered with dust from head to foot, but he thought he had never seen her look so pretty.

While she talked, Mr. Thorpe came through the godown and stopped for a moment.

"My daughter, your honour," said Moung Byoo; "she has been in the mill."

"Oh! your daughter, Moung Byoo. And what is your name, pretty one? Miss Sweet Flower is it? And a very good name for you." Mah Pan, the colour darkening her face, laughed shyly, and answered, "Yes, your honour," too confused to know what she was saying. At this Mr. Thorpe laughed, Moung Byoo and Mah Hehn joining in; but the smile Pho Lone called up was rather sickly; he felt suddenly jealous of the gentleman.

"So you think this a wonderful place. Very wonderful? Well, then, should you like to see my house?"

Mah Pan's eyes lightened, and she looked to her mother to answer.

"Your honour is kind," said Mah Hehn promptly, "she would like to see your house."

Mr. Thorpe said it was good, and went away; he had no time for talking in the busy season.

"When shall we go?" asked Mah Pan.

"It was only his politeness; he did not mean anything," said Moung Byoo.

Mah Pan's face fell, and she looked at her mother. Mah Hehn said nothing, but it was plain that she did not think Mr. Thorpe's words mere politeness whatever her husband's opinion was.

The evening in the godown was even busier than the day. The whole of the mat floor was covered with heaps of grain, and a fog of grey dust filled the place when Moung Let's boat arrived, a little before the sky shut. He explained that the fire-boat, having gone a long way in search of Hpo Chit's body, overtook them on its way back, and hearing whither they were going, passed a line and towed them up.

"It is good luck," said Pho Lone. "We shall measure by the lightning lamps, and in the dark these black dogs will not see what I do."

Till that moment Mah Pan had forgotten her father's words about Bah Loogalay's punishment. Now she told Pho Lone he had better not cheat, lest he also got a beating.

" Nobody will see," said Pho Lone ; " I shall be very careful."

Mr. Thorpe had two ships waiting for cargo, Moung Dway said ; and upon this account they were in haste to measure up paddy, so Moung Let's had better be landed this evening. Moung Let was quite willing, and when his boat had been unloaded he called upon Moung Maw and Pho Lone to gird up their pasohs and do the measuring. Now, Abdool Latif, the Chittagong man, who kept tally for the godown was old, and though he had slept all day in order to work at night, seemed only just awake. The nearest electric light shone down feebly through clouds of dust, and unless Abdool Latif had looked very closely he could not see whether the measuring was done properly. Moung Let, also sleepy, and confused by the roar of the mill and other noises, sat on the floor, keeping count on slips of bamboo, and giving all his mind to it ; and Moung Maw did not care whether Pho Lone did the work fairly or not, it was no affair of his. Over a hundred baskets had been short measured before Moung Dway came by. Pho Lone, not seeing him, scooped out a lot of paddy in levelling the basket.

"Hé!" called Moung Dway. " You young man, I see you cheat."

" No," said Pho Lone ; and Abdool Latif, not wishing to have his pay docked for carelessness, said there had been no cheating. As the tallyman denied it, Moung Dway only said, if he saw more cheating he should report and have the paddy measured over again. He waited to see a few baskets passed and went his way. As soon as he had gone Pho Lone began to cut as before.

" They will catch you," whispered Moung Maw, " then you will be sore."

" Nobody is here to see," said Pho Lone ; " I shall not be caught."

Even while he spoke, Moung Dway, having passed round a mountain of grain behind them, was watching close by, but Pho Lone did not see him and went on cutting till the tallyman saw it.

" That is very bad," he said in his broken Burmese ; " the other man must use the stick."

Moung Maw had just taken it from Pho Lone's hand when Mr. Thorpe walked up with Moung Dway behind him.

" Who was cutting ? " he asked sharply.

" That man, sir," said Moung Dway ; " two times I saw it."

He pointed to Pho Lone, but Mr. Thorpe, seeing the measuring stick in Moung Maw's hand, stepped forward and gave him a slap that made his ear sing.

" Not that one, sir ! " cried Moung Dway. But Moung Maw, stung to fury, raised the heavy pin to strike back. Mr. Thorpe caught him by the throat and flung him backwards on the paddy.

" I did not do it," roared Moung Maw, all the

fight knocked out of him by the fall. "I had just received the stick."

Moung Dway repeated that Pho Lone was the man, and Mr. Thorpe, saying to Moung Maw, "I will speak to you in a minute then," caught Pho Lone by the wrist.

"Will you go to prison or be whipped?" he asked.

Pho Lone only begged for pardon; so Moung Let, frightened at the mention of prison, said, "Your honour, pray give him a little beating."

The cane fell on his bare skin and Pho Lone howled; howled so loudly that every one near came running to look on. "Eight, nine, ten!" concluded Mr. Thorpe; "now, young man, next time you will go to prison without choice."

"Where is the other man?" he asked when Pho Lone had fled, pressing both hands behind him.

"He has gone away, your honour," said Moung Let, who felt rather anxious lest his own turn should come. "I am very sorry, your honour; being an old man, my eyes do not see well in this dark light."

"Why, I know you, don't I?" said Mr. Thorpe, turning on him. "Are you not an advance-man?"

"Lord, for many years I have received from your hand three hundred rupees each season to buy paddy."

"You must be more careful in future about the men you employ," said Mr. Thorpe.

"It was my own son that your honour whipped with the cane," said Moung Let sadly; for many people had seen it, and he was disgraced. Bassein is an old-fashioned place.

"Well, he won't cheat again, I think," said Mr. Thorpe. "Perhaps the whipping will make him honest like his father. I should not have struck the other fellow had I known he did not cut with his own hand, but he must have been in league with your son."

"If your honour had not knocked him down he would have killed you," said Moung Let; and he spoke the truth.

It was late that night when Moung Let went to his boat to sleep. Pho Lone was there, ashamed to go near Mah Pan after what had happened. Moung Maw had not come to the boat. Shway Toon, who had helped to row, said that the carpenter had run by shouting that he should not return.

"I think he will go to the jungles," said Shway Toon. "He is proud and very angry, having been wrongfully beaten."

Moung Let said nothing; he thought it well that Moung Maw should have gone, otherwise Pho Lone would probably have received from him a worse beating than Mr. Thorpe's. However, the business was over now, and it was useless to

be unhappy about it. After all, he himself had
escaped easily, for no word had been said about
calling in his advance money as he had feared.
Pho Lone had behaved very badly, but he had
had a severe punishment. Moung Let was turning over in his mind whether he should give him
a scolding to make him more honest or two rupees
to console him when he fell asleep.

When Moung Maw ran out of the godown he
had no idea where he was going or what he meant
to do. He was mad with rage, and had he come
upon Mr. Thorpe or Pho Lone in the dark it
would have gone hardly with either. He came out
of the mill yard upon the road behind, and the
lights of the town catching his eye he went in
that direction. The night was very hot, and
people sat outside their houses talking. Nobody
spoke to him, for men are less friendly in the
town than they are in the jungles, and Moung
Maw reached the dimly lighted bazaar before he
recovered himself sufficiently to think what he
should do to pass the time. Having walked fast
he was thirsty, and it suddenly came to him
that it would be good to go to the liquor shop
kept by Ah Chain, the Chinaman; he had no
money, but Ah Chain knew him and would give
credit. The shop was a wooden house with a
big, white sign-board over it; all the front was
open to the street, and many lamps made the
bottles on the shelves at the back twinkle like

rows of stars. A number of white men, whom
Moung Maw knew at once to belong to ships,
were in the shop drinking and making a noise;
but he walked in, and waited for Ah Chain or
his man to see him. The sailors saw him first,
however. Having been ashore only a few hours
after many weeks at sea they were very happy,
and three or four at once began to make signs to
him to drink at their expense. They were so
hearty and good-tempered that Moung Maw
nodded and joined them. He could not understand a word they said, but when Ah Chain told
him they wished to know what he would drink
and he said "berrandy," they roared with laughter
and slapped him on the back.

"They say you are a good man," laughed Ah
Chain; and when Moung Maw saw they slapped
each other on the back he laughed also, and
thought the ship-men very good fellows. He had
one glass of liquor and then another, and after
that a third. The ship-men caught the word
thouk from Ah Chain's mouth, and were so
pleased with themselves that they made Moung
Maw understand that he must thouk with each
one of them in turn. Now, three glasses of
brandy, particularly bazaar brandy distilled only
Chinamen know how, are more than enough for
a sober jungle man, and there were eight of the
sailors. Moung Maw felt the liquor in his brains,
and told Ah Chain to say that he could not

thouk any more. The bar-keeper told the sailors what he said, and they cried like one that that was mean; he must thouk with each of his new friends in turn or they should be offended. Ah Chain repeated their words, and said if Moung Maw were wise he would humour them, for the sailors had had much liquor and their temper would very easily turn. So Moung Maw, against his will, drank two more glasses.

Whether he reached the eighth glass or a twentieth he never knew. He had some recollection of falling against a sailor and feeling a dash of something wet on his back, then there was crashing of glass, fighting in the road, and a great shouting. After that he knew nothing, except that he would not go into a house because he did not want to drink any more and was carried in by the arms and legs. After that, blank darkness.

When he awoke in the morning he knew what had happened; the police had taken him up with the only sailor drunk enough to be safely caught, and they two were to be sent before the magistrate. The sailor groaned a great deal, but Moung Maw, though his head beat terribly, and he felt sick, sat quietly looking out through the bars of the thannah cage. After the policemen had given him rice and a drink of water he got better, and asked what would happen to him.

"I expect only five rupees fine, or one week,"

answered a good-natured constable. "You did not beat the police."

Having no money with him, Moung Maw was alarmed at this; but he had little time to think about it, for he and his companion were soon called out and marched off. He was very much ashamed when the police made him follow the sailor on to a railed platform, where all the people in the court could stare at him. He crouched on his heels with his hands pressed together before him, and wondered at the coolness of the sailor, who leaned on the rail swinging his hat.

The magistrate, a young man in white clothes, came in from behind a curtain, and sat at a great table under the punkah. He spoke one word, and a policeman stood forward, and told a long story.

The sailor was dealt with first; the magistrate talked to him in English, so Moung Maw knew nothing of what was said. But presently he was told to stand up, and the magistrate spoke in Burmese.

"The policeman says you were drunk. Is that true?"

"Lord, I was very drunk indeed," said Moung Maw.

"And fighting in the street also?"

"Lord, I cannot tell; I was too drunk to know."

How came he to be drinking and fighting with English sailors?

Well, having done much work in Mr. Thorpe's godown, he was thirsty, and went in to drink a very little liquor; yes, was a son of the jungle, and seldom drank anything; did not wish to drink much; the sailors made him drink; was afraid to refuse. Thus he got drunk; felt very ill this morning, and thought he should die; yes, he was a fool—a very big fool. Had never been in court before.

The magistrate then spoke again with the sailor, and Moung Maw knew their talk was of himself.

"This Englishman says your story is true," said the magistrate, at last. "Therefore you may go. Do not be foolish and drink with white men again."

The police hurried him out of court before he quite understood that he was to be neither fined nor sent to gaol, and he squatted outside on the verandah to wind on his head-kerchief, feeling very happy. While he did this, the sailor came out with a black stranger, who seemed to have been waiting for him.

"The ship-man says you and he got off easily," said the black stranger. "He says, will you come and drink a little on that account."

Moung Maw stared at the sailor; he imitated the action of drinking; there was no doubt what he meant.

I

"Mad!" thought Moung Maw; and he hurried away as fast as he could towards the river, for he did not feel safe in the town with mad shipmen about, and also thought a swim would do him good.

The trouble in the godown had sunk out of sight behind his later adventures, and while he bathed his only fear was lest the Myothit boats should have gone while he was away. In spite of this fear he spent some time in the river; for though the sun was very hot, the wind blew softly, so it was very pleasant splashing in the shallows. He wondered whether Mr. Thorpe would attack him again when he went back through the godown. The gentleman had beaten Pho Lone severely, but he deserved it; and Moung Maw, wallowing up to his chest, thought of the young man's howls, and chuckled. He was not ill-natured, but it was all Pho Lone's doing that he himself had got into trouble.

While Moung Maw was bathing, Mah Hehn and Mah Pan were enjoying the greatest treat that had ever come in their lives. Mr. Thorpe's invitation had not been empty politeness; for early next morning, when he saw them in the godown, he came up and said they were to eat rice with him presently; meantime they must come to his house and see it. Fortunately, Mah Hehn, intending to go up to the bazaar, had brought silk tameins, clean linen jackets, and gay neck-kerchiefs for them both in her rush-work box, so they were able to dress properly.

"It is very good," said Moung Byoo, as they came out of the little cabin ; "it is well to wear good clothes to go to his honour's house. Take a little present in your hands—three bundles of cheroots; his honour will be pleased, they being rolled by Mah Pan."

Mah Hehn said it was a wise thought, so they chose three bundles of the best, tied them with paper bands, and Mah Pan carried them on her head in the big lacquer tray. Mr. Thorpe was in his office under the house when they arrived, so of course they could not go upstairs ; to do so would have been to heap ignominy upon him by standing over his head ; moreover it would spoil his charms if he happened to have any about him ; therefore, they sat in the office verandah and waited.

"Now, follow," said Mr. Thorpe coming out and leading the way upstairs. "First you will drink lemonade with ice in it." Mah Pan knew what "lem'nay" was, but had never heard of ice. It was certainly very agreeable to drink the sweet stuff from a long tumbler with a lump of solid water tinkling in it. As she frankly admitted it burned the inside, and the tumbler grew so hot she had to pass it from one hand to the other, and was finally obliged to put it on the floor. However she finished it to the last drop and tried her best not to shriek when at the gentleman's suggestion she took the remaining ice in her mouth.

The lemonade finished, Mah Hehn, failing to persuade Mah Pan to do it, offered the cheroots.

"They are very well rolled," said Mr. Thorpe, lighting one. "I think the Sweet Flower rolled them."

"She rolled them with her own hands," assented Mah Hehn proudly, "she rolls better than any girl in the village."

"Will you make some for me?" asked Mr. Thorpe.

Mah Pan blushed and promised to send five hundred next time her father came.

"The price is one rupee eight annas a hundred," said Mah Hehn.

It did not seem fair to overcharge the gentleman thus. One rupee was the proper price; but her mother's eye forbade Mah Pan to speak. Mr. Thorpe, however, said lightly that it was a little price for cheroots rolled by the Sweet Flower, and that he would buy a thousand if she would send so many.

Never had Mah Pan, or her mother for that matter, seen so beautiful a house. The walls were smooth boards painted light green and hung with English pictures of horses and dogs, hardly any of which had the glass broken. Instead of dark and dirty rafters white canvas was stretched overhead; there was only one hole of any size in the whole ceiling ; that was in the corner where a great brown stain appeared, and Mr. Thorpe explained that owls had had their nest there till he cut the canvas with a knife tied to a bamboo and let a basketful of rubbish with two young birds among it fall into the dining-room. Mah Pan was not interested in owls at any time, and now the furniture and the glass on the sideboard took up all her attention. The chairs were delightful, particularly those with long arms in which one could lie down ; and she lay in them by turn, her admiration increasing with each. The coloured wine-glasses were finer than anything she had ever seen, but she was afraid to touch them they looked so fragile. In the whole house, however, the thing she liked most was a great mirror in the vacant bed-room ; for the first time in her life she saw Mah Pan, and she studied her for quite a betel-chew ; she thought one would never feel alone if one had a glass like that. The matting on the floor was the only thing in the house she did not admire ; it had many great holes in it and her bare feet tripped very often. " I should take it up if it were in my house," she said, forgetting that Mr. Thorpe spoke almost as well as a Burman.

"It is very old and bad," he said laughing, "When you come and see me again I will have new matting down."

"For me ? "

" For the Sweet Flower."

" We have no matting on the floor in our own house," said Mah Pan. " Nor such a mirror as your honour has ; " and she sighed.

" I wish that mirror would keep your picture," smiled Mr. Thorpe.

" You do not want my picture," said Mah Pan pertly.

Breakfast was her dream for weeks afterwards. It was strange to sit on a chair and eat at a table covered with a cloth very nearly white ; it was not so good as sitting on the floor, but finding she could raise her feet on the chair without being seen she made herself comfortable and hoped it was not improper. As she told her father that evening you could not tell how rich Mr. Thorpe was till you ate with him. He, her mother and herself had separate plates, while the fish, chicken, curry, and the sweet mess called—mother would remember its name—yes, poo-ding, were handed round each on its own dish by two kullahs who, further, gave a new plate for each kind of food.

" I should like to live in a house like this," she remarked, as they sat smoking in the darkened verandah after breakfast.

" Should you ? " said Mr. Thorpe, thoughtfully.

" Your honour has much business," said Mah Hehn, after a short silence, " and we must go to the bazaar. Is there leave to go ? "

" There is leave," said Mr. Thorpe rising. " Look,

Sweet Flower ; bring the cheroots yourself if your mother allows it."

" She shall bring them in her own hand," said Mah Hehn ; and they came downstairs, Mah Pan carrying a large paper bag of sugar which Mr. Thorpe had ordered his servant to bring her.

" It is a very beautiful house," said Mah Pan, looking back.

" Thaw' thekin is a very kind gentleman," said her mother.

" His voice is kind ; and I should love to live in a house like that."

Passing through the godown, they met Moung Maw ; his red swelled eyes showed he had been drinking last night, and he must have known that his face betrayed it, he looked so uneasy.

" We come from Thaw' thekin's house," said Mah Pan through a mouthful of sugar. " We have eaten rice there."

Moung Maw only nodded ; he felt very sick still and was on his way to the boat to sleep.

" English gentlemen do not get drunk," said Mah Hehn, as the carpenter moved away.

" It is very disgraceful to be beaten for cheating," said Mah Pan, half to herself.

CHAPTER VIII

"You should have waited, my son," said Mah Tsay when she heard about it. "It is good that parents talk first of these matters." Pho Lone had no reply to make to this.

"Also you chose a bad time to speak," continued Mah Tsay. "Many of the neighbours had seen you beaten, and a girl does not love a young man when he is shamed."

It was all Moung Byoo's fault: he in his good nature had sought out Pho Lone before starting on the homeward trip, and asked him to come back with them; Mah Pan, he said, was very sorry and angry that he had been beaten, and Mah Hehn would give him for his back some of the English medicine she had bought in the bazaar. Hence, when the boats crept away from the godown in the moonlight, Pho Lone pulled his oar on Moung Byoo's boat, instead of rowing in his father's as he intended.

The women were very good to him. Mah Hehn gave him medicine at her husband's order; a very little, but as she said, it was expensive.

Mah Pan sympathised with him, saying it was bad luck to be caught cheating and he would remember she advised him not to; but she was sorry. She was so sorry as they sat together next night, the boat being anchored for the tide at Tawchoung, that Pho Lone had mistaken her mind, and asked her to marry him.

"I think Mah Hehn and Mah Pan are very proud, having eaten in Thaw' thekin's house," said Pho Lone, "they boast that the gentleman, sitting at the table, ate with them."

"It makes a woman proud to be thus treated," said Mah Tsay, nursing her knees as she rocked idly to and fro, "a male dog stealing the offerings is higher than a woman saying prayers at the pagoda. No wonder a girl likes to marry an Englishman."

"I shall still keep very near her," said Pho Lone, his thoughts flying away with his tongue, "perhaps she will change her mind."

"Perhaps," said his mother; but her voice was doubtful.

It was past noon; not a leaf stirred; you could scarcely step on the verandah where the sun struck; it pained the eyes to look down the street, and even sitting quite still in the house water started all over the skin. There was no work just now, nor would there be until the time came to load the boats for the next trip to Bassein, so every one was glad to lie in his house and sleep away the hot silence of the days.

Though there was no work, much business had to be done in the cool mornings of those days on which the Books say it is lucky to buy and sell. The boats returned from Bassein empty and light on Tuesday afternoon's tide, and as Wednesday, like Thursday and Friday, is a good day for trading, all the men in the village, whether boat owner or cultivator, met at sunrise under the bamboo clump near the pagoda to do business. Nobody knew whether the price of paddy would rise above the Rs 85 paid by the merchants for the first arrivals, or fall below it ; so as every man and his wife had their own opinion about this, trade was very brisk indeed.

"Take a hundred and fifty baskets," said Ko Moung Galay to Moung Byoo. "I will give a hundred and fifty."

"No," said Mah Hehn. And Moung Byoo said, "No."

"It is a good price for five days' hire of the boat," said Ko Moung Galay.

Moung Byoo had nothing to say against the offer, as an offer. But he repeated that, like the head-man, he believed the price of paddy must go up, and therefore he wished to buy outright from neighbours who held the contrary opinion, and take his chance of making money. He thought prices must go up.

"Go up!" echoed Oo Yan in his cracked voice. "Bet you——" and he paused to glance round.

"Go on, neighbour, your wife is not by," said Shway Toon.

"Bet you twenty baskets the price is under eighty-five when you sell again," said Oo Yan ignoring the laughter.

"No, no, it will certainly rise," cried Zah Nee, "there is news from the Karen village that more great fire-ships have passed up."

"Bet?" asked Moung Byoo, for Mah Hehn was making faces at him.

"Yes: twenty-five rupees."

"Good! if it falls, I save that much money."

"I have eight hundred baskets to sell cheap," said Moung Ket Kay. "It is better to sell to a neighbour than that dog's son, the chetty to whom I owe so much money."

Mention of the Madrasi money-lender caused business to stop for a moment : there was always a little joke about him.

"Say the black animal's name, Ko Ket Kay," cried Moung Maw, and the rest shouted, "Yes! Say his name."

"It takes too much time," replied Moung Ket Kay, laughing slowly; he was the only man on the creek who could say the chetty's name, and was proud of it.

"Well, then," he said, after a little more pressing, "When you speak to the animal you must call him—you must say 'Teeroopalaythoray Annasawmy Soobramaneyam Chetty;' for that is his name."

"Good! Oh very good, such a name!" laughed everybody.

"How did you learn it off like that?" asked Moung Maw, after a pause.

"From the *hoondi!*"* replied Moung Ket Kay drily; and the neighbours laughed more than ever.

"His interest is very big, like his name," said Moung Ket Kay, relapsing into business; "if he seizes my paddy he will pay as little as he pleases," and saying this, he got up and stepped round to Moung Byoo's side.

"Now, friend, if I put the grain into the boat will you pay fifty rupees a hundred baskets for it?"

"Forty-five is a good price," said Mah Hehn.

If his wife had not been at his elbow, Moung Byoo would have closed the bargain at fifty, for it was cheap enough; but he knew that if he did, he should be scolded about it after, and hesitated.

"Fifty is a good price," urged Moung Ket Kay.

"Forty-five is better," put in Mah Hehn.

Moung Byoo looked first at his neighbour and then at his wife.

"Toss you, fifty rupees or forty-five," he said, and Mah Hehn scowled.

"Look friends! we toss," cried Moung Ket Kay

---

* *Hoondi* = promissory note.

gaily, as he drew out a rupee. "Fifty rupees, neighbour Moung Byoo pays, or forty-five."

"Flower!" he shouted, as the coin fell. "Ho, ho! good neighbour, you pay fifty!" and he jumped up to dance a little, while every one laughed except Mah Hehn. She got up and walked away without speaking; but Moung Byoo knew by her face that she would have something to say by-and-by.

"Never mind," said Moung Ket Kay, "it is a good bargain for you at fifty. Bet you the price goes up."

"Twenty rupees it is under eighty-five when I sell," said Moung Byoo.

"Baskets," suggested Moung Ket Kay; but Moung Byoo preferred rupees.

"It is a bet," agreed his friend. "Go! It grows hot."

"It is fully rice-time now," said two or three, getting on their feet; and business ceased for the day.

"You are a fool," was Mah Hehn's greeting to her husband, as he stepped into the house, "a stupid-head and a fool. He must sell, and you could have bought for forty-five. A baby would make a better bargain than you."

"Moung Let would have paid fifty, I think," said Moung Byoo easily; "and I bet him twenty rupees that the price will fall."

"A wise man would have bet forty," retorted

Mah Hehn. "Look where you put your feet, you have killed many little insects."

Moung Byoo looked, and saw a thin stream of ants pouring across the floor ; he had trodden on it, killing many, as his wife said.

"It was an accident," he remarked ruefully.

"More expense," grumbled Mah Hehn; " you must give alms to atone for breaking the law ; one rupee worth of rice gone under your clumsy foot." She went to take the pot off the fire outside, calling, " Hé, dog ! " for a big pariah was snuffing about it hungrily.

"One rupee worth of rice to the Lord Ruler for breaking the law by killing," she scolded. "Go, dog !" and the pariah tucked in his tail and fled, yelping from the boiling water she tilted over his yellow back. "You will say that one rupee worth is not enough, I daresay," she went on, as she brought in the pot and set it to steam. For Moung Byoo was a very devout man.

"Being an accident, I think a little alms will atone," he answered, idly watching the pariah which, still shrieking with pain, had crawled under the house over the way to curl up and lick the hair off the great red scald. "Yes, certainly, a very little will be enough."

Mah Hehn sat grumbling to herself, while Moung Byoo ate his rice, and then called to Mah Pan and Mah Noo to eat with her.

"It is not such food as we ate ate at Thaw' thekin's," she said, as they crouched over the rice.

"That is true," murmured Mah Pan; "I feel the poo-ding now in my mouth."

Moung Byoo got up and strolled over to Moung Maw's; he had heard rather much about Mr. Thorpe's style of living already, and the English method of women eating with men had been pressed somewhat frequently upon his attention. It was not good that women-folk should visit white men; it made them too proud.

As he crossed the street he forgot these matters, for people at the further end were coming out of their houses and gathering round somebody who sat on Moung Let's verandah, drinking from the chatty. He had evidently just arrived, and in haste, for women stood in their houses calling to ask what the news was; a man does not come from a distant village in the heat of the day for nothing; and Moung Byoo went down to learn what he came to tell.

The visitor was Shway Gyee of Ngatheing. He had been running ever since the sun looked over the jungle, to escape and to bring warning to Myothit; for Boh Tah's gang had attacked Ngatheing, and by this time everybody there was killed, the village burned, and all the property in the place carried away.

"I cannot see smoke," said Ko Moung Galay,

looking anxious. "Had the dacoits come when you left ? "

They had not actually arrived ; a boy had run home to say he saw them coming, and certainly when the dacoits had burned Ngatheing they would come on to Myothit ; if the people were wise they would cross over the creek at once and hide in the jungle.

"We have much money," said Ko Moung Galay. "I think it is good to put the rupees and property in a boat ready to take away when the dacoits come."

Everybody was quite satisfied that Boh Tah would come ; the only question was, when ?

"Not yet, I think," said Ko Moung Galay ; "there will be plenty of time for us to go and hide before the sky shuts. The dacoits have not burned Ngatheing. Therefore I think they eat rice there and sleep."

Every eye strained eastward seeking smoke ; but the sky was clear, and Oo Yan said he thought the head-man's words were good.

"There are guns in Ngatheing," said Ko Moung Galay, wishing to calm his people. "Dacoits want guns far more than rupees, and we, having none, will perhaps not be attacked."

"Ko Bah Too, our head-man, was loading his gun when I ran past his house ; he cried to me : 'Stop, I shall shoot the dacoits when they come.'"

"You were wise to run then," said Moung Let,

" the dacoits will be very angry if he fires at them, and will certainly kill every one."

Shway Gyee had always thought Ko Bah Too a fool; he was just the stupid man who believed he could fight dacoits, charmed against all kinds of death though they were. Fools like him were not common, and the Ngatheing people were unlucky having one of them for head-man.

" Well then, friend," said Ko Moung Galay, " you have run very far; come to my house to eat and sleep. We will go presently to the jungle."

" I think it will also be time to take our money when we go ourselves to hide," remarked Moung Let, as the head-man moved away followed by Shway Gyee. " For my part I wish to sleep just now."

" You speak well, neighbour," said several. And like him they went back to their houses, glad to get in from the street. It really was too hot to think of carrying heavy bags of money and bundles of clothes all the way to a boat.

The sun stared down upon the dusty brown thatch; the boats at their moorings rubbed sides on the flow, and you heard the clack of a pariah's teeth as he snapped at the flies which shared the cool darkness under the house; the brown birds hidden in the bushes woke up to clutter and laugh, ceasing suddenly as if the sound of their own voices frightened them in the stillness; and all Myothit slept.

K

When Pho Lone opened his eyes he saw that
the shadows rippled right across the creek, and
rose quickly, girding up his pasoh as he went
down the ladder.   Thanks to the patrol constable
he had nothing to carry away with him.   Finding
that his mother sat in her place against the wall,
smoking stolidly, he asked whether his father had
yet gone ; of course she would not go to hide ; an
elderly woman, ugly and deformed, runs no danger
at the hands of dacoits except being killed, and
we must all die some time or other ; besides Boh
Tah and his followers might want food, and it was
well for somebody to stay and prepare it for them
lest they should be displeased.

"He went long ago," said Mah Tsay.   "All
have gone now.   I thought you slept late, my
son."

Pho Lone was frightened, and he went out
behind the house to look whether a canoe had
been left.   Moung Byoo's and other large boats
remained, but every craft that one man could
work was gone, and knowing where to look he
soon made out the stern-pieces of canoes and
small boats peering from a tiny cove smothered
with jungle.   It was useless to call and ask the
men who were hidden over there to send over for
him, even had it been wise to speak loud when
the dacoits were probably very near ; so he went
back to ask his mother's advice.

"Go and lie down in the jungle beyond the

pagoda," she said. "The sky will soon shut, and
dacoits will not find you even if they pass that
way."

Pho Lone lingered, rubbing one foot against
the other.

"I do not like to hide alone," he said. "What
was that noise?"

"Buffaloes striking their horns together. But
go, my son. If the dacoits come they come soon."
She blew smoke through her nostrils and watched
it float and curl. "Go quickly."

"I shall certainly be killed, I know——"

A sound of twigs, pressed stealthily aside,
stopped him; and darting behind the house he
raced along the creek bank, never pausing till he
reached the jungle which grew up to the worn
brick paving about the pagoda. It was too dense
to force one's way through, so looking fearfully
towards the village he crept along by the bushes
to the narrow path which came out behind the
pagoda, and turning down that began to look for
a hiding-place. He did not go far, partly because
he was afraid, and partly because he wanted to
know what the dacoits did; so finding a place
where he could creep below the undergrowth, he
curled himself up and listened. The path was
very near his hiding-place, but the dacoits were
not likely to see him if they passed along, and he
felt tolerably safe.

As soon as her son had gone, Mah Tsay got up

and let down one of the mats hinged to the beam
below the eaves to form the front of the house;
it was heavy in its wooden frame, and it was as
much as she could do to lower it without a crash.
By this means she made a dark corner in which,
unless a dacoit came on the verandah and looked
into the house, she could not be seen. The noise
in the jungle came nearer, and each moment she
expected the yell which dacoits give when they
rush into a village, and which hurts one's very
inside. Her heart jumped like a newly caught
fish as she held her breath to listen—a helpless
old woman who could not even stand upright
without her staff. From down the street now
came the clink of cocoa-nut shell ladles in chatties
as the dacoits drank. Then they talked together,
and she could hear a voice ordering the men to
search the houses. It was curious that there
was no shouting. Mah Tsay could hear them
in the neighbours' houses pulling about the
boxes and turning them over to shake out the
contents, but even when money was found they
did not call to each other as she expected.
Nearer they came, taking house by house in
turn. They were next door now, and she could
hear them grumbling at the poor clothes they
found.

"Not a man in this place has a silk pasoh," said
one.

"I have taken four rupees and a broken silver

bangle of one rupee weight," said another, with a
sulky laugh.

"Nothing here worth carrying," said the dacoit
who had spoken first.   "Let us go to the next."

Mah Tsay pressed her hands on her breast to
still the heart-beat as the verandah creaked to
footsteps.

"Have care, friend," said a voice at her elbow,
"there is some one in there."

A man's head came cautiously round the mat
edge. For half a breath Mah Tsay, her lip shaking,
stared at him. Then she shut her eyes, and all
her pent up terror burst in a scream. It was
such a terrible cry that when the men hiding
across the creek heard it they sprang up and flew
through the jungle, tearing their skins on the
thorns. Pho Lone heard it, and scrambled out
upon the path to listen. Another scream, another,
and more. The dacoits were killing his mother,
and he turned to run, anywhere, nowhere. When
one is frightened one must run, and he sped along
the path with flying hair, dashing round the
corners like a deer. Running so blindly he fell
over a stone, and while getting up thought he
heard the sound of feet behind; yes, and now
breathless voices urging haste. He flew on again;
but now the path wound suddenly out of the
jungle and across open land with a bamboo clump
here and there, and the dacoits were close behind.
When they saw him running they would certainly

shoot him dead. He pulled up and dropped, panting, on his heels, with hands pressed together, just as the dacoits poured out of the jungle. They hesitated for a moment when they saw him, and then advanced.

"Kill," said the leader who was evidently angry; and having flung the word to his men walked past.

Pho Lone threw himself upon his face. "Lord, do not kill me. I will follow. I am your lordship's slave! Master of Nine White Umbrellas, have mercy! Do not kill a slave whose desire it is to follow your lordship."

Now the dacoit leader was out of temper and felt that the sight of blood would be very pleasing; the men had already cleared Pho Lone's long hair off his neck and were quarrelling for the honour of striking first blow. This delay had given Pho Lone time for his petition and the leader time to change his mind. He was not the chief, and he knew his chief wished to get more men, for he had been out for only one season and his following was by no means so strong as he could wish, numbering only thirteen. He had one gun, and a bamboo bound with wire, which when charged with powder made a very alarming noise, and on that account was of much service in attacking villages at night, though no man dared hold it in his hand to let off. All the men had dahs or spears, some of them, two; but until a dacoit chief has at least three guns and a score of men he cannot hope for a really successful season.

"Send for his lordship," said the dacoit squatting, "his lordship will decide." Two young men ran off, and after a long time came back walking behind the real chief of the band.

"Do not kill," said Boh Tah, and the men fell back. "Hé, you!" kicking Pho Lone as he lay sobbing and praying by turns, "Can you show villages where there are guns?"

"Yes, yes, my lord; the Ngatheing people have three guns."

Mention of Ngatheing village caused a little silence; Pho Lone was wondering why, when the dacoit who had ordered that he should be killed dropped on his heels near the Boh's feet and pitching his voice high sang rather than spoke :

"Listen!" he cried, "we were led to Ngatheing village this day. In the village were guns and money, jewellery and silk, and we had but to take. Yet his lordship, of his great clemency and might, was pleased to hear the prayers of the people who are as dirt below his feet. They prayed for mercy and he bade us leave them. So great was the kindness of this Destroyer of Cities that he took not one rupee. Lord!" and he shiko'd to the Boh.

"These are true words," cried the men, eagerly; "the words of Moung Toke are true."

Pho Lone took courage also to shiko to the chief, behind whom he caught sight of a young man re-settling a bloody cloth about his arm ; it crossed his mind that Mah Tsay had scratched or perhaps bitten him before she was killed.

"Has the head-man of this village a gun?" asked the Boh of the man who had sung his praises.

"May it please his lordship, no man in Myothit owns one," said Pho Lone when the question had been passed on, "but the head-man of a village three days from here has a fine gun."

"What village?" asked the Boh through Moung Toke as before.

"Kyouksay on the river, by his lordship's favour. It is only three days' march through jungles, but there are three creeks to cross."

"His lordship's magic dries up creeks at his word," said Moung Toke severely. Pho Lone shiko'd again, and was relieved to see that the chief's face cleared somewhat.

"The young man will follow," he said. "I spare his life because he gives information. But if it prove that there is no gun in Kyouksay village he shall be cut in pieces."

"It is good," said Pho Lone clasping Boh Tah's feet, "I follow."

He was quite at ease in his mind now, for he knew that the Kyouksay head-man had not only a gun but also some powder and large shot. He had seen these treasures each time he had stopped at the village on the way to Bassein, for the head-man of course was very proud of possessions which proved that the Deputy Commissioner thought well of him.

"Follow!" said the Boh; and Pho Lone got up to take his place at the end of the line as the men filed past.

The sky was shutting now, and before they reached the jungle on the further side of the open stretch it was quite dark. The young man with the rag about his arm was next to Pho Lone, and as he could not walk as fast as the others, the two fell behind a little on the narrow path; presently the cloth slipped down and they stopped to tie it again.

"You have been shot with a gun," said Pho Lone, surprised as he saw the wound, "this cloth is not good now;" and throwing the blood-soaked rag aside he took off his head-kerchief and used that for a bandage.

"Yes, it is a shot-hole," said the dacoit. "At Ngatheing some one lay in his house and fired poung! when we came in the street."

Pho Lone remembered Shway Gyee's words that the head-man of Ngatheing had loaded his gun to fight the dacoits; but he said that without doubt there were a great many police with English officers hidden in the village.

The dacoit thought so too; he had followed his comrades as quickly as he could, but was much afraid that he should be taken prisoner owing to the wound which bled very much.

"I think you will die," said Pho Lone tying the last knot, "your face is sick and your arm is very large."

The dacoit thought not; the shot had gone right through the flesh without hurting the bone; the wound would be well in a few days.

"Did you take many rupees from my village?" asked Pho Lone as they moved on again. He did not like to ask if Boh Tah had killed his mother, as the dacoit might think it not polite.

"We took very little," said the dacoit, "we had news that there was much money in the village, the people having returned from Bassein."

Pho Lone explained how it was that large sums were not found; but he said he thought some would have been left behind.

"We might have taken more," said the dacoit; "but while searching in the houses, we heard great screaming, and being much frightened ran away very fast."

"My mother was in her house; everybody had gone across the creek. She, having a bent back, remained."

"It was a very terrible screaming," said the dacoit.

"I myself ran away when I heard it," said Pho Lone. "Go! it is not good to walk alone thus in the jungle at night; let us come up with the other men."

CHAPTER IX

"I THINK that is the noise of oars," said Ko Moung Galay, suddenly sitting up on his mat. "Listen!"

"Each day since Boh Tah came you think of dacoits," replied Mah Doh; but nevertheless she sat up too, and strained her ears.

It was very still outside. Ko Moung Galay heard the perspiration drip from his arms on the mat as they listened.

"It is certainly a boat," he repeated.

"Yes, it is; but boats bring others than dacoits," retorted Mah Doh. "Another gang would not so soon follow Boh Tah's, there being nothing left to take."

"Boh Tah took nothing," yawned Ko Moung Galay.

"How shall other dacoits know that?" asked his wife, getting up: for her ear caught the flutter of clothing and swift patter of feet outside. Ko Moung Galay heard it too, and rose also to throw open the big teak box which stood in the dark corner of their sleeping room.

"Well?" he said, as Mah Doh reappeared.

"Hasten," she said, "the people are running away. Certainly dacoits are coming."

Ko Moung Galay needed no urging; he plunged into the box, and with shaking hands gathered the money and gold ornaments together, while his wife went down again, to run to the jungle he supposed.

"It is strange," she said, standing on the stairs, and looking in with a puzzled face, "the dacoits neither shout nor beat gongs."

"Boh Tah and his men crept into the village like snakes," said Ko Moung Galay, tying up the bundle. "I think all the people have gone now. I shall be last of all," he added fearfully.

Mah Doh, more inquisitive than frightened, went out again, and presently she called from the bank.

"Stop! put back the money and things."

"Why?" asked Ko Moung Galay, on his way downstairs, hugging the bundle.

"Put that back in the box, quick," said Mah Doh, bustling across the street. "Get the dah quickly, and sit outside as if waiting to fight."

But Ko Moung Galay, having made up his mind to run, still hesitated. He did not understand, and said so.

"It is the police," said his wife. She took the bundle from him, and tossed it into the sleeping-room, out of sight; then, wiping the perspiration

KO MOUNG GALAY'S GALLANT DEFENCE OF MYOTHIT

from her forehead, pointed to the dah hanging against the wall.

" But I must go and shiko the officer," objected Ko Moung Galay. " It is not respectful to wait sitting in my house."

" Can you see the police ? " demanded his wife, forcing the dah into his hand. " Do we not hear dacoits, in fear of whom all the people have run away ? "

Ko Moung Galay looked at her for a breath or two, and understood. He nodded gravely, gripped the weapon, slipped outside, and sank down in an attitude.

" You are sure it is police ? " he said ; for the dogs bristling and barking told that the boat was very near now.

" I see the white helmet of the officer," said Mah Doh, standing on tip-toe behind him, and screwing her eyes to look out in the glare, " and now his face. I think it is a gentleman, and not a half-caste."

" Good," said Ko Moung Galay ; and he looked fiercer than ever. The boat swept up on the tide, and the pariahs bolted under the houses as it turned to run in just opposite Ko Moung Galay's.

" Now go and shiko," said Mah Doh as the prow seethed on the mud. " Take also the umbrella to hold over his honour's head."

" Are you the only people in this village ? " asked the officer, springing ashore.

Ko Moung Galay replied that, by his honour's leave, he and his wife were alone in the village. "Every one else having run away in great fear," added Mah Doh.

"In great fear?" echoed the officer. He was a young man with little hair on his face, but he spoke well. "What were they afraid of?"

"Dacoits, your honour," said Ko Moung Galay.

"Yes, dacoits, your honour," added Mah Doh hastily. "Hearing the oars they ran to hide in the jungle. My man remained to defend the village, he being the head-man."

"Yes. Being the head-man, I stayed to fight the dacoits," said Ko Moung Galay, nursing his dah. "But I am glad that police and not dacoits are come."

"I shall remember this," said the officer, taking the open umbrella offered him, and looking with much approval upon Ko Moung Galay. "I shall report in your favour to the Deputy Commissioner."

Ko Moung Galay replied that he should always pray for his honour's continued good health and immunity from all the Accidents, Misfortunes, and Diseases, also for his rapid promotion. Then, having shiko'd again very profoundly, led the way across the street to his house, stooping that his pasoh might hide his feet.

The officer's Burmese servant, having placed

his chair in the shady verandah, and given him light for his cheroot, Ko Moung Galay squatted at a respectful distance to answer questions. Mah Doh, he saw, was anxious to talk, but he waved her into the background. The gentleman did not ask much. Ko Moung Galay had to tell him what day Boh Tah visited the village, how the dacoits neither killed nor hurt anybody, nor obtained any booty worth speaking of, owing to the care the village people took to leave nothing behind them.

"You ran away yourself that day, then ?" said the officer.

"We went across to hide our property," said Mah Doh. "While in the jungle the dacoits came, and they had gone when we came back."

"Exactly," said her husband.

"I see," said the officer, smiling a little. "Well, which path did the dacoits take when they left ?"

Ko Moung Galay replied that they took the path through the jungle to Ladaw village, two days distant. If his honour proposed to give chase, he begged leave to recommend the jungle path ; the creek shallowed a tide's journey higher up, and a large boat could not go there.

The officer was silent for a breath or two, and then he sent Ko Moung Galay to tell the policemen to came ashore and eat their rice before marching. This was Mah Doh's opportunity ; she waddled on her heels to the gentleman's chair and

began to ask questions. She had, however, only
ascertained that his clothes cost fifteen rupees in
Rangoon, that he liked hunting dacoits, and that
his name was Mah Kin Lay, when the police sergeant interrupted by coming to ask for orders.
He was much too proud to take orders through
the mouth of a jungle head-man.

"Sell rice," he said to Mah Doh on receiving
orders to buy supplies for two days.

Mah Doh loved bargaining as well as another
woman. She had taken her cheroot from her lips
to say, "Two rupees a basket," when a clever
thought struck her. "I have none to spare," she
replied with an effort; "but the people are now
coming back, and the broken woman, one Mah
Tsay, has plenty. She will sell rice to you."

The people were coming back; they might be
seen creeping along behind the houses and round
the corners into their verandahs, whence they
emerged boldly with an air of surprise as if they
had been very sound asleep and had only just
awakened. It was terribly hot; every man's
pasoh clung about his legs, and the perspiration
ran in heavy trickles down back and breast; but
in a betel-chew every soul was squatting in the
sun before Ko Moung Galay's house; for a white
man had not visited Myothit since Thaw' thekin
came to shoot ducks three years ago. They sat
patiently blinking at him, comparing notes on his
appearance, and wondering whether he would

take off his coat when his skin would be seen; or eat, which latter is a particularly interesting sight.

Mr. McKinlay did neither of these things. After accepting a drink of cocoa-nut water, which Mah Doh offered in Moung Maw's tumbler borrowed for the purpose, he turned his chair to face the crowd, flicked the ash from his cheroot, and began to speak. Each person felt that the gentleman addressed him direct, and by consequence whenever he paused all pressed their hands together and said, " Lord, yes, certainly," in chorus.

He began by saying he had been this morning at Ngatheing and had learned that when Boh Tah attacked that village the head-man fired his gun, driving the gang away. By doing this Ko Bah Too had gained much favour with the Government, and for reward his village would pay no taxes for one whole year. People who ran away and left their property for dacoits to take incurred the displeasure of Government.

The crowd murmured, " Lord, certainly," but sorrowfully; and Ko Moung Galay, creeping a little forward on his heels, begged leave to point out that when he and his people ran away they took all their goods with them, whereby the dacoits got nothing. He hoped Government would make a small rebate on the year's taxes upon that account.

Mr. McKinlay was afraid that any petition for

L

remission of taxes on that ground would be re-
jected, and advised that such should not be sent
in.   He should not, however, forget that on his
arrival to-day he found the head-man armed with
his dah in readiness to defend his house against
dacoits.   The Government would approve that
action, which was no doubt due to the excellent
example set by the Ngatheing head-man a few
days back.   ·

"It was, your honour," said Mah Doh readily.

"He would have been killed, had dacoits and
not police come," said Moung Byoo, much surprised
to hear that his neighbour had been so rash.   He
himself had been among the first to fly.

"Yes!" said Mr. McKinlay, throwing out his
arm so sharply that every one shiko'd ; "but if all
you men remained to fight the dacoits would run
away."

"His lordship does not think of the dacoits'
magic," said Moung Byoo, forgivingly ; "white
people do not understand these things."

The neighbours murmured assent, and eyed Mr.
McKinlay more hopefully, for he was unbuttoning
his coat.   It was disappointing when he began to
speak again without taking it off ; but this time
his words were more interesting.

He said he had heard that they did not like the
patrol system.   ("We do not like it at all, your
honour," said Mah Doh.)   Well, then, if they had
any complaint against the patrol constable they

could always come and lay it before himself and he would inquire into it. It was the patrol man who brought the news of Boh Tah's visit to Ngatheing, thus enabling the police to start at once in pursuit. Now they could see how useful the patrol system was.

"It is a wise plan," said Mah Doh, "but it would be better if a gentleman like your honour came to the village. Your honour would not say, 'the pen is bad, give me two rupees to buy you a new one,' the price of pens being about one anna each, I think. Two rupees!—the thief!" and she nursed her knees, puffing viciously at her cheroot.

"The woman talks nonsense, your lordship," said Ko Moung Galay, scowling at his wife and wishing the neighbours would not giggle. "I shall certainly report if the patrol constable asks for presents."

Before Mr. McKinlay could reply the sergeant came up to say that his men had eaten and that he had bought a basket of rice.

"Very good; we go at once," said Mr. McKinlay, rising from his chair. "Well, mother, what do you want?"

"Lord!" cried Mah Tsay, holding out an eight anna piece, "I have received only this money for my rice, the price being one rupee."

"Of course the price for a full basket is one rupee. Sergeant! What is this?"

"The woman lies, your lordship," replied the
sergeant easily. "I paid her one rupee; Constable
Bah Twin is witness. Moung Bah Twin!"

"Lord, Sergeant Moung Kya paid one rupee
into her hand," said Bah Twin, dropping on his
heels behind his superior. "Constable Shway
Hlaing also saw it. Moung Shway Hlaing!"

"Lord, I saw the money, one rupee, paid into
this woman's hand," said Shway Hlaing, dropping
on his heels behind Bah Twin. "Moung Poh also
saw it. Moung Poh! Ho, Moung Poh!"

"Lord, I saw the money paid," said Moung
Poh, dropping on his heels behind Shway
Hlaing.

"How much did you see paid?" demanded
Mr. McKinlay, whose sharp eye caught Shway
Hlaing turning his head to speak to his comrade.
"Stand up you; attention! How much did you
see paid?"

Moung Poh opened his mouth and shut it,
opened it again and gaped round helplessly. The
village men chuckled; and Mah Tsay cried that
that policeman was not present.

"Constable Shway Hlaing called me to witness," said Moung Poh, rubbing his knees together.

"That will do. Moung Kya will give the
woman one rupee more, and it will be cut from
his pay."

"Now," said Mr. McKinlay, hitching up his
sword, "Are all the men here? Go!" and

nodding to Ko Moung Galay, he strode off up the village at their head.

"Policemen are liars," shrieked Mah Tsay after them. "But for the white stranger they will rob their mothers. Policemen are thieves and lepers, and sons of she-dogs, and——"

"Be silent!" struck in Ko Moung Galay. "Will you make all these enemies for one half rupee? Besides, you have received the price and more."

"It was the order of the officer with the woman's name," grumbled Mah Tsay. "If he had not been here, I had been robbed."

"They are great liars," said Moung Byoo; "I laughed when his honour caught Moung Poh lying."

"It is true," said Oo Yan, "I know the police. In the thannah all tongues are one against a son of the village."

But Mah Tsay was whimpering again, and the men, who were beginning to relate stories of police mendacity, stopped.

"I have sold rice to the dog's sons who will shoot my boy," wept Mah Tsay, and her voice was shrill. "Why have I done this?"

"Because—because the price was good," said Ko Moung Galay lamely.

Mah Doh, swelling with importance, put her husband down with a word and explained.

"It was my thought. The sergeant said to

me, 'Sell rice,' and I said to him, 'Buy from my good neighbour, Mah Tsay.'"

She paused; the silence was flattering as she could wish, and she went on.

"If the police catch Pho Lone" (Mah Tsay howled), "if the police catch him," repeated Mah Doh, fixing her good neighbour with the eye of reproach, "Mah Tsay will be witness, saying, 'I am his mother, and sold rice to the police. The son of a helper of the Government is not a dacoit.'"

"Very good; very good indeed," cried all the neighbours. "Truly that was a very wise thought."

"Yes," agreed Mah Doh.

"But nobody ever heard of police catching dacoits," said Moung Let, who saw that his wife was not much consoled. "Besides, somebody must have sold rice to them."

"Why? they are not dacoits," said Moung Maw, drawing lines in the dust with his great toe. "Police do not beat us for refusing it. Boh Tah will be very angry."

"Yes, he will," said Mah Hehn, scowling at Mah Tsay.

"Then it's a pity you offered to sell to the sergeant, neighbour," retorted Moung Let; and the rest laughed so much at this that Mah Hehn got up and went to her house in a huff. Mah Hehn was too anxious to make annas and pice to be loved in the village.

"We have not heard yet how it was you stayed to fight," said Moung Byoo, addressing the head-man. "Tell!"

Ko Moung Galay grinned and wagged his elbow at his wife, who explained how the idea had come to her; and the story amused her neighbours so much that they agreed it was nearly as good to gain the favour of the Government as of Boh Tah.

"Mah Kin Lay thekin is our friend now," said Ko Moung Galay. "Next we shall gain the ear of the Deputy Commissioner himself."

This was ambitious, but Mah Tsay remembered the head-man's words a few days later.

    *   *   *   *   *

It was one night a week or ten days afterwards. All the people who had not gone on the second trip of the season to Bassein were sitting on the creek bank watching for the return of the empty boats; not that they were particularly interested in their coming; but the night was so still and close that no one could sleep and they sat together outside for company's sake. It was terribly hot; the scorched earth was pouring out the day's heat, and the wooden walls still glowed where the sun had fallen. The world was awake; pariahs trotted about snarling over garbage, or baying the full moon; you could hear the mosquito-teased buffaloes stamping at their pickets and blowing great sighs for freedom to go and wallow in the

mud ; the crows scuffled among the branches,
croaking crossly as they fluttered from perch to
perch ; the crickets shrilled in the jungle, the wall
lizards chirped and the tuctoo bawled his name
from a tree close by.   Over the group on the bank
you might see the mosquitoes hovering in swarms.

"It is too late this tide," yawned Oo Yan,
nodding at the creek where the moon shone down
as on a black-bordered mirror.

"No !" cried a little boy knee-deep in the water.
"A boat comes."

The screech of oars came from far away, but
soon a dark shadow crept in moonlit ripples round
the bend.

"Ho, neighbours !" cried a voice all knew as
Moung Let's.   "Ho, neighbours."

"What is the news ?" called Oo Ket Kay
lazily.

"There is news," replied Moung Let, and the
oars were still as he spoke, "the daughter of
Moung Byoo is married to Thaw' thekin !"   The
jungle echoed "Thaw' thekin" sharply ; but the
people answered "Mother ! that is news indeed.
Mah Pan is a lucky girl."

"I heard it as we pushed off from the godown,"
shouted Moung Let, proud to be first with the
great news.   Moung Byoo called to me, "His
honour marries Mah Pan."

Other boats arrived before the tide set down,
but Moung Byoo's was not among them.   This

was a little disappointing, but the bare fact gave food for a whole night's talk, and the red star had risen before Myothit went to bed.

Moung Byoo and Mah Hehn came on the morning's tide; it was boiling time; but every pot was left to take care of itself, for every one wanted to hear exactly how the marriage had come about. Moung Maw was the only person who did not seem interested; but as he had pulled an oar in Moung Byoo's boat he had heard all about it; perhaps more than he cared to, some of the women said slyly. However, he did at last stroll over to Moung Byoo's and stand on the edge of the crowd which packed the floor. Mah Hehn had just begun to tell the story over again as he came in; so he sat down and listened.

"His honour said to me, 'Three hundred and fifty rupees,' and I said: 'My Lord, it is my great wish to earn Merit by building a new monastery for the reverend monk in my village; this work will cost much money!' At this Thaw' thekin lay back and laughed very much; so much that his little ship-dog got up and barked; never have I seen a white gentleman laugh so."

"How very strange," said the neighbours, "Why should he laugh so much?"

"I cannot tell," said Mah Hehn perplexedly, "but he did. Presently having wiped his eyes he said, 'Very well, O female builder of a monastery, four hundred rupees.' To this I made answer, 'I think if Mah Pan were not happy she would wish to return home. She would be happy if I were able to build the new monastery.' His honour then looked a little cross. He said, 'Four hundred rupees is a large present,' and I said then, 'I will take it.'"

"Thaw' thekin must be very rich," said one.

"He is very rich," said Mah Hehn, "but not I think, very generous."

"She is a most fortunate girl," said several, "most fortunate."

"And when will the work be commenced?" asked Ko Moung Galay.

"Very soon," replied Moung Byoo. "The boards are bought; we took the four hundred rupees which Thaw' thekin's clerk paid into our hands and went to the Chinese carpenter to give order for the boards and other timber. As soon as we have found good posts Moung Maw will begin."

"Yes, I picked the planks," struck Moung Maw so suddenly that people started, "sixty, of good teak, scarcely any having beeholes; also boards for the floor and stout pieces for the rafters and joists, and shingles."

"Mother!"

"Yes, the roof of the new kyoung will be of shingles, not thatch," said Mah Hehn. She had right to expect that the neighbours would be surprised, for not a house in Myothit, or Ngatheing for that matter, was roofed with the wooden tiles which give such a respectable look; they are expensive compared with thatch.

"Will there be carving too?" inquired a voice respectfully.

"Yes, there will be carved pieces at each corner of the roof," replied Mah Hehn.

"Truly, it is a great work!"

"All must give the work of their hands in this building," said Mah Hehn graciously. "It is my wish that all shall join in it."

Every one said that it was very good, and without doubt the new kyoung would be one of which the village might be proud. And as it was now very hot and much after rice-time, Mah Hehn's visitors began to go their way; in the best of good humour, as well as they might be, for such an opportunity to earn Merit does not come every day. Mah Hehn was entitled to much respect, and the women whispered to each other that after very few more existences she would certainly be a man.

"If my son were here, he also would earn Merit by helping to build," sighed Mah Tsay as she crept down the street after Moung Let, "but he is gone with the dacoits and we shall never see him again."

Both the parents were very unhappy in these days. Nothing had been heard of Pho Lone; the men had made search for his body, and not finding it, knew what had happened. It was no new thing, but all were sorry because Pho Lone was his mother's only son.

"He will come back when the monsoon breaks," said the neighbours hopefully. "When the rains come, Boh Tah will send his men home to their villages."

At first Mah Tsay had listened gratefully ; but after Mah Kin Lay thekin and his police went in pursuit she gave way to despair. They would hunt the Boh and kill him and all his followers ; and if they did not kill Pho Lone they would catch him and cut off his hair and send him over the sea to be kept in prison for the rest of his life. The thought that she had sold rice to the men who would do this clung to Mah Tsay ; and she would crouch in the corner all day sobbing to her knees, while Moung Let sat brooding over his cheroot, only opening his mouth to say, "The woman speaks truth."

In vain their friends tried to reassure them. Who, they asked, ever heard of police catching dacoits ? How, they desired Moung Let to say, could mere police catch a Boh whose magic was the talk of the country side ? Mah Kin Lay thekin and his men would walk here and walk there, stopping at every village to ask questions, while the Boh got further off every day.

They were sitting silent and unhappy on their verandah that evening when Moung Byoo came.

He had something important to say concerning Pho Lone, and did so without any beating about the bush.

"When I go to the godown again," he said, "I shall say to my son-in-law Thaw' thekin 'Pho Lone was a good lad who lived with his mother. He was taken against his will to follow the Boh, and I beg your lordship to speak these words in the ear of his honour the Deputy Commissioner.' His honour, being a friend of Thaw' thekin, my son-in-law, will listen. Thus, if Pho Lone is caught by the police, the Deputy Commissioner will sign an order, and the good youth will be set free, not even his hair being cut."

These were very good words; Moung Let and Mah Tsay were comforted, and told Moung Byoo his talk was as English medicine to a pain in one's inside.

"I was a little sorry when I heard the girl had married Thaw' thekin," said Mah Tsay, when Moung Byoo had gone; "but I am now very happy it is so. Through Thaw' thekin poor jungle people can now speak in the ear of the Deputy Commissioner himself."

"His honour must speak for us," agreed Moung Let, "having married a daughter of our village."

CHAPTER X

"His lordship's order!" cried Moung Toke hoarsely, as a man who has just awakened. "Listen to the words his lordship commands that I speak!"

Those of the men who had not yet drawn their pasohs from their faces, did so quickly and sat up yawning. The sun had risen; through a rift in the foliage above, you might see where his rays touched a lofty tree; but down in the jungle was twilight.

"His lordship has dreamed a dream;" sang Moung Toke, and his voice echoed through the gloom. "The omen is evil. In his dream his lordship walked by a ruined pagoda, and from the bricks came a snake which bit his sacred foot, so that he should die. Lord! Wherefore this being a most evil omen his lordship will not to-day attack Ladaw village. Lord!"

Repeating "Lord!" Moung Toke shiko'd, and crept back to his place by Boh Tah's mat, which was spread against a tree a little way off. "It is a good place to rest," Pho Lone heard the chief say, "therefore we remain here; if there is a good omen to-night we will go to-morrow to Ladaw."

Moung Toke replied that his lordship spoke wisely, in which Pho Lone silently agreed, for he had been made to work very hard since he followed the Boh. His duty was to carry the rice bag, the big iron cooking-pot, tools for digging, and the chief's mat, in which various pieces of silk, and, judging by the weight, a good many rupees were rolled; and as the others had only their dahs and what little property they had stolen, they could march much faster than Pho Lone. In consequence he often lagged, and then Moung Toke would wait behind and beat him with his spear shaft till he trotted up to the rest. It would be a pleasant change, after three days of such toil, to sleep away the heat in this cool jungle, with the little stream close at hand to bathe in. There was no danger of being found by the police either, for the underwood was thick and a person passing along the path a bowshot distant could not see the fire.

He set about his work of cooking the morning rice quite cheerfully, and as Moung Chaik, the young man with the wounded arm, helped him, not being able to bathe like the rest, they soon had the fire blazing, and sat down to tend it and talk.

"I think there is only rice for one more meal," said Moung Chaik, eyeing the limp bag from which Pho Lone had filled the pot, "that is bad for us."

"Good for me who must carry it," laughed Pho Lone, weighing the bag in his hand, "there is enough left for two little meals, I think."

"Wonder if his lordship will dream well to-night," remarked Moung Chaik, "that was a very bad omen he dreamed."

"It was indeed," assented Pho Lone: for he knew the Dream-book as well as another, and could have repeated word for word the page which tells that the Snake signifies an enemy and its Bite defeat.

"I don't know what his lordship will do if he has another bad dream," sighed Moung Chaik. His arm gave him pain and he slept little at night, so he was apt to take a gloomy view of matters.

"We shall be all right," said Pho Lone, whom the prospect of an idle day had put in the best spirits. "For my part I am happy."

If Moung Chaik had not been suffering he would have had faith in the Boh; but as it was he felt obliged to show that they were in a very bad case. Here they were three hours from Ladaw, and unable to attack, having rice only for to-night's eating and no prospect of refilling the bag. They had counted on getting food at Ladaw to take them to Kyouksay four days farther on. How did Pho Lone propose that fifteen men should march four days having no food?

"Well there is plenty for to-day," said Pho Lone easily, as he raised the lid to see how the rice got on. "Let to-morrow take care of to-morrow."

By the time the men came up from the water, the rice was ready and heaped in the pot-lid for lack of anything more convenient ; and Pho Lone, having received permission to bring the Boh his portion, joined his comrades who were already eating.

"No dried fish, no ngapee, not even a chilli," grumbled Moung Chaik, plunging his fingers into the steaming white mass. "I wish," he glanced round and dropped his voice, "I wish I were back in my village."

The other men ate and said nothing. The Boh had pulled them through worse straits ere now, and they were content to take things as they came. They finished the rice to the last grain, strolled away to take a drink at the stream, and came back to enjoy the idleness.

It was good to lie on one's back and smoke, or chew betel till the red juice trickled from the corners of the mouth, for it was yet very cool in the jungle. Here and there the sun pierced the foliage and struck a broken patch of light on the tree trunks to make the dark shades pleasanter by contrast; the doves cooed sleepily in the distance, and the splash of the flying squirrel as he leaped from bough to bough startled the

stillness.   The sun-patches crept slowly down the
trees and one by one the men fell asleep.

Pho Lone stayed awake sucking his cheroot
and watching the blue smoke curl and wreathe
unshaken by a breath of air ; to-day he liked being
a dacoit much better than he had done during the
three days he had followed Boh Tah.   When his
life was spared he had made up his mind to make
the best of his misfortune and enjoy himself as
much as he could ; and the tales his new companions told that first night after eating rice had
excited his fancy.   He had pictured himself returning to Myothit with a bag of rupees so heavy
that his shoulders ached, and a great bundle of
silk pasohs and tameins, in which gold jewellery
was hidden, on his back ; for that was exactly what
each man of the gang expected for himself.   The
picture had become a little dimmed in these three
days ; his shoulders ached from the rice bag he
had been made to carry as the last enrolled
member of the gang, and his thighs were sore
from Moung Toke's spear-shaft ; it seemed as
though a fellow had become a slave instead of a
dacoit ; but no doubt other new men would join
very soon and then, if he could gain the favour of
the Boh, he would be relieved of this coolie work.
Certainly he did not stand very well with the
chief at present ; only last night Moung Toke
had warned him that if he lagged again it was
their intention to hang him by the feet to a

tree and leave him with a fire lighted under him. But then Moung Toke had lost at play last night and was cross; so perhaps he said more than the Boh meant. Anyhow his threat did not seem real this morning, and Pho Lone was enjoying the envy and admiration of Moung Maw and the neighbours when sleep overtook him.

The cooking fire was black out, and had been made on bare ground for convenience sake, so it must have been a live cheroot, falling from drowsy fingers, that set the dry grass smouldering; but whatever the cause it was the sudden burst of heat from blazing underwood that woke the men. Pho Lone sat up to see the flames leap and the leaves high overhead dance and shrivel in the smoke, while the blaze spread with a savage roar that drowned the orders shouted by Boh Tah. There was no need for him to tell them to run; nobody can tell where a jungle fire will stop, and every man caught up his dah and bundle and fled through the thorns to the stream. At first they thought only of escape from the fire, and after crossing the shallow stream and wide stretch of sand beyond, stopped to look back at the flames leaping higher among the trees.

"Will it cross to us?" asked Pho Lone of the man beside him; but before he got an answer the Boh was shouting to them.

"Go!" he cried. "If the police come, they

come quickly to see who made this fire. Go then!"

"The wisdom of his lordship is as the wisdom of Bhudda himself," said Moung Toke in a very distinct voice, as he snatched up the bamboo gun and ran after the leader. "Hasten all of you!"

They ran along the watercourse until they struck the path which clove the steep flood-worn banks. Boh Tah took the way to Ladaw without pausing, and sped along. The roaring of the flames was faint in their rear when his run slackened into a rapid walk, and presently crossing an open glade he stopped to look back. They could no longer hear the fire, but above the forest a great column of smoke tapered, to spread in purple clouds and reflect the glow.

"That will be seen two days' march away," remarked Moung Chaik gloomily, "and will bring the forest guards if not the police."

That seemed to be the Boh's thought also, for he jerked himself on to his feet, and called to the men to follow. Moung Toke waited till Pho Lone passed, to give him a word of advice.

"I think the bad omen of last night means that the police chase us to-day," he said. "If you fall behind now, his lordship will to-night give the order to spit you from buttock to shoulder upon a bamboo."

He glowered savagely, and trotted on to take his place next the Boh, while Pho Lone hunched

up his load and drew his pasoh tighter about his
hips, before he started again to bring up the
rear. The track was very narrow, and wound
sharply through dense jungle, so that the leaders
of the file, as it strung out, were seldom in sight
of the hindmost. Pho Lone did his best to keep
up, but the thorns caught in his load, detaining
him so often that he was continually in fear of
Moung Toke's coming back to beat him. The
sweat dripped from his elbows as he strove to
hold his load steady, and trickled down his brow,
half blinding him. He longed to put the things
down and rest his tired back, but he dared not,
and stumbled along as best he might, full two
bamboos' length behind the last man, seeing and
hearing nothing for utter weariness.

Turning a corner which showed the path
straight for a little distance, he shook the hair
from his face, to see how far behind he had fallen
before making an effort to catch up. As he did
so, he saw the Boh's gun held high, and the file
suddenly halt; a moment's pause, and every man
flung his weapon far into the jungle, and leaped
like one in the opposite direction, to vanish like
deer, and with as little sound. For a breath Pho
Lone hesitated; then he dropped his own load
carefully behind a bush, and stole along the path
to seek a hiding-place, for now he too heard the
tramp of feet which had caught the more prac-
tised ears of his companions. He was stepping

gingerly off the track, for the jungle was thorny, when a shout stopped him, and he looked up to see a white officer striding along with levelled revolver, and a party of police crowding behind him. Pho Lone drew back from the bushes, and crouched on his heels, hoping that the pot and bag had not been seen.

"Who are you, and where do you come from?" demanded the officer, lowering his pistol.

Now if Pho Lone had been less in awe of Boh Tah and Moung Toke, whom he knew must be hiding close by, he would have confessed the truth, although he saw prison and chains for life before him. But he was too much afraid of the chief, so replied that he was Moung Gyee, son of Moung Loogalay, of Ladaw village.

"And what are you doing in the jungle when the sun is high, so far from your village?"

Fear quickened Pho Lone's wits; he answered that, with the officer's permission, he was seeking a few medicine leaves.

"You were trying to hide," said the officer, eyeing him keenly.

"Lord, I heard many feet, and being greatly in fear of dacoits, did try to hide myself."

"Stand up and show your body."

Pho Lone rose, thankful that the Boh had contemptuously refused Moung Toke's proposal to tattoo him. Not only had he no charms particularly affected by dacoits—he had not even taken the most ordinary precautions; was neither gun-proof nor sword-proof; the only protection he had against jungle perils was that against snake-bite; and the person who has not two or three blue spots below his ankle, where the medicine has been tattooed into the skin, is not to be found in town or country. Pho Lone therefore stood up confidently to be examined, and was relieved to see that the officer's face now showed disappointment.

There was a little silence while the white man put his pistol into his belt, and drew off the thick cord which secured it to his wrist. Pho Lone stood, straining his ears to catch a rustle which might betray the presence of Boh Tah or his men, but all one could hear was the cluck of a lizard and the heavy breathing of the police who had been travelling fast since they saw the fire.

"Is there any talk of Boh Tah's gang in your village?" inquired the officer in a less severe tone.

"We had news that he burned Ngatheing and Myothit villages, after killing many people," replied Pho Lone, wishing to please the chief, if he chanced to be listening.

"Now, look here. The jungle has been fired about one hour and a half from this place. Did you know that?"

Pho Lone denied it, but looked much

frightened. Luckily the officer misunderstood his fear, and went on to say, if he did not want to fall into the dacoits' hands, he had better run home to his village as fast as he could.

"Wait a bit," he added, seeing that Pho Lone was about to go; "where does the path lead to which meets this one two hours march back?"

"To the creek, your honour, to a very small village where fishermen live. I hope the dacoits have gone that way, being afraid lest the fire should bring the police."

"With your lordship's leave," struck in the sergeant, dropping on his heels, "I think this jungle-man speaks truth; he must have seen the dacoits had they come this way, there being but the one path."

"That's just what they have done," said the officer viciously, and he drew his cheroot case from his pocket and lighted one while he seemed to be considering.

"I suppose they have many boats at the little fishing village you speak of?" he said presently.

"They have three or four large boats at Panmaw village," replied Pho Lone, glad to be able to speak truth again; "boats that pull many oars and good for shallow water. Your lordship, I think these dacoits will steal boats to escape in," he added for the Boh's benefit.

The officer made no answer. He turned on his heel, called "Right about turn, march!" and strode away, leaving Pho Lone to shrink off the path as the policemen passed. There were nine men with rifles, and Pho Lone thought Boh Tah would need all his magic to deal with a party so well armed as that. The steady tramp of the officer's boots died in the distance, and still he crouched among the bushes afraid to move. He felt sure that the dacoits would kill him for being caught, and wished the police had taken him away prisoner.

Fully a betel-chew passed before Boh Tah and Moung Toke stole out upon the path. Pho Lone trembled and crawled out to beg for mercy, but before he could speak the Boh addressed him mouth to mouth for the first time.

"You have done well, young man; I am pleased with you."

"I am your lordship's slave," said Pho Lone, so astonished and gratified that he did not know what else to say.

"You are appointed my Life-guard; henceforth you carry the gun. Moung Toke will give the rice and baggage to another man."

"Your lordship heaps favours on his slave," said Pho Lone, shikoing once more. A reception so different to that he had looked for set his head whirling; he could hardly believe his ears. The Boh smiled condescendingly, and Pho Lone was his follower at heart from that moment.

"He threw them completely off our path," said

Moung Toke. "They will go to Panmaw, which is two days from this place. Before they find out their mistake we shall sack both Ladaw and Kyouksay."

"I give orders what shall be done," said the Boh, and Moung Toke shiko'd and collapsed.

"Forty police dogs each having a rifle," remarked Boh Tah presently. "That is without counting the Englishmen."

"Nothing escapes his lordship's eye," cried Moung Toke. He had counted only nine himself, but if the Boh said there were forty it was not his place to contradict; and for a little time the three squatted on the path, reflecting upon the danger from which they had escaped.

"What are your honour's commands?" inquired Moung Toke, as the chief rose thoughtfully and felt in the fold of his pasoh for a cheroot.

"Follow those policemen, kill them all, and take their guns and cartridges. What was that?" he added, taking one step into the jungle.

"It might be the police returning," replied Moung Toke, whose keen eye had caught a monkey shaking a bough, "but I do not think it is. Will it be pleasing to your lordship that I call the followers together?"

The Boh assented. So Moung Toke, having first recovered the gun, which the chief passed to Pho Lone with another gracious smile, went to collect the men. This was easy, because he had

merely to shake a little tree and imitate the
cry of the lizard ; but finding the weapons and
baggage was a very different matter, as it must
be when a gang is well disciplined. Frequent
false alarms had given Boh Tah's men practice,
and now they executed the manœuvre so well
when the signal to hide was given that it sometimes took an hour and a half to find all the
weapons when danger was past.

After much searching, at the cost of skin and
clothes among the quickset, everything was recovered except the bamboo gun, which was
Moung Toke's especial charge. He thought he
had marked the spot where he flung it, but it
was nowhere to be found. And when it seemed
that they must leave it for lost, the chief's brow
grew so black that Moung Toke's knees began to
shake. Iron wire of the strong kind necessary
to bind a bamboo gun can only be got in the
bazaar of a big town, and Moung Toke could
scarcely have done worse had he lost the bag of
large shot. This was Pho Lone's lucky day, as
everybody said that evening. It was he who
spied out the missing weapon sticking upright, a
man's height above the ground, in a thick bamboo
clump. He pointed it out to Moung Toke while
the Boh was looking the other way, and so made
the lieutenant his friend. While the men were
searching each one took a chance of telling Pho
Lone how glad he was to hear of his promotion,

and begged him if he found himself short of betel, cheroots or anything, to confer on his friend the favour of asking for what he wanted. It was very likely Pho Lone would find his supplies of these things run short, because up till now the men had helped themselves from his box to save their own.

Moung Toke divided the load Pho Lone had carried between Moung Chaik and Shway Dway, who happened to have been somewhat lax of late in paying their respects to him; and this having been settled, the Boh was informed that all was ready for the march.

"We have come far and fast to-day," said Boh Tah. "I will lead you to a safe resting-place, whence we shall go to Ladaw to-morrow."

"We shall not follow the police to kill them and take their guns, then?" asked Pho Lone. He was fairly drunk with good fortune, or would never have said such a thing. The men stared with amazement, and Moung Toke, pressing forward, whispered in his ear, "Fickle is a great man's favour. Still tongue, wise head," and drew back again, nodding at him earnestly. Another Boh would most likely have ordered the young man to be thrown down and flogged with split bamboos; but Boh Tah knew when to be severe and when kind, and he lost nothing in the eyes of his followers by seeming not to hear.

"The fool," said Moung Toke to the man next

him; "does he think fourteen men with dahs can kill forty policemen with rifles?"

"He is young and will grow wiser," said Shway Dway, whose hair was touched with white, "to-day the youth has had great good fortune, also," and he sighed; he had been dacoiting at intervals for many years, but had never had much luck.

The Boh was in no haste to start, and the sun was declining when he gave the order to march, and led the way in the Ladaw direction. He moved slowly, for that village was now less than one hour distant, and he did not wish to be seen by people who might be out in the jungle to gather firewood or on some other errand. He followed the path a little way, and then, the jungle being thinner, turned aside to look for water, near which they might camp for the night. He found a place which pleased him in the bend of a deep water-course, along whose sandy bed a tiny stream trickled; the elephant bamboos met overhead at this spot making it very dark. Pho Lone's heart sank when he saw the chief throw down his dah.

"There is night here," he whispered to Moung Toke, "it being yet day outside. I think there are many evil spirits in this place."

"Dark camp, good camp," said Shway Dway, who heard his complaint. "See the print of the deer's feet, good son; nobody ever comes here."

When rice had been eaten that evening, Boh Tah called Pho Lone and told him to tell Moung Toke that, unless anything happened to-night to prevent it, they should attack Ladaw next morning, and he must therefore make the usual preparations.

"It is a trouble," said Moung Toke when he received the message, lying at full length on the sand; "but it must be done. Ho! Shway Dway, Bah Chet, bring the mamootees, we go to prepare for to-morrow."

"Why do we carry the digging tools?" asked Pho Lone, as they felt their way out of the gully and back to the path.

"To dig the hole for his lordship, of course," replied Moung Toke.

"I don't understand," said Pho Lone.

Moung Toke, albeit much surprised that Pho Lone should have followed for four days without discovering a fact so important, explained, as they walked stealthily along in the direction of the village. His lordship was not a common fighting leader; his charms were so powerful and therefore so precious that he must not run any risks; if he were killed his charms would be spoiled, and then his followers might as well go home to their villages.

"On that account he does not fight himself?" said Pho Lone, much impressed.

"Exactly," assented Moung Toke. "His lordship is a Pit-hiding Chief. We now go to dig the hole in which he will hide to-morrow, while we fight the village men; his charms being thus safe from hurt will protect all into whose hand his lordship shall give a little magic rice."

"Then shall I myself be commanded to stay and protect his lordship?" inquired Pho Lone.

"We cannot tell what he may order," replied Moung Toke; "now, we come near the Ladaw paddy kwins and must be quiet."

They walked on in silence until the jungle came to an end and straggled out in low bushes to meet the cultivated land. Against the soft light of the night-sky the roofs of Ladaw stood out, about half a mile away. You might walk across the fields straight to the village, or by threading your way through the jungle get round unseen till the nearest house was but a stone's throw distant. Moung Toke looked about and finally selected a spot at the foot of a great tree, between whose buttress-like roots six men might crouch and be hidden from the village.

"This is a good place," he said, "the roots being large we need not dig deep, being tired after so much marching to-day. Also the wild swine have loosened the earth for us." He signed to Shway Dway and Bah Chet, and they, having muttered a prayer to the spirits of earth

and forest, whom they were about to disturb,
tucked up their pasohs and bent their backs to
the digging.   They worked with a will; but the
many voices of the jungle night smothered the
noise of their tools.

CHAPTER XI

THE day was breaking. Pho Lone, drawing his pasoh from his face, lay watching the ragged patches of sky through the leaves grow lighter. He would have risen, but as he awakened he caught the voice of the Boh speaking to Moung Toke and thought it good to listen.

"And this I dreamed last night," said the Boh, making an end of speech.

"Indeed a very good dream, your lordship. It is written in the Book, he who dreams that he eats the flesh of an enemy slain in fight dreams well. The layman dreaming this thing shall certainly soon receive a Government appointment; and the official thus dreaming must look for much honour and promotion."

"It means success in my undertaking," said the Boh. "Without doubt it foretells great measure of success; for I, having awakened after dreaming, saw, by the sinking moon, that the hour of midnight was long past."

"Dreams which come before midnight are not good to read as omens," remarked Moung Toke,

for lack of anything better to say; "when one
eats at the evening meal food that is a little
strange, or much curry that is highly spiced,
one's inside is troubled and dreams follow quickly
upon sleep. Such dreams must not be read as
omens."

"I know, I know," said the Boh, a little angry
that Moung Toke should tell him what every child
knows; "as I have told, I wakened and knew that
the dream came long after midnight."

"Lord," said Moung Toke respectfully.

Pho Lone lay listening with strained ears, but
for many breaths he heard only the drip of the
dew.

"Your lordship will no doubt command your
servants to attack the village to-day?" said Moung
Toke presently.

"Having again fallen asleep, very happy by
reason of the good omen," said the Boh, paying
no heed to the question, "I dreamed yet another
dream."

"Another dream!"

"In this dream, O friend, I, lying upon my mat,
saw come down to me from the darkness of the
heavens the full moon, like burnished silver, and
having many bright stars hanging from his rim.
Whereupon I, saying, 'O King, Grandfather Moon!
speak, why do you come?' the moon made
answer, 'Conquest awaits the bravery of your
followers and your own very great wisdom.' And

having spoken these words the moon faded up again into the sky of the night."

" What fortune is his lordship's !"

" Yes, I dreamed this dream when I slept, having already dreamed that I ate of the flesh of an enemy," said the Boh.

" Two such omens !" said Moung Toke under his breath.

"This second dream, just before I woke at the dawn," said the Boh thoughtfully. " We shall attack to-day. I go now to learn the propitious hour."

Pho Lone, lying as though still asleep, heard the mat crackle as the Boh rose, and presently heard him brushing through the jungle above the water-course. He sat up and saw Moung Toke smoking. He rose and coiled up his hair, for it is not very respectful to address a superior with one's hair hanging loose on the shoulders.

"His lordship's dreams last night were full of the best omens," said Moung Toke. " Listen, I will tell you all that he dreamed."

Moung Toke was so eager to repeat the dreams which had come to their chief that Pho Lone squatted and heard them again from his mouth.

"Without doubt there are none more favourable in the Book," said Pho Lone, when he finished.

"None," said Moung Toke, with conviction. "His lordship has already gone to the jungle to learn the auspicious hour for attacking Ladaw village."

" What a leader ! " said Pho Lone.

" There is not such another in all the land," said Moung Toke. " Two such dreams in one night, and nearly in the hour when one can see the veins in the hand ! "

" The best of hours," said Pho Lone.

Somebody yawned loudly at this moment and Moung Toke moved away. It was good to repeat such news to Pho Lone, who enjoyed his lordship's favour, but he was not going to tell every one in this friendly way. Time enough for that when the Boh returned and commanded him to relate the dreams with proper ceremony. In the time one takes to smoke a cheroot the chief came back, and sitting upon a fallen tree trunk ordered silence ; and all having shiko'd Moung Toke sang with long-drawn breaths the dreams which the chief had dreamed.

" And it is the order of his lordship," he went on, having lent ear to the Boh for a little time, " that the attack be made two hours after noon, that hour being found by his lordship the propitious hour. Lord ! And the gun being fired by me, his lordship's servant, all shall rush upon the village with very great and fierce shouting, that the people being awakened from sleep in fear shall run from us. This is the order of his lordship. Lord ! "

All shiko'd. Pho Lone did so, wishing the Boh
had discovered that two hours before noon was a
propitious hour, for he was hungry and there was
no rice left. The others looked as though the
same wish was in their hearts, but nobody spoke,
for the chief was now holding something out
beyond his knees in both hands, while he gazed
over it into the gloom.

"By my order"—he spoke as a man speaking
to himself—"By my order, a little rice was saved
last night when the bag was emptied."

He opened his hands and all could see that his
lordship held his head-kerchief tightly rolled in a
ball. "That my followers may escape from death
by gunshot or by sword and from capture, I give
each a little of this rice which I have charmed by
magical arts."

Every one shiko'd again. Pho Lone felt a little
frightened, for the gloom and the tone of the Boh's
voice made him think of Oo Boo Nah and his evil
smelling house far away by Ngatheing. Holding
the cloth carefully in one hand, the Boh unrolled
it slowly, and at a word from Moung Toke the
men crept forward one by one to receive in up-
raised hands a few grains of the magic rice. Pho
Lone, looking respectfully upon his, thought it
was like rice that had been stirred in curry stuff.
Perhaps the chief had used turmeric in working
his charm; he was so clever at magic that he
could produce wonderful results with the simplest

means.   It was the first charm against dangers
of war that Pho Lone had ever possessed, and he
took care that the Boh should see him wrap the
yellow rice in a rag and tie it about his neck.

Having given out the rice, the Boh sat for a few
moments gazing into the shades, then slipped off
the log and stalked quietly up the gully to dis-
appear in the jungle.

"His lordship goes to work more charms and
make offerings," said Moung Toke in an under-
tone, "it is good that he should do so we having
had but little fortune in the last few villages."

"It is certainly very good," said all. Pho Lone
spoke with the rest and, remembering the cause
of the band's ill fortune at Myothit, hoped no old
woman of Ladaw would scream, at all events
until they had got a basket or two of rice.

The morning passed very slowly. It was the
Boh's order that no one should go ten bamboos'
length from the black spot which marked last
night's fire, or Shway Dway, who cared little for
the Law, might have tried to catch a few fish in
the pool which could be seen from the bend below
the camp. They stayed hunger by drinking much
water, and sat round in the brightest place
nursing their knees and talking of the great
deeds they were to perform. The jungle grew
still under the rising of the sun they could not
see, and talk languished ; some slept and others
whiled away the time playing a child's game with

pebbles on the sand. It was not a very good
game and hardly served to keep the players
awake until Shway Dway said, " Last time I
played this game was in the sawyer's shed of
Henzada gaol where we were always locked on
Sunday afternoons with nothing to do."

" Why do you talk such talk just before we go
to work ? " snarled Moung Toke rising to his feet,
" I think you are an old fool."

" It is very unlucky to speak of such places at
this time," said Moung Chaik.

"I shall report him to his lordship," said Moung
Toke dropping on his heels to continue play.
" His lordship will punish him."

Shway Dway blinked solemnly and rolled his
chew, for the angry grumblings of his comrades
made him ashamed. He said he should go and
make an offering with prayers to dispel the bad
omen of his thoughtless words and strolled away
into the jungle.

He had been back some time and the men were
beginning to ask each other if the sun were not
now much past the meridian, when the Boh
suddenly appeared in their midst and gave the
order to march.

" I give my English gun to Pho Lone," he said
taking it from the heap of bundles against which
it leaned, " it will kill ten men when fired." He
handled it fondly before he raised the hammer
and poured fresh priming into the pan. It was a

very short gun with a thick barrel much eaten by
rust; but, as Shway Dway said, any one who
knew about guns could see what a fine weapon it
was; and Pho Lone heard the murmur of envy as
the chief gave it him and showed him how to let
it off.

" Go then," said the Boh, " the omens are the
best; great success awaits us."

This was very cheering to men in rather low
spirits by reason of their long morning of hunger
spent in the gloom of the choung.   At the chief's
words they drew themselves up and flourished
their dahs; but for Moung Toke's warning they
would have shouted.

" March next to his lordship, most favoured
one !" said Shway Dway smiling to Pho Lone.

" His lordship has done the Myothit son great
honour," said Moung Toke, " march forward,
friend."

Accordingly Pho Lone led the file behind the
Boh, feeling very proud as he heard the men
speak of the honour conferred upon him.

" He will lead the attack, I think," said Shway
Dway; and the others echoed, " Yes, he will lead
the attack."

Now Pho Lone was very proud of the honour,
but he did not wish to lead the charge upon the
village; so when Moung Toke bade them all wait
in the jungle while he went on to guide the Boh
to his hiding hole, he crept to Shway Dway's side

and offered him the gun saying, " You are very brave and have so much experience ; I think the honour of using his lordship's gun should be yours."

Shway Dway took the gun, passed his hand along the barrel and sighed as he gave it back. He should dearly like to take it and lead the attack, he said ; but Moung Toke would certainly tell his lordship, who would be angry at his favour being thus set aside. Pho Lone said he would explain to the Boh, but Shway Dway was firm ; so he offered the gun to Moung Chaik. Moung Chaik also declined it, as did all the others in turn : each man said how much he should esteem the honour, but not one would accept it, because the Boh would be so angry with Pho Lone. Hence when Moung Toke returned saying, " His lordship is pleased to say I chose a good place for the pit," Pho Lone still squatted with the gun between knees which shook in spite of his arms round them.

" Now be silent and follow," said Moung Toke.

The men rose and started to creep through the jungle behind him. They had not far to go to strike the little path which curved with the edge of the forest and from which the open kwins and the distant village could be seen. The sight of the houses brought the sweat in great drops down Pho Lone's face ; he could hear his heart beat as he stole along, and he looked round to see

how the others were feeling. Each face was set
and yellow ; only Shway Dway appeared happy ;
he chewed betel as he walked, and grinned
pleasantly to Pho Lone as he caught his eye.
The way seemed long because Moung Toke was
so careful. If a twig snapped under foot his
hand went out, and the band dropped on their
heels, lest any one in the village, having heard,
should look. It seemed unnecessary to do this,
when Ladaw was still a gunshot distant, but all
obeyed Moung Toke's smallest sign. Thanks to
the skill with which he led the advance, they
came to the end of the jungle, where it trickled
out in a point a bowshot from the nearest house,
without even a dog having barked ; but the pain
of creeping forward like this in silence was so
great that, had they had much further to go,
Pho Lone felt he must throw down the gun, and
fly into the jungle. He was quite glad when,
there being but a few bushes before them, Moung
Toke put down his bundle, and motioned the men
on in front.

"All are here," he whispered, as they passed
and crouched close under the shrubs. "Now,
when the village men hear the poung !"—he laid
the bamboo gun carefully on the ground and un-
wound the rag from the touchhole—"I think
they will wake in a fright and run away. But
lest any stay to fight, you must go first and shoot
them with his lordship's gun."

The men, craning forward to listen, nodded
approval, and somehow Pho Lone, without moving,
found himself in front and Shway Dway at his
elbow whispering encouragement. Shway Dway's
words were sweet, but Pho Lone was frightened
when he looked in his face. There was that in
his eyes and the way he was balancing his dah
which fairly pulled up his heart.

"Don't fear; you lead and I keep near you,"
said Shway Dway.

"I shall certainly be killed," stammered Pho
Lone, with bloodless lips.

"Only if you run the wrong way," replied
Shway Dway, whipping off a twig with his dah
to show its edge. "When the gun goes poung!
lead with great shouting."

Pho Lone watched Moung Toke laying the
train to fire his bamboo gun, and wondered how
long he would take. He was very slow; he
could not shake out the powder properly, and
when at last he got the train laid he tried many
times before he could strike a match. At last he
saw the blue smoke leap, and Shway Dway gave
him a little push. The gun went off, and something seemed to break in his head. He knew
that he screamed as he ran, for Shway Dway's
first yell was so terrible. He had a glimpse of
people flying and great splashing in the creek;
but when a hand seized his arm, and a voice bade
him stop, he felt as if he had dreamed and was

now awakened in the Ladaw street surrounded by breathless men.

"You are a leader," panted Shway Dway. "You fired the gun."

Pho Lone felt a pain in his chest, and saw a bruise. It was there that the gun kicked him, he thought.

. "He is indeed a leader," cried the rest; and one added: "I think his shot wounded a boy. I saw him stagger, and his mother swung him upon her hip."

"Every person in the village has fled," said another man, looking up and down the ragged row of houses which faced the narrow creek.

"Our great shouting frightened the dogs," said Pho Lone proudly. "They are very much afraid of us."

Moung Toke now limped up. He explained that when he fired the bamboo gun it jumped and struck his foot. Upon that account he fell down, and was not able to charge with the rest.

"However, the work is now done," he said. "Moung Chaik, Bah Chet! Go, tell his lordship the village is captured. We light a fire to cook before we search the houses."

It was a most successful attack. The people had been in such haste to escape that they had taken nothing in their hands. Not a box was open; some of the women had even left their neck-kerchiefs, with the keys tied to them, on the mats whence they had been roused by the firing and shouts.

"This plan of making great noise is much the best," Pho Lone said to Shway Dway. "I am glad I so advised his lordship."

Pho Lone was beginning to give himself airs; but Shway Dway did not wish to quarrel with the Boh's favourite, so he said that Pho Lone's advice was certainly very good.

"Come, little chief," he said, "let us search this house, which looks as if it might belong to a rich man."

It was good to be called "Boh galay" by the most experienced man of the band, and Pho Lone held up his head as Shway Dway addressed him thus. It was nearly as good to climb the steps to the dark sleeping-room and find two large teak boxes, both locked.

"Something worth having here," said Shway Dway, lifting one by the handle.

"Money!" exclaimed Pho Lone, whose ear caught the rumble and clash of rupees. "How can we open the box?"

"The jungle-man's key," laughed Shway Dway, raising his dah; and with a few quick blows he cut away the wood about the hasps and prised up the lid. "There, little chief, turn it out while I open the other."

Pho Lone groped in the box till he found a

bundle of rupees tied in an old cotton pasoh, and lifted it out in triumph.

"I told you so," he cried. "Five hundred rupees and more by the weight."

"Turn it quite over," said Shway Dway, chopping at the other box. "Spread a cloth and turn it upside down."

Pho Lone did so, and was rewarded by finding a diamond ear ornament and a gold bracelet.

"This is better than being a cultivator," said Shway Dway. "What do you think?"

"The life of the jungle for me," laughed Pho Lone gaily. "Look at this silk pasoh; it must have cost forty rupees."

"Go then, little chief. I think we have taken everything, and I am hungry."

Pho Lone had forgotten his hunger in the excitement of the search, but now he felt that he could eat three men's portion of rice, and followed Shway Dway out of the house, laden with booty.

There was already quite a large heap of property in the street, though the men had not yet searched half the houses. Pho Lone put his bundle with the rest, and after reckoning that the money taken amounted to quite six thousand rupees, picked up the Boh's gun and went to join the rest, who were beginning to eat in the head-man's house.

"We shall be laden like coolies now," remarked

Moung Toke, through a mouthful, as he glanced
out at the pile.

"No; we shall march like a Royal army," said
Bah Chet, stepping upon the verandah, "I have
seen an elephant standing under the tree over
there."

Bah Chet's words gave great joy; the Boh
himself looked up from his rice, and before
Moung Toke could repeat the news, asked,
"Who can drive an elephant?"

"Your lordship's slave has been an elephant
driver," said Bah Chet shikoing.

"Then I appoint this man driver of my
elephant," said the Boh; and Bah Chet shiko'd
again, with a prayer for his lordship's prosperity.

When rice had been eaten, the chief called
Moung Toke aside, and the two sat talking in
the far corner of the verandah. Pho Lone in his
pride would have joined them, but Shway Dway
said, "Disturb not tigers eating," and he took
the old man's advice, much as he wished to show
that he enjoyed Boh Tah's favour. A heavy
meal makes men lazy; so, although many houses
yet remained unsearched, none were anxious to
go out in the still heat and finish the work.
There was plenty of betel-nut in the head-man's
house, for his wife kept a little shop for the sale
of such things; and it was good to find half-nuts
neatly made up with pink lime and fresh soap-
leaves ready for chewing; the men helped them-

selves and settled down to enjoy a quiet afternoon. The village people were hiding in the thick jungle just across the creek, for once or twice Pho Lone heard a child's cry checked short, as if by a hand over its mouth ; but though he watched with the eye of fear, lest the village men should suddenly plunge through the bushes and across the creek to kill them all, not a leaf stirred until the shadows stretched and the evening breeze moved the hot air.

The Boh and Moung Toke sat long in talk, and at last called Shway Dway to them. Shway Dway had passed all his life in the jungles, except when in prison, and knew the forests better than any man of the band. Once Pho Lone had asked him, "What is the name of your village?" and Shway Dway made answer, "Jungle-town, which lies between the great sea and the Ngawoon River." And Pho Lone saying, "A large village, truly," Shway Dway replied that the police could not find him there ; the police were his enemies because he had a bad name. He could not dwell in peace in his own village, which was below Ngapoota : he had tried many times ; but whenever a dacoity occurred, though a hundred miles away, the police always came and arrested him. Upon that account he preferred the jungles ; during the fine weather he followed some Boh, and when the rains came he used to lie up in a tiny hamlet called Nyounglay, which was, he said, known to very few people. When Shway Dway was asked if it was a good village to hide at, he said, "The hair of many at Nyounglay is short," so it was easy to guess what kind of place it was.

Pho Lone would have been glad to lie idle till the order was given to start; but the chief, looking round, gave, through Moung Toke's mouth, the order to finish searching the houses at once, and he got up feeling a little angry.

"I want to do mischief," he said to Moung Chaik, as they went out.

Moung Chaik said he felt the same, so they went together.

It was while they were searching the last house that a bright thought came to Pho Lone. He caught sight of the three little earthen jars, which stood on a high shelf to contain the sadahs* of the house-owner, his wife and children.

* The sadah, or horoscope, is drawn out in mysterious cabalistic squares on a strip of palm-leaf for every child when he or she is about three years old. It sets forth the exact moment, day and date of birth, records the planet under which the owner was born, and sundry other details. It is extremely important that these particulars should be kept private, because any evilly disposed person possessed of the information set out in your sadah would be in a position to work charms and spells against you. The jars are kept where they can be seen, high up to show them respect, and also to avoid risk of accident. It would be the height of discourtesy even to refer to a neighbour's jars or their contents.

"Let us carry away all the sadahs we can find," said Pho Lone, with a malicious laugh.

"What would be the good of that?"

"Think of the fear the people will be in when they find them all gone," sniggered Pho Lone, knocking down the jars with the gun he carried. "Mind that scorpion!" as the pots shattered on the floor. "There, five sadahs. Let us go to the next house."

Moung Chaik was not much pleased with the plan, but rather than offend the Boh's favourite, he went. They smashed the pots so as to show the village people what they had done.

"Now what are you going to do with them?" asked Moung Chaik as Pho Lone added the last to his bundle of strips.

Pho Lone had not quite made up his mind. He thought it would be very amusing to throw the whole lot down in the street, when the people on their return would have a fine sorting and each would see every one else's before he found his own. Then everybody would be uneasy because his neighbours had seen his sadah and would not know what spells might be worked against him. While he squatted, turning the palm leaves about in his hands, Moung Toke called him to the headman's verandah, where he still sat with the Boh.

"What have you there?" inquired the chief; and seeing, before Pho Lone could reply, he smiled more graciously than ever.

"This youth is the best man among my following," he said to Moung Toke. "He collects the
sadahs that the people, knowing I thereby hold
their fate in my hands, may become very submis-
sive. You have indeed done well, O Myothit
son!"

Pho Lone had not thought of this valuable use
to which the sadahs might be put; but he was
wise enough to shiko and express gratitude for
his lordship's good words, without confessing this.

"This young man will one day be a very great
chief, leading hundreds of men and having many
elephants," said Moung Toke with a touch of envy.
He had had many opportunities, but it had never
come to his thoughts to hold villages in his hand
by such simple means.

"He certainly will," agreed the Boh. "There
is leave to go, friend. Give order to bring my
elephant and see it loaded with the property I
have taken; we march very soon for Nyounglay,
having so much to carry."

The elephant was brought up and Pho Lone
gave, through Bah Chet, orders to load it. It
was a great work for inexperienced men to pack
all the loose property safely in the riding basket,
but Pho Lone squatted at a little distance giving
his orders and did not lift so much as a betel box.

"All is ready now, neighbour," said Bah Chet
cheerfully as he tugged at the last knot, "shall I
bid the elephant rise?"

Pho Lone took no notice, so Bah Chet stepped astride the elephant's neck and repeated his words. Pho Lone scowled.

" Does your lordship give order that his servant bids the elephant stand ? " said Bah Chet, slipping quickly to the ground and crouching on his heels.

" Bid the elephant rise," said Pho Lone, throwing the command over his shoulder without looking at Bah Chet ; and Bah Chet shiko'd.

CHAPTER XII

"Who makes that great crying which has awakened me?"

The Boh always slept a little apart from his men, so he was the last to be disturbed by the groans and cries which had roused the whole camp. His voice was sleepy and harsh, and Shway Dway trembled a little as he called across the darkness that the Myothit son was very ill with great pains in his inside.

The men who sat yawning and blinking round Pho Lone, edged away as they heard the chief's mat crackle.

"Make fire that I may see," said the Boh, stepping among them. "I must have light to discover the nature of this sickness."

They hastened to blow up the dying embers of the pot-fire till it lighted all the glade and showed Pho Lone's face drawn with pain as he sat with bent body on his sleeping mat. He did not answer when the Boh spoke to him but cried continually that he had been bewitched.

"I fear the good son is indeed bewitched," said

the Boh, squatting at his side and studying him
closely.

There was a sleepy murmur of assent from the
men, and Moung Toke remarked it was well for
Pho Lone that his lordship's powers were greater
than those of a Kaway, a born witch versed in the
twenty-four branches of sorcery.

"I can guess what has brought this sickness on
the little chief," said Moung Chaik, in an under-
tone ; "among the sadahs which he brought away
from Ladaw village is the sadah of a witch : this
is her revenge."

"I never thought it well to take those sadahs,"
said Moung Toke ; but in a whisper, for he did not
wish the Boh to hear.

The Boh had been too much absorbed watching
Pho Lone to notice what his men said, but now
he began to mutter charms while he drew cabalistic squares on the ground. When he did this
Pho Lone groaned more than ever, and the men,
now wide awake, looked on in silence.

"A little time, only a very little time," said
Shway Dway, clasping his knees and looking up
at the fire-flecked foliage, "and the witch-sign
will show."

"By my order !" exclaimed the Boh, rising to
his feet, and speaking very loudly ; "by my order
the witch has entered into the body of my friend."

At these words, Pho Lone straightened his
back with a jerk, flung out his hands, and

dribbling from the mouth, swung round and round from the waist like a failing top.

"See!" cried Moung Toke, "look all of you! By his lordship's order the witch has entered the youth. You see he rolls his body. Were his sickness merely of the belly he would rock to and fro thus."

"Moung Toke would teach the babe to take the breast," said Shway Dway, impatiently.

"Or give his lordship lessons in magic," added Moung Chaik.

Moung Toke pretended not to hear what they said; he was always telling people what they knew already, and if he had not enjoyed the Boh's favour would have been told often and plainly what the men thought of him.

Pho Lone continued to roll, and threw his arms about, until the Boh held out his hand so that all could see the long yellow thread he held.

"Be still, witch!" he commanded; but Pho Lone only writhed and howled the more.

"A bamboo," said the Boh, looking round; "a stout one."

Somebody crept forward and handed his lordship a staff used to carry bundles. He drew the yellow thread carefully about his neck that it might not fall to the ground and so lose its virtue, and fell to beating Pho Lone till the bamboo split and drew blood from his back.

"That has made her obedient," said Shway

Dway to himself, as Pho Lone ceased rolling and groaning.

The Boh threw the stick aside, and bidding the witch be still if she did not want a worse beating, tied the yellow thread about Pho Lone's arms. This magic bond tamed her as though it had been an iron chain ; Pho Lone sat quite still, shivering a little, though the perspiration streamed down his face and breast, and the witch, through his mouth, answered the Boh's questions very meekly, showing that her powers were much inferior to those of the chief.

It was exactly as Moung Chaik thought. Among the sadahs taken at Ladaw was that of Mah Too ; she desired the document back ; she was the slave of the sorcerer who had thus compelled her attendance and would do his bidding ; she implored that he, of his great justice and mercy, would grant her prayer for reparation.

The Boh pretended to consider her request, because it is never a good plan to consent readily to a witch's prayer, however reasonable ; and after thinking for the space of a few breaths he bade Moung Chaik bring the sadahs to the fire that he might look them through. Moung Toke stirred the fire till the sparks leaped in the smoke among the boughs, and the Boh sat down to turn over the bundle of dingy palm leaves.

" This is yours, witch," he said holding one up.

Now the witch showed her power ; Pho Lone

sat ten paces from the fire, and she could not have read one letter or figure on the sadah; but she replied at once that Boh Tah's wisdom spoke the truth, for the sadah he held was indeed hers.

"Take it, then," said the Boh, stepping to his follower's side; and the witch took it with Pho Lone's hand, blessing the might, glory, wisdom and justice of the Boh through Pho Lone's mouth, which was very wonderful to see and hear.

"Well," said the chief, "because my follower has done you injury he shall make reparation with offerings. It is not convenient to me that he should return to your village to lay them outside your house; you must accept his offering here in the jungle."

To this the witch made answer that she was only anxious to please her master in every way; whereupon the Boh spoke these words.

"Witch! This patient is my friend and follower. Therefore, under pain of death, molest him no more!"

He loosed the yellow thread from Pho Lone's arms, and the witch, having received permission to go, went as mysteriously as she had come, Shway Dway, it is true, said he saw a fruit-bat pass above the fire, but Moung Toke was certain it had been about since rice-time.

"You are now freed from the spell," said the chief; and Pho Lone lay back on his mat and was very sick indeed.

"You are freed now," repeated the Boh, when he sat up looking red and watery about the eyes.

Pho Lone replied that owing to his lordship's great might, wisdom, and control over evil things, he was quite well again. If it was his lordship's order he would at once go and make his offering, placing the sadah with it that the witch might come and recover it.

"Make the best offering you can and quickly," said the Boh, as he stalked away to his mat in the dark shadows across the glade.

"You should offer cheroots, betel, a very little pickled tea, because we have not much, and the jack fruit we have left," said Moung Toke, eager as usual to display his knowledge.

After leaving Ladaw they had passed through a grove of jack trees and had filled the elephant basket with great green fruits twice the size of a man's head. Even when quite ripe jacks are not very wholesome; but the men had eaten them greedily at evening rice.

"It is a pity to offer the only two we have left," said Pho Lone, eyeing them wistfully, "they would be nice to-morrow morning."

"You found them nice last night, judging by the quantity you ate," retorted Moung Toke. "Do as you please, but remember that it must be the best offering you can make."

Pho Lone said no more, but he sighed as he lifted the great spiny fruit on to the tray.

"Don't put the offering on the ground, you know," said Moung Toke, as Pho Lone balanced the heavily-loaded tray on his head. "A fallen tree would be a good place, or a large stone."

"Yes," replied Pho Lone meekly. He knew how to make an offering quite as well as Moung Toke or any one else, but felt too weak to resent being treated like a young child.

He stole into the jungle, and found a fallen tree by nearly tumbling over it. He balanced the tray gingerly on this, prayed the witch to accept his offering in reparation, and ran back as fast as he could, for it is never good to be in the jungle alone at night, and one feels it the more gloomy and bad just after having been bewitched.

The ease with which Boh Tah had relieved him from the witch's spell made Pho Lone his slave; the chief, in the young man's eyes, was the greatest and most powerful sorcerer in the land, and Pho Lone could not help shikoing whenever the Boh glanced in his direction. As they marched, hour after hour, through the jungle shades, his mind was always busy with thoughts of pleasing the chief, and showing his devotion. In view of his lordship's wondrous magical powers, Pho Lone thought it a little strange that they were not led direct against Kyouksay; for the season was drawing on, and another two weeks at most must bring the rains.

But the Boh, for some reason which in his wisdom he did not make known, had announced his intention of leading the band first to Nyoung-glay, where Shway Dway was sure more men would join. It was hearing what the old man said to the chief on this point one evening, while the bags of rupees were being taken from the kneeling elephant, that gave Pho Lone a good thought. Two or three of the men whom he honoured by asking their opinion were much struck with it; and strengthened by their praise, Pho Lone begged leave to speak when they halted for the night half a day's march from Nyounglay. The Boh graciously consented to hear him, and Pho Lone explained. His lordship went to Nyounglay to enrol more followers; well, his very humble slave urged that his lordship receive the respects of the village folk seated upon the money taken at Ladaw, which should be strewn on the floor as a mat. Thus, the Nyounglay men, seeing his lordship regard money so lightly as to rest the body upon it, should be very greatly dazzled, and pray leave to follow.

The Boh smiled, and said that this was indeed a very good thought; what did Shway Dway think?

Shway Dway was quite of opinion that the wisdom of a leader shone in Pho Lone's mouth; but at the same time he spoke without knowledge of the men who lived at Nyounglay.

Those men were friends of his own; wherefore it was his advice that the money be buried here, and committed to the care of the demons of the forest.

"What do you think?" said the Boh to Moung Toke.

Moung Toke begged leave to think with his lordship.

"I think both ways," said the Boh.

Moung Toke shiko'd, clasped his knees, and fixed his eyes on the stars. It would be well to wait until his lordship had made up his mind.

The chief drank smoke and thought over the counsel given by his followers. Pho Lone's plan had taken his fancy, but he could not deny that Shway Dway's might be the wiser. He sat, puffing his cheroot, and turned the matter over in his mind, while he idly watched the movements of his men about the fire. The drone of their voices was nearly drowned by the screaming crickets and the night wind whispering in the trees, like the sea on shingle. From the blackness of the jungle came the leathery flap of the elephant's ears, and the clink of his chain as he foraged for tender branches.

"Your advice, friend, is very good," said the Boh, at last to Pho Lone, "but yours," to Shway Dway, "is better."

"Much better," put in Moung Toke.

"It is my order, therefore," continued the

chief, "that the money and jewels taken at Ladaw, except thirty rupees, be buried in this place."

Moung Toke was understood to say that the wisdom of his lordship was as the wisdom of a Bhudd; and that such might, glory, and majesty as his needed not displays of gold and silver for their enhancement.

"Fortunately," said the Boh, taking no notice of Moung Toke, "this is Saturday, which is a lucky day for my purpose, in this month of Kasone. You two friends, carrying tools to dig, will follow while I seek a spot proper for the burying of the money."

A suitable place, at the root of a great oil tree, was found, and with beating hearts—for this is a fearsome task at night—Pho Lone and Shway Dway dug the hole while Moung Toke toiled to and fro, carrying the bags. When the treasure was buried, and the earth tramped down, the Boh dismissed them, saying he must be alone while he spoke the invocations, and worked the spells which should compel the forest demons to his service. They were glad to go, and hurried stealthily back to their comrades, marvelling at this fresh evidence of the courage and power of the Boh. Pho Lone felt that this was yet another bond in his allegiance to the chief. The spirits of the jungle own for master only him who is brave enough thus to enslave them, and will tear in pieces any man who dares approach treasure given into their charge, unless their master, by the exercise of magic, restrain them. He, though far away, can bring them to receive his orders, and they must obey; by this means, very simple to one so gifted, Boh Tah retained control over all the treasure.

It was well they were within half a day of Nyounglay village, for that night, while they were asleep, the elephant came very quietly and ate all the rice. Bah Chet woke at dawn, in time to see him shaking the empty sack, and having hobbled him, pricked his trunk hard with a spear; whereat the elephant groaned and screamed so loudly that he woke the whole camp, and Moung Toke bade Bah Chet desist.

"He has eaten our rice, and there is an end of it. You needn't make him call the police now."

The rest laughed, but not heartily, for they were hungry. Bah Chet dropped his spear, and after calling the elephant all the bad names he could think of, promised him a pair of leathern anklets with spikes inside to wear every night for a month.

The sun caught the tree tops and the birds awoke. Boh Tah, who looked haggard after spending many hours of the night working charms, gave the order to march as soon as he was told there was no food, and the elephant suffered again

when Bah Chet took the driving rod in hand.
It is ill marching on an empty belly, and all were
glad when the jungle gave place to rolling grass
land, and Shway Dway could point to the site of
Nyounglay village. They could not see the place
itself, and never a curl of smoke rose to tell that
there was a village on the low hill which
shouldered out from the forest clad range behind ;
only when they came very near and saw the
crows fluttering over the trees, did they see that
men lived there.

The flanks of the hill were grown over with
thorn bush as high as a man's breast, and so close
that a pariah could not find a way through.
There was no sign of a path on the dusty grass,
and the men were beginning to ask how they
were to get up to the village when Shway Dway,
laughing, turned sharp to the left, and led the
way to an outcrop of rock at the bottom of the
hill, and pointed out the track, smooth and narrow
across its steepest face.

"I thought I would see if any one could find
the path," laughed the old man, as he led the
way up.

"Go forward and tell your friends I come with
my followers to eat rice at their village," called
Boh Tah from the elephant ; and Shway Dway
stepped out, the perspiration trickling down his
back as he climbed the steep in the glare.

The men were tired and their pasohs drenched

BOH TAH'S VISIT TO NYOUNGLAY

with sweat when they reached the crown of the hill, and across the bald top saw the village a bow shot off. It clustered against the forest line as though shrinking from notice, and was, Pho Lone thought, the dirtiest and poorest village he had ever seen. It was very small; there was neither kyoung nor pagoda, and half the houses were in ruins, mere skeletons of mat and rafter, from which hung shreds of ragged thatch. Several men were squatting round Shway Dway in the shade of a tree, when Boh Tah's band arrived, but these gave no greeting such as new-comers expect; they looked over their shoulders in the surly fashion of dogs disturbed at food, and did not move even when Moung Toke sang with many honorific phrases that his lordship was come to Nyounglay. There were other men and women certainly, who sat on their verandahs, and came out shyly to greet the Boh; but these did not seem more pleased than the others to see the party, and gave no invitation to enter their houses. The Boh took no notice of their rudeness; he slid from the kneeling elephant, shook out his pasoh, threw a glance over the villagers as a cultivator looks at plough cattle, and stepped up the ladder of the nearest house, unasked but unhindered. Pho Lone, though faint with hunger and heat, stood nursing the chief's gun, rubbing one foot against the other, uncertain what to do.

" Go, little chief," said Shway Dway, stepping

out from the group which surrounded him.
" Enter this house. The order is given and rice
is cooking. Drink ! "

Pho Lone sat down on the verandah, drank the
cocoa-nut shell of water which Shway Dway
handed him, and felt better. He laid down the
gun, and coiled up his hair which hung in draggled
wisps down his back.

" Are these men your friends ? " he asked ; and
his tone was not that of a little chief.

" Prison friends," replied Shway Dway.

Pho Lone went to the corner of the verandah
to see them more closely, and liked their looks no
better. Two or three wore head-kerchiefs with a
corner drooping, as if carelessly, to hide the
shortness of their hair ; the rest were bare-headed,
and while some had hair of a finger's length,
others had enough to fasten on false tails, which
allowed short locks to betray themselves. One
man, whose back was turned, had curious straight
scars half hidden by his pasoh.

" Perhaps he was once bewitched and his
friends beat the witch who possessed him," said
Shway Dway, with a twinkle in his eye, when
Pho Lone asked whence those marks came.

" Or perhaps he was flogged in gaol," retorted
Pho Lone, who knew that prisoners were sometimes beaten. " What are those marks each man
has on his ancles ? "

" If one gets a bad leg, they take off the iron

till it heals," replied Shway Dway, covering his own right foot with his pasoh as he spoke, "hence those marks."

He did not speak loudly, but one of the men looked round and said: "My son, put a little wet sand often on your ancle-ring, when you want it taken off."

The others laughed so much at this that Pho Lone thought it wise to laugh also; but as he laughed, he shrank from these people, and forgetting his devotion to Boh Tah, wished with all his heart he were at home with his mother. He felt the stiff weals on his own back, and the thought that these men might think he had been in gaol and beaten, stung him with shame till he remembered that his long hair proved him. Half unconsciously he shook out his hair that it might be seen.

"Go, let us eat," said Shway Dway, "they call that rice is ready."

Pho Lone went with him gladly; the old man had spent years in gaol but he had not the prison taint like the others; his jungle life had purged it.

"I hope very much his lordship will not allow any of these dogs to follow," he remarked as Shway Dway showed him the house where the men were gathering, "I think they are bad men."

"They have been caught," said Shway Dway; and Pho Lone had nothing more to say.

After eating, they slept until the shadows grew

long, when Moung Toke sent men round to
announce that there was leave for all who would
to come and pay their respects to the Boh. All
the band went as a matter of course and sat round
to receive visitors. The village men seemed in
no haste to come, but after Shway Dway had
slipped quietly out for a few minutes and come in
again, seven men slouched in and sat on their
heels in the attitude of respect.

"These fine fellows pray for leave to follow
your lordship," said Shway Dway, speaking very
distinctly.

"His lordship orders me to say that he has
plenty of good men already," said Moung Toke.

The seven laughed, and sat still.

"They are very fine fellows," said Shway Dway,
"and friends of mine. I pray your lordship's
favour for them."

"What arms do they possess?" the Boh asked
Moung Toke.

"Your lordship, each has a dah, very good and
sharp," said Shway Dway.

Boh Tah looked the seven over, one by one,
as they sat.

"Let them follow then," he said at last; and
the band forthwith welcomed them as brothers.

"Does that fine young man also wish to follow?"
asked Moung Toke, seeing somebody hanging
about outside. "Ho, neighbour! do you desire
leave to follow?"

For answer the man turned his back and pulling down his pasoh from the waist, shouted, "I have had enough."

"His lordship has a charm which will prevent the worst flogging from giving pain," said Moung Toke. "But none who follow so great a chief will ever be in danger from mere police dogs."

"His lordship's followers can never be caught or killed," cried all; but the man outside laughed, and strolled away, deaf to the jeers hurled after him.

"Don't you try to escape from prison, neighbour," grinned one of the new men to Pho Lone. "That man was flogged because he tried it."

"Friend!" said Shway Dway dropping behind the speaker. "You must treat this young man with respect. He is the little chief."

"I did not know it," said the man anxiously, as he shiko'd. "I beg your lordship's favour. Will your lordship honour my poor house by deigning to eat rice there when the sky shuts? And will your lordship spread his sleeping mat on the raised place?"

The man spoke so respectfully that Pho Lone, who had shrunk from him at first, smiled graciously and replied that he would eat and sleep in his house; whereat the man said the honour done him was the very highest; and he edged away muttering that he must go and seek food proper to place before a Boh.

" This young fellow also prays for your honour's favour," said Shway Dway, indicating a man with very short hair who crept forward and shiko'd. Pho Lone recognised him as the one who had offered advice about ancle rings, and looked him down haughtily.

"The prayer of your lordship's servant is that your honour will condescend to accept a small gift at unworthy hands," whined the short-haired man. "A silk kerchief to cover the head that is sheltered by nine golden umbrellas."

" Bring it," said Pho Lone without looking at him ; and the man crawled away, saying the honour done him was far greater than he deserved.

" Little chief," said Shway Dway that night as they lay down to sleep, " you will one day be a great leader ; you know how to treat these dogs' children."

CHAPTER XIII

BOH TAH had never concealed from his lieutenants that he viewed with dislike the custom of dispersing at the approach of the rains, when it is no longer possible to live in the jungles. The system, in his judgment, was a bad one; in the first place, men were likely to be questioned concerning their long absence by those prying dogs the patrol policemen; then there was the danger that men might grow lazy and resume their old occupation as cultivator or carpenter, or what not, and refuse to follow again; and, in any case, there was always the delay in assembling them when the fine weather returned, a delay which he had known extend to several precious weeks. His trouble hitherto had been the want of a place where the band could dwell during the rainy season; but the discovery of Nyounglay dispelled that difficulty in the happiest manner. Hence no one was surprised when, on the morning after the new followers had been enrolled, Moung Toke came round and announced in each house where men lay, that his lordship had bidden him make known that he should look with favour upon those who, after the visit to Kyouksay, decided to continue with him during the rains at Nyounglay. It might have been Moung Toke's own opinion merely; but he added that he understood it was his lordship's intention not to divide the spoil taken at Ladaw and what they expected at Kyouksay until the rainy season was over, four or five months hence. Anyhow, Moung Toke was able to return to his lordship with the news that all his followers begged leave to remain with him.

"I am sorry," said Pho Lone to Moung Chaik afterwards, "because I want to go home to my old mother, and also to show the neighbours the money and other property which falls to my share. I know my mother wants very much to see me."

"A Boh, little or great," said Shway Dway, who squatted near, rolling a chew, "has neither mother nor father nor relations."

"It is no use going to one's village empty-handed," said Moung Chaik, "but I want to go to mine because a very clever doctor lives there." For Moung Chaik's wound did not heal, and he was growing thinner each day.

Pho Lone's disappointment was forgotten that evening, for his lordship sent for him to receive a *loon* pasoh, the uniform of a Boh. It was a very fine cloth of woven silk, and on Pho Lone's fine figure showed well; he walked up and down the village wearing it till the sky shut.

The Boh did not give his men time to fret over the arrangement: the next day, as it happened, was a lucky one on which to begin a new enterprise, and orders were given to put the village into a state of defence. Even those who most wished to go home to their villages had to admit that if they were to spend the rains with the chief it would be hard to find a better place than Nyounglay. No stockade was required, as the dense thickets which clothed the hillsides were far better protection from assault; the path through the jungle at the back wound up hill and down through forest which grew darker and deeper as it rolled away up to the hill-tops; but whither it led, after crossing the rill where the women drew water, only the sambhur and leopard could tell. All that had to be done to defend the village was to block the path by which they had come, and this Shway Dway undertook to do in half a day; he of all the band, save Moung Toke, was really glad to stay at the Boh's bidding, for he was more at home in Nyounglay than in any other village.

"How will you block the path so quickly?" asked Pho Lone.

"Is there not a cart over there under that house, little chief? Yes, it is very old, and broken as to the sides, but the wheels are sound; we only want those wheels and a few bamboos."

Pho Lone had not thought of the wheels : they were great heavy, solid things, more like millstones than wheels, with two holes shaped like new moons in the centre to receive the split axle. Now Shway Dway mentioned it, he remembered having heard how dacoits had held the police at bay for days on a narrow path blocked by a cartwheel, and scarcely required Shway Dway's explanation, which he gave, when one wheel had been rolled halfway down the hill, and braced with bamboos across the path.

"See, now, little chief, two men can sit behind it thus ; and being unseen themselves keep watch through the axle holes. Then, if an enemy comes you wait till he is quite close, and putting your gun through the hole shoot him, poung !"

"No policeman would come near when he saw the gun muzzle peeping through," said Pho Lone, levelling the Boh's gun and aiming through an axle hole. "How could he, I being able to shoot him dead ?"

Shway Dway got up, laughing a little.

"Last time I was taken—no, the last time but one, I sat behind a wheel on the jungle path waiting to fight police. When I had fired one shot the black dogs would not come on ; but the little officer, finding the jungle too thick, came all alone, jumping like a deer as he ran, and though I fired again, jumped right over the wheel upon my back. Thus I was made prisoner." And

Shway Dway added, as if to himself, "That time, five years."

Pho Lone stood up and looked over the wheel down the steep path ending in bushes a bow-shot below. "No white officer could run up here if I sat behind with the gun," he said. "He must be shot."

"We have chosen a very good place, little chief; but go! there is yet another wheel to be set in a place not yet chosen, and much more to do besides."

The sun was high when the second wheel had been fixed, and they returned to the village. Many of the band sat in the verandahs working with dahs at bamboo stakes. Pho Lone disdained to ask questions before the new followers, but Moung Toke seized such a chance of giving him instruction, and Pho Lone lay down with his eyes shut pretending not to listen, though what Moung Toke had to tell was very interesting.

"Learn to make foot-traps, my son," said Moung Toke, "they are very good to defend a path, particularly at night when the policemen cannot see where they tread. You take a bamboo, thicker than one's thumb, and about one cubit long; one end you make very sharp, like a pen, thus. Then you dig a hole in the path and plant the bamboo very firmly with the point a fingers' breadth below the level of the ground, and fill up the hole lightly with earth. You see!"

"It would go through the foot that trod upon the point," said Pho Lone, sitting up and pressing the sharpened end on his hand.

"Yes; I, lying hid in the jungle close by, have seen a policeman fall with his foot pierced through," said Moung Toke, as he delicately finished off another stake.

"Would it go through the boots an officer wears?" asked one of the new men.

"It will pierce the boot a white man wears when he wishes to move very silently," said Moung Toke. "I have heard of one officer who was thus lamed for many months."

"I know what kind of boot that is," struck in Pho Lone. "I have seen the merchants wear them when they played a running-about game with a ball over a little net."

"I daresay they use them for that purpose too," said Moung Toke, "but I think their proper use is to wear when in the jungles shooting deer."

"Or men," said Shway Dway in a tone which made the rest laugh.

It seemed as though Boh Tah expected the police to hunt him, for besides arranging defences on the village path he commanded that thorn balls should be prepared in readiness for the retreat from Kyouksay.

"Why does his lordship give this order?" asked Shway Dway; "is there a bad omen for the attack?"

Moung Toke had not heard so ; but his lordship was unlucky enough this afternoon to forget that the day was Wednesday and attended to his finger nails, which needed cutting.   It was a pity ; but the mischief was done now.

Shway Dway really would not have believed so good a chief could do such a foolish thing.   Every child knew that to trim the nails on Wednesday would bring trouble upon him either through his own fault or that of some one else.   It was the very worst day of the week to choose for this purpose.

"His lordship's nails were very long," said Moung Toke, "but——"

"Then why could he not have cut them yesterday," interrupted Shway Dway ; "what more propitious day for nail-cutting than Tuesday ?"

"Yes, that is true," said Moung Toke ; " Cut the nails on Tuesday and live happily a hundred years.   It was very unlucky," he added, tossing his cheroot butt out on the road.   " His lordship says nothing, but I think he is sorry, and fears lest trouble follow : upon that account he gives the order to prepare thorn balls ; we had best send people at once to the jungle to bring a great quantity of thorn-threads, it being the order that we march to-morrow."

One finds in the jungle, very plentifully in some places, a climbing plant which drops from the trees long tough tendrils like thin string set at

every finger's length with strong thorns in groups
of three; these are very troublesome, for they
catch one's arm or neck and whip round, tearing
the skin; but they are useful to make balls to
lame the police.

At Moung Toke's request Pho Lone went out
into the village and ordered women and boys to
go and bring in thorn threads, threatening them
with the Boh's displeasure if they failed to bring
enough; and as the displeasure of a Boh usually
takes a very painful shape, all hastened to obey.
Afterwards they wished they had refused; for
when they brought in the tendrils gathered at the
cost of many scratches, Moung Toke ordered them
to set to work at once and twist the thorn threads
into balls the size of a hen's egg; whence were
many sore fingers among the Nyounglay women
that night. However it was done, and soon after
evening rice, an old woman, with blood dripping
from every finger, brought to the house where
Moung Toke slept a large kerchief full of
thorn balls, which she laid before him praying
in her heart that he might tread upon them
himself.

It was only two days march to Kyouksay by the
direct path, but it was impossible to go straight
there, because Kyouksay lies due south of Nyounglay, and it is not at all advisable to march due
south in the month of May, the dragon's head
being on the west of the Meroo mountain and

therefore pointing north.* Boh Tah, therefore, when he reached the foot of Nyounglay Hill, skirted round it and bade a son of the village show a path through the jungle towards the

* Burmese mythology is entangled in a peculiar and slightly inconvenient way with geography as taught by Burmese science. The scheme of the universe is charmingly simple in its symmetry ; this world consists of four large circular islands grouped round the Meroo Mountain which rises from the sea in the shape of a sugar-loaf. There are also one thousand more small islands, five oceans, five large, and five hundred small rivers, whose positions have not, I believe, been fixed with any precision, but which are not involved in the important matter under notice. Which is this : In the sea at the base of Mount Meroo lies a great dragon whose length is three-fourths the circumference of the mountain. This dragon's influence on the inhabitants of the four islands is mysterious and powerful, so that if you wish to enjoy good health and freedom from accident, disease and other ills, you must never journey towards the dragon's mouth. Fortunately his movements are as regular as those of the sun and very much better understood, so there is no excuse for your marching towards his mouth by mistake. During the first three months of the Burmese year—March to May inclusive—his head is on the west of the mountain, pointing north; and as he moves (in the direction of the hands of a watch) one quarter round the mountain every three months, so completing the circuit in a year, one always knows in what direction it is bad to travel ; and if you happen to be a native of the Western Island which contains Europe, where these important matters are not properly understood, you may be sure that when you travel in Burma, which lies in the South Island, the better-informed people of that country will not let you go wrong—if they have to accompany you. In the circumstances, Boh Tah's choice of route, forty miles along one side of a triangle and forty along the other to avoid going fifty miles on

south-east. It was broad day when they started, and by the time they reached the shade every man was wet as though he had swum the creek, though none carried more than his dah or spear; rice, sleeping mats, and other things being packed on the elephant. Moung Sin,* one of the Nyoun-glay sons, said he was the follower of his good namesake, who carried the poor man's food, and not of the Boh, who shouted " Go, go!" when-ever a fellow sat down to rest; for the Nyoun-glay men had not been in the jungle before this year, and the soul of Moung Toke was vexed within him that he must spare the spear shaft on those who lagged, and drive only with his tongue. He was tired out with running back to urge up stragglers who only laughed when he spoke of his lordship's anger.

" Why walk so fast ?" the dawdler would ask. " Does his lordship eat rice in the police thannah on a certain day ?"

" His lordship desires haste, that we may return before the rains come," Moung Toke re-plied patiently, though his fingers tingled to strike.

" Surely so great a sayah will bid the rains hold off for a day or two. I follow, friend, when I have drunk yet a little more smoke."

---

a base line due south, was therefore as natural as would be an Englishman's preference for a ford a hundred yards out of his way to wading a torrent up to his saddle bow.

* Moung Sin = Mr. Elephant.

The Boh had ordered patience with the new followers, but he also was angry when the doves' cooing told it was time to halt for the night, and they had come but half a day's march.

"I think it would be very good if your lordship commanded that I hang one of them by the feet for the night," said Moung Toke. "The youth Pho Let is weak and rather ill with fever, and upon that account is not much use to us. Shall we punish him?"

"If we journeyed in a boat so that it were more difficult to escape," said the Boh, "I would give order, 'take the weakly youth and cut him slowly in pieces from the feet up.' But these Nyounglay sons have but lately come out of prison and having done nothing since need not fear the police. Were we to beat one, all would run away and perhaps might lay information against us."

Moung Toke said his lordship's wisdom gave light even as the sun by day and the moon and stars by night.

"Nevertheless we cannot march again as we have done to-day," continued Boh Tah, "is there none among my own followers who may be punished for the others to see? There is that wounded man; he grows weaker each day and I think will die very soon. Also he fell behind often to-day. Beat him very severely because he did this."

Moung Chaik ate no rice that evening; when

they untied his hands and legs from the tree, they
had to drag him to his mat, where he lay on his
face, while the blood dried on the ground about
him and the great red ants swarmed on his back.
Many times he cried for water but none dared
give it while Moung Toke was by. The Nyoung-
glay men spoke very little after eating, and slept
early, unrolling their mats as far from Moung
Chaik as they could. Moung Toke and the Boh
sat apart talking in low tones till the moon was
high ; nobody spoke much till they parted and lay
down to sleep.

"I have never seen a man so beaten," Pho
Lone whispered to Shway Dway, "I think he
will die."

"Having bled a great deal he will certainly
die, being ill with fever before," replied Shway
Dway. "Moung Toke's arms must be tired I
think."

Shway Dway yawned, and presently slept ; but
Pho Lone lay watching the bright moon and
listening to Moung Chaik's moans. When the
beaten man cried for water again, Pho Lone sat
up, and having made sure that the Boh and
Moung Toke were asleep, rose and filled a cocoa-
nut shell for him.

"You are going to die, neighbour," he said, as
he held the shell to Moung Chaik's mouth.

"Yes, I shall die very soon," replied Moung
Chaik. "Give more water."

Pho Lone brought it, and squatting, tried to brush the swarming ants from Moung Chaik's stiffening wounds; but he groaned so much with the pain that the men about began to stir.

"I will make the Offering for you," said Pho Lone, in a hurried whisper. "If you die before we march I will perform the offices."

"It is good of you, neighbour. I shall certainly die before the second crowing of the cock. Sooner, because the ants eat into my inside."

There was a little movement in the darkness where Moung Toke lay; the mosquitoes sang loud in the still hot night, perhaps they had disturbed him.

"I go," said Pho Lone, when all was quiet again; and he stole warily across the glade to his own mat, to pick the ants from his toes before he lay down again.

Moung Chaik cried once more for water, and this time the answer came from Moung Toke, "Silence, dog! or I kill you in the morning."

But when morning came the vultures were already wheeling overhead, so low you might count the wing feathers; and the flies buzzed, a shining swarm, over Moung Chaik's body, as he lay, on his back now, his teeth bared in a grin of pain.

"Hasten now," cried Moung Toke, "we march before eating."

"The man is dead," said Moung Sin, from the

group squatting round Moung Chaik. " Mother ! how much blood !"

"What of that ? Do not all men die ? Go ! He died of being too slow, friends. Leave him to the birds and dogs to bury, and help load the elephant."

They got up and obeyed, working as usual with talk and laughter ; but Boh Tah noticed that they moved quickly and told Moung Toke he had done well. In a betel chew all was ready and Bah Chet led the way on the elephant.

" March forward, little chief," said Moung Toke, seeing that Pho Lone lingered. "See, all are now on the path."

"I follow quickly, friend ; I have forgotten something."

Moung Toke, in good humour, though his arms were stiff, turned and followed the last man, while Pho Lone ran back to the camping-place and squatting by Moung Chaik's body, drew out his betel box, and pressed a nut carefully over the swollen tongue into the dead mouth.

"For the Ferry, for the Ferry," he muttered. Then he rose and drew off the silk head-kerchief which the new follower had given him at Nyounglay, looking round for a convenient bough.

"That will do," he said to himself, and hastily tied the bright kerchief by the corner. "Great Lord, Great Lord !" he whispered, shikoing at each word; and turning, he sped like a deer after the band.

"I know why you went back," said Shway Dway, when the Boh ordered them to halt for rice near mid-day. "You went to make an offering to the spirits of the jungle."

"Yes, yes; but say nothing; his lordship might be very angry."

"It will be reckoned to you for Merit," said Shway Dway, thoughtfully. "May I find a friend to do it for me should I die like a dog in the forest."

"Have these fellows been marching better? asked Pho Lone in a loud voice, for Moung Toke had come up, and sat by them.

"The last came in a bamboo's length from the first," replied Shway Dway, "they learned something last night; did they not, neighbour?"

"I taught them," said Moung Toke; "we shall reach Kyouksay in five days after all, I think."

The shade was so deep that they could march all day, and the Boh did not allow much time for eating rice. Indeed the men had hardly time to get water to drink before he called to Moung Toke to make ready for the start again.

"Give me a chew," said Moung Toke, rising and holding out his hand to Pho Lone, "my box is empty."

"So is mine," sighed Pho Lone. "Nothing left but a leaf or two and the cutter."

CHAPTER XIV

" No," said the Boh, "it is not good to attack with shouting."

Pho Lone shiko'd and drew back into his place among those who sat in respectful silence near his lordship's mat. The Boh had given audience to such of his men who knew Kyouksay village and could say how much money might be expected there; and when Pho Lone and Moung Sin of Nyounglay had spoken he had been gracious enough to say that if any follower wished to offer council, concerning the best mode of attack, his ears were open to hear. Moung Toke and the others merely expressed their confidence in the wisdom and magical powers of his lordship, and were a little surprised at Pho Lone's boldness when, receiving leave to speak, he urged the same tactics as his lordship had ordered at Ladaw. The Boh was not angry with the young man; on the contrary, he accepted his words as a tribute to the wisdom of the commands which had brought success at Ladaw; but his tone proved that his mind was quite made up, and the men of any experience at all agreed with him.

Moung Sin, indeed, had said, "that place cannot be rushed by day," the moment the band came out of the jungle into the sun glare, and saw the Kyouksay paddy land stretching far on either hand to the river on whose bank the village stood. There were trees about the houses of course ; but for a gun-shot all round neither clump nor bush gave cover. Any but a very young dacoit, like Pho Lone, could see at once that the Kyouksay head-man with his gun would shoot every man of the band while they were crossing the open. They eyed the village hungrily as from noon to sunset they skirted the paddy plain, keeping just within the jungle for shade and concealment ; for, as Shway Dway said, "So much good land means plenty of rupees for us."

The moon was high now ; sitting there round the Boh's mat they could hear the village dogs baying, and through the trees see the faint glow of house lamps to remind them that they must light no fire. The tide was running up, and many paddy boats were creaking by, some near the bank, others far out to get the strength of the flood. The song of the rowers rang clear across the dark water, and loudest the voices of Karens, who could be known by the tunes they sang. Shway Dway, who knew a great deal, said the Karens sang English prayer-songs.

"These Karen dogs sing thus because they receive Government guns on the word of their sayahs," said the Boh, hearing his follower's words.

"Lord!" said everybody, shikoing.

"Would the sons of jungle-dogs be Klistan if they got no reward?" demanded the Boh, as though somebody had contradicted him; and all made answer, "Lord, never!" Shway Dway joined in the reply as a matter of form. He knew many Karen people, and did not like them; but he did not believe that they turned Christians merely to get Government guns; more likely they wanted Government appointments. His lordship now said that his followers had permission to go; so all shiko'd, and returned along the bank overhanging the water to the spot where they lay smoking and chewing. It was good to lie there in the moonlight, enjoying the soft night wind from the river, for they had marched far that day and were tired. The Nyounglay men had needed no driving since they saw Moung Chaik beaten to death, and the Boh had been pleased to tell Moung Sin that the new followers should receive a full share of the goods taken at Kyouksay and at any other villages they might visit before the rains brought the season's work to a close.

They were telling stories of the great deeds they had done in the past and meant to do again to-morrow, when his lordship was heard calling from the darkness of the jungle, where he sat alone; and Moung Toke presently came to summon Pho Lone to the Presence.

"My order is this," said the Boh, "the gun belonging to the head-man of this village must be taken before I order the attack, or how shall my followers escape being shot? The Myothit son, being a friend of the head-man, shall go and demand the gun."

"Good," murmured Moung Toke, "very good. What wisdom!"

But Pho Lone did not think the plan a good one.

"Lord!" he said, "I do your lordship's commands. But Moung Hla will certainly shoot me."

"Why should he shoot you, his friend?" demanded Moung Toke.

"I think," said Pho Lone, drawing on the ground with his finger, "if I came from my father's boat, saying, 'Lend me your gun, neighbour.' Moung Hla would refuse, saying, 'It is against the order of Government.' Moreover, all the country side knows by this time that I am the follower of his lordship, wherefore Moung Hla would laugh at me demanding the gun."

"True," said the Boh, half aloud. "Of course all the world knows he is my follower."

There was silence for a few breaths, and then Moung Toke begged leave to suggest that the Myothit son should take his lordship's gun and shoot Moung Hla to-night as he lay asleep.

" I wish the gun to be taken to-night, but it must be done quietly," said the Boh, " otherwise the people, being frightened, will gather their property and run away to hide. Also, many boats are passing on the river ; some, as we hear by their songs, being Karens, who may have guns."

" Such wisdom ! " exclaimed Moung Toke.

There was another silence while the Boh drank smoke, and thought. Presently a plan came to him.

" Listen, O Myothit son ! you shall take a spear, very long and sharp, and go quietly to the village to-night : the head-man will be lying asleep in his house, and you shall kill him with a thrust through the bamboos of the floor. Then, when much blood falls, you will know he is killed and can go in and carry away his gun."

" Your lordship's words are commands," said Pho Lone, " but I cannot do this."

The Boh was too astonished to speak. He took his cheroot from his mouth and stared, first at the rebel, then at Moung Toke, and back at Pho Lone again.

" Why can you not do this ? " demanded Moung Toke. " You know the man's house."

" Yes, I have eaten rice with him many times, but——"

" You know where the man spreads his mat."

" My father and I have slept many times in the room, but——"

"Then you know exactly where to thrust through the floor."

"You do not let me speak," whined Pho Lone, for the Boh's brow was growing darker and darker. "I cannot do this because the floor of Moung Hla's sleeping-room is made of junglewood boards, and not of bamboos. No spear could kill through thick boards."

"Well, that is unfortunate," said Moung Toke; "I never thought that the floor might be of boards. Nor did his lordship, who graciously proposed this plan for your guidance."

"I am sorry to hear what you say," said the Boh. "I think you must go into the room and kill the head-man."

Pho Lone would certainly try and do this; but to his certain knowledge Moung Hla had very excellent charms against death in all shapes; he had seen him try to stab his own arm and leg with an English knife bought in the bazaar, and the point turned on the flesh as on a stone. Many men were present to see that wonderful thing. He feared lest Moung Hla should awaken and shoot him before he could be killed, when the poung! would cause that very noise which his lordship's wisdom wished to avoid. Besides, Moung Hla made a practice of wadding his gun with shreds of his wife's old tamein, and the very best charms against gunshot—— Pho Lone stopped suddenly, for the moonlight showed that in his lordship's face which dried up speech.

"Shall such means destroy the virtue of charms given by the hand of his lordship?" inquired Moung Toke, after an awful silence.

The Boh said nothing; but his terrible stare made Pho Lone gather himself into an attitude of the profoundest respect.

"By his lordship's gracious leave," he began, but his lips trembled so that he could hardly speak the words. "What I would have said was this: that the dog's son, Moung Hla, is a strong man, and so rash that he will certainly shoot when he is attacked. If he will shoot at his lordship, upon whose skin bullets flatten like water-drops and whose hands catch bullets like falling leaves, who shall venture to take him alone? If it be his lordship's command, his lordship's slave awaits his order to go and kill Moung Hla."

The Boh spoke in a low tone to Moung Toke, and it was from his mouth that Pho Lone received orders, showing that his lordship had withdrawn his favour.

"It is commanded that you go now, and, seeking out a very safe place, cause a very deep hiding-hole to be dug."

"An arm's depth," said the Boh.

"A long arm's depth," said Moung Toke.

"Behind a tree," added the Boh.

" Behind a great tree," continued Moung Toke.

All slept very lightly that night, for when the tide ebbed it brought down many empty boats, whose rowers sang loudly, and often swept so close by the bank that the more cautious followers braved the mosquitoes and still heat of the jungle, preferring to hide under the bushes than lie out in the open where the cool breeze fanned their weary bodies, but where the boat people might see them and tell the police. The men on whom was conferred the honour of digging the hiding hole did not lie down till the moon was sinking, for each passing boat bade them cease work lest the strokes of their tools should be heard. Whether digging or resting they looked round often and fearfully; for all his lordship's magic, the gloom might hide offended ghouls and goblins which would pounce suddenly from above to tear them limb from limb.

Hence, when Moung Toke awoke a little before the dawn he found the whole band sitting up, scratching their mosquito bites and yawning.

" Bring rope from the elephant gear," he said, " and listen. Bah Chet will carry the rope and march behind me, Shway Dway will take the bag of thorn balls, and all will follow with closed mouths. The order is to enter the village silently, as jungle dogs track deer, that we may find the head-man sleeping. We shall bind him and bring him away as a hostage until the followers have taken all they can find and have brought the booty here to place upon the elephant."

"I think the omens are bad," said Pho Lone to Shway Dway.

Shway Dway thought so himself, but it did not seem good to admit it. So he merely answered that it would be wise of the little chief to lead swiftly to the head-man's house and get the business over.

After dwelling so long in the jungle Pho Lone shivered when he found himself out on the open kwins far from shelter, and at every step he stared round fearful of being seen. It seemed a great way to the village, and indeed the dawn light was in the eastern sky when the houses gave back the echo of their feet. How the dogs howled as they rushed down the street! Pho Lone's heart beat his ribs as he ran.

"The house!" he gasped, pointing; and Moung Toke, calling "Follow!" jumped on the low verandah. The house, of course, was open, the nights being so hot, and as the men sprang in a figure lurched up from a mat spread on the lower floor, asking sleepily, who came. For answer a dozen men threw themselves upon Moung Hla and held him to be bound, threatening death and torture if he resisted.

Moung Hla was rash, and also very strong. He fought hard and so fiercely that Pho Lone, who had remained outside lest he should be recognised, thought what excellent charms he must have. But one man cannot fight twelve, and presently the struggling throng stood round to jeer at their prisoner lying with arms and legs tied.

"Well, then?" panted Moung Hla, glaring at them, "well, then?"

"Give up your gun, dog's son," said Moung Toke. "Where shall I find it?"

Moung Hla raised his head and stared at him. The day was brightening, and it was light enough now to learn a face.

"Answer quickly," shouted Moung Toke, jabbing the tied arms with his spear.

"In the sleeping-room," said Moung Hla, jerking his head.

Seeing that men stood all round the prisoner, Pho Lone stepped into the house and stole quietly across the floor to the ladder. He wanted to get the business over as quickly as possible, and was also anxious to draw the charge from Moung Hla's gun. He was particularly afraid of Moung Hla's gun, for the scraps of his wife's old tamein, which he used for wadding, were quite enough to destroy the best charm against gun-shot.

He glided up the steps, followed by Moung Toke and others, and pushed the creaking mat-door back. There was one small window on the floor level, but Mah Hlaing, the headman's wife, spread her mat there for the air, and the dingy old cotton mosquito net, hanging tent-wise over her, shut out what light there was. Mah Hlaing sat up and screamed as the men came in.

"We have faggots and kerosene oil for scream- ing women," said Moung Toke, turning on her fiercely. The threat did its work; Mah Hlaing had heard of women being burned alive by dacoits; she stopped screaming, and wept.

But the men were turning the room upside down as they groped about for the gun, and presently the splintering crash told Mah Hlaing that they were breaking open the big teak box where the money was. She screamed again. Pho Lone saw the light glint on the spear as Moung Toke made his thrust, and Mah Hlaing's scream died in a choking groan, as the blood spurted from her neck, and splattered on the floor.

The sun broke pale over the far horizon across the river, and looked in at the window; the fan leaf of a young toddy palm trembled as it threw shade to hide the heap below the bloody mosquito net; but the sun rose higher, and played brightly on the mat wall, flooding the room with light.

"Here it is!" cried Moung Toke in triumph, as he snatched up the gun, and shook it over his head. "Go quickly now."

The crows were beginning to flutter and croak as the men poured down the ladder. Moung Hla lay where they had left him, and smiled as they came. Moung Toke saw it, and stopped short.

"Listen!" he said. "What is that noise?"

All held their breath. The crows chattered, and the pariahs growled over something they lapped below the sleeping-room. Moung Hla lay still, and smiled.

"It is like the sound of a mill when one is far away," said Pho Lone.

Moung Toke pushed him aside, and stepped down into the street, to peer between the houses over the river.

In the silence, the drip from the sleeping-room floor and the lapping of dogs' tongues was loud. Moung Hla heard it and laughed, but his laugh was not good to hear. The hum seemed drawing nearer, and the men strained their ears to listen, hardly daring to meet each other's eyes. Moung Hla, with his arms bound so tightly that the flesh swelled purple between the ropes, listened also.

"The little police fire-ship comes down the river from the town," he said.

Moung Toke, crouching outside to peer between the houses, heard his words, and dashed off down the street, while the rest fell over each other in their haste to get away.

Pho Lone led, his eyes staring in sheer terror. He heard only the scuffling whisper of feet and laboured breathing behind him, but soon he felt that the hum was growing louder; and as the band faced the open kwins, Shway Dway cried

that the launch came up the river, not down, and
cursed Moung Hla for a liar.

"What shall we do?" asked Pho Lone, crying.
"See! the village people wait over there to kill
us, and we cannot hide in the houses."

Shway Dway glanced to the right, and saw
that the coming of the launch had given the
village men courage; to the left, and saw the
launch cutting the brown water into fans from
its bow. He said no word, but started to run
straight for the jungle, whence they had come at
dawn, while the village men shouted, and the
launch swooped round in a swirling froth, to run
in under the bank. Pho Lone dropped the Boh's
gun, and ran for his life, jumping the bunds,
which cut the plain at every stone's throw, like
a stag. A splashing, the rustle of withered grass,
and a bow-shot on the left rifle-barrels glittered,
and policemen rose over the crest of the bank.
Pho Lone felt his knees weak, but he flew on,
sobbing. He heard an English voice say one
word, and there was the clack of breech-blocks;
one more word, and his back-bone turned to
water, for a ragged volley burst, and bullets
whizzed by, the hard earth spitting dust at his
feet. Behind, he heard a fall and a scream, and
a smothered curse as another stumbled. Pho
Lone's eyes started from his head as he ran, for
more bullets came, kicking up dirt about his legs.
But the jungle was near now, and he could see

the path like a slit in the trees. Only one more
bund to jump. He gathered himself, and sprang
clear over—into a mud hole that took him nearly
to the waist. It was a buffalo-wallow; and his
heart-strings cracked as the band sped by. He
was out now, and flying again, for the fire was
hot, and he knew the police were shooting at
him; each poung! went through him, but he was
not touched. The men in front were closing on
the path, and struggling, as they wedged their
way in; he heard a crack, as though a dog bit
bone, and saw Moung Toke fall against the
bushes, while the police shouted. Moung Toke
yelled, and clutched at the men, so that he was
carried on a little by the rush; but his leg was
smashed below the knee, and he fell again,
screaming, for the bullets came ripping through
the trees, bringing down leaves like raindrops
from a rope.

"Throw him aside!" called Shway Dway, for
Moung Toke's struggles blocked the path.
"Throw him aside, and run."

Moung Toke shrieked that he would kill the
man who touched him, but the hustling carried
him off his one foot, and he fell again, howling.

Shway Dway backed into the bushes off the
path, and squatted to open his bag of thorn-
balls.

"Pass on," he cried, "go quickly! Who follows
me needs iron feet."

The path was clear now; the men strung out, and soon the patter of feet told how they raced along its windings.

"Stop, little chief," said Shway Dway, as Pho Lone hurried by. "Stop! the police dogs will not come quickly into this jungle."

He opened his bag, gingerly drew out thorn-balls, and shook them from his fingers on the path as he walked. Moung Toke, lying hid a few steps on, groaned. Shway Dway looked up, set his bag carefully on the ground, and let the dah-loop on his shoulder run down his arm. Moung Toke, watching him, ceased groaning and his face, drawn with pain, grew grey as Shway Dway gripped his weapon. Neither spoke. Moung Toke pressed his hands together, and made as if to rise, but Shway Dway, leaning over, reached for his long hair, and drew him out on the path. Moung Toke's arms went up, but the flat of the dah pressed them down, as Shway Dway squatted. A feint for aim, a stroke with all the strength of Shway Dway's arm, and there was that between Moung Toke's quivering shoulders which hurt the eyes to see.

"Carry that with you, my son," said Shway Dway, bowling the head in a whirl of hair and blood, "and now run, for the police dogs come."

Pho Lone snatched it up by the hair and ran, the blood whisking as it spun against his legs.

Shway Dway came behind, scattering thorn-balls, and chuckled when he heard the police calling that the wounded man was of no more use to give information than the dead one out on the fields.

CHAPTER XV

THE shadows were drawing out, and one by one
the men who had spent the day helping to build
Mah Hehn's new kyoung dropped off and sat
down in the shade, until Moung Maw was left
alone measuring and sawing planks. The air was
so still that never a leaf stirred; the cheroot
smoke floated up in blue wisps to melt away in
the foliage overhead, and the screeching of the
carpenter's saw was the only sound to be heard in
all the village; for in these last and hottest days
of the hot season most people slept till sunset.

"Soon the rain will come," said Moung Byoo.
"It will be good to have the rains."

Somebody made this remark every evening,
and, as usual, every one said slowly, "Yes, it will
be good."

They sat there nursing their knees until Moung
Maw, having sawn the last board, stretched his
back and threw down his tool with a grunt of
content. He had been working hard all day.

"Do you think we shall finish to-morrow,
neighbour?" asked Moung Byoo, as Moung Maw

stepped over the litter of wood scraps and joined the rest.

"Without doubt," replied the carpenter, surveying his work with pride. "I said the monastery should be finished before the monsoon came, and it is done all but a few hours work."

"There is not another carpenter on the creek who could make such a kyoung," said Ko Moung Galay, rising.

"Where do you go, neighbour?"

The head-man nodded at the old kyoung close by, in the darkness of which one might see a still figure sitting cross-legged against the wall.

"Go," said Moung Byoo, getting on his feet; and the men rose and lounged into the kyoung to pay their respects, as was customary of an evening.

The hpoongyee did not move or acknowledge the respectful shikos of his visitors. He remained with his eyes cast down, clasping his beads in his shrivelled hand. He was very strict in his observance of the Law. Moung Byoo raised his voice and spoke.

"The work of the Lord Ruler's supporters is nearly finished. Save for the boards of one side the new kyoung is ready for his honoured presence."

The old monk took no more notice than if a lizard had chirped. He had only to raise his head to see the new monastery, which in a few weeks had

grown up under the great tree ten paces distant.
The faint, sweet smell of fresh-cut wood had been
in his nostrils day and night, and sometimes the
shouting and laughter of men and women, happy
in sharing the good work, must have disturbed
his meditations. But as is becoming in one who
has withdrawn from the world, he knew nothing.
Moung Byoo reported progress each evening, but
the hpoongyee heard what he had to say without
even looking up. He had never referred to the
new kyoung since Moung Byoo first told him they
were about to begin building. This evening,
however, he relaxed a little as the offering was
so nearly completed.

"My woman," said Moung Byoo, clearing his
throat to speak well, "my woman feels great
happiness in giving this monastery to be the
dwelling of the Lord Ruler."

"The disciple who, having means to acquire
Merit, employs it thus is fortunate," said the
hpoongyee, speaking as one whose thoughts are
of other things. "But let her be humble; for
the respect of many gives a proud heart, and
pride is a sin."

"She shall hear the Lord Ruler's wise words,"
said Moung Byoo, and he meant it. His reverence
spoke well; Mah Hehn had grown much too
proud of late between her white son-in-law and
the sweet words of her neighbours concerning the
new kyoung.

THE OLD KYOUNG

"By consenting to dwell in this monastery," said the hpoongyee, rousing himself a little, "I shall be the instrument whereby much Merit is earned."

"We are most grateful," murmured all, mindful of the part they had borne in the building.

"It is a very beautiful monastery," said Moung Let. He spoke wishing to please Moung Byoo, who had often renewed his promise to speak for Pho Lone; but the hpoongyee caught him up quite sharply. Any hut, any hole in rocks, was meet dwelling for a monk, he said. What need had yahan of beautiful houses, of fine clothing, of rich food? A shelter of leaves or a cave, a few rags, and a little food given in charity that he should not starve in his meditations on the Three Precious Things: this was the portion of a yahan.

Moung Let listened very respectfully while his reverence addressed them thus; but as he strolled home in the starlight it would come to his mind that before the new kyoung was built or even spoken of the hpoongyee would often say to his supporters: "This roof is broken, and the rain falls on old bones which have much pain. Great Merit is gained by him who supplies the wants of a servant of the Lord Bhudda;" or, "This yellow robe is so tattered a stranger would think the wearer had no supporters." But since the new monastery had been commenced he had grown much more strict in his views concerning the wants of a monk.

Mah Tsay had watched the growth of the new kyoung very anxiously. She had earned Merit herself by handing nails or tools, which was all her weakness allowed; but what she so greatly desired was that Pho Lone should come back in time to do a little, if only a day's, work so as to gain Merit like everybody else in the village. But the building and the hot season were drawing to an end together and no word had been heard of Pho Lone, save the meagre news given by some Ladaw men who stopped at Myothit on their way to Ngatheing to buy salt, and told how Boh Tah's men had stolen all the money and goods in their village; and these had not seen Pho Lone. True, Oo Boo Nah, whom Moung Let had, of course, consulted a day or two after his son's disappearance, had examined Pho Lone's sadah, and had calculated by astrology that he would return soon after the monsoon burst and bring with him rupees enough to build a great pagoda, and cover it with gold leaf to boot. This was very reassuring, for Oo Boo Nah's predictions always came right unless some error crept into his calculations, as had been known to happen; or, what he could control still less, the person prophesied about upset the natural course of things by doing some particularly good or particularly bad action. Moung Let had been four times altogether to see Oo Boo Nah, and had done him honour to the extent of two rupees

each time ; but it was well spent money, for on
each visit the old sayah made fresh calculations
which produced the same result. Pho Lone was
alive and well, was conquering towns and villages,
and gaining great wealth.

"It is due to the care we take to do nothing
unlucky," said Mah Tsay.

"Yes, good wife. We have never slept with
our heads to the north or the west."

"Never, Ko Moung Let. Always we lie with
our heads to the east. And you never eat rice
facing the north. Nor do I."

Oo Boo Nah had proved with such certainty
that Pho Lone would not return till his birth-
planet entered the same house with Saturn, which
would happen soon after the monsoon burst, that
when early the next morning a murmur of excitement passed sleepily through the village, bringing
the neighbours out in the glare, Mah Tsay scarcely
looked up from her fire-making under the lee of
the house.

"They say Pho Lone comes. Ho, neighbour
Mah Tsay, they say Pho Lone is come!" called a
girl from over the way.

Mah Tsay dropped her fire-fan, grasped her
staff, and hobbled out into the street. A crowd
was coming slowly along, swelling as it came, for
every one was running to see. Mah Tsay called
out, but her thin old voice was not heard, and she
made what haste she could to join the throng.

"Here is your son, mother!" shouted fifty voices. "A dacoit chief. See! he wears the loon pasoh!"

It was Pho Lone. He looked hungry and tired, but he bore himself proudly, and received the greetings of his friends with an air. The pasoh Boh Tah had given him at Nyounglay was stained with mud and flapped raggedly about his calves, but the wavy pattern in the once brilliant silk was plain to see.

"Yes," called Shway Toon to Moung Yeik, who could not force his way through the crowd, "it is he, and he wears the loon pasoh!"

"Mother! Pho Lone a chief!" exclaimed Moung Yeik in awe.

"Do you not want to speak to him?" Moung Let asked Ko Moung Galay, for something is due to the head-man of the village.

"Presently I will speak," said Ko Moung Galay.

"The head-man looks a little gravely on you," said Moung Let in a low tone to his son.

"He has nothing to fear," replied Pho Lone kindly. "Let him come and speak if he will," and he smoothed out his pasoh.

"My son!" cried Mah Tsay, standing in his path as the people made way for her, "my dear son!"

She waved her shrunken old arms and moved her knees as if she would dance with joy. She had forgotten the wealth Pho Lone was to bring;

she saw he was thin and ragged and carried only
a staff in his hand, but he had come home at last
and she wanted nothing more. Pho Lone smiled
upon her, and she stood aside to be carried on by
the crowd. They moved slowly, and Mah Tsay
hobbled along, unable to take her eyes off the
fine young man who threw out his chest and
swaggered like the hero in a play.

"I am hungry; let rice be brought," he said,
as he stepped upon the verandah of Moung Let's
house and squatted on the mat Shway Toon
crouched to spread for him. "I have travelled
far since the last fight when we killed the police."

The sun scorched their bare backs, but the
people, close packed on the road outside, sank on
their heels to hear what he would tell.

"Was it a great fight?" Shway Toon respectfully inquired of Moung Let, who sat on the edge
of his son's mat.

"Hardly a great fight," said Pho Lone. "The
dogs ran away too soon; but we killed many. I
myself always led the attack, carrying his lordship's own gun. I killed a man the very first
time I fired it."

"Mother! Always led! that is why he wears
the dress of a chief; and he used the Boh's own
gun! killed a man with it!"

Pho Lone listened to the ripple of admiring
talk with the smile of one who has just given a
taste of what is to come.

" I suppose he has a great deal of money buried in the jungle," Mah Hehn said to Moung Yeik, who put the question through Moung Let.

" An elephant's load of rupees, gold and diamond ornaments and fine silk is committed to the care of the demons," said Pho Lone. " His lordship, by the power of his magic, vanished from our sight when we dispersed, or I had brought my share—a chief's share—with me."

Mah Tsay laughed aloud ; it was the first time she had been heard to laugh for many weeks.

" I bring rice, good son," she said, beaming on him, " thou art hungry."

" I will eat also young bamboo shoots, curry, and a little ngapee," said Pho Lone. Mah Tsay looked aghast, for she had no dainties in the house ; but several young men crept forward and begged leave to bring what was required.

" Will the Boh come again to this village ? " inquired Moung Byoo.

" I cannot tell what his lordship's pleasure will be," replied Pho Lone, " though he always desired my advice."

Moung Maw who had twice addressed Pho Lone mouth to mouth without getting an answer, cried, " Did he ever take it ? " but was scowled down by his neighbours, and Pho Lone took no notice.

" You will perhaps speak to his lordship in favour of our village," said several, very respectfully; and Pho Lone said, Yes, he would do this, and did not doubt but that Boh Tah would extend his protection to their village on payment of the usual tribute. At these words Ko Moung Galay was seen to rise on the outskirts of the crowd and walk away to his house, followed by Elders Oo Ket Kay and Oo Shway. Moung Let remarked it and twiddled his cheroot uneasily; for he knew what was in the head-man's mind, and began to be afraid lest he should wish to perform his duty. He was about to whisper Pho Lone not to speak more of Boh Tah but that young chief stopped him by calling again very fiercely for food; and as the curry and other things were at this moment passed up to the verandah, the crowd remembered that it was long past rice-time and melted away.

In the head-man's house, the elders sat chewing betel and discussing the matter. Ko Moung Galay, fearing the displeasure of the Deputy Commissioner, said he thought it was proper to report to the patrol constable when he next called at the village, and Oo Ket Kay was of the same opinion though fearful lest this measure should give offence to Boh Tah. Oo Shway, however, thought otherwise; he reminded Ko Moung Galay that fully half the people in Myothit were blood relations of Moung Let or of Mah Tsay and that all these would be strongly opposed to giving up Pho Lone to the police. He himself as the brother-in-law of Moung Let's second cousin, Oo

Yan, should not feel justified in advising the young man's arrest, and he was quite sure all Pho Lone's relations would be equally against it.

Ko Moung Galay fully recognised Oo Shway's point of view and should be very sorry to do anything that would breed dissension in the village, but Oo Shway would remember Mah Kin Lay thekin's visit? Well, they had all heard what he had said; and since then, he must remind his friend that Moung Paw Thin, the patrol constable, had brought news that it was the intention of Government to impose fines on villages which were successfully attacked by dacoits, and to punish with great severity all persons who were found harbouring dacoits. Was it wise to run these risks? Oo Shway confessed he was rather surprised that so sensible a man as Ko Moung Galay did not see that his own arguments pointed to the wisdom of ignoring Pho Lone's adventure; in the first place Boh Tah would never again attack Myothit, a son of the village having followed him, so there was no chance of being fined on that ground. Then Pho Lone was now no longer a dacoit, but a youth of good character living with his mother; if nothing was said, nobody would be any the wiser.

"Certainly, the young man did not follow the Boh of his own accord," said Oo Ket Kay thoughtfully. He was not related to Pho Lone's family, but as he had a grand-daughter, and therefore might become so, he did not wish to see bad blood.

"I will think it over," said Ko Moung Galay. "I wish the youth no ill, but such talk as his is not good."

"True, neighbour; but who shall stop a young cock's crowing?" asked Oo Shway, rising to leave.

No work was done on the new kyoung that morning. Until the sun declined, the people were gathered in and about Moung Let's house, which was not big enough to hold one quarter of those who wished to hear about Pho Lone's doings since he followed the Boh. Ko Moung Galay was the only man in the village who stayed away, and he lost nothing, because the neighbours, sorry for a man who always used his authority mildly, dropped in from time to time to tell him Pho Lone's tales. Ko Moung Galay listened, but when he looked down the street, and saw how the young bloods bore themselves, howling and pretending to fight as they left Moung Let's house, his face grew more and more grave. If only half the young man's stories were true, the position was much more serious than he had supposed. Moung Hla was not the man to see his people killed and their houses robbed, and the whole village burned, without reporting to the Government as quickly as he could. Ko Moung Galay did not believe that all the police

had been killed in the fight after the sacking of
Kyouksay, but he saw no reason to doubt that
Ko Moung Hla had appealed for mercy to Pho
Lone; and this was what troubled him most, for
Ko Moung Hla would assuredly denounce Pho
Lone to the police. The patrol constable was
due to make his usual visit to Myothit in a day
or two at farthest, and he was sure to have heard
about the Kyouksay dacoity; indeed it was quite
likely that he would arrest Pho Lone on suspicion, for on the two occasions he had lately
visited the village, he had inquired about the
young man, and last time had pressed Moung Let
to explain his son's absence, until Moung Let,
being greatly confused, lent him twenty rupees.

Ko Moung Galay thought over the matter
until the sun was low, without being able to
make up his mind; and at last he got up, and
went away down the street to talk it over with
Oo Yan; for Oo Yan, being the oldest man in the
village, had had much experience, and could give
good advice.

"I think Ko Moung Galay is not very glad that
I have come back," said Pho Lone as he saw the
head-man pass without even turning his head.

"Never mind him," shrilled Mah Tsay, "how
good it is to see the neighbours sit and listen
to thy speech! But thou wilt not follow again,
good son."

When Pho Lone entered the village that morning he was so glad to be back, having eaten nothing but wild fruits for three days, that he had had no thought of following Boh Tah or any other chief again. But having eaten, and being drunk with the admiration of the neighbours, he could not say he would never " follow " any more ; so he smiled upon his mother, and said no man might dwell in the jungles during the rainy season and live ; time enough to think about jungle life when the cold weather came round.

" This has been the day of my life," said Mah Tsay, thinking of the silence which held the neighbours while Pho Lone told of his marches and battles, and of the magical powers of the Boh. " But, my son, the sayah foretold that you should bring money; much money, enough to build a great pagoda."

" I have enough to build two pagodas, each with rest-houses all round," said Pho Lone, boastfully. " I must see his lordship and arrange to get this money."

" My dear son, the Builder of a Pagoda," murmured Mah Tsay, looking up the street where she could see Mah Helm's Work of Merit, its newness gleaming in the setting sun, " that woman is a kyoung-tagama. How much better is a payah-taga."

" The Ladaw men said you took everything," said Moung Let, rolling a chew. " Ladaw is a rich village, is it not ? "

"It was," replied Pho Lone, grinning, and
Moung Let laughed.

"I wonder where his lordship went when he
vanished out of sight," remarked Moung Let
thoughtfully, "you said he took the elephants with
him?"

"I did not say those words. I said that when
his lordship by means of his sorcery vanished, we
no longer could see the elephants."

"Truly a great sayah," said Moung Let. "It
is good for the village that we shall henceforward
enjoy his favour."

"Speak no more on these matters," said Mah
Tsay, "the head-man with Oo Yan comes and I
think to our house."

Pho Lone frowned darkly, but his look of high
displeasure gave way to one of anxiety as Ko
Moung Galay stepped on to the verandah and sat
down without taking the least notice of him. The
manner of the old men hurt him after the beha-
viour of the neighbours, and he wished he had
gone upstairs to his room before they entered. It
would not be polite to do so now, so he sat waiting for them to speak.

"We are very glad, neighbour," began Ko
Moung Galay, a little awkwardly, "we are all rejoiced that your good son has escaped unhurt from
the bad men who compelled him to follow them."

"It has been a happy day, indeed," said Mah
Tsay.

"You would grieve much if you should lose him again," said Oo Yan to Moung Let, for one does not address a woman in such matters, "yet, neighbour, there is that danger. Without doubt it is in your mind how constable Paw Thin asked many searching questions when he was last here."

Moung Let said it was; he added that in his opinion Moung Paw Thin was a great thief. Pho Lone listened while his seniors talked, and began to feel very uncomfortable.

"Our fear is," said Ko Moung Galay, after a little silence, "that Moung Hla of Kyouksay, having recognised Pho Lone in the company of the dacoits who robbed his village and burned it, killing many people also, will tell his name to the police."

"But the dacoits did not rob Kyouksay, nor burn the houses, and only one woman was killed by mistake," put in Pho Lone, much frightened.

"The youth was there with the dacoits and Moung Hla saw him," said Ko Moung Galay; "he will therefore certainly be arrested by the police."

"They made me follow; I had been killed else," moaned Pho Lone, looking from one to the other.

"We are anxious to save your son," said Ko Moung Galay, "it is not good that a son of the village should be sent over the sea with chains on his legs [Mah Tsay howled], we wish to save him from this."

"What do you advise?" asked Moung Let, "Peace, woman!"

Ko Moung Galay nodded to Oo Yan, and Oo Yan clearing his throat, spoke:

"We have talked much of this thing and we are of one mind. The young man shall go to Bassein, taking with him a letter from Ko Moung Galay in which shall be written: 'Pho Lone, the son of Moung Let, of Myothit, on the Ngatheing creek, is a young man of very good character. He has lived with his mother. He does not drink berrandy and he does not eat opium,' these being evil things and much disapproved by the Government," explained Oo Yan. "And the letter shall also say: 'The young man desires to serve on the Government-side as a policeman, and begs for this letter recommending him to the kindness of Moung Wah Gyee, Head Constable of Police; for whose long life and freedom from all the Accidents, Diseases, and Misfortunes he will ever pray.'"

Oo Yan rolled out the last words and looked round for approval.

"Very good words," said Ko Moung Galay.

The sky had shut now and the house was dark. The silence was broken by Mah Tsay's sobs and a muffled sniffle from where Pho Lone sat.

"I will write this letter to-night," said Ko Moung Galay. "The youth must go very quickly lest the police arrest him on Moung Hla's report."

"But the police will put him in prison," cried Mah Tsay.

"No," said Oo Yan, "there is but one tongue in the thannah. Should Moung Hla come, saying, 'I have seen this young man with dacoits,' the sergeant will reply, 'Your words are lies, he is one of Us; be careful how you speak against him lest you incur the displeasure of Government,' when Moung Hla will be silent, fearing to make enemies of the police."

"Ko Moung Galay, I beg you to write the letter to night that I may go on the next tide," cried Pho Lone. "It is my great desire to be a policeman."

"I go to write it in my house," said Ko Moung Galay rising.

"This village is happy in the wisdom of its head-man," said Moung Let a little sadly.

"His wisdom is as the wisdom of a Bhudd," said Pho Lone.

But Ko Moung Galay had yet one more word to say, and he was not sorry to see many neighbours standing round to hear.

"I do this because your father is my friend. Go, fool! take off that pasoh, wrap it about a stone, and throw it in the creek."

Pho Lone went.

CHAPTER XVI

"A CHEW," said Constable Moung Eik.

Pho Lone pushed his betel box along the floor, and when his comrade had helped himself, reached for it again: he did not want the box, but he liked to hear his new police-belt creak. The noise of the rain was deafening; now and again Pho Lone bent forward to look at the sky, but there was never a gleam of light in the misty grey above: the spout at the roof corner shot a torrent clear over the gutter to eat a hole knee-deep in the metal of the roadway, and the muddy water sheeted sullenly into the brick-lined drain at the verandah edge.

" We ought to go on beat," said Pho Lone.

" I was eager to go out and be seen in my uniform when I first joined," grinned Moung Eik. " Who shall see you in this rain ? "

Pho Lone laughed and fingered the bâton he was so proud of; he had worn the blue serge coat and red pasoh for only two days, but Sergeant Moung Nee had taught him his business, and he was now fitted for duty.

" I have taught you to stand tensin and sah-loo' when a gentleman passes," said the sergeant when dismissing his pupil, "and also I have taught the duty of a constable on beat. If you find cattle or goats straying on the road you bring them to the pound; if you see a house take fire you come to the thannah and report; if you see a thief running away—what will you do?"

"Come and make report," replied Pho Lone.

"Quite right," said the sergeant, "to-morrow you go on beat."

Pho Lone was to have taken his first turn of duty at eight o'clock this morning; but the rain being very heavy, and Constable Moung Eik, who had been directed to show him the limits of his beat, having no umbrella, they decided to wait under shelter until the sun came out. It was early in the monsoon when the rain falls for days and nights together, so they spent the hours in the back verandah where the inspector would not see them, smoking and chewing, sleeping and talking by turns.

It was late in the afternoon before the rain ceased and the sun pushed his way out below the leaden clouds; and when the road began to steam and glisten Pho Lone suggested that they should go; he was eager to enjoy the respect of the townspeople. Moung Eik said Pho Lone could go if he chose; for his own part he hated sitting about in the wet, and should let the world dry up before he went on duty.

"You know your beat perhaps," he said, "on the riverside road from Thaw' thekin's mill to the Chinese pig-dealer's quarter."

"That road! Yes, I know it well; also I know Thaw' thekin and his wife; Mah Pan is the daughter of Moung Byoo of my village."

"Ah," said Moung Eik, "I know her too. She called me in one day to arrest a kullah servant for stealing. How angry she was! I remember that his honour let the man off. She is a very pretty woman."

"Yes, she is," assented Pho Lone, squirting betel juice: he laughed lightly, "she was my madah* once."

"Was she now?" asked Moung Eik, growing interested. "She is pretty; but not very sweet, I think, and very proud."

"It is so long since I saw her that I forget," said Pho Lone carelessly. "But I ought to go on beat."

"There is leave," laughed Moung Eik; "come back at eight o'clock and report everything all right."

Pho Lone shook out his pasoh and strolled off past the Court-house down to the road which runs along the river bank, straightening his back a little as some coolies drew aside to let him pass. Moung Eik's words had brought Mah Pan and his court-

* Madah; Burmese slang, equivalent to 'Arry's "My girl."

ship back to his mind again, and he debated
whether he should go now and visit her. He had
been four weeks in Bassein, but until yesterday
had not wished to seek out any of his town friends.
When he presented Ko Moung Galay's letter to
Head Constable Moung Wah Gyee, that officer had
said : "There is now no vacancy in the force, and
I must know something about you before I can
recommend you for enrolment. I will take you as
my servant till a vacancy occurs, so that you may
learn something of police duty." Had Pho Lone
not been afraid to go home he would have made
answer that he was no man's servant to cut wood
and run errands ; but as the village elders had
hinted that they should report him to Moung
Paw Thin if he did return, he could only shiko the
head constable and pray for his favour. He felt
very humble being a servant, after having been
shiko'd himself as a dacoit leader, though Moung
Wah Gyee was very kind, and treated him as a
son. He had been a servant for two weeks, and
had gained his master's favour, when Moung Maw
came to see him. Pho Lone was home-sick and
glad to see any one from Myothit, but Moung
Maw was the more welcome because he brought
the very thing of all others a man in bad case
desires : this was nothing less than the potent
peeyah thadee* charm which compels the granting

---

* "Peeyah thadee," Pali for "Completed Love." The charm
consists of a few red-stained cotton threads passed through two

of any request the owner may prefer. Mah Tsay had been to see Oo Boo Nah, and had honoured him with many rupees for it. Pho Lone treated the charm with jealous respect. He kept it in the breast pocket of his linen jacket, never carrying it near his waist, much less below it; he set it in a high place at night and scented it with frangipanni till his room reeked; these precautions being necessary to preserve and excite its virtue. Then, on a lucky day, he begged the head constable to appoint him a policeman soon.

Moung Wah Gyee yielded to the influence of the charm at once, saying: "If your good father wishes it I will make a vacancy." When Moung Let received this message from Moung Maw's mouth he tied thirty rupees in a cloth and came to tell the Head Constable that he wished very much his son should be " on the Government-side," but being a wise man he added that he would take leave to pay his respects again after Pho Lone had been enrolled. When he had seen the young man in his uniform he said: "It has been a great expense, but we are proud that you are a Government officer : when leave is given, come to the village to gladden the eyes of your mother."

Pho Lone rejoiced in his release from house

tiny gold cylinders. The one in my possession has always been well treated, but has never produced any effect upon publishers and others on whom it has been tried. Probably they owned more potent talismans.

service, and he was also glad to wear his uniform
and enjoy the people's respect. It had, moreover,
come to him that the officer who had caught him
that day after the jungle fire near Ladaw, might
recognise him when they met again face to face,
as they must do sooner or later in the course of
police duty. He had misdirected the officer, and
had thereby proved himself, if not a dacoit, at least
in league with dacoits; and if the officer knew his
face Pho Lone knew that nothing could save him
from chains and a shaven head. When Moung Let
first saw him in uniform, he said : " Now who
would know that smart officer for my son ? " and
thus Pho Lone was in hopes that the gentleman
who had seen him with hair disordered, and only
a ragged old pasoh about his thighs, would not
recognise him again.

It was very reassuring when, on the road above
the Strand where the Chittagong men draw up
their boats, he met one who had known him so
well as Thaw' thekin, and that gentleman did not
know him, though he looked at the uncouth constable, who forgot to salute when he passed. Pho
Lone was so busy wondering if the gentleman
would know him that the sergeant's teaching was
forgotten. He watched Thaw' thekin ride by and
went on his way with a lighter heart. Surely if
Thaw' thekin, who had seen him so often, and
had once given him a beating, did not recognise
him in his new uniform, the officer would not.

It was good to feel that one was once more above other men, for a proud man does not like to be a servant even though his master address him "younger brother," or "nephew," and expects to be called "uncle." It had been very easy and pleasant to do the bidding of Moung Wah Gyee; but Mah Gway his wife was not like him. Pho Lone's gorge rose as he remembered her cross voice, "Hé, Pho Lone! Hé, lazy one! Go quickly to bring water!" that all the street might hear. He clutched his bâton and stalked over the road to threaten the driver of a bullock cart with instant arrest if he let his gharry stand blocking the way. The coolie salaamed, praying for indulgence, and Pho Lone relented; the salaam did him good though it was only a black kullah's.

There was nothing to do on beat, and Pho Lone squatted on the low culvert wall just outside Thaw' thekin's garden gate, to rest and roll a chew. He wanted Mah Pan to see him that he might enjoy the respect she would naturally pay to an official; but he was doubtful about going to the house which he could see a stone's throw distant through the red flowering trees. She would probably be in the great verandah over the porch, and when she begged him to honour her by coming up he should have to pass under her feet to reach the stairs, a humiliation he was not inclined to risk. Besides, would it accord with the dignity of a Government officer to go out of his way to visit a woman, fellow villager and friend though she were ?

"Hé! do not sit there; you will frighten my lord's pony when he comes."

Pho Lone looked over his shoulder; he had heard the dragging clatter of a woman's sandals on the path within, but it had not occurred to him that the wearer might be Mah Pan. Mah Pan it was, nevertheless; prettier than ever, and richly dressed in silk tamein and white silk jacket; she wore diamond nadoungs in her ears, and a gold necklet. She held a small Burmese umbrella over her shoulder to shade her head from the sinking sun, and it formed a background which showed off her face. Pho Lone did not get off the wall; he turned a little and faced her as she stopped a few steps from him.

"Moung Pho Lone!" exclaimed Mah Pan, her tone changing from sharp command to gracious condescension; "Why, the last news was that you followed Boh Tah. You are in good health?"

"I am of the police," said Pho Lone haughtily; he was glad to see Mah Pan, but she must be taught that "Hé!" was not the way to address a Government officer. She must show respect before he could hold converse with her.

"And what do you do here?"

"I have charge of this part of the town at present," replied Pho Lone, with a responsible air. He looked up the road and down for somebody on whom to vent his authority; but there was nothing, not even a stray goat.

"I hope you will arrest any one who steals flowers from the garden, then," said Mah Pan, "or my lord will complain to the superintendent again. How long have you been of the police?"

"Two days," replied Pho Lone, digging at the cracked cement with his bâton to hide his confusion. "And are you going to buy rice in the bazaar?" he inquired, making a sudden effort to put her down in the woman's place.

Mah Pan laughed. "I send my servants to buy rice. I go now to visit my friend Mah Pyin who lives in that large fine house at the corner." She raised her hand to point and the sparkle of diamond rings angered Pho Lone; she, to wear many precious stones on her fingers, who three months ago treasured a silver ring worth two rupees!

"Mah Pyin? That is Thaw' thekin's old broker's wife?"

"No," corrected Mah Pan, smiling, "she is the wife of Ko Moung Loo, the junior magistrate."

Pho Lone had seen Ko Moung Loo in court; policemen crouched on their heels when he spoke and always said "Lord."

"The Wheel has turned for you, neighbour Mah Pan."

"I am still your friend," smiled Mah Pan. "Should you like promotion? Shall I bespeak Ko Moung Loo's favour for you?"

"It would be very good," mumbled Pho Lone, digging viciously at the cement again. Mah Pan was such a great lady, she had no respect for a policeman now ; and how humble she used to be to Moung Paw Thin!

"Come and see me in my house," said Mah Pan. "It will please me to hear of Myothit people. I shall tell Mah Pyin of you, that she may speak in the ear of Ko Moung Loo."

Pho Lone could endure her airs no longer.

"I'm going," he said, and swinging his feet off the wall he turned his back and marched down the road.

"Yes, the inspector will no doubt punish you if he finds you sitting to gossip," said Mah Pan.

He pretended not to hear. If only he could arrest and walk her through the town in hand-cuffs! If only she had seen his entry into Myo-thit that morning when all the neighbours ran out to see him and pray for his favour! The big Coringa coolies who strolled along singing through their noses and throwing their mushroom spools as they wound cotton, hustled one another out of the way, for they saw a very fierce young policeman who might bring a false charge if offended. Pho Lone liked to see them make way, and by the time he reached the end of the fence which enclosed the now silent mill and its grounds, his anger had passed, and he began to think it would be pleasant to see some of the old friends whose houses backed

T

against the palisade in this far corner; so after a glance townwards, lest the inspector of whom Mah Pan had spoken might be about, he crossed the plank over the flooded ditch and entered by the narrow slit which served as gateway.

The only man to be seen about was white haired Moung Woon the broker, whose wife Pho Lone had supposed Mah Pan was on her way to visit. Moung Woon squatted on his verandah smoking, and called " Ho, neighbour! " for he was rather blind with age and saw only a constable.

" You do not know me," said Pho Lone, approaching and speaking with the respect due to one so old.

" I know your voice, my son," said Moung Woon. " Your good father came only two days since and told how you were now in the Government service. That was very good news. Enter and talk with me."

Pho Lone took a drink from the water chatty and sat down, remarking that he had just seen Mah Pan.

Moung Woon's face became a little grave at mention of Mah Pan's name. " Yes," he said, " of course you know her; she is a Myothit daughter."

" She is grown proud, I think," said Pho Lone, who saw that the old man did not think very well of Mah Pan. " I suppose she is proud having married his honour, who gives her so many beautiful jewels."

Moung Woon's face relaxed.

"They are my wife's jewels," he said, chuckling. "Mah Pyin is fond of the foolish girl ; and when Mah Pan comes, saying, 'Lend me jewellery, that I may do my lord honour,' she laughs and lends. Thaw' thekin give her diamonds ! One day there will be—Missi' Thorpe, for whom Thaw' thekin will no doubt buy diamonds, also rubies and other precious stones."

"I thought the gentleman would not give such things to a jungle woman," said Pho Lone; and he told how Mah Pan had affected to laugh at the idea of visiting Moung Woon's wife.

"I shall tell Mah Pyin," said the old man, with a chuckle. He rolled his cheroot in his mouth and went on, "Often have I sat in this place hearing their women's talk. The jungle girl would be ruler in that house, and indeed it is in my mind that his honour is too easy tempered. But three of his old kullah servants remain, the others having refused to obey the orders of Mah Pan. The cooking man remains because he makes much money buying in the bazaar ; also his honour's body servant, a big man of the fighting race whom Mah Pan fears, and the groom, who is not at her order."

"And his honour allows this !" said Pho Lone. He had never thought white men permitted women to rule in their houses thus.

"What is it to him ?" said Moung Woon. "He is all day working in his office below——"

"Her feet over his head!"

"Englishmen think it no shame; how often have I seen it! Well then, he has much business, and leaves the household to the woman's care. Servants come and go, and what is it to him?"

"Is he kind to her?" asked Pho Lone, half hoping to hear that Thaw' thekin was not kind.

"Yes, yes. His honour is not like the engineer who married that Henzada girl and beat her. He is very kind, and gives her presents. Once she brought much paddy to us by smiling upon the Chinaman who had stored it; his honour gave her the brokerage and a silk tamein."

Moung Woon paused and laughed to himself.

"Why do you laugh?" inquired Pho Lone.

"I sat in the office doorway when his honour gave her the tamein. I heard his honour say to her, 'Here is a gift, because you brought that ten thousand baskets to me. I give you this tamein which cost fifty rupees.'"

Moung Woon paused to chuckle again, until Pho Lone said, "And then?"

"Then Mah Pan, handling the silk as women do, said, 'Has my lord paid fifty rupees for this?' and Thaw' thekin saying, 'I shall pay all that money,' Mah Pan made answer, 'My lord has been cheated, for it is worth but twenty. Let my lord pay fifty rupees into my hand, and I will buy value for the money, returning this to the cheat who asks fifty.' So his honour had to give her the fifty rupees; the price of the tamein being but twenty-four, as he well knew, having bidden the clerk, Hpo Youk, pay not over twenty-five for the rag. It is fool's work teaching women the price of finery."

Pho Lone laughed at the way Thaw' thekin had blundered, saying he was well served for saying the tamein was worth more than the real price.

"I think Mah Pan must make a great deal of money," he added.

"No," said Moung Woon, "Mah Pan no doubt would dig for turtle eggs going to the pagoda,* but it is not good. She cannot be his honour's broker and also his wife. It was her pretty face that brought the Chinaman to us; just a chance; so we brokers did not complain, having tried to buy his grain and failed."

"She seems very happy," remarked Pho Lone.

"Why not? His honour allows her to invite friends to the house; she goes whither she pleases and does as she likes. The girl who was married to the gentleman who was here many years ago was a good girl; she learned to mend his clothes and socks, as I am told Englishwomen do for their lords. Mah Pan never does that; she prefers to amuse herself."

"She worked at the loom at home," said Pho

---

* "Combine business with religion," or, "Kill two birds with one stone."

Lone ; " if English ladies do such work why does not she, wishing to be like them ? "

" She knows nothing of English ladies," said Moung Woon, " save what she would rather not know."

" And that ? "

" They come to play the ball game with his honour. Then Mah Pan stays in the house watching from a window, very jealous." Moung Woon stopped to laugh. " Some day there will be trouble, I think. But we have spoken too much of the girl ; tell me of yourself. They say you were carried off by the dacoit Boh Tah ? "

" I was," replied Pho Lone, " and I saw many terrible things in the jungle ; as soon as I could I escaped and returned home, joining the police lest I should be caught as a dacoit." For Moung Woon was a good man and much respected in the town. He often told how the Deputy Commissioner sent for him and explained what Government were doing that he might tell the people in his quarter. Pho Lone knew this of old and was not going to boast of his dacoit doings to Moung Woon.

" When they catch Boh Tah they will hang him for killing Moung Hla's wife at Kyouksay," said Moung Woon.

" The police will never catch him," said Pho Lone, " how can we catch one whose magical power is so great." It was on his lips to say that it was not the Boh but Moung Toke who had speared Mah Hlaing, but reflected that the less he spoke of such doings now the better.

Moung Woon lighted a fresh cheroot and stared out across the rank jungle which choked the yard. Presently he asked Pho Lone if he knew where the Boh would lie up during the rains.

"Nyounglay village, I think," said Pho Lone.

"Then you may be a sergeant when you choose," said Moung Woon. "If you guide police to that place and they catch the Boh the Government will assuredly give honour and promotion."

"I am too much afraid," said Pho Lone; "the Boh would certainly kill us all."

"He didn't kill many police at Kyouksay, the only time he met them," said Moung Woon drily.

"I will tell the head constable, Moung Wah Gyee where the Boh may be found, and thus gain his favour."

"A wise young man would wait till report of the Boh came to the thannah; then he would go to Bay Lee thekin and tell what he knew offering to guide the police," said Moung Woon; "think of your good father's happiness, you being made a sergeant so soon! Besides, if you do not offer to go you may be sent."

"I will think about it," said Pho Lone; and as the sky had long since shut and the gong at the mill gate had rung seven o'clock some time ago, he got up to return to the thannah.

Moung Woon's words touching Boh Tah were

not very good, to his thinking, and he would have
forgotten them but for a piece of duty he had to
do a day or two later, when orders came for ten
policemen to be at the wharf and meet the creek
steamer to escort some dacoits to the lock-up.
Pho Lone marched down with the rest in fear and
trembling; but when he saw the dacoits, men
whose chests were covered with charms, tied up
with cords and cowering before the kullahs who
had brought them, Moung Woon's words came
back to him, and he began to think that the
Government must have some very potent spell to
be able to control dacoits like this. Why, every
one knew that Boh Tah's charms would enable
him to break iron rods with his fingers; yet these
men followed every movement of the police with
their eyes, and scarcely dared wriggle their bound
hands. It was, however, when they were cutting
off the cords and putting the prisoners into the
cells that Pho Lone discovered he himself was
endowed with the mysterious power which tamed
dacoits and made them helpless. A man refused
to enter the cell saying one of those inside was his
enemy and would kill him. Pho Lone said fiercely
"Go! son of a she-dog," raising his bâton, and the
man ran in praying for mercy! Next morning he
helped to escort the prisoners to the Court-house,
and tried his power over them again on the way;
the men shiko'd him and obeyed; then Pho Lone
resolved to follow Moung Woon's advice.

CHAPTER XVII

THE rainy season was nearly over. When the sun shone the still air was thick in the throat, so that one felt the veins swell and the head tight, while sweat ran as in the hot weather. Myothit was half buried in the rank jungle which had sprung up, round and between the houses, till one needed a dah to cut the way through : round the boats, drawn high on the creek bank, the jungle had grown up as though their day were done. Thorns and hairy-leaved creepers smothered the paths outside the village, but this did not matter as planting out was long since finished, and the young paddy rolled a green sea to the distant hills. The people rose at dawn to eat and smoke and sleep by turns, till night came again.

"It is very dull," yawned Pho Lone to his mother as they sat on the verandah watching the sun-drawn steam roll along the wet street like smoke from burning stubble, "so dull that I do not wish to live here any more."

Pho Lone had received a few days leave to visit his mother, who had sent messages that her eyes ached to see him again. She continually praised his appearance in uniform, only sorrowing that he had not brought the rifle and gun-spear he had described; the neighbours, too, showed much respect, but nevertheless the village was a poor place after the town. One reason perhaps was that so many people were ill. Moung Maw lay in his house with fever, Moung Yeik was also sick, and several other young men who might otherwise have made up parties for play in these long days, for it was cool enough when the rain fell. Every body who was not ill was listless, and Pho Lone, glad as he was to see his father and mother again, was cheered by thinking that in four days more he must go back to duty.

"There is much sickness," said Mah Tsay, who, never having lived anywhere else, did not know what her son meant when he said it was dull. "Many of the neighbours have fever or other sickness and Oo Yan will die I think. Mah Khin thinks he will die."

"Doctors have seen him?" asked Pho Lone, for there were no doctors in Myothit.

"Sayah Moung Byan, the drug doctor, came from Ngatheing village, and gave him medicine," said Mah Tsay, who loved to talk of medical matters, "but when Oo Yan had taken what Sayah Moung Byan gave for half a month and was no better, Mah Khin said to the sayah, 'I fear it is not your excellent medicine that my man

MAH TSAY

requires or he must have recovered his health by
now. It is the wish of his friends to call in Sayah
Bah Pay, the diet doctor.' So Sayah Moung
Byan received four rupees for fee, and we sent for
Sayah Bah Pay who comes one day in each week
to see Oo Yan ; he will come to-morrow, I think,
unless much rain falls."

"Oo Yan is an old man," said Moung Let, "if
dieting does not cure it will kill."

"Sayah Bah Pay is the best diet doctor on the
creek," said Mah Tsay; "he knows more Pali
rhymes than Sayah Moung Byan, and he knows
more about the stars than Oo Boo Nah himself."

"The woman thinks much of doctors," said
Moung Let soothingly, for his wife's tone was
angry.

"Theirs is an honourable profession, and one
respects the doctor nearly as much as the official,"
said Mah Tsay, "doctors are more respected than
rich merchants and such people ; do they not earn
Merit each time they prescribe ?"

"Of course they do," said Pho Lone, "but tell
me, did Oo Yan fall ill suddenly ?"

"At first he was only a little ill. I helped
Mah Khin to examine the cocoa-nut. It had hung
in the house for only one year but we found it
rotten.* She got a new one and made obeisance

---

* In every Burmese house hangs a cocoa-nut dedicated to the
guardian spirit of the dwelling. This serves the purpose of a
health preserver. When any one falls ill, the first thing done

to the house nat; but Oo Yan getting no better, we sent for Sayah Moung Byan."

"Many people have been ill this rainy season," said Moung Let, twisting off a long green shoot which had pushed through a crack in the wall planks. 'I myself believe that Ko Moung Galay is right when he says evil spirits have caused the sickness. Old people and young besides have had much fever and other diseases."

"I expect he is right," said Pho Lone.

He had hardly spoken the words when Mah Tsay said, "the goung comes," and they saw him walking carefully along the pathway whose loose bricks squelched and bubbled to the tread. He looked very grave as he stepped upon the verandah and scraped the dirt off his feet.

"I have spoken with the elders," he said, unrolling a paper he carried in his hand, "and they think with me that it will be very good to post this notice on a tree at the end of the village. I will write another in the same words, and post it on a tree at the other end also. Shall I read what I have written?"

Moung Let begged him to do so, and the headman squatting, held up the paper and read these words in the sing-song voice:

is to examine the cocoa-nut, and if it be either rotting or sprouting it must at once be replaced by a new one. The sick person will get well then; if he does not, you know the old cocoa-nut was not to blame, and had better send for the drug doctor.

ORDER OF THE VILLAGE GOUNG.

"The Village Goung, who is the Builder of a Rest-house, gives this order :*

"Some of my people are afflicted with headaches, vomiting, coughs and other diseases, caused by wicked beeloos, ghosts and nats. I pray to the Yahans that the people who live within my jurisdiction may be free from all dangers, and I command you wicked beeloos, ghosts and nats to quit my jurisdiction and to betake yourselves to forests, oceans and other distant places. I also order the good nats to drive you away, and to watch over and protect my village."

"Very good," said Moung Let, as Ko Moung Galay ceased reading and looked at him for approval, "but it is in my mind that such an order will not be obeyed unless it be issued by the Great Glory himself."

"It is said in the town that he is no longer king in Mandalay," said Ko Moung Galay. "If this is so, none can command the nats and demons."

"The Ingalay Mahgyee,† might," said Moung Let dubiously. "They certainly will not obey your order, friend."

---

* An "Order" in these terms was found posted on trees on the outskirts of one of the most flourishing towns in Lower Burma two or three years ago. The official responsible for this sanitary measure was a Magistrate of the First Class, and not a mere jungle village head-man.

† "Great English Lady" = The Queen.

"I cannot think of anything else to do," sighed the goung.

"Put it up," said Moung Let recklessly, "only do not let the neighbours see it, lest they laugh saying, 'Ko Moung Galay is become the Great Glory, with a palace in Myothit.'"

Sayah Bah Pay arrived on the tide next morning in a boat with two rowers, and a third to steer, for a doctor with any practice at all must travel in some style. The day was sunless, and there was a breath of air stirring, so all the village turned out to pay respect to the sayah and follow him to Oo Yan's house. Pho Lone strolled down the street and sat on the verandah while the doctor examined his patient. Sayah Bah Pay was clever beyond doubt; even Pho Lone, whose town experience made him inclined to look disdainfully on jungle village sayahs, was obliged to admit that. He felt Oo Yan's pulse and looked at his tongue just as one sees the English doctor do in the Bassein hospital; when he had done this he asked a few questions in a low tone, and shook his head very gravely at Oo Yan's replies.

"I will see if I made any mistake in my calculations," he said; "let me see; you are sure you told me the date and hour of your birth correctly? That is very important."

Oo Yan was quite sure he had told the exact date and hour; it was written in his sadah so there could be no mistake. The sayah went over his calculations carefully, drew a few cabalistic squares, and said he had made no error.

"The moon was at the full two nights ago," he said to Mah Khin, "you remembered the change of diet?"

Mah Khin had given her man exactly the foods the sayah had prescribed: dried fish, eggs and bamboo shoots while the moon was waxing; and the day after the full moon she changed at once to pumpkins, cocoa-nuts and plantains; he always had as much rice as he wanted, but ate very little.

The sayah looked graver than ever as he cleared his throat, and began to repeat the Pali rhymes proper for such sickness. He did not understand them himself, and the people knew it, but he rolled them out in a solemn voice, glancing now and again at Oo Yan, who listened with half shut eyes, but never once said he felt better. He must have been very ill indeed. For nearly half a betel chew the doctor repeated rhymes, and then shut his mouth with a snap and sat staring out over the heads of the people who squatted in the street. Mah Khin left her husband's side and went up-stairs to fetch one rupee which she laid before the sayah who took it without a word.

"You are going to die very soon," he said, as he stood up to leave. "You are beyond the skill even of the famous Sayah Ko Tha Bwin under whom I studied. I shall not come any more.

Oo Yan said yes, he should certainly die very soon, and Mah Khin said the same. As the sayah was stepping out upon the verandah Oo Yan called in his feeble voice :

" Will you, honoured sir, kindly make a calculation and tell us in what hour I shall die ? "

The sayah was in haste to go and see Moung Maw and other patients, but being a man of courtly manners he at once sat down and drew out his palm leaf almanack again. He ascertained that Oo Yan would die next morning when the red light was in the sky, and then went up the street, followed by some of the people, to visit Moung Maw, who had seen Sayah Moung Byan, the drug doctor, and said he felt worse after his physic.

Ko Moung Galay, Moung Let and all who were related to Oo Yan, remained to talk with him and hear his wishes concerning his funeral ; he seemed to have gained a little strength, for when Mah Khin at his bidding put a pillow under his head, he spoke in the clear voice of health.

" It is my wish to make offerings at the pagoda. Let three large cocoa-nuts, a bunch of plantains, and much rice, with one jar of oil be offered ; also let candles be lighted and placed in the niches at my day corner and with them a praying flag having written upon it the day of my birth."

Ko Moung Galay and Moung Let, being Oo Yan's cousins, rose and set about collecting the

offering, Pho Lone and others helping. The head-
man brought paper, and cutting a slip one finger's
length by two fingers' breadth, wrote upon it
" Yahu," * that being the day on which Oo Yan
was born ; then he mounted it on a slip of bamboo
and stuck it among the plantains on the tray.
Oo Yan raised himself and said a prayer, after
which he sank back and signed that the offering
should be taken to the pagoda.

"I think you will not live till morning, neighbour," said Ko Moung Galay, as with Moung Let's
aid he set the tray upon his shoulder. "You fail
very fast and I think the sayah has made a little
mistake in the calculation."

"He was much hurried," said Mah Khin who
was busy preparing candles ; and every one said :
"Yes, certainly the learned and honourable man
was in a hurry."

"It is fortunate that the Wednesday corners
are the most sheltered of all," said the head-man
as he walked up the street with Moung Let who
carried the candles and matches. " Were our
relation's day Sunday, we could hardly light the
candles."

Ko Moung Galay spoke truth ; the light air of
the dawn had grown into a gale which lashed the
creek into froth-tipped waves, and kept the
bamboos groaning as their feathery crests whipped
and swayed. Banks of black cloud were racing

* Half Wednesday : noon to midnight.

up too, warning the men to make haste in their pious duty. The wind screamed round the pagoda, laying flat the rank grass which the rains had brought up through its brick paving; but the Wednesday corners were the most sheltered of the eight,* and after a few failures Moung Let succeeded in lighting the candles he set in the niches.

As they turned their faces to the village again, they saw the rain-storm advancing over the paddy fields, blotting out the world as it came, with a hissing roar that grew louder until great drops striking the earth bade them run for shelter. The kyoung was the nearest roof and thither they ran, Moung Let shouting that it was their duty to tell the Lord Ruler how neighbour Oo Yan was sick unto death. They reached the kyoung just as the storm swept upon the village, and found the hpoongyee rousing himself from meditation. He had already heard the news, but at Ko Moung Galay's request he promised to lend his presence in the house after Oo Yan was dead. It is very good that a hpoongyee sit in the house where any one lies dead, because his sanctity is the best protection against the evil spirits which come about at such a time. Then as the rain still fell very heavily, he threw his yellow robe from his

* The base of every pagoda is either heptagonal or octagonal, Wednesday being divided into two days in the Burmese calendar, thus making eight days in the week.

shoulders and gave a short exhortation on the vanity, emptiness, and sorrow of human life. The lightning played white and blue and the thunder crashed and rolled in the very street; but the two supporters sat hearing the priest's solemn words. When he ceased speaking the storm had passed and the sun came to warm the chilled air.

Oo Yan was lying very still when they returned to the house to eat rice. Pho Lone told them that since they left he had spoken once to say he wished rupees to the number of the years of his life to be spent in alms for the hpoongyees of Myothit, Ngatheing and Ladaw and for the poor of those villages.

"Seventy-one rupees," said Ko Moung Galay. "Well, our friend has money enough for that. We must invite his friends from up the creek and down to come to his funeral. It is your wish that friends from Ngatheing and Ladaw attend the funeral feasts, is it not, neighbour?" he added, addressing Oo Yan. The sick man understood when Mah Khin repeated the question, and whis- pered that Ko Moung Galay spoke his desire.

All that afternoon the old man lay on the low wooden bedstead, seeming to watch the wall where the sunlight played from the dancing water of the creek, while the neighbours sat round talking in low tones of his virtues and good deeds; for Oo Yan had passed his whole life in the village, and all held him in respect as a just and charitable man.

They had eaten the evening rice and were beginning to grow weary of the watch ; the sky had shut and the night was still, save for the shrilling of the crickets and the slow hoot of an owl across the creek. The moon rose, and the dog below the house whimpered as he plashed out into the open street. Oo Yan moved a little, and those of the neighbours who were talking in low tones stopped, and drew nearer round the bedstead ; for the sick man began to speak as one in pain :

" Lord, Lord, the All Merciful ! May the sum of Merits outweigh——"

The pariah outside gave tongue in a swelling howl, taken up by a hundred dogs along the street. For a few breaths the watchers sat still listening to Mah Khin's sobs ; then Ko Moung Galay rose and said : " Let us light the lamps and place candles on the bed-posts. Moung Pho Lone go to the kyoung and pray the Lord Ruler to grant his sacred presence in the house of death."

It was past midnight when the ceremonies were finished. The house being made light with lamps and candles, they drew the bedstead to the front between the house-posts, and washed the dead man before they swathed him in clean white cotton cloth. Then they put on him his Mandalay silk pasoh and a clean white jacket, and Ko Moung Galay placed in the mouth a new rupee for Ferry

THE FUNERAL OBSEQUIES OF OO YAN

hire across that river which the dead cross but which flows none can tell whence nor whither. They set his great toes together and tied them with a strip of cloth, his thumbs also. Then, the body being made ready, most of the friends went home to sleep, leaving Mah Khin with the women who had come to sorrow with her, and Moung Let with a few more listening to the pious words of the hpoongyee.

The funeral band arrived from Ngatheing next day and, the weather being fine, sat playing dirges in the road outside the house where Oo Yan's body, dressed for the grave, lay in sight of passers by. Many people came from Ngatheing and Ladaw for the funeral, and brought their share of food for the feast, which went on from dawn to midnight. All who could rise from their mats followed in the procession to the burial ground, and Mah Tsay assured Mah Khin that so great a funeral had never been seen on the creek before; and Mah Khin, though the rupees her man had left in the box were few after the alms had been given, spared nothing to do honour to his memory in making the feast afterwards.

While the people sat eating in the house on the day after Oo Yan's burial, Pho Lone, who in virtue of his office and relationship to the deceased had had much to do, was drawn aside in an idle moment by a Ladaw son who said he had a message to give.

"Boh Tah, whom you followed, has sent word to our village that he will be our friend if we say to you, 'the Boh waits at Nyounglay for his men.' Those were his words," said the young man.

"Then the band scattered before the rains came?" asked Pho Lone.

"We cannot tell. How should we know? I tell you the words that he sent by the mouth of a woman who stayed only to eat rice, and returned the way she came."

Pho Lone squatted and drew lines on the earth. It made his heart beat to hear that the Boh had him in mind, and wished him to follow again; it brought back the old feeling of Boh Tah's power, which was not good now he wore the police uniform. He had done duty in the gaol also, and the clank of leg-irons was louder in his ear now than the yell of attack. His hand shook as the Ladaw man repeated:

"The Boh will be our friend if you go, we having given his message."

"Does he know I am now of the police?" asked Pho Lone, for a thought had come to him which made his heart leap at its daring.

"We could find means to let him know."

"Then tell him these words from me: 'Pho Lone, the little chief, being now of the police, will come to your lordship at Nyounglay, bringing many constables with rifles and ammunition, to follow and eat the country."

"We will send that message," said the Ladaw man, rising and laughing with pleasure ; "but will your comrades go ?"

"Why not? all the world knows that policemen have often turned dacoits before now. They tell in the thannah how, but a few seasons gone, a sergeant and six men robbed the treasure-chest placed in their keeping, killed the myooke and such of the village men as refused to follow or did not run away, and went to the jungles, the sergeant himself being their chief."

"I have heard of it," said the Ladaw man ; "but look ! the Boh seeing many armed police approach, may think them enemies, and kill them by his magic. Shall we tell him you will come alone first ?"

"No," replied Pho Lone, with decision. " Tell him these words : 'Your lordship shall know that the constables are your followers because their leader will carry a white paper in his hand and wave it when within sight of the village."

"That is very good." The Ladaw son repeated the words, and said again, "We shall now be no longer afraid of the Boh, who robbed our houses last season, having gained his favour by this service."

"Stop !" said Pho Lone, as the man turned towards the house where the neighbours sat eating and enjoying themselves, evidently bent on telling his friends the good news. "Stop ! I forbid you to speak of what I have said till you are back in your village; if you tell about it now, you must send no word of mine to the Boh."

The man's face fell; but in a breath he saw the wisdom of the order. "I will say no word, neighbour; of course, if people got talking, you would be in danger of arrest." He smiled wisely and went slowly back to his friends.

When Pho Lone took leave of his mother next morning, before taking boat for Bassein, he told her to be of good heart, for ere next harvest were reaped he should certainly be promoted sergeant.

CHAPTER XVIII

"Look here, bearer! I told you to take these clothes out and dry them once a week over the basket: you didn't do it."

"Sahib, the order was obeyed."

"Bearer! it was not. See! the finger goes through the cloth become rotten with damp." Mr. Thorpe spread his fingers and thrust them severally through the back of a tweed coat. "What shall I say to you?"

"Protector of the Poor, it is by reason of the much rain that falls in this country."

"It is by reason of the disobedience of the bearer who obeys not orders, and whose pay is therefore cut five rupees."

The bearer represented that he was a very poor man, but without the fervour he would have imported into protest against a fine of four annas; he made the representation merely as a matter of *dastour* and principle, knowing well that the master had prickly heat, and that prickly heat is a magnifying medium, whose effects are not likely to continue until pay-day. If master had meant business he would have cut eight annas at most.

The bearer, laden with garments smelling of mould, disappeared in the back verandah to hang them over the gigantic skeleton beehive, which covered a pan of glowing charcoal : the master found the book he had been seeking, tossed aside the damp-released binding, and strolled out to lie in a long arm-chair under the punkah in the front verandah, where he smoked and read, and wriggled after the manner of those afflicted with the most irritating of harmless skin affections; battling with mosquitoes at intervals by way of a change.

"I wish Mah Pan were in to give me tanakhet," he growled, rubbing his shoulders against the chair, "it's the only thing on earth that's any good for prickly heat."

But Mah Pan had gone out to visit a friend, and the fragrant powder she smeared upon her cheeks was concealed in some hiding-place, and further secured by one of the twelve or fourteen keys she loved to display, tied to her neck-kerchief.

"Hang me," said Thorpe, with another desperate writhe, "hang me, if I go out again, though all the snipe in Asia are reported across the road. It's fagging after them in the sun that has brought it on."

Mention of snipe reminded him of a duty forgotten, for he laid down his book and called the bearer, whom he ordered to send six birds to the

house of the padre, with salaams to the memsahib.
Then he shouted to the punkah coolie to pull
harder, and strove to forget his sorrows in the
schemes of Becky Sharp. The perspiration trickled
down his brow and hung upon his eyelashes, and
the Burmese pasoh he wore settled in clinging
folds about his legs : the thermometer marked only
ninety degrees in the verandah, but earth was a
cauldron over the pit of hell.

The pitiless sun glare wavered, and suddenly
faded in a twilight so gloomy that Thorpe was
roused from his book : a hundred and four inches
of rain had fallen since May, but the monsoon keeps
its most violent outbursts for its parting, and now
the skies wept till the spouts shot clear of the holes
they had burrowed in the path below during the
last few months.

"Bearer! put clothes to dry for the gentleman
who comes to breakfast. Stop, punkah!" for the
thermometer was falling like mine shares in scare
time.

The storm was at its worst, an occasional splutter
drumming ponderously on an exposed corner of the
verandah floor, when Thorpe's ear caught the mash
of footsteps on the path, and then the squelch of
water-logged shoes on the stairs. "Come up,"
he shouted, wondering who it might be, for only a
white man would enter shod, and the visitor was
on foot.

"Oh Thorpe, excuse me," said a voice trained in

elocution. " I shall make your house in a terrible mess. I was caught in it."

"Come along up and get into dry clothes, my dear padre. By good luck I told the bearer five minutes ago to air them for Bailey, who is coming down to breakfast. You will stay, of course."

The Rev. Mr. Melling reached the top of the stairs and paused there to pull off the soaked pith hat which had settled over his ears, and wring the weight of water from the sleeves of his black coat. He was a well-built man, over middle height, who looked as though he might once have been an athlete ; but there was a careworn, anxious look in his face, which suggested that the grey in his hair was premature.

" My wife expects me back to tiffin at one," he said doubtfully, as he plashed across the verandah to the bedroom, flinging a shower at every step. " Could you let her know ? "

" I'll send a man up at once. Were you walking, padre ? "

Mr. Melling confessed that he had been walking, with an air of guilt as though exercise of that kind were at least a social offence.

" Why on earth couldn't you tell me you'd like a pony ; the two of 'em are eating their heads off in the stable, as you know."

" Well, you see, Thorpe, I don't ride often now. I never was much of a horseman, and last time you lent me a pony it bolted, and I had to walk home five miles in the dark." Mr. Melling let the bearer pull off his wet flannel shirt, and looked round for a towel. "I say, just tell your man not to put my shoes too near the fire," he added anxiously, as the bearer pounced upon them. Thorpe's eyes rested on the shoes as he gave the order : whole and respectable clothing in this country is something in the nature of a luxury, particularly in an out-station during the wet season ; but sound foot gear is a necessity, and the condition of Mr. Melling's shoes told their tale plainly as any bank account. Leaving his guest to enjoy a rub down in the bath-room with a charcoal-smelling rough towel, Thorpe went out into the verandah to meet Mr. Bailey, the District Superintendent of Police, whose gharry had just rattled under the porch ; the rain was passing off, but a grey fog of waters still hid the town half a mile up the river.

"Hullo, Bailey ! what's happened to you ? "

"I was clawed by a Chinese gambler this morning. I only hope his infernal nails were clean," he felt his lacerated cheek tenderly. " I'd rather have a clout from a leopard than a Chinaman ; dirty savage ! "

"But what is the chief of the police doing arresting gamblers with his own right hand ? "

"Thank you, Thorpe, yes, sherry and bitters, I think you said." He spread himself luxuriously on a cane lounge as Thorpe called for the drink. "Now," twirling his glass, "I'll tell you. I've

had my eye on Mr. Boon Sing for months past.
I knew his house was nothing but a gambling den,
but my brilliant bobbies couldn't get evidence to
convict.   So, when that Norwegian barque came
up to-day, I went on board and came ashore dis-
guised.   I caught Boon Sing with two pals red-
handed, and we had a rare set-to before my false
beard came off.   Lord ! you would have laughed
to see them collapse when they recognised me.
How are you, padre ? " to Mr. Melling who now
emerged from the curtained door of the bedroom,
in a shapeless suit of white drill, clean but crying
loud for scissors at the frayed cuffs, collar, and
seams.

" Do my shoes fit you ? " inquired Thorpe.

The shoes fitted as if made to measure.   Mr.
Melling said it with a sigh, and glanced round the
verandah.

" Your house has been done up since I was
here last," he said.

" You haven't been near me for about five
months ; I have had things put to rights to some
extent."

" New matting in the front room ; ceiling re-
strained and whitewashed.   Thorpe, I believe
you're going to be married ! "

" Come on in to breakfast," said Thorpe, colour-
ing slightly.   " You don't catch me marrying on
four hundred dibs a month, padre."

" I'd be sorry for you if you did," said Mr.

Melling, and the lines on his forehead grew deeper. He drew three hundred and fifty rupees a month himself, and had a wife and family to support therewith; "and what with these whining Eurasian loafers, and no Easter offering to speak of," Mrs. Melling was wont to say in unguarded moments of confidence, "I don't know how we get along at all."

"Snipe!" exclaimed the padre with a brightening eye as the khitmagar presented the dish. "Now I haven't seen a snipe this year." He raised the knife and fork, but hesitated. His face fell; for to-day was Monday and probably, most probably——

"I got seven couple this morning in an hour and a half," said Thorpe, who was blessed with that mental ability to be in two places at once, which men call tact; and the fork went home in a plump breast followed by a sigh of relief. Mr. Melling had denounced Sunday shooting, Sunday tennis, and other Eastern irregularities from the pulpit and privately, till he recognised that persistence in attack on recognised institutions would only impair his power for good, when he wisely refrained, but made the rules for his own conduct the more rigid to atone.

"I'm glad it wasn't yesterday," he said frankly, "Your cook knows how to do snipe, Thorpe."

"You haven't been up at the tennis court lately," remarked Bailey, who shared the universal liking for Mr. Melling, though, as he often said, he couldn't quite understand him.

"I have not played of late." An explanation seemed about to follow, but did not : the padre did not care to say it was because his tennis-shoes were worn out, and he could not spare ten rupees to buy another pair; and he was too simple-minded and honest to frame an excuse.

"I think of taking up the study of Burmese," he said, by way of turning the subject. "I have so much time on my hands, and I often feel that residence out here would be more tolerable if I knew something of the people."

"Now there I'm with you," said Bailey, who spoke the language like a native, and understood the Burman and his ways of thought much better than he did Mr. Melling and his views. "Once you break the back of the language it's all plain sailing, isn't it Thorpe? You must have learned a lot lately."

"Yes; I always make a point of talking with the brokers and people during the rainy season when we're all idle," replied his host, accompanying the words with a warning kick under the table.

"It seems strange to have lived out here so long and to know as little of the people as I did on the day we landed," said the padre.

"They don't come in your way; you would soon pick up the language if they did," said

Thorpe, "come outside and have a rubber if you don't mind dummy."

"Well, Thorpe——"

"All right, old fellow, we play for love here."

"*What?*" demanded the suppresser of gamblers, pausing in his choice of cheroots from the hot-water plate.

"We'll have a private chick on the rub if you like, Bailey, or a gold mohur if that's your form, but no points."

"Done as to the gold mohur," said Bailey, drawing in his chair at the whist table. "Hooray! dummy and I. Well!" for the khitmagar was standing at his elbow. "A policeman begs leave to speak? What a nuisance these fellows are; he may come up here, Thorpe? Thanks."

The constable was accordingly called up, and squatted on his heels four yards away till bidden come nearer.

"Tell me what it's all about if there is no secret," said Mr. Melling to Thorpe.

There was nothing of a private nature in Pho Lone's errand. He begged his lordship's leave to bring important news; by his lordship's favour he had been to see his friends at his village, and had there received information concerning the dacoit Boh Tah.

"O-ho!" Bailey dropped the cards he had been "making" while the man spoke and faced round.

X

"You heard news of Boh Tah, did you? Now what did you hear?"

"A Ladaw son came to my village, and said: 'The Boh is at Nyounglay village;' he said those words to me."

"Oh, and why did he say those words to you?" inquired Bailey, who knew by long and sad experience that the police were not usually the confidants of village men in such matters.

Pho Lone supposed it was because he, by his lordships' favour, was a policeman; no, the Ladaw son was not his friend; he had never seen him before that he remembered. Having received this news he thought it proper to report at once to his lordship.

"I confess I don't quite understand it," said Bailey in English, "but we'll come to that afterwards. Now see here, my man, did the Ladaw son say what the Boh was doing at Nyounglay?"

Pho Lone thought it very likely he was collecting men.

"Your views are no doubt of value, but I don't want them: did the Ladaw son say, 'The Boh is collecting men'?"

Pho Lone fenced with the question, but finally driven into a corner gave in and answered: "Yes, he did say so."

"Bailey," struck in Thorpe, "pardon the interruption, but perhaps I can throw a little light on the mystery. Ask him his name and village. I thought I knew him," as Pho Lone gave his name and that of his father. "Moung Let is a most respectable old chap; his hopeful son here was carried off by the Boh last hot weather. Moung Let came and begged me to get him a pardon in advance. I thought I mentioned it one night at the club when Boh Tah was a good deal talked about, but perhaps you weren't there."

"I've forgotten if you did," said Bailey. He pulled thoughtfully at his cheroot, and thought for a minute before addressing Pho Lone again.

"Well then, my man, as you know Nyounglay village, and also the face of the Boh—now don't be a fool: this gentleman has just told me how you were made to follow, so you needn't take the trouble to tell lies."

Pho Lone laughed shamefacedly, saying he ran away from the Boh as soon as he could.

"You can show the path to this village and can swear to the Boh? Yes; very good. Therefore you will guide me there: we shall start in one hour; you will take a note to the sergeant in charge of the thannah at once."

Thorpe called for writing materials, and Mr. Melling looked on with respectful admiration while Bailey wrote a note in Burmese as fast as he could have done it in English.

"There it is," tossing the paper to Pho Lone. "What is that you say about promotion? Wait till we have got the Boh, my man; time enough to talk of promotion then."

Pho Lone shiko'd and crept away downstairs. Bailey sat still for a few minutes ruminating.

" You said that young man's father is respectable, Thorpe ; have you known him long ? "

" I've only known him myself for six seasons ; but he has been on our books for the last twenty years.   I remember that I licked the son for cheating in the godown once ; but that doesn't affect my belief that it's quite a true bill about his being carried off against his will.   I don't believe he has the pluck to go dacoiting of his own accord."

" I'll forgive him his dacoity, if he puts me in the way of laying Boh Tah by the heels.   Mackinlay, my assistant, nearly killed himself last hot season, hunting the rascal through the jungles ; he very nearly collared the whole gang after the Kyouksay affair."

There was no whist that afternoon.   Bailey had no thought for anything but the news Pho Lone had brought, and chafed impatiently till a pony was brought round, when he threw his farewells over his shoulder, and cantered off in the sweltering heat.

Left alone with Thorpe, Mr. Melling reverted to his idea of learning Burmese ; and from that found his way to the care which lay so heavily upon him —the education of his two boys, aged respectively six and seven.   Without private means, interest, or hope of advancement, the educational outlook was a blank one indeed : meantime the two children ran wild under the bare bungalow, happy in their freedom from clothes worthy the name, and living in a world of their own, created from a blend of English, of Tamil picked up from the Madrasee chokra, and of Burmese acquired heaven knows how.

"There are schools in the Hills of course," remarked the padre, "but I don't even see my way to them, much less to an education at home. It's hard enough to scrape up the few pounds we send to the wife's mother to dress the girl we left with her eight years ago. It's no country for a poor man with a family," he continued, thoughtfully. "I was thirty-three when we left Smallwood-under-Barton, and I thought I was doing well—in the worldly sense— to exchange the hundred and fifty pounds I got there for three hundred and fifty out here. It was a mistake. My rector urged me to come out; I remember he was great on the idea that there were no poor to tax the parson's pocket in this country. He had never heard of the Eurasian. I cannot put up with those wretched creatures, their vanity and lies." The padre threw away the end of his cheroot with a vicious jerk. "I offered one who came begging the other day a rupee to do half an hour's carpentering in the house; he said that was native's work, and asked if I thought it a Christian thing to insult a fellow European because he was poor."

"I'm afraid your own profession is to blame for a good many of these loafers. The missionaries go about rescuing the youngsters from a pasoh and idle bliss for trousers and idle misery. Rescue! If they were cleaner I should object to them less; but dignity in a dirty shirt nauseates me. Going to the root of the evil, it's a matter of money to a great extent. Fellows come out here and slave on pay that won't let them marry till they've burned out their vitality in early old age."

"Government can't afford to increase expenditure nowadays," said the padre, who shrank from discussing the social aspects of the knotty Eurasian question: but Thorpe did not observe his disinclination to dig up the "root of the evil."

"Lots of men I know would rather marry, even in a jungle station, than—live alone; but marriage is discouraged by the high-minded people at headquarters. I know their end idea is reasonable enough; they must be able to move a man at a few days' notice, and a bachelor is a more mobile item than a married man. Young Wauchope, who married a girl in Maulmain, told me that his chief advised him not to saddle himself with a wife, as the Government wouldn't spare him a single move on that account. And yet Government House has a periodical outbreak of imbecility which it works off in moral circulars."

Mr. Melling listened and swung his hand nervously ; Thorpe relighted his cheroot and went on again. "And mind you there is another thing to consider. I don't think it's playing fair to go home and marry a girl whose notion of this country is a muddle of palm trees, niggers and elephants, with a sandbank in the background, and then bring her out to some ghastly jungle station where there isn't another petticoat within fifty miles or more. It's all right for us ; we have our work and a bit of sport thrown in now and again to keep us going. I have enough to do and manage to have a good enough time all round ; but if I married to-morrow on four hundred a month what would my wife do with herself all day ?"

Mr. Melling did not answer at once. His thoughts flew to the naked bungalow near the church, which he got cheap because it had a leaky roof, uneven floors, and doors and fittings uniformly dilapidated. He looked inside and saw his patient wife under a punkah still for lack of a servant to pull it, stitching at the jacket for little Willy and soothing the sickly three-year-old girl who seemed so likely to follow her two brothers to the station cemetery—a place where graves, when you could see them for jungle, were oftener troughs than mounds. Other Englishwomen had a native tailor in to do such work ; but the durzee charged one rupee a day, so his aid was out of the question.

"I rather think she would find enough to do if

she had little ones, Thorpe," he said at length,
" but you won't be here many seasons more ? "

" No ; I get a run home the year after next,
and they have promised me a move to Rangoon
when I come out. I shouldn't mind being married
in Rangoon, there's plenty for a girl to do there."

" Wait till you're a partner in the firm ! Don't
make the awful mistake of marrying on inadequate
means out here. We've buried two in that
horrible place beyond the maidan : both boys ;
both of fever ; and a few hundred rupees to send
them away would have saved both. And as
things are, I sometimes think you know, Thorpe,
much as we both felt it——"

He broke off abruptly and saying it was time
he thought of going home, swung himself on his
feet.

" Why, there's our chokra with a note," he
said suddenly.   " Be quick, you boy ! "

" For Thorpe sahib," said the boy quickening
his pace.

" Our little girl is seedy and I get anxious,"
explained Mr. Melling with a nervous laugh, " I
might have guessed that the wife had sent a line
of thanks for the birds."

By some fatality the padre's shoes had met
the fate he had dreaded ; they were scorched to
cinders and useless when the amazed bearer produced them.

" Now you needn't say any more, Thorpe," said

Mr. Melling in despair of stopping the flood of apology and regret. " I'll just walk off in yours, and if it will keep you quiet I'll keep them."

"That's a good fellow, I'm so glad they fit."

" I wonder now," said Thorpe to himself as Mr. Melling picked his way down the path, "I wonder if he has any suspicion how those old wrecks got burned ; hope not."

It was on the evening of this day that the padre wrote one of those honest letters which did something to impair his prospects of preferment. It was to the Secretary of the Anti-Opium Society who had written begging his services to collect evidence to lay before a famous Commission.

" *I much regret,*" he wrote, " *that I feel unable to lend the assistance you desire. I am of opinion that the evils resulting from the use of opium are insignificant in themselves, and as nothing by comparison with another social irregularity peculiar to the East, and which can only be removed by greater liberality on the part of the Imperial Government towards its junior officers in all services ; also by private employers. I am disinclined to do even my little in a movement that seeks a change calculated to produce large decrease in the revenue which is already unequal to the calls upon it.*"

From which it would appear that Thorpe's care to avoid wounding his susceptibilities had been labour wasted.

CHAPTER XIX

"Go slow, my man, go slow! His lordship said to you, 'I cannot permit the policemen, your comrades, to approach my person carrying guns;' were those his words? They were. Well, then, what did you say to that?"

"Lord, I made answer, 'I am your lordship's slave.'"

"And the Boh said?"

"The dacoit thought a space, and said to me, 'It is my order that the policemen leave their guns in the jungle, and come one by one to make obeisance. I shall then lead all my followers to bring the guns in.' Those were the words of the dacoit."

"Wary old bird is Boh Tah," remarked Mr. Bailey, throwing his leg over his knee. "Really, he displays wonderful acumen. I'm afraid that plan would not suit us," he added in Burmese.

"Your lordship's servant hoped that the dacoit would be taken in by the plan named to the Ladaw son," said Pho Lone.

"My servant was a little too trusting, it seems;

I never thought myself he would be such a fool, and I don't think I should have cared to risk my reputation by letting you try your plan if the Boh had consented."

" Lord ! "

" To-morrow morning, therefore, when there is light to see the veins in the hand, you will follow me to the village and point out the house in which the Boh sleeps."

"Your slave is a little lame in the right foot," said Pho Lone, turning yellow ; this plan did not fit in with his ideas at all.

Mr. Bailey regarded his slave with an air of indulgent scepticism.

"Your right foot will be well to-morrow morning," he said, slowly ; and Pho Lone shiko'd and crept away.

Mr. Bailey had brought his force of ten constables to within a couple of hours of Nyounglay, which was as near as he thought risk of premature discovery allowed, and had sent Pho Lone on alone to ascertain that Boh Tah still lay there. Now he had been satisfied on this vital point, it remained to decide how he should best set about making the arrest. He wanted to take the man alive, partially as a matter of credit, and also because he had an eye to the moral effect to be wrought by parading through the villages on the march home a notorious dacoit leader in handcuffs like a mere pickpocket. For, despite disheartening experience, he still clung to the idea that such exhibitions must shake the mischievous faith of the people in the potency of dacoit magic. He half despised himself for indulging in this notion ; for none knew better than he how easily police successes of this kind were explained away—not that the people often required such explanation ; as a general rule, they politely declined to believe that the prisoner was the man the police declared him to be.

" Really, I don't know that I care much if I do have to drop the brute," thought Bailey, as he stepped off his chair into the high cot he always used for jungle work. " I've only got one witness who can swear to him, and the beggar is as likely as not to get clear off on appeal, if I take him alive. The man *I* want to shoot is the Judicial Commissioner, with his fantastic notions of evidence," and with this savage reflection against the legal chief of the province he fell asleep.

A little conversation with his comrades had induced Pho Lone to reconsider the state of his foot, the sergeant having assured him that the whole force would go ; and though he limped a little for form's sake when summoned next morning, he professed himself able to walk as far as Nyounglay. Mr. Bailey expressed his gratification with an earnestness that made his men laugh, and for Pho Lone's encouragement did a little magic on his own account by the light of the lamp on his folding camp-table.

"You will observe that I put in this cartridge large shot to the number of nine, that being a sacred number, and therefore very fatal to the virtue of all charms; and also because the cartridge won't hold any more."

Pho Lone, much impressed, said, "Lord!" and wondered why Sergeant Moung Nee chuckled in that disrespectful way.

"This machine screwed upon the edge of the table is also a very wonderful magic appliance. You see the shot in the cartridge? I put the cartridge in, turn this handle a sacred number of times—three, and the shot do not fall out when I toss the cartridge about. Had the Boh any magic things like mine?"

Pho Lone could truthfully declare he had none; and though he began to feel a lurking suspicion that the gentleman who was so stern and unapproachable in town was not above poking fun in the jungle, he was sufficiently puzzled by the work of the cartridge-turner to forget his limp when they started five minutes later. The moon was low, and they had to feel their way step by step through the darkness that hid the jungle path. Mr. Bailey refused to allow a lantern, not knowing when they might come out upon the open ground in sight of the village; so the advance was slow enough. It was five o'clock when they emerged from the forest and struck across the park land, through knee-deep grass, for the outcrop of rock which marked the path up the hill-side. Arrived here, Bailey halted his men and asked Pho Lone about the track.

"H'm, the rain has washed away the earth so that what spikes are left stick up a hand's breadth; also the growth of the bushes has displaced the cart-wheels. I'm afraid this shows a lack of attention to detail on the part of Boh Tah; I had thought better of so judicious a man. The bush grows within a bowshot of the houses; say, seventy or eighty yards; and thins out so that men can hide? Yes, my man, so I supposed; it would without doubt be very good that you lie down hidden when you call the Boh's name; but it will be still better for you to obey my order."

He led the way up the path in the doubtful light of the sinking moon, treading softly in his heavy shooting boots, dodging the twigs which caught and broke away with a noisy rustle; for the jungle on either hand was shoulder high, denser and thornier than ever since the rains, and bulged over the narrow track in places so that the men had to force a passage. He found a stake or two, uncovered and aslant, and stamped these down as he passed; he had picked men behind him who understood the business, and they reached the crest of the hill without mishap as a tinge of colour flushed the cold grey horizon.

It was not yet light enough to make snap shooting desirable with dangerous game ; so Bailey bade his men take cover, and sat himself down to smoke contentedly till dawn should break. The forest-clad hill-tops beyond the village were smothered in white cloud and on the slopes wisps of vapour hung about the trees like dewy spider webs ; the air was chill and damp ; night-birds and crickets were hushed, and the silence was intense.

"Another twenty minutes," said Bailey, drawing his cheroot into a brighter glow to read his watch, "and then."

Involuntarily his thoughts flew back to his first exploit of this kind ; when the challenged murderer, decoyed from his hut, fell dead, shot in the act of stooping to seize his gun. If Boh Tah had the sense to do what Pho Goung did not— peep through the matting when he was called, instead of coming out straightway—well, the betting was there would be some promotion going. Promotion ! Bailey smiled as he thought of his mother's letter after the Pho Goung incident ; how she wrote praying that the sin of bloodshed might be forgiven him, and hoping the promotion it brought meant higher pay. He looked round eastwards ; the heavy cloud rims were glistening white and the jungle outline struck clear against the sky ; as he looked a cock in the village flapped his wings and crowed ; he jumped up, drew the cartridges, saw the barrels clear, and reloading, softly closed the breech.

"Load quietly," he said, and singling out Pho Lone with his eye, beckoned him to follow. The swish of the grass seemed loud as they crossed the open ground towards the huts, shut and silent, against the jungle.

"Which house?" he asked, stopping within twenty yards, and throwing aside his cheroot.

Pho Lone pointed, but his hand shook till it took in half the row.

"That won't do, my man. Unknown traps are half the fun at Hurlingham, but with this kind of bird they don't do. Come now," in Burmese, "count. End house? No. Next one? No. Is it the next? It is; good. Now call. Lie flat if you like." For Pho Lone had sunk upon his heels, his knees unequal to the strain.

"What words?"

"These words: 'Ho, friend! Is his lordship the chief there?' Go on, be sharp, the dogs will wake everybody," as a watchful cur gave tongue.

Pho Lone drew a long breath and called. Only the echoes and the village dogs replied. Bailey tapped his gun stock impatiently.

"Call again."

A muffled voice replied from within the closed house, and Pho Lone cried once more, "Will your lordship deign to speak?"

Bailey caught the sound of movement within,

and brought his fowling-piece to the "ready."
The hanging mat creaked out and a figure swathed
in a pasoh slid into sight.

"Boh!" choked Pho Lone.

"Will you come into Bassein?" roared Bailey,
feeling the triggers. "Move and I shoot you
dead."

Between the hammers for one eternal second his
eye met Boh Tah's.

"Your servant will come," said Boh Tah,
hoarsely.

"Then lie down! flat on your face!"

"Mother!" exclaimed Pho Lone; for the Boh,
whose sorcery was great as the sorcery of the
Bahmai Sadaw himself, who, had he chosen, could
with a word have called down the lightning or
brought legions of demons to his aid, made obeisance to Bay Lee thekin, knelt, and then threw
himself on his face crying for mercy.

"Is there any one else in that house?"

A woman, who must have been waiting for the
order, pressed her way out and shivered as she
faced the levelled gun; her tamein touched the
head of the Boh where he lay. Pho Lone saw the
dingy cotton drag on his head as she knelt, and
yet the Boh never stirred. Was he a Man?

Another call and a man appeared, to crouch
with his hands raised in supplication.

"Are you all?"

"Lord, we are all in this house."

Y

"Come up, men!" shouted Bailey, lowering his gun; and the police raced forward, Sergeant Moung Nee clinking the handcuffs. They dropped their rifles and, pouncing upon the Boh, dragged him down to the ground and chained his wrists.

"Sit," said the sergeant fiercely, and the Boh, meekly shikoing, squatted.

"Here, constables Tha Loo, Pho Lone! Guard these three people, while we search the houses."

Mr. Bailey went off with the rest of his posse to seek more dacoits, and Pho Lone and his comrade stood over the little group; they preferred guarding prisoners to peering about in dark houses where men might hide with dahs, but Pho Lone caught the Boh's eye and quailed. "It would be better to chain his hands behind——" he began, when the chained hands flew out and gripped his throat, and he fell under the Boh, whose eyes blazed like a jungle cat's.

"He kills me!" he shrieked.

There was a sound like a blow on rotten wood, and the Boh rolled over stunned by Tha Loo's rifle butt.

"What is this!" inquired Mr. Bailey, returning.

Pho Lone explained that this dacoit had attempted to kill him; adding that he thought it would be a very good plan to shoot him dead at once.

"Tried to kill you, did he? Now, really it

does not surprise me;" and from the way the gentleman looked at him Pho Lone thought that he thought it would not much have mattered if the Boh had succeeded.

Some of the men wanted must have contrived to escape while the first house was being cleared, for only three whom Pho Lone could recognise as old acquaintances were taken.

"There is one Shway Dway who told me he lived here," he remarked to the sergeant, as they escorted the prisoners down the path behind Mr. Bailey. "He must have got away."

"Yes. Shway Dway; I know him well," said the sergeant. "The quietest man we ever have in the gaol; no trouble at all with Shway Dway. I am sorry we did not catch him instead of that little tiger who attacked you. We shall have trouble with him, I think."

"He is very rash," said Pho Lone, "and will run away if he can."

"We must watch him closely," said the sergeant; and being a cautious man, he resolved to chain the Boh by the ankles every night when Bay Lee thekin was not looking; which he did, sleeping the sleep of the just with the handcuff-key in his pasoh. It was doubtless owing to these precautions that the Boh was unable to work magic that would have killed the whole escort, and that he was safely consigned to the lock-up, very stiff in the arms, five days later.

Pho Lone waited anxiously for several days after they got back to Bassein for news of his promotion, but none coming he took courage to creep into Bay Lee thekin's office and present the petition, which he had drawn up with the aid and advice of all the constables in the thannah.

"So you want promotion," said the gentleman, turning in his chair, and looking at Pho Lone with his head on one side. "I can't say anything about that until you have been tried, you know."

"Tried! your lordship?"

"Yes. Section 121 of the Indian Penal Code: 'Waging war against the Queen Empress.'"

"But I never made war upon the Ingalay Shinboyin Mahgyee," said Pho Lone.

"Yes, you did; you confessed it to me in Thaw' thekin's house, and must be tried for it. It won't do you any harm, and if the Lord Judge does not condemn you to be hanged or transported, we shall see about promoting you. There is leave to go."

Bay Lee thekin's half-caste clerks were laughing, so Pho Lone went out of the office more puzzled than fearful. It was evidently a joke of some kind; but nevertheless he was a little anxious when Sergeant Moung Nee told him he must be in court to-morrow when Boh Tah was tried.

He became very much afraid when, the Boh and two of his followers having been placed in the dock, he was ordered to enter it also, and stand while the interpreter repeated the charge. As Bay Lee thekin—who sat at the pleader's table —had said, he, Pho Lone, was charged with waging war against the Queen.

"Do you plead guilty or not guilty?" asked the interpreter again, having repeated the usual words.

"Well," said Pho Lone, much distressed, "I do not know. If the Court says to plead guilty, I will plead guilty; if I am told to plead not guilty, then I will do so. I am the servant of the Lord Judge."

"Your plea of not guilty is accepted by the Court," said the interpreter, after the Lord Judge and Sayah Wil-ber-for', the Government-side pleader, had spoken a little.

Pho Lone shiko'd, and resting his hands on the dock-rail, waited uneasily till the two-tongued man should speak again; for Bay Lee thekin and the Sayah Wil-ber-for' were talking together, and in a few breaths the sayah rose and said something to the judge, who addressed Pho Lone through the interpreter.

"No evidence is offered against you. The Court gives you leave to go."

"His Lordship, Bay Lee thekin, said I was to be tried," said Pho Lone, sorely puzzled.

"Well, then, you have been tried, and cannot be tried any more," said the interpreter, after referring to the Court. "Go away a free policeman."

Pho Lone shiko'd, and crept out of the dock, very glad to have people between the Boh and himself, for each time his late chief moved, he felt his hands about his throat.

"Do not go away," said Sergeant Moung Nee, "you have to give evidence."

And almost as the words left his lips, the call for constable Pho Lone came, and he was in the witness-box. Bay Lee thekin rose, and having spoken with the Lord Judge, turned to him, and said these words :

"You must remember that you have been tried for waging war, dacoity and other crimes, and no evidence being offered against you, the Court finds you not guilty. You cannot be tried again for past offences. Therefore answer all the questions put to you truthfully, fearing nothing."

Pho Lone took the oath, and in answer to Mr. Wilberforce, told everything. How the Boh had caught him, and had made him follow ; how the gang had looted Ladaw ; how the Boh had buried the money after enlisting more men at Nyounglay village, and fortifying the path, had gone to Kyouksay, where Moung Toke, now dead, had killed Mah Hlaing : and how, being chased by the police, the band had dispersed without waiting orders from the Boh, whom they left as usual in his hiding pit.

"Where?" asked the lawyer.

Pho Lone explained how the chief conducted attacks, and as he did so, saw that Sayah Bair' who also sat at the pleader's table, looked pleased, and began to write with his pen.

"Now, witness," said Mr. Wilberforce, reaching for something which lay behind the books on the table, "Did you ever see this gun before?"

Pho Lone started, for the gentleman held up the Boh's gun which he had been so proud to carry.

"Well, you recognise it as the prisoner's property; when did you last see it in his hand?"

"Being his, the prisoner's bodyguard, I was ordered to carry it," replied Pho Lone uneasily, for he saw Sayah Bair' making notes again.

"But it was the prisoner's property, and he made you carry it? Yes, very good," and Mr. Wilberforce sat down.

Pho Lone was very tired of answering questions by the time Mr. Baird had learned all he wished to know. It seemed to him that the gentleman, who was trying to get the Boh off, wished to convict Pho Lone himself of having led the gang to attack villages; for he was called upon to swear that Boh Tah always lay hidden in his pit, never fired and never even carried the gun produced, and was not within rifle shot when Mah Hlaing was killed. When Mr. Baird sat down, Mr. Wilberforce got up again, and when he had asked about forty questions more Pho Lone had to beg for a drink of water before his tongue could answer those the Lord Judge himself put. However, it was over at last, and he left the witness-box to go out on the verandah and talk with his comrades while Bah Chet, the elephant driver, who had turned Queen's evidence, and Moung Hla of Kyouksay were examined.

"I have never had to speak so much in all my life," he said ; "my jaw is very tired and my mouth is dry."

"You have given very good evidence," said an old kullah Jemadar of military police, "very good indeed. I listened."

"We all listened," said the policemen, "it was good."

"Well, younger brother," said Sergeant Moung Nee pleasantly, "you have done well."

"Do you think the Government will give promotion ?" asked Pho Lone.

"You will be a nai-kah * in a very few days, I think," said Moung Nee confidently ; "a great thing for a young officer like you who has been but four or five months in the service. Yes, you will certainly be appointed nai-kah."

Pho Lone said it was good, but at heart he was a little disappointed. As a constable he drew

* Burmese corruption of the Hindustani "naique."

twelve rupees a month ; as nai-kah he should get twenty and have much power ; but he had hoped to be made outright a sergeant on thirty rupees. It was not so much pay as position he coveted ; why, an inspector who draws sixty-five rupees a month can arrest any one he likes, and consequently can live at the rate of two hundred rupees a month.

" My old mother will be pleased," said Pho Lone. " She always——"

" The Lord Judge is going to deliver sentence," said a man from one of the many doors which gave upon the verandah, and the policemen crowded in to hear.

It was long before Pho Lone forgot the speech the Commissioner made to Boh Tah ; he said hard things which showed how little he understood about magic, and in a way, moreover, which proved that he did not mind displaying his ignorance in open Court. He said that he had had before him many bad and cowardly men, but never one so cowardly and contemptible as Boh Tah.

" Imposing upon your foolish followers," said his honour, " with tales of magical powers, you sent them into danger while you hid your worthless body in a hole where no hurt could come to you. Your cowardice and trickery has been so far successful that I cannot, and I regret it, pass upon you sentence of death. The sentence is that you be transported for life and do forfeit all your property ! "

As the judge spoke the sentence he seemed to grow larger; he raised his voice and hurled the last words at Boh Tah, who shrank cowering against the back rail of the dock till the policemen closed round and hustled him away.

Pho Lone thought the Lord Judge might as well have left out the words about forfeiture of property, for all the prisoner possessed in the world was the cotton pasoh he was wearing when they caught him. Perhaps he was thinking of the buried treasure; but would the demons give it up on a mere order by the Court?

If his honour had had the treasure in his mind, he evidently did not intend to make any order at present, for he finished scribbling off his judgment, passed the sheets to his kullah clerk and called on the next case. Pho Lone went out with the crowd and presently found himself beside the court interpreter who recognised him with a smile.

"I have heard the gentlemen speaking of you," he said. "Bay Lee thekin and the Sayah Baird."

Pho Lone was naturally anxious to hear what they said, so the interpreter, having ascertained that he was not wanted in the new case, took Pho Lone into a quiet corner and told him.

"The sayah said, 'That policeman ought to get ten years,' and Bay Lee thekin made answer, 'He will get promotion instead.' The sayah then said, 'The thief catches the thief. Your constable is himself a dacoit;' to this Bay Lee thekin replied laughing, 'Such thieves are very good in the police; that constable is a nai-kah.'"

"Were those his words?"

"He said that," replied the interpreter, "I am glad to give you good news."

"It is indeed very good news," said Pho Lone; and he forthwith went out to the bazaar to buy a new blanket as a present for his mother; the price was five rupees, but being in uniform he got it for three and a half.

CHAPTER XX

"IT is good that my lord is well again; very often I have feared greatly lest he should die."

"A little fever does not kill, my flower."

"My lord had great fever; many times I have known people die of that sickness."

Thorpe, yellow and wasted from ten days of malaria, lay on a cane lounge in the verandah over the porch, enjoying the comparative cool of the April evening, in his shirt sleeves. Mah Pan sat on the floor by his side, dividing her attention about equally between the baby, squirming on its mat with the purposeless industry of thirty days, and her lord. She had been an attentive nurse, but scarcely a cheering one to European ideas. When one is weak from fever, and the starvation it compels, one's funeral is not the topic best calculated to exhilarate the healthy minded patient, and Mah Pan of course had held that ceremony her sick lord's most legitimate and proper interest. His condition had been such that she had been forbidden to talk with him until the crisis was well over; but the corner turned, the obsequies

which might still be his and the ceremonies
Mah Pan should perform in event of his demise,
were ever uppermost in her thoughts. She had
indeed gone so far as to make tentative inquiries
concerning a black silk tamein, to the amazement
of the bazaar stall keepers, who sold such only to
very old women who had renounced the vanities
of life. Whether she should have courage to
appear in a dress so ugly and unbecoming if
occasion unhappily arose, was, she honestly confessed to Thorpe, doubtful. Apprehensions on
this score, however, had been allayed for the
present by her lord's recovery. He had shaken
off the fever, but was so pulled down that there
was no appeal from the doctor's, " home at once,"
and he was only waiting for the river steamer,
which would land him in Rangoon in time to catch
a direct boat home.

" Ah, the sweet little one ! " cried Mah Pan,
catching up her child. " He cries ; he is crying
because his father goes so soon away to his
country—to In-ga-lan."

" Because an ant is biting him, more likely,"
remarked his other parent, " Turn him over and
look, my flower."

Mah Pan found the insect and set it carefully aside to crawl away, repeating that the
little Tum cried because his father was about
to go.

" And shall you cry when I go ? " inquired

Thorpe. He asked the question idly ; he had no
fear of "a scene," such as friends of his had experienced on similar occasions ; Mah Pan was a
sensible girl.

"Yes my lord. I shall be very sorry." She
put the child down and her gaze wandered wistfully round the wide verandah and into the cool
darkness of the rooms beyond. " But my lord will
come again in eight months time, and send for me
to my mother's house."

"You will go to your village ? "

Mah Pan would go to Myothit. Her mother
wanted her, and all the women wanted to see
bay bee. "My mother said I should learn my
lord's speech," she remarked, when Thorpe corrected her. "I have learned very little, I think ;
and I have an In-ga-liss son !"

"You know many words : say the words I have
taught."

"Many I have forgotten while my lord lay
sick ; but some I remember. Looking ga-lass,
dee-nah, tea, bah-lek-fass, soo-gah, loo-pee ; no my
lord I cannot say r-roo pee," concluded Mah Pan,
with charming effort.

"Those are the words you remember best ? "
said Thorpe with the ghost of a smile.

"Yes my lord ; also bay bee."

"You forget some very good words."

"One, two, tha-ree, sikkis, ten ? " inquired Mah
Pan laboriously.

"No; but never mind now. When I come back I will teach you more."

"Why should I learn when my lord speaks like one who has been to the kyoung school all his life?" she inquired. "I can ask for all I want in my own tongue."

"That is true." The wrinkles came at the corners of Thorpe's eyes again.

"Tum will speak English," said Mah Pan, catching up the baby and pressing its face against her neck. "He is English, for his skin is white as my lord's under the sleeve."

Thorpe looked grave. The plaything of to-day was the social excrescence of to-morrow, shunned by his father's race and shunning his mother's. For a time he lay still, listening to the heavy boom of the mill.

"And when I go away, in two days' time, you will return with the child to Myothit village?" he remarked presently.

"Yes, I shall go. Never has woman on our creek borne so fair a son. They call me fair, but, my lord, am I not brown by his whiteness?"

"Not very brown, my flower." He could say it truthfully.

"See, see! He watches the little dog," cried Mah Pan pointing a finger at the baby's wide eyes which followed Thorpe's fox terrier, "he looked upon the dog." Snap, fresh from his bath, and exhaling carbolic soap, wagged his way to his master's side, to be invited up on the lounge. "My lord looks more upon the dog than upon our little Tum."

"When Tom can walk and speak, I shall notice him much more."

"The dog does not speak," objected Mah Pan.

"Yes, he does. He said to me 'May I not kill that big naked rat on Mah Pan's lap?'"

For answer Mah Pan laid the child on her lord's chest, and bade him nurse Tum for three betel chews. "By which time you shall know your own son and so teach the dog that he is no rat, but an English baby."

"He is a little Burman," replied Thorpe, drawing up his knees to make the child comfortable, "he will go to the kyoung to learn *Kahgway, Kahgyee;** he will be tattooed upon these little fat thighs and wear the pasoh and head-kerchief."

"No!"

"Wear the pasoh and head-kerchief, so that all will say, 'there goes a fine young man.'"

"No!"

"Is it then good that people shall say of him, 'only a *Kabya?*'" asked Thorpe.

Mah Pan took the child upon her lap again. He had an Englishman's skin, but the sun would brown it dark as hers, ere he went to learn his alphabet at the monastery her mother had built; and in the dress her lord proposed for him, none

* The Burmese equivalent for "A B C."

should know that he was not a Man. On the other hand, who, seeing a youth with such skin as this in the town school wearing trousers, coat and sun-hat should say " He is only a half-caste ? "

" I think," said Thorpe, lazily folding his hands behind his head and gazing out over the river, oily in the stillness of the evening flood, "I think when I have been away a few months, my flower will forget her English lord in her own village. What is the name of that fine young bachelor of whom she has spoken—Moung Maw ? "

" Moung Maw ! A jungle village carpenter like the talouk who takes my order for work in this house. I marry him ! No, my lord ; I may marry as I will, for who would not love to call this sweet little Tum his son ? "

" I think it is not good to call him by an English name," said Thorpe gently. He had for months past been haunted by visions of a lantern-jawed half-caste reproachfully pressing on him claims he could not deny ; and yet, as he spoke, he felt a curious twinge at the reminder that her great possession made Mah Pan more desirable in the eyes of her own countrymen.

" He is English," said Mah Pan, obstinately ; " Tum is his name ; I will have an English son."

" Poor Tum ! "

There was much to be done during the next two days ; the work had to be given over to the man who had come round from Rangoon, and who was none too pleased at the prospect of spending the rains in this jungle station ; then there was a certain amount of packing, and homes found for the ponies and Snap while their master was away ; and when necessary arrangements had been completed, the onerous task of providing every man in house, mill, and godown with a three-line " character," occupied a few hours. Altogether Mah Pan had reason to feel that she and her son were rather neglected in these last days, though she enjoyed, at least, a quiet hour or two in the verandah by his side after dinner. No further reference was made by either to their child's future. Thorpe saw that no good end could be attained by discussing it now, and Mah Pan's mind was too full of matters of more immediate importance. She had thought her lord generous when he said she should receive thirty rupees a month during his absence ; but a little conversation with Mah Pyin, the old broker's wife, had given her new ideas on this subject. Mah Pyin had acknowledged the liberality of Thaw' thekin's arrangement, but, re membering a case in which a gentleman had died while away in England, advised Mah Pan to ask for a sum of money down, instead of a monthly payment.

" He is ill," said Mah Pyin ; " see how the bones of his face stick out as they never did before. He might die, and if he dies who will pay you the thirty rupees ? "

These were the words of wisdom, and Mah Pan

lost no time in following the old woman's advice.
She went to the young clerk in the office, who was
always so obliging, and got him to do a little sum
for her, and having ascertained from him the
amount due, went upstairs and begged Thaw'
thekin to sign a *chit* for two hundred and forty
rupees.

"Myothit village being very distant, no man
comes to the town in the rainy season. Upon this
account, will my lord pay all the money into my
hand?"

"Pay you the money at once, my flower. I'd
do it, and gladly, but I have not got it."

"Have not got it!" echoed Mah Pan, thinking
of the thousands and thousands of rupees which
one might see any day in the clerk's office, "my
lord plays with me."

"Indeed I do not, my garland of flowers. I
have already spent the pay of this month and of
next."

Mah Pan looked at him, and seeing he was
quite serious began to feel rather uneasy.

"Only a year ago, or a little less, my lord gave
four hundred rupees to my mother."

"That is true; also, that is why I have no
money now."

Mah Pan sat silent for a time; her ideas had
expanded during her residence in this large beautiful house; two hundred rupees a month passed
through her hands in one way or another, and she

had learned to regard money lightly, measuring
her lord's wealth by the piles of rupees she saw
handled daily in the busy season. She began to
think there was better reason for getting the
money now than that Mah Pyin had suggested;
perhaps when her lord had gone away the clerk
would say, " His honour left no money in my hand
for you, and I cannot pay you one rupee."

" I should like the money very much if my lord
could give it."

Thorpe stopped in his task of sorting clothes to
be given or thrown away and sat on the edge of
the bed stroking his chin.

" I did not intend you to come for the money
each month, my flower. I was going to arrange
that the little broker should go to your village
with it. Do you want it so very much ? "

" My lord, it is my wish to show the neighbours
how generous my lord has been to me."

" Very well, I will see what can be done."

" To-day ? It is my desire to go on this evening's tide, because a neighbour. Moung Let, returns
to-night."

" I will tell you this afternoon," replied Thorpe,
coldly.

Mah Pan said it was good, and went away to
make her own preparations. When she arrived a
year ago, a rushwork box, which she could carry
easily on her head, contained all she possessed;
but now a teak box, larger than Moung Byoo's

own, was too small to hold everything, and Tum's clothes, which he was never required to wear, filled the old pah.

"I wish I could take the mirror," she said to Mah Pyin, who had stolen in by the bathroom entrance to help her. She stood before the wardrobe and surveyed herself sorrowfully. "My lord gives me all I ask ; I shall beg him to let me take this till he returns."

"You could not take it to your jungle village," said Mah Pyin, "the people would laugh at you. Now what is this beautiful little brush used for ?"

Mah Pan forgot the mirror in her eagerness to display her knowledge ; the little brush, she explained, was very good to scratch the back with ; her lord certainly did not use it for that purpose, but rubbed his teeth with it.

Mah Pyin, much interested, tried the tooth brush on skin and teeth and gave it as her opinion that Mah Pan put it to the proper use ; she should buy one for herself if it were not too expensive.

How or where Mr. Thorpe obtained the rupees Mah Pan never knew, but when the shadows were creeping across the verandah that afternoon he called her and said the clerk had orders to pay the money into her hand.

"Shall you be glad to come back to me ?" he asked, an hour after, when the men had carried the boxes down to Moung Let's boat, and Mah Pan with Tom on her hip came to say she was going.

"Yes, I shall be glad, my lord." She looked round the house with regretful eyes, "I shall certainly be very glad."

"If I am sent to Rangoon we shall have only a little jungle house," said her lord, who must have marked her look round. "Do you think you and Tum could live in a little house after dwelling in this great one ?"

Mah Pan could live anywhere with her lord : she should be sad until his return, for he had always been kind and good, very kind and good. She prayed that he might quickly become quite well, and enjoy freedom from all the Accidents, Diseases, and Misfortunes.

In speaking the last words Mah Pan's voice broke, and the tears came.

"Only a few months, my flower."

"It is such a long time, my lord," and, hitching Tum higher on her hip, she went swiftly downstairs, through the great godown to the boat.

"So little sister, you come back to us," said Moung Let, smiling down on her from his perch in the stern. "Mother ! what a lovely baby. What will the neighbours say of so fair a child !"

Mah Pan hugged Tum proudly, and laid him on his mat : a little sob rose in her throat, but she kept it back. After all it was a pleasant leaving, for the mill kullahs showed respect, and also her mind was now very full of the sweet words the neighbours would speak when they saw Tum.

"I have been to the thannah to see my good son, Pho Lone," said Moung Let, shading his eyes to steer clear of the boat crush and out into the current. "He has been nai-kah now for several months, and they say will soon be a sergeant."

"Yes, I spoke for him," answered Mah Pan at random, for she was busy making the baby safe and comfortable under the dhunny-leaf tunnel which covered in the rear third of the boat. "There, beautiful one! When I have tied the mosquito curtain above thou shalt sleep. How shall we get on without the kullah servant to wait upon us, my little son?"

The mosquito net secured, Mah Pan drew herself out to sit near Moung Let, and glance back at the house, fast disappearing behind the trees, as Shway Toon and Moung Yeik jerked at the oars. "I think our house in Myothit will be very small after that large fine house," she sighed.

"All will be glad to see you again, little sister," said Moung Let. "Also Pho Lone will soon get leave and come to the village; then you will see him."

"I have often seen him on duty in the town," said Mah Pan, "once or twice I stopped to speak to him."

"That was kind," grinned Shway Toon, stooping to ladle a shell of water over the rattan loop of his oar, "very kind."

Mah Pan had spoken neither to him nor Moung

Yeik since she stepped into the boat: she had always been proud, and was now prouder than ever, the young men said to each other.

"I was anxious to be kind to him," said Mah Pan graciously. "At his desire I spoke in his favour to my friend the town magistrate's wife."

"He was promoted for good service," struck in Moung Let, partly to prevent the quarrel he saw was coming, and partly because he wished Pho Lone to have all the honour that was his due. "All the world knows that it was not by favour of any man, but because he caught the dacoit Boh Tah. I, myself, by favour of the sergeant of the gate guard, who is Pho Lone's friend, was allowed inside the gaol, where I saw the Boh with chains on his legs : they told me he would be sent over the seas to live. All Pho Lone's doing."

"It is a bad place, the gaol," said Moung Yeik, who had been with Moung Let. "I was glad to come outside ; were you not glad to come out, good uncle ? "

"I was," said Moung Let thoughtfully; it was in his mind that but for Ko Moung Galay's wise advice, Pho Lone might have been among the evil looking prisoners he had seen.

"It is a bad place," said Moung Yeik again ; he drew a long breath and looked round to enjoy the freedom of space ; "let us not speak of it."

But Moung Let had still much to say, and talked until, the sky being long shut, Mah Pan lay down to tuck Tum within her arm, and be lulled asleep by the screech of oars and bubbling whisper under the boat's side.

When she awoke the boat lay at the bank under the houses of Kyouksay, and the men were asleep, for they had rowed till far into the night when the tide turned. This Mah Pan saw from under the mosquito curtain, for there was light in the sky and people were moving in the village : it was very close under the boat roof, so, softly lest she should disturb Tum, she drew herself out to sit on the stern piece, and coil up her hair in the sunrise. It felt strange to wake up thus in a boat once more, after a year in Thaw' thekin's house : her life there seemed a dream as she sat gazing up the river and down, at the endless jungle of the banks ; it did not seem possible that she should ever go back to her lord, so far away was he and all that was his.

Bustle and laughter on the bank where the shore sloped hard and sandy, made her turn to see several girls coming down to bathe. It was long since Mah Pan had bathed thus with friends in the river : when she sighed to bathe, Mah Pyin, the town magistrate's wife, had said "Bazaar girls and jungle women wash in the river"; after which, of course, Mah Pan could only look on and envy the godown sewing girls when they climbed down the ballast of an evening to romp and splash. Mah Pyin bathed in her bath-room, so Mah Pan had done the same ever since those words had been spoken. Now she sat, thinking how good it would be to join the girls; it was such a beautiful bathing place, as good as that at Myothit, and clearer water. While she looked and longed in the growing heat, one of the bathers saw her, and whispering to another, called, "Ho friend, come in with us!"

"I come!" replied Mah Pan; and in three breaths she was letting herself carefully overside into the clear shallow. Mah Pyin's teaching drifted away on the flood back to the town it belonged to as she dipped and splashed among the Kyouksay girls.

"She is now no longer proud, Thaw' thekin's house being out of sight," said Moung Yeik that night when, having stopped for the tide, they sat smoking on the prow under the stars. "Her speech to-day was neighbourly, and she boiled the evening rice for us."

"I think Moung Let's words to her this morning were very good," said Shway Toon, "when rice being ready, she said, 'I eat always with my lord,' he said to her, 'the little sister forgets the usage of her own people,' upon which she sat apart till we had eaten."

"With this child, a woman must be a little proud," said Moung Let good naturedly, "its skin is wonderful to see. I wonder if Pho Lone has seen the baby."

"Does Thaw' thekin come back from his country,

can you tell, uncle?" inquired Shway Toon carelessly.

Moung Let did not know.

" Uncle, when does your good son come on leave
to Myothit?" asked Moung Yeik, yawning.

Moung Let thought he might come about the
end of the rains.

"She is divorced if she pleases, her husband
having left her," said Shway Toon.

" Yes, certainly, she is free to marry any man,"
agreed Moung Yeik, " I think she does not like Pho
Lone, neighbour? What a pity it is she has so
much money. One cannot marry a girl who has a
lot of money."

" Has she much money?" asked Shway Toon
anxiously.

" Thaw' thekin is very generous, and her box
was extremely heavy to carry," said Moung Yeik,
"therefore I am afraid she has money: it is a
pity."

" Ah friend! you were thinking——"

" Not at all—but that little Tum is a very
beautiful child."

" He is indeed—I think I shall sleep now
neighbour."

CHAPTER XXI

MAH PAN had been glad to return home for some reasons; life in her father's house was so much more free than in Thaw' thekin's, though the restraints her lord laid upon her were light. It was particularly pleasant to have friends dropping in at all hours; to sit on the verandah looking on the road, and call in for a smoke and a chat any one who passed. Thaw' thekin had told her she might ask friends to his house, but she must tell him first who they were. Anxious to please, she began by inquiring if his clerks might visit her; their manners were beautiful and they spoke English, so she thought them just the friends her lord would like her to receive. When she mooted it she was much surprised to be answered: "Ask no man employed in my office or godown;" and after this mistake concerning his tastes she had always felt a little shy about asking his permission, though it was never again refused. In this respect therefore life at home was pleasanter than in the town. The food of course was very different, and at first she spoke very often about it, but Mah

Hehn having said once: "Eat or leave your rice," she ceased to compare home dinners with those at the mill-house.

While the hot season lasted she enjoyed being in her father's house again. Beside the village people, boats were always passing up and down, and very many travellers stopped at Myothit just to walk up to Moung Byoo's and admire his daughter's white baby. This was extremely agreeable; but, of course, when the monsoon came an end was made of these visitors, and she began to tire of the village, and to think much of the town. At Thaw' thekin's, even when the rain roared its loudest on the roof, she had only to say a word to the servant, and a carriage stood under the porch to take her in her best clothes wherever she wished. Here when it rained her mother and sister said: "We cannot go out," and lay down to sleep; and as it often rained for days and nights without ceasing, life was very dull.

When the sun shone out, it was not much better, for the men went off to plough, returning at evening mud-splashed to the neck, and too weary to speak after they had eaten; and the women picked their way along the glistening street wearing their oldest tameins and no sandals. Everybody here looked poor and shabby after the people in Bassein, who came out like butterflies on dry days to buy in the bazaar or worship and talk at the pagoda; and what made matters worse, the neighbours did not seem to understand when Mah Pan said : " It is very dull in Myothit."

The house too was displeasing to her. Moung Byoo's was one of the best in the village, but the roughness of the plank walls, and the bare floor befouled by muddy feet, hurt her eyes accustomed to the neatness of her English lord's house.

" I think of the pony-house at the back of the garden when I look round," she said.

" Certainly this is a poor place after his lordship's," said Mah Noo, who had seen and envied with a great envy, " but very soon you will go back."

"It is yet many months before my lord returns," sighed Mah Pan.

She thought sometimes that Thaw' thekin might send a message which she would repeat to the neighbours who would flock round to hear it. But when she said so, her mother replied : " Why shall his lordship send a message, being far away in his own country, and having paid you all the money before he left." And to this Mah Pan had no answer ; for what message could his lordship send ?

By reason of the quietness of Myothit that rainy season seemed a very long one : but it passed away at length, and gave place to the after heat of earth-born steam. The paddy was waist-high now, and the men who had done nothing

since planting out time, began to speak of building
the bird scarers' huts against the ripening of the
grain. But the wet season makes people lazy, and
they put off cutting bamboos till the paddy began
to yellow, and Ko Moung Galay said suddenly one
day : " Go, let us work ! " Then they began, and
slaved daily from dawn to dark till huts, scares,
and even clapper-poles were finished.

The cold weather came bringing harvest time
when every one woke up. All were busy except
Mah Pan. She went out on the kwins it is true,
but only for company's sake. She said Tum
needed all her care, so she sat in the shade of a
cart-tail all day playing with the child and talking to the young men who dropped their sickles
to come and chew half a betel by her side.
Moung Maw was hard at work upon the boats as
usual at this season, and therefore came seldom
to the harvesting ; when he did he took much
notice of Tum, but said few words to Tum's
mother ; for Mah Pan had seemed to shun him
when he gave her a neighbour's greeting in the
early days of her return : nevertheless, the gossips
smiled when they saw him squat making toys of
straw for the fair skinned child.

Tum had grown fast : he was able to stand
holding his mother's tamein or by Moung Maw's
finger, and gurgled nosily at the crows when they
hopped near his mat. Like every other little boy
his head was shaved bare save for a tuft on top,

and a bead necklace was all his clothing. Tum sunned himself in the dust before his grandfather's house, when the sun broke through the morning mists, and sprawled away the heat in the shade of the mangoes, pulling the legs of the great tawny pariahs which bristled and barked if they saw a white man a bow-shot off.

"A-a-h!" Mah Pan would cry when his fat yellow fist closed on her cheroot. "Thou art a little English son, and my lord has said English boys drink not smoke till they be grown men."

"He will be English by-and-by," said Moung Byoo. "Let the good little one be happy now." Then he would talk of the kyoung school, and of the day when the tattooer should be called in to tattoo his grandson's thighs; but to such words Mah Pan would not listen.

"See how big he grows!" she would cry, "his father will not know him when he returns."

"When does he return?" asked Moung Byoo.

"Very soon now," said Mah Pan, hopefully. "I look for his message every day. I pray always for its coming."

"Thus the cricket chirps to the mountain, and listens for the echo," said Moung Byoo to himself; but to Mah Pan he said, "Without doubt you will soon receive a message, daughter."

So the cold season faded like its own mists; the men laid aside their English blankets, and those who had them, their fur-lined coats, and looked to the great basket-work hats which protect the head and neck when one goes abroad at mid-day. The crows were building in the mangoes along the street, and the sparrows screamed and quarrelled over the straws they trailed up to the eaves. But no message came from Thaw' thekin.

Mah Pan was patient. When there came to the village a broker's runner, seeking news of the crop, or a kullah trader selling prints and cottons, she would bide her time, and ask the man for tidings. Only once the stranger did not reply "I cannot tell," and then she received for answer, "Thaw' thekin is not yet come."

"I shall prepare to go," she said, when the boats were in the water ready for the grain heaps which grew daily by the threshing floors. "Each tide now a canoe may come with a messenger. My lord said, 'In eight months I shall return, and send for you,' and he is now fully nine months gone."

Thaw' thekin had always kept his word about coming back. He would say, "I go to Rangoon, and return in a week's time;" and so surely as the creek steamer arrived, it brought him. Therefore Mah Pan began to feel a little uneasy; but she had packed her great teak box, and locked it, ready to start.

"Do not be unhappy," said Mah Hehn. "Ingalan country is a great way off, they say; upon that account there is delay." For Mah Pan was beginning to spend much time sitting on the bank when the tide flowed, and grew low-spirited when the ebb set in and no canoe-man had come.

Mah Hehn was kind, and said all she could to reassure her daughter. She reminded Mah Pan that Thaw' thekin's country was many weeks' journey distant by the largest fire-ship, and that the date of his honour's return must of necessity be uncertain, by reason of the nature of the journey, if it were as Thaw' thekin had described; though for her own part she thought his honour was making fun when he said you did not see land for weeks together. Anyhow it was clear that one could not tell exactly when so long a journey would end; it was different travelling in the boat when one knew to a tide how soon one should arrive, unless there was very much wind, and the boat went faster; and it was also another thing going by road when you could tell to a day how long a distance would take if the cart did not break down or the bullocks become lame by the way.

The boats were laden and ready to start as soon as Oo Boo Nah should ascertain a lucky day. Ten months had passed since Thaw' thekin's departure, and Mah Pan was beginning to fear she should never again dwell in the big house by the mill, when Moung Let came back from Ngatheing, whither he had gone to see the wizard, bringing news that to-morrow would be a very propitious day to start for market.

"I shall go with my father," she said.

But Mah Hehn gave other counsel, saying it was not good to go unbidden; so Mah Pan yielded, and took Tum out to watch the boats drop down the creek with all the usual shouting, dancing, and noise. She had of late grown the more anxious to go away from Myothit because Moung Maw's sister, Mah Htone, had come often to speak in praise of her brother, and the people said, "That clever tongue wags between two again." Mah Htone had a clever tongue: there was no denying that. More than one marriage had been brought about by her good offices. A love-sick young man would say to his mother: "Let Mah Htone go to speak in my behalf to her father and mother;" and Mah Htone would do this out of sheer love for match-making. Ko Moung Galay said it was a pity she did not live in a great town, for there she might arrange marriages every day, and so be happy, beside making a good income by the business; he was sure there were many professional match-makers who were not as clever as she was. All previous affairs Mah Htone had conducted very well; but in dealing with Mah Pan she had been indiscreet by reason of her great anxiety that her brother should become the father of Tum. She saw plainly, as did everybody, that it angered Mah

Pan to say, "I do not think Thaw' thekin will come back," yet she could not help saying words she wished to be true; and as she came every day to Moung Byoo's house, Mah Pan was quite weary of hearing it.

"If it prove that my lord does not return any more," she said, on the evening of the day that saw the boats start, "I shall leave the little one here, and become a nun."

"What!" cried Mah Noo. "You will shave your head naked like the Lord Ruler! Wear white robes, and live apart! Good sister, you have sickness of the brain to think of such a thing!"

"I shall become a nun," repeated Mah Pan, feeling her hair, to make sure the flowers were straight, for some young men were passing. "I shall go to the pottery village near Bassein where there are many rest-houses, and shall live there, sweeping out the houses, and keeping the chatties supplied with water for worshippers."

When Mah Hehn came in Mah Noo told her what surprising ideas Mah Pan had in her mind. Their mother laughed a great deal.

"Our pretty flower turn nun! Well, that is a joke. Why, if she did she would flirt with the supporter of the rest-houses she swept, and marry him as soon as she tired of good works; and I think she would very quickly tire of sweeping and carrying water."

"Nevertheless I hope my father will bring news of Thaw' thekin," said Mah Noo.

"If his lordship returns, he does, and if he does not, he does not," said Mah Hehn. "It is disagreeable to be uncertain, but what is the use of making oneself unhappy?"

Mah Pan in the sleeping room heard her mother's words and, being made a little ashamed, said no more about forsaking the world lest the neighbours should laugh.

Mah Htone however, heard what she had said, for in the village nobody's speech is her own, and she went to her brother urging him to go and visit Mah Pan; but Moung Maw would not listen.

"She says she looks for Thaw' thekin's order to go to him again. Shall I go at bachelor's time to see a woman who speaks thus?"

"You are too proud, good brother. I feel sure that his lordship will never come back."

"How can you tell? Wait till there is news," and saying this Moung Maw went out to join the men smoking in the street that he might hear no more. He was angry with Mah Htone, for the neighbours had said, "Her tongue is on your side and you will marry Moung Byoo's daughter;" and it is not well that a sister should do unasked what a fellow's mother does only at his express desire.

Nevertheless, when a few evenings later, Tha Tway paddling in the shallow, called, "Ko Moung

Byoo's boat comes," the gossips remarked that Moung Maw was one of the first to stroll over to the creek side where Mah Pan with Tum on her hip as usual was already waiting. There was nothing else to do, so of course every one in the village was out on the bank by the time the great boat, crank in its lightness, swayed round on the flood and the rowers let their oars trail to pole her in shore. Moung Byoo was in his place on the steering chair, but though Mah Pan called, " Is there news ? " he only shook his hand without speaking.

" He brings bad tidings I think," said Mah Hehn with a troubled face ; and Mah Pan called no more.

It took a very long time to bring the boat in so that Moung Byoo could let himself over the side and come ashore by the logs that formed the landing stage. Then at last as he stepped up the slope and the neighbours gathered round, he said in answer to Mah Hehn, "There is much news, which I will tell."

It was clear to all that Moung Byoo brought important tidings, he took so long to begin ; the sky was shutting when he sat down under the bamboo clump with the neighbours pressing round to listen, and the cricket struck up his song before he spoke.

" I bring news," he said, and those who still stood, sat down and craned forward to listen.

"There is come to the mill a new gentleman who sits in Thaw' thekin's office and in his chair. From his mouth I have received news of Thaw' thekin." He stopped for a few breaths and rolled his cheroot; Mah Pan, crouching at his side, eyed him hungrily but did not speak.

"The new gentleman has received from Thaw' thekin a letter in which his honour writes that he is in bad health."

"His honour had fever," murmured the neighbours as Moung Byoo paused.

"He is in bad health," repeated Moung Byoo with point. "Also he has become very rich by reason of the death of a relation who leaves him many lakhs of rupees."

"Mother!" exclaimed the neighbours, for Moung Byoo paused again.

"Upon this account, his honour will never come any more to Bassein."

The neighbours murmured, "A-a-a-h!" in sympathy, looking at Mah Pan; and there was silence while the wavelets lapped sleepily and the reeds across the water whispered in the rising night wind.

"This is all your tidings?" asked Mah Hehn as their daughter said no word.

"There is more. Thaw' thekin has given order that the new gentleman shall pay into Mah Pan's hand one thousand rupees; also twenty rupees each month for the little son till he be grown a man. This is all my news."

"Did you bring this money?" asked Mah Hehn.

Moung Byoo did not answer; he looked sadly after Mah Pan who, when he ceased speaking, had risen quickly and pressing her way through the people, vanished into the dark.

"His honour has been very generous," said Mah Htone.

"Very generous," chorused the neighbours, and again was silence. Moung Byoo still sat there in the dark shadow of the bamboo clump, so nobody moved; there might be more to hear from his mouth, for the glow and wane of his cheroot showed that he drank smoke hard, as one who thinks deeply.

"Such things have happened before," said a voice slowly, "but we are very sorry."

"I had looked for this," said Mah Hehn, "but not yet."

"*If you pull the tiger's tail he bites,*"

"*If you love the Englishman you are a fool,*" quoted Mah Tsay.

"A true saying!" murmured the women. "Yes, that is a true saying," and one added, "but no girl of this village has before pulled the tiger's tail."

"I think the Government order is to pay ten rupees a month," said Mah Hehn. "Thaw' thekin pays double, which is very good."

"The hag thinks only of rupees," said Moung

Maw in a low voice to Ko Moung Galay. "She is just like a black coolie animal."

His wife's words seemed to rouse Moung Byoo, for he said, "I forgot the tidings I brought for Mah Tsay. Ho, mother!"

"I am here," came Mah Tsay's cracked voice; "Pray tell the news. Is it of my son the official?"

"It is of Pho Lone, mother. Your good son will come very soon to the village. This was told me by Moung Let, who has seen him."

"Now that is good news," shrilled Mah Tsay. "What day will he come, uncle?"

Moung Byoo could not tell: but Moung Let would be home on the next or following tide.

"The next, I hope," said Mah Tsay, and her bent figure, resting on her staff, rose above the sitting throng. "This is good news indeed," and she hobbled slowly away, as Moung Byoo got up to go to his house.

For a few days after this the neighbours saw little of Mah Pan, for she did not come out, and went up to her sleeping-room when any one came to the house. Mah Htone, though now more than ever anxious to plead her brother's cause, refrained from going to see her till her sorrow should be over. She felt that there was no time to lose; Moung Let had made known that his son would come in half a month, and Mah Htone feared Pho Lone as Moung Maw's rival. Mah Pan had not shown that young man much favour in the old days; but between Pho Lone the cultivator, and Pho Lone the official, dwelling in town, was a vast difference; and Mah Htone was afraid.

Passing Moung Byoo's house one evening before sunset she saw Mah Pan with the baby sitting once more in her accustomed place against the wall, and turned aside to speak with her.

"This is now the richest little man in the village," she said, by way of a beginning.

"Yes, and I am the richest woman, they say," replied Mah Pan dully. "I think often what I shall do with all the money. I do not want it."

"Buy a boat and trade in paddy."

"My mother said that, but I do not wish to buy a boat : there would be much trouble. I think it would be better to spend the money building a very beautiful rest-house yonder by the pagoda."

Mah Htone said that such a meritorious work would without doubt afford much pleasure to all the village.

"It seems the best plan, I think," said Mah Pan.

"I am sure my brother, Moung Maw, will be glad to build it for you."

"He is certainly a clever carpenter," said Mah Pan, glancing up the road at Mah Hehn's kyoung.

"Shall I tell him to come and see you ?"

"I cannot prevent any young man coming to see me," said Mah Pan ; but she smiled a little saying it.

"I will tell him of your plan," said Mah Htone; and as the matter she had so much at heart was at last in train she turned to praising Tum's white skin and pink palms.

After she had eaten her own rice that evening she went down to Moung Maw's house and sat in the dark to wait till he came.

"You here again!" he said; "well, what now?"

"Mah Pan speaks of building a rest-house, and would speak with you, brother."

"Let her speak when we meet to-morrow."

"Go to her at bachelor's time," pleaded Mah Htone. "I have been with her this evening, and she will be sweet."

Moung Maw sat nursing his knees in silence for a time.

"If I go at that hour," he said at last, "all men will say 'The carpenter seeks a wife who can give him his rice.'"

"No! for all the village knows you used to visit her before she married Thaw' thekin. She wishes to build the rest-house in order to spend money she does not want."

"Then she won't do it on the cheap plan her mother approved?" said Moung Maw, chuckling.

Mah Htone laughed, for Mah Hehn's attempt to save money over the building of the monastery had amused the village for months. When the work was nearly finished she had come to Moung Maw and speaking in his ear said that the neigh-

bours were much distressed because he of all the
village was the only person who gained no Merit
by that building, for the reason that he received
payment for the work of his hands; and did he
not wish to earn Merit like others? To which
Moung Maw had answered, " 1 wish much to earn
Merit but more to earn the twenty-five rupees you
agreed to pay me for the job." He told everybody
about it and though Mah Hehn said the story was
untrue she always spoke of the carpenter as a man
who cared nothing for the good opinion of his
neighbours; so they knew who spoke truth.

Moung Maw thought much over his sister's
words after she left his house. Now Thaw' thekin
was gone Mah Pan evidently wished to rid herself
of wealth which would keep self-respecting suitors
at a distance, and to build a large rest-house was
a very good plan. It was not wanted in the least,
but of course that was no matter. He resolved
that he would go and see her about it.

He let some days pass, however, not feeling very
anxious to go at bachelor's time and not caring to
visit her under the eyes of all the village. He
might never have gone but for Tum. Strolling
across the road one evening Mah Pan came along
carrying the child who cried to him.

"The little one wants you, neighbour," said
Mah Pan.

Moung Maw turned aside to meet her and take
Tum on his shoulder.

" And whence does the elder sister come ? " he asked politely.

" I had taken the child for Mah Tsay to see."

" Yes ? And is there news when her son comes ? "

" I believe he comes soon ; I forgot to ask," said Mah Pan, looking away, " but neighbour, I want to speak with you touching the rest-house I am going to build."

She sat down on the brick pathway as she spoke. Her voice was soft ; Moung Maw sat down too.

" But I will not stop now," she said, rising, " I must go and put the little one on his mat."

Moung Maw got up and held Tun to her.

" He wants to stay on your shoulder. Bring him if you will."

Her voice was very sweet. Moung kept Tun and walked with her.

" It is long since the elder brother has been to our house. When will he come—to speak of this matter of the building ? "

" This evening ? " suggested Moung Maw as he put down Tun.

" Come this evening," smiled Mah Pan, with a glance.

CHAPTER XXII

"I TRUST we see you in good health," said Ko Moung Galay.

"I enjoy the best health by reason of your good wishes," replied Pho Lone cordially. "I hope that my prayers for the welfare of your much-respected person are answered."

Ko Moung Galay said his health was very good, and Pho Lone, making a little obeisance to the elders who sat with the head-man, passed on with his father and mother.

"The young man has improved in his manners," said Ko Moung Galay, "he knows now what is due to his seniors."

"His manners are certainly better," said Oo Ket Kay, "but will any one tell me why he should come in a hired boat with three black kullahs when there are at Bassein many friends who would gladly bring him home for nothing?"

"Who shall prevent the young cocks from crowing?" said Ko Moung Galay, good humouredly. "I daresay we tried to cut a figure before the girls when we were young, neighbour. Pho

Lone is young, and also he is proud, being an official."

"I have no patience with these cocks whose feathers are scarce grown," said Oo Ket Kay testily. "In the town I have known a young fellow spend all his money in hiring every evening a pony cart which he drove up and down the street where his girl dwelt."

"I have known a young son of the town do just the same thing," said Oo Shway. "I have also known a young clerk take a bundle of law papers from his English master's office and walk about with them under his arm that his girl might think much of his importance; they all do something of the sort; but an end of this woman's talk! We were speaking of the matter of Moung Byoo's daughter."

"Yes," said Ko Moung Galay, "but what have we more to say? Thaw' thekin is gone and therefore Mah Pan is free; he has divorced himself, as one may say, so what need of decree of divorce from us? The thing is done."

"None at all," said Oo Shway, for the sun was growing hot and he wanted to go home. "Moung Byoo's daughter is free to marry whom she will."

"Yes, and we think the whole affair very creditable to all concerned," said Ko Moung Galay, who liked to say a kind word. He glanced up the road at the monastery and then to the vacant ground by the pagoda where Moung Maw in sun-hat and

tightly girt pasoh was busy measuring with a
light bamboo. "Our village will gain a name for
the pious works of its women."

While the elders sat talking thus on the creek
bank Pho Lone was receiving the friends who
came to Moung Let's to see him. All the young
men and many of the girls came, and they showed
so much respect that Mah Tsay afterwards said
she was reminded of the morning when her son
returned home from following the Boh.

"Shall you go and visit Mah Pan?" she asked
as they ate rice that evening, "she has been asking
when you would come."

"She was asking, was she?" said Pho Lone
carelessly.

"Yes, several times she has brought the child
here and always asked when you were to arrive.
I think she wants you to go and see her."

"I daresay she does," said Pho Lone drily; for
it was in his mind that Mah Pan gave herself
great airs when she was Thaw' thekin's wife and
he was only a constable. Without doubt she
would now be very glad to have a police nai-kah
come courting her.

"I daresay she saw me arrive this morning," he
said.

"She was watching. I saw her," said Mah Tsay;
and Pho Lone straightened his back and smiled a
little. That eight rupees spent on boat hire had
not been wasted.

When Moung Maw went to see Mah Pan that evening he found her dressed in her best town clothes and wearing more jewellery than usual; she was so sweet to him that he spent a long time in the house, and good-natured Shway Toon, who had come with him, quietly went away after sitting outside for a couple of betel chews.

"He did not come last night," Mah Pan said to her mother in the morning.

"Give him only a neighbour's greeting when you meet," said Mah Hehn. "And remember that the carpenter wants you to go and give him instructions about the new rest-house this morning."

Mah Pan did not remember that Moung Maw had said anything about instructions, but it is well to be guided by one's mother, and accordingly she spent much time that morning under a shady tree watching Moung Maw at work; other men and women were there, so she showed the carpenter much respect and attention.

That evening Moung Let gave a feast to celebrate Pho Lone's return. The young official had brought many good things to eat from the town, and the fellows said that such a feast had never before been seen in Myothit. The jam in tin pots and preserved milk to eat with it were finished to the last drop, and Moung Maw had difficulty in securing two of the biscuits with pink sugar to keep for Tum. The strange meats from tins were

2 B

also very good ; but much of these was left over
because when one has eaten a great deal of jam
and milk one does not care about meat.   There
was no liquor, because, as Moung Let said more
than once to his guests : "My son being an Official
it would not be proper for any one to get even a
little drunk in his presence."   It was a very
delightful evening, and if Pho Lone was a little
proud it was no more than his friends expected ;
even Moung Maw said he was not such a bad
fellow, while Pho Lone declared that his friend
the carpenter was the finest chap on the creek.

"He is a fine fellow," said Shway Toon who
was one of the last to go, " a very fine one. I know
somebody who thinks much of Moung Maw."

"A girl, without doubt !" laughed Pho Lone
who was in the highest spirits.

"A girl you visited once."

"Mah Pan ! She would never marry a jungle
carpenter !"

"You think so ? She has eyes for no other
man."

When strolling down the village before sunset
that evening Pho Lone had met Mah Pan, and
she passed him by with scarcely a word ; true, his
own greeting had been very off-hand, because
after what Mah Tsay had told him he meant to
show her that the Wheel had turned again ; but
he had thought at the time, " I have only to smile
upon her to see all her sweetness."   Shway Toon's

words gave him an unpleasant feeling, that his
mother might have mistaken Mah Pan's purpose
in asking about his return ; but he answered with
an air :

" My good fellow, I think you don't understand
women very well. I confess I did not till I lived
in the town ; but now I rather think I know
something about them. Why, I tell you, I have
only to——"

" My son, my son ! "

"It is my old mother who calls," he said, breaking off. " I must go and hear her."

Shway Toon went away, and he turned to step
back into the house where Mah Tsay, now the
guests had gone, was hastily saving the ends of
the limp and guttering candles which smoked over
the remains of the feast.

" You called me, mother."

" You would marry the girl ? " she asked, blinking gravely at him over a handful of candle ends.
" If you would, do not speak such words as you
were going to say to Shway Toon. He would
repeat your boast to her, and your chance would
then be small. She is proud, you know."

" Perhaps you are right, mother. But I
think——"

" Perhaps ! I am sure of it. There, go ! it is
time to sleep."

Shway Toon's words proved so far wrong that
when Pho Lone met Mah Pan next morning, and

said pleasant things concerning Tum, she was gracious to him. He sat down on the brick pathway to talk to her, and heard all about the new work of merit. The fact that the carpenter was building it of course made frequent mention of his name necessary, but to Pho Lone it seemed that it came to her lips more often than it ought.

"See the pretty cakes Moung Maw brought Tum this morning," she said holding up the little fist.

"He was at our house last night. I shall take him up for stealing," said Pho Lone.

Mah Pan laughed at his joke; this was an encouraging sign.

"You know I am now naikah of police?" he said.

"Moung Maw told me," said Mah Pan innocently.

"He comes often to your house?"

"Yes, often. Tum and I like Moung Maw."

"Do you not sometimes wish to live again in the town?" asked Pho Lone presently.

Mah Pan loved the village best. She should not care if she never saw the town again.

"I sometimes wish for the jungle, I must say," said Pho Lone, "but having gained the favour of the head of the police I must live in town, for I hope some day to be promoted inspector."

"That will be a very fine position," said Mah Pan really impressed.

" And you say ' I like him much.' "

" I might also say, ' I like much the police nai-kah Pho Lone.' "

" Oh ! you might say that ! Then I shall come and see you at bachelor's time."

" I cannot prevent you." And saying this, Mah Pan rose and fled back to the house where she found her mother. Mah Hehn listened with interest, nodding her head as if to say " Just what I expected."

"But suppose Moung Maw comes first to-night," said Mah Pan, when she had told all that had passed, " I do not wish him to come any more now."

" Give the carpenter sweet words, but not too sweet ; you are not sure of him yet ;" but by " him," Mah Hehn did not mean Moung Maw.

Mah Pan tossed her head at this ; but her mother's advice had proved so wise that she resolved to follow it again.

When Moung Maw came along the street that evening, he said to Shway Toon who was with him as usual, that he should not go in to-night ; and Shway Toon glancing into Moung Byoo's, saw Pho Lone and Mah Pan sitting together in the lamplight.

"Come to my house and play cards instead," said Shway Toon, " we will get Moung Yeik and some other fellows also."

" That will be good," said Moung Maw, " let us go and play."

The young men played until far into the night; Moung Maw was the noisiest of all, and drank the most; when the party broke up he was so drunk that Shway Toon and Moung Yeik had to hold his arms and lead him home. From that day forward he went no more to Moung Byoo's house, though Mah Pan came every day to look on at the building he directed and gave him words sweeter than she had ever spoken before.

It would have been strange if a man of spirit had gone to see her again, for each night people who chanced to stroll in the street at young man's time to enjoy the cool air of the night, might see in the lamplight Mah Pan in her best, with Pho Lone at her side.

"They will marry," said the gossips; and the only question was whether they would marry before Pho Lone had to return to duty.

This doubt was cleared up in a few days time, when Moung Let in his silk pasoh and a clean white jacket walked with Mah Tsay, also in her best clothes, to Moung Byoo's house. All knew what their errand was, and all who held themselves of kin near enough to be present made haste to the house. Nearly every one in the village was a cousin at least of a parent on one side or the other, so when Moung Let came in followed by his wife, the neighbours squatted four deep all round the mats which had been spread for the special guests in the middle of the floor; the elders were there

wearing the white muslin fillets with which old
men replace the bright head-kerchief worn by
others, and for them clean mats had also been laid.
Mah Pan was not present; but the creaking of the
partition which shut off her sleeping-room, a
man's height above, told those whose ears were
sharp that she was listening and perhaps peeping
down on them.

The day was still and so hot that the crows in
the tree outside crouched on the boughs with
open beaks and drooping wings. Moung Let
wiped the drops from his face with his sleeve as
he entered, and sat down with Mah Tsay at his
side, but a span behind. Moung Byoo inclined
his head gravely as his neighbour begged leave to
sit, and with downcast eyes waiting for him to
speak.

"You know the purpose of our coming," said
Moung Let cheerfully, as one who knows he is
welcome.

"We are pleased to see you," said Moung
Byoo; and Mah Hehn murmured, "Pleased to
see you;" though the woman should keep closed
lips on these occasions.

"Our son," said Moung Let, raising his voice a
little, "our son loves your daughter, and wishes
to make her his wife."

"We are honoured," said Moung Byoo, "much
honoured." Then again was a little silence for it
was Moung Byoo's turn to speak, and he sought

pleasant words to say what duty requires of a
girl's father. Overhead the partition creaked,
and one might hear eager whispering. " I believe,
good neighbour," said Moung Byoo at last, " I am
sure that your admirable son is of good blood ;
that in his family on either side has never been
any taint of slave blood ? That none of his fore-
bears have been King's slaves, nor Pagoda
slaves ? "

" There is no slave blood in our family," replied
Moung Let.

"No, no! surely not," murmured the assembled
friends.

" And we are also sure that he has in his veins
no taint of the Grave-digger class ? " continued
Moung Byoo.

" Neither the ancestors of myself nor of my
woman have had any strain of Grave-digger
caste," replied Moung Let.

And the neighbours again murmured, " Surely
not," in politeness.

Moung Byoo paused again to find words for the
other formal questions, and dug splinters from the
mat with his nail as he thought.

" He is a very fine young man. We feel sure
he is healthy."

" Our son does not suffer from leprosy nor
scrofula, nor from other evil disease that is
properly held disgraceful. He is clean and
healthy."

"We were sure of it," said Moung Byoo, relieved that his task was nearly over. "Well,
then, good neighbour, in the presence of our
friends and neighbours, we consent to your excellent son's marriage with our daughter; and we
shall pray that long life, fertility, and much
happiness attend their union."

"It is very good," said Moung Let gravely.

"We all wish the young people freedom from
the Accidents, Diseases, and Misfortunes; and
very great happiness," said Ko Moung Galay;
and the head-man having said these words, everybody burst into talk.

All were agreed that the match was most suitable, and could not but be a happy one; and all
of course were very much surprised, not having
dreamed for a moment that anything of the kind
was impending. Moung Byoo and Mah Hehn
received much sympathy for that their son-in-
law would dwell for so brief a space in their
house after the wedding; but they were re-
signed.

"We are sorry," said Moung Byoo, "but an
Official of course," he sighed, "an Official has very
important duties to perform, and Pho Lone is
required by the Government in the town whither
he must take his wife."

"Yes, yes; it is the case," said the neighbours
very solemnly, and by slow degrees the gathering
melted away, leaving Moung Byoo to take off his

THE BRIDEGROOM

jacket with the tight sleeves, and exchange his
silk pasoh for the old cotton one he always wore.
His face was grave as he sat with his back
against the wall, smoking; for he was sorry that
his daughter should leave him again. Mah Hehn
upstairs was all bustle and chatter. Once Moung
Byoo heard her say, "A sergeant's pay is thirty
rupees a month," at which he shook his head
looking graver than before.

Moung Let and his wife were also grave as they
walked down the street in the heat, for a married
son is a lost son.

"You will marry her to-morrow, I expect?" said
Mah Tsay sadly to Pho Lone, when she returned
to the house where the young man had been
waiting with a friend or two.

"Yes, to-morrow, good mother. Moung Yeik
has promised to bring the bullock cart to take my
goods to Moung Byoo's house."

Pho Lone's goods in Myothit were very few,
consisting of a mat and a pillow, a change of
clothes, and a betel box; but he had more property
at the thannah, and his friends would lend him all
he needed to make a respectable show in the cart
which would follow him.

Before the sun was hot next morning, Moung
Yeik drove the cart before Moung Let's, and pulled
off the mat he had thrown over various boxes and
other matters of his own which he had lent for the
occasion. Pho Lone tossed his bundle into it, and

settling his belt, led the way along the street, returning with smiles the good wishes of the neighbours who stood on their verandahs to see him pass, the bullock cart squeaking and groaning behind him. A few neighbours had assembled at Moung Byoo's, and these were admiring Mah Pan's dress, for she wore her best tamein, a white silk jacket, and a new pink silk kerchief about her shoulders carefully arranged that it might not hide her necklet.

"The rice is ready, my son," said Moung Byoo, as Pho Lone stepped into the house; and as he spoke, Mah Hehn set on the floor a new lacquer tray with a little boiled rice.

"Eat from the same dish," said Ko Moung Galay, "eat from the dish, Son and Daughter."

Pho Lone sitting ate a mouthful, and Mah Pan, taking her place beside him, did the same; they smiled to each other.

"It is done," said Ko Moung Galay, "they are man and wife."

After the sky was shut Pho Lone and Mah Pan listening, heard the dull thud and rustle of a heavy stone on the roof.

"The bachelors are come," said the bride.

The stones came thick and fast upon the thatch, but no word from the young fellows in the street without; for this is a ceremony performed in silence to prove unmarried envy.

" And it was long ago my thought that I should throw stones upon this roof for Moung Maw," said Pho Lone.

And Moung Maw throwing with good will said in his heart, " Other girls are left."

GLOSSARY

Aing-sohn, *the guardian spirit of a Burmese dwelling.*

Bund, *a low, flat-topped bank of earth.*

Chatty, *earthenware vessel used to hold water or for cooking.*

Chetty, *Madras money-lender.*

Choung, *a water-worn gully.*

Dah, *sword-knife; shape varies according to purpose.*

Goung, lit. *"head," the head-man of a village.*

Hpoongyee, *Bhuddist priest.*

Kabya, lit. *"half," a Eurasian.*

Kullah, *"stranger from the West," commonly a native of India.*

Kwin, *paddy land.*

Kyeezee, *a small triangular gong.*

Kyoung, *monastery.*

Loon pasoh, *a silk waist-cloth of peculiar pattern.*

Mamootee, *a species of hoe, like a large adze.*

Nadoung, *ear ornament of amber, glass or ivory, in shape like a stick ferrule, solid or hollow; sometimes jewelled.*

Nat, *fairy, sprite, kelpie.*

Paddy, *growing rice; also rice unhusked.*

Pah, *an oblong rushwork receptacle with a cover as deep as the box; used by Burmese and Europeans.*

Pasoh, *man's waist-cloth.*

Sayah, *learned man.*

Sit-boh, "*war chief*," *officer*.

Sohn, *spirit*.

Talouk, "*stranger from the East*," *commonly a Chinaman*.

Tamein, *woman's skirt*.

"A betel chew," *the time required to chew a betel nut*, 15 *or* 20 *minutes*.

"A bamboo's length," 30 *or* 40 *yards*.

"A bow shot," 60 *or* 80 *yards*.

"Courting Time," *also called* "Young man's" *and* "Bachelor's Time;" *in the country villages from soon after dark to about* 9 P.M.

"Sky shuts," *nightfall*.

"Red star rises," 2 *or* 3 A.M.

Printed by BALLANTYNE, HANSON & Co.
London and Edinburgh

www.ingramcontent.com/pod-product-compliance
Lightning Source LLC
Chambersburg PA
CBHW021325110726
47900CB00005B/1361